Claude E. Savary

Letters on Egypt

With a parallel between the manners of its ancient and modern inhabitants, the present state, the commerce, the argriculture, and government of that country - and an account of the descent of St. Lewis at Damietta - Vol. 2

Claude E. Savary

Letters on Egypt

With a parallel between the manners of its ancient and modern inhabitants, the present state, the commerce, the argriculture, and government of that country - and an account of the descent of St. Lewis at Damietta - Vol. 2

ISBN/EAN: 9783337238568

Printed in Europe, USA, Canada, Australia, Japan

Cover: Foto ©Andreas Hilbeck / pixelio.de

More available books at **www.hansebooks.com**

LETTERS

ON

EGYPT.

WITH A

PARALLEL BETWEEN THE MANNERS OF ITS ANCIENT AND MODERN INHABITANTS, THE PRESENT STATE, THE COMMERCE, THE AGRICULTURE, AND GOVERNMENT OF THAT COUNTRY;

AND AN ACCOUNT OF THE

DESCENT OF ST. LEWIS AT DAMIETTA;

EXTRACTED FROM

JOINVILLE, AND ARABIAN AUTHORS;

ILLUSTRATED WITH MAPS.

BY MR. SAVARY,

AUTHOR OF THE LIFE OF MAHOMET, AND TRANSLATOR OF THE CORAN.

IN TWO VOLUMES.

VOL. II.

DUBLIN:

PRINTED FOR L. WHITE, No. 86, DAME-STREET, AND P. BYRNE, No. 108, GRAFTON-STREET.

M DCC LXXXVII.

THE

CONTENTS

OF THE SECOND VOLUME.

LETTER XXXII.

ROUTE FROM ACHMIN TO DENDERA.

 LET-

LETTER XXXIII.

LETTER XXXIV.

LETTER XXXV.

LETTER XL.

GOVERNMENT OF EGYPT.

LETTER XLI.

HISTORY OF ALI BEY.

LETTER XLII.

SEQUEL OF THE HISTORY OF ALI.

LETTER XLIII.

OBSERVATIONS ON THE AGRICULTURE OF THE COUNTRY.

LETTER XLIV.

ACCOUNT OF THE TEMPERATURE OF THE CLIMATE.

LETTER XLVII.

LETTER XLVIII.

LET-

LETTER XLIX.

LETTER L.

LETTER LI.

LETTER LXII.

OF MNEVIS AND ONUPHIS, SACRED BULLS OF ANCIENT EGYPT.

LETTER LXIII.

OF THE TERRESTRIAL SERAPIS, A SYMBOLICAL DEITY WHICH BORE A RELATION TO THE NILE.

LETTER LXIV.

OF ANUBIS, A SYMBOLICAL DEITY OF THE EGYPTIANS.

 dog;

LETTER LXVIII.

OF CANOBUS, A PRETENDED DEITY OF THE EGYPTIANS.

LETTER LXIX.

OF THOTH, A SYMBOLICAL DEITY OF THE EGYPTIANS, AND REGARDED AS A CELEBRATED MAN BY THE GREATER PART OF WRITERS.

LETTER LXXIII.

To Mr. LEMONNIER, *Physician to the* KING *of* FRANCE, *First Physician to* MONSIEUR, *and* MEMBER *of the* ACADEMY, *of* SCIENCES.

PLAN OF AN INTERESTING VOYAGE, AND WHICH HAS NEVER BEEN PERFORMED.

LETTERS ON EGYPT.

LETTER XXXII.

ROUTE FROM ACHMIN TO DENDERA.

Description of Souadi, on the west of which are two old monasteries surrounded with ruins, which fix the situation of the ancient Crocodilopolis. Observations on Menchié *and the ancient Ptolemais, the ruins of which are at a small distance. Description of the fields in its environs. Observations on Girgé, the capital of Upper Egypt, and on Abydus towards the west. Here are vestiges of the celebrated temple of Osiris, where singers and musicians were strictly prohibited from access. Account of* Farchout *and its delightful orchards. Description of the antiquities at Tentyra, situated near Dendera. Hatred of the ancient inhabitants of Tentyra towards Crocodiles.*

To Mr. L. M.

Grand Cairo.

LET us take our leave of *Achmin*, and the serpent Horidi. Passing to the other side of the

Nile, we ſee the burgh of *Souadi* governed by a Cachef, and proceeding to the weſtward, two Coptic monaſteries, ſituated at the entrance of the deſert. Their churches are ornamented with Corinthian pillars, with a croſs in the middle of the capital, and are paved with red granite, covered with hieroglyphics; their architecture ſavours of the decline of taſte amongſt the Greeks. They are thought to have been built by the Empreſs Helena. In the ſpace between them, the ground is ſtrewed with antique marbles. Theſe remains point out the ſite of *Crocodilopolis* (*y*), which was far from the river, and which Ptolemy places after *Aphroditopolis*, or the city of Venus.

Aſcending towards the ſouth-eaſt, we croſs a plain ſhaded by various trees, covered with harveſts, and interſected by rivulets. It leads to the burgh of *Menchié* decorated with a large moſque. A conſiderable market is held here.— The bazards are ſtored with all ſorts of articles. They ſell a conſerve of wheat here, in high eſtimation in the country. It is compoſed of corn ſteeped in water for two days, then dried in the ſun, and boiled to the thickneſs of a jelly. This paſte thus prepared is called *elnede* dew. It is melting, ſugary, and very nouriſhing. If this ſort of confection dried in the oven would keep at ſea, it might be a very great reſource in long voyages.

(*y*) Ptolemy, l. 4. This is the ſacred city of that name. But the former ſituated in the *Feioum*, was better known by the Name of Arſinoé.

On

On an eminence to the south of *Menchie*, are to be remarked the remains of the entablatures of cornices, and trunks of columns. The river is lined by a quay in this place. A projecting mole serves to protect the boats from the winds and currents. These ruins, and oriental works, recal to mind the great *Ptolemais*, which Strabo (z) compares to Memphis for its extent and population (*a*). Ptolemy calls it *Ptolemais* of *Hermes*, because the symbolical deity, Mercury, was worshipped there.

Whilst the wind is driving us towards the south, cast your eyes on the rocks which project on the eastern side, you will there perceive the little convent of *der Hadid* placed in the middle of a desert beset with barren points, and grottoes which the fervour of the primitive ages of Christianity peopled with pious Anchorites. Can there be a more frightful solitude so near an enchanting country? On one side we discover nothing but barren sands, hills burnt up by the sun, from which the reverbation is suffocating. On the other we admire all the treasures of abundance. Already the dourra, with all its reedy leaves shoots up its vigorous stalk, and is crowned with large ears. The corn, whose surface is kept waving by the wind, is near the period of its growth. Vast fields are covered with sugar canes. The flax flourish close by. The date reddens on the summit of the date tree. The palm of the Thebais displays its leaves in the form of a fan, and the golden melon hangs over the edges of the

(*z*) Strabo, l. 17.——(*a*) Ptolemy, l. 4.

river. Such is the aſpect of theſe plains at the beginning of December.

We land at the port of Girgé, the capital of Upper Egypt. This town, which is a league in circumference, has ſeveral moſques, bazards, and public ſquares, but no remarkable buildings; it is ſurrounded by well cultivated gardens. It is governed by a Bey. His ſoldiers commit innumerable outrages. The Copts are not permitted to have churches here. To aſſiſt at divine ſervice, they are obliged to go to a convent ſituated on the other ſide of the Nile. Girgé affords no veſtige of ancient edifices. It appears to be a modern town, for Abulfeda does not ſpeak of it.—Proceeding for about an hour towards the weſt, we fall in with the ruins of *Abydus*, where Iſmandés built a magnificent temple in honour of Oſiris: It was the only one in Egypt which the ſingers and dancers were forbid to enter. This city, reduced to a village under the empire of Auguſtus, preſents in our time nothing but a heap of ruins without inhabitants; but to the weſt of theſe ruins we ſtill find the celebrated monument of Iſmandés (*b*).

We firſt enter under a portico raiſed about ſixty feet, and ſupported by two rows of maſſy columns. The immoveable ſolidity of the edifice, the huge maſſes which compoſe it, the hieroglyphics it is loaded with, ſtamp it as a work of the ancient Egyptians. Beyond, is a temple which is three hundred feet long by one hundred

(*b*) Strabo, l. 17, calls it Imandès and Memnon. He ſays that this is the ſame Pharoah who built the Labyrinth.

and

and forty-five feet wide. On entering we remark an immenſe hall, the roof of which is ſupported by twenty-eight columns fifty feet high, and nineteen in circumference at the baſe. They are twelve feet diſtant from each other. The enormous ſtones that form the cieling perfectly joined, and incruſted as it were one in the other, offer to the eye nothing but one whole platform of marble one hundred and twenty-ſix feet long, and ſixty-ſix feet wide. The walls are covered with innumerable hieroglyphics. One ſees there a multitude of animals, of birds and human figures with pointed caps on their heads, and a piece of ſtuff hanging down behind (*c*), and dreſſed in open robes deſcending only to the waiſt. The clumſineſs of the ſculpture, announces its antiquity. It is art in its infancy. The forms of the body, the attitudes, the proportions of the members are badly obſerved. Amongſt theſe various repreſentations, women are to be diſtinguiſhed ſuckling their children, and men preſenting offerings to them. In the midſt of theſe deſigns, engraved on the marble, the traveller diſcovers the *divinities of India*. Monſieur Chevalier, formerly governor of Chandernagor, who paſſed twenty years in that country, where he rendered great ſervice to his own, carefully viſited this ancient monument on his return from Bengal. He remarked there the gods *Jaggrenat*, *Gonez*, and *Vichnou*, or *Viſtnou*, ſuch as they are repreſented in the temples of Indoſtan. Have

(*c*) Theſe caps ſtill form the head-dreſs of the Egyptian Prieſts on their days of ceremony.

the

the Egyptians received these divinities, from the Indians or the Indians from the Egyptians? Were this question resolved, it would decide the antiquity of the two people.

At the bottom of the first hall opens a great gate which leads to an apartment forty-six feet long, by twenty-two wide. Six square pillars support the roof of it. At the angles are the doors of four other chambers, but so choaked up by rubbish, that one cannot enter them. The last hall, sixty-four feet long, by twenty-four wide, has stairs by which one descends into the subterraneous apartments of this grand edifice. The Arabs in searching after treasure have piled up heaps of earth and rubbish. One discovers in the part one is able to penetrate, sculpture and hieroglyphics as in the upper story. The natives of the country say, that they correspond exactly with those above, and that the columns are as deep in the earth, as they are lofty above ground. It would be dangerous to go far into these vaults, because the air of them is much infected, and so loaded with mephitic vapour that one can scarcely keep a candle lighted.

Six lions heads placed on the two sides of the temple serve as spouts to carry off the water.— You mount to the top by a stair-case of a very singular form. It is built with stones incrusted in the wall and projecting six feet out, so that being supported only at one end they appear suspended in the air. The walls, the roof, the columns of this edifice have suffered nothing from the injuries of time. Did not the hieroglyphics, corroded in several places, mark its antiquity, it would

appear

appear to have been newly built. The ſolidity is ſuch, that it will laſt a great number of ages, unleſs men make a point of deſtroying it. Except the coloſſal figures, whoſe heads ſerve as the ornament to the capital of the columns, and which are ſculptured in *relievo*, the reſt of the hieroglyphics which cover the inſide of the temple are carved in ſtone.

To the left of this great building, we ſee another much ſmaller at the bottom of which appears a ſort of altar. This was probably the ſanctuary of the temple of Oſiris. I have already obſerved, that the ſingers and muſicians were not allowed to enter it. The Egyptian prieſts invented ſeven vowels, and gave to each of them a ſound approaching our notes of muſic *(d)*. To preſerve this beautiful diſcovery, they repeated at certain periods theſe vowels in the form of hymns, and their various tones ſucceſſively modulated, formed an agreeable melody. This doubtleſs is the reaſon why they baniſhed from this temple all muſical inſtruments. The Greeks drew from this ſource, in compoſing their muſical language, ſo admirably accented, that a diſcourſe well delivered had all the effect of a pleaſing air. If the *Piccini*, the *Glucks*, the *Sacchini*, make us like even the harſh ſounds of the French language, by the ſcientific combinations of their harmony, what would they not have made of theſe ancient tongues? Ceaſe your aſtoniſhment therefore at the marvellous effects the ancient muſic of the Greeks is ſaid to have produced; they had in their hands

(*d*) Plutarch. Treatiſe on Iris and Oſiris.

all

all the treaſures of melody, all the riches of an imitative language, and ſpoke at once to the heart, to the underſtanding, and the ear. Let us take our leave, Sir, of the antique monument of Iſmandes, around which Strabo deſcribes a foreſt of Acacia, conſecrated to Apollo, the remains of which are ſtill viſible on the ſide of *Farchout*.

The dominion of the Turks, from *Girgé* to Sienna, is in a very precarious ſtate. A part of the lands is poſſeſſed by Arabs, in general independent. Such as inhabit the mountains to the eaſt of *Girgé* pay no tribute, and afford an aſſylum to all the malecontents of the government. They even frequently eſpouſe their quarrel, and furniſh them with arms to re-enter Grand Cairo.

The Iſle of *Doum (e)* is not far from *Girgé*. Above is the port of *Bardis*, a ſmall town dependent on the Great Scheik. This prince, whoſe government is very extenſive, has his uſual reſidence at *Farchout*, where a branch of the Nile runs. He poſſeſſes there a vaſt encloſure, where he cultivates the palm, and the date, the acacia, the nabe, the vine, and the orange tree; the Arabian jeſſamine, tufts of ſweet baſil, and clumps of roſes are diſperſed here and there amongſt the trees. Though theſe plantations are made without taſte and without a plan, they afford notwithſtanding moſt delightful thickets. Did art but give the

(*e*) *Doum* is the name given by the Arabs to the Palm-tree with leaves ſpreading like a fan.

ſmalleſt

ſmalleſt aid to nature here, delicious gardens might be formed at ſmall expence; for this happy climate unites a fruitful ſoil, abundant waters, the moſt odoriferous ſhrubs, and the pureſt ſky.

The village of *Beliéné* depends alſo on the Grand Scheik; its ſituation between two canals renders it a very agreeable abode. Oppoſite to it are ſome hamlets, inhabited by Arabs, who infeſt the river with their piracies, eſpecially during the night. Paſſing the arm of the Nile, which goes to *Farchout*, we arrive at *Badjoura*, from whence one diſcovers a handſome iſland, and at a diſtance the village of *Attariſſ*. The Burgh of *Hau*, placed on an eminence, commands the country to the weſt; it ſtands on the ruins of *Dioſpolis Parva (f)*, the ſmall city of Jupiter. The works of the Egyptians had placed it out of the reach of the inundation. *Hau* ſtill poſſeſſes this advantage. Whilſt the adjacent plains are under water, it riſes up amidſt them like an iſland. For this reaſon the inhabitants of Badjoura, and the neighbouring villages, bury their dead here.

In this place the rocks ſtretch off from the eaſtern bank. We remark there the villages of *Caſr* and of *Fau*: the former was heretofore a town, of which Abulfeda gives us the following deſcription: "*Caſr* is a day's journey to the "ſouthward of *Cous*. This town, ſituated on

(*f*) Strabo, l. 17, and Ptolemy, l. 4, lay down Dioſpolis between Abydus and Tentyra, on an eminence, a ſituation which perfectly agrees with the Burgh of *Hau*.

" the

"the eastern bank of the river, is surrounded "with fields abounding in grain, and palm trees. "A great quantity of earthen jars are fabricated "here, which are conveyed into the west of "Egypt." Since the time of Abulfeda, the town of *Casr* has lost the greatest part of its commerce, and of its inhabitants *(g)*. At this day it is no more than a village of little importance.

The western border of the Nile, more pleasant, and better peopled, offers to the sight, woods of date-trees, and of *Doum* dispersed around the dwellings, rich plains of wheat, and pastures covered with flocks. The Burgh of Dendera has nothing remarkable; but about a league to the westward we find the ruins of ancient *Tentyra*. Heaps of rubbish, and ruins of a great extent, mark the grandeur of the city, where, according to Strabo *(h)*, Isis and Venus were adored. After crossing these remains, one admires on a little eminence two ancient temples, the largest of which is only two hundred feet long, by one hundred and forty wide. Around it is a double frize; the interior is divided into several very lofty apartments, supported by large columns, with a square stone by way of capital, on which is carved the head of Isis. The walls are covered with hieroglyphics, separated into different compartments. The angles of the temple are ornamented without, by colossal figures. Ten flights of stairs lead to the top.

(g) Abulfeda. Description of Egypt.
(h) Strabo, l. 17.

The

The ſecond, ſituated on the right-hand, is ſmaller; the cornice which goes round it, and the gate at the entrance, are decorated with falcons, with their wings ſpread. A double ſquare ſtone forms the capital of the columns which ſupport the roof. On the walls are ſculptured ſeveral figures of men, of birds, and animals. Theſe hieroglyphics compriſed the hiſtory of the time. By reading them we ſhould learn probably, whether theſe monuments are the temples of Iſis and of Venus. We remark the ſame ſolidity in them as in thoſe of *Abydus*, but they have leſs grandeur and magnificence.

I ſhall not finiſh this letter, Sir, without laying before you what Strabo (*i*) ſays of the averſion the Tentyrites preſerved for the Crocodile, worſhipped in ſo many other cities. " The inhabi-" tants of *Tentyra* abhor the Crocodile, and " wage continual war againſt him, as the moſt " dangerous of animals. Other men looking " upon him as pernicious, avoid him; but the " Tentyrites induſtriouſly ſeek after him, and " kill him wherever they meet with him. It is " known that the Pſylli of Cyrène have a cer-" tain empire over ſerpents, and it is generally " believed that the Tentyrites have the ſame " power over crocodiles. In fact, they dive and " ſwim boldly in the middle of the Nile, with-" out any injury. In the ſpectacles given at Rome " ſeveral crocodiles were put into a baſon. " There was an opening on one of the ſides to " allow them to eſcape. One ſaw the inhabi-

(*i*) Strabo, l. 17.

" tants

" tants of Tentyra throw themſelves into the " water amongſt theſe monſters, take them in a " net, and draw them out. After expoſing them " to the Roman people, they took hold of them " intrepidly, and carried them back into the " baſon."

This fact atteſted by a judicious hiſtorian, an ocular witneſs of it, cannot be called in queſtion. In our days, do not the Caribs, armed only with a knife, fight advantageouſly with the ſhark, one of the moſt dreadful monſters of the ſea? Determined men are ſtill to be found in Egypt, who dare to attack the crocodile. They ſwim towards that formidable animal; and when he opens his mouth to ſwallow them, thruſt into it a plank of fir, to which a cord is faſtened. The crocodile, by violently ſhutting his jaws, buries his ſharp teeth in it ſo far that he cannot diſengage them. The Egyptian, holding the cord with one hand, then regains the banks of the river, and ſeveral men draw the monſter on ſhore, and kill him. This attack is not without danger; for if the ſwimmer is not ſkilful, he is immediately devoured. I never was myſelf a witneſs to this tranſaction, but many perſons at Grand Cairo have aſſured me it was true.

I have the honour to be, &c.

LETTER XXXIII.

DESCRIPTION OF GIENE, COPHTOS, COUS, AND OF THE ROUTE FROM THESE TO COSSEIR ON THE RED SEA.

Cophtos and Cous successively enjoyed the trade of the Red Sea. Giéné now in the possession of it. The efforts of the Ptolemies to protect it. True state of this commerce. Description of the route from Giéné to Cosseir. This place only a large village with a good port and a convenient road for ships. Precautions necessary in travelling through the Desart. Means of improving this road. The advantages which would result from such improvement.

To Mr. L. M.

Grand Cairo.

OPPOSITE to *Dendera*, Sir, we discover *Giéné*, built on an eminence. The ancients who called it Cœnœ, (*k*) mention no remarkable monument there. It is not now more flourishing, though it be the rendezvous of the caravans which set out for *Cosseir*. A canal runs near it which was formerly navigable. The negligence of the Turks has suffered it to be choaked up, and it has no water but in the time of the inundation.

(*k*) Ptolemy, l. 4. calls it Cœnœ, or the New City.

dation. If *Giéné* contains no edifice worthy to attract the attention, its environs merit well to be remarked by travellers. They are occupied by gardens which produce excellent oranges, dates, lemons, and exquifite melons. The trees collected here form fhades which are invaluable, under a burning fky.

Above *Giéné* are the ruins of *Cophtos (l)*. This town, fituated on an eminence furrounded by the waters of the Nile, was advantageoufly placed for the commerce of the Red Sea. Strabo thus defcribes it *(m)*: " A canal cut from the " Nile paffes by *Cophtos* inhabited by Egyptians " and Arabs. Ptolemy Philadelphus was the " firft who opened a high road from this town " to Berenice, acrofs a defart without water. " He made them conftruct public buildings " where travellers on foot, and horfemen found " neceffary refrefhment. The dangers of the " navigation towards the narrow extremity of " the Red Sea, determined him to execute this " project, the great advantages of which evinced " its utility. The produce of Arabia, of India " and Ethiopia, were fpeedily conveyed to " Cophtos by the Arabic gulph. This town is " ftill the emporium of the merchandize of the " eaft. It is no longer landed at Berenice, which " affords nothing but a road infecure for veffels,

(*l*) The Arabs having no letter *p* in their language, fubftitute the *b*, and call this town *Cobt*.

(*m*) Strabo, l. 17.

" but

" but at the port of Rat (*n*), which is not far " from it, and where a navy is maintained. At " first men travelled by night on camels, and " steered their course, like mariners, by the " stars. It was necessary, too, to have a provisi- " on of water sufficient for six or seven days " journey. At present they make use of what " they find collected in deep wells and cisterns, " formed for the purpose. In the isthmus one " crosses over, are found mines of emeralds and " precious metals, which the Arabs search af- " ter."

The riches *Cophtos* derived from the trade with India, rendered it very flourishing. It became a celebrated town; its prosperity lasted till the reign of Dioclesian. Its inhabitants having embraced Christianity, were exposed to the persecutions of that Emperor, and revolted. He marched his troops against them, and their town

(*n*) The Greeks and Romans called it so, because it is small. The Arabs in calling it *Cosseir*, little, have preserved its ancient denomination. This passage stands in need of explanation. Strabo places *Berenice* at a small distance from the port of Rat, now called *Cosseir*. Ptolemy and Pliny lay it down almost under the tropic, that is to say, more than twenty leagues farther to the southward. It was eleven or twelve days journey, therefore, at least from Cophtos to Berenice, and Strabo calls it only seven. It is evident that this historian, who never made the journey, and who contented himself with taking informations on the spot, was deceived at the time that this ancient road was no longer frequented. By consulting the best geographers, there is no doubt that Berenice was situated on the coast of the Red Sea, and in the parallel of Sienna. Father Sicard and several other travellers are of opinion that *Cosseir* is the ancient Berenice; but this is a mistake.

was

was rased to the ground. In the time of Abulfeda it had lost all its splendour, and was no more than a hamlet, elevated amongst ruins. At this day no inhabitants are to be seen; they have retired to a village a mile above, which they call *Cobt*. The marbles, and fine remains of monuments dispersed amongst the sands which cover the ancient city, attest the barbarism of Dioclesian. The great bason which served it as a port, is still subsisting, with two bridges thrown over the canals that encompass it.

Cous, formerly the city of Apollo, rose from the disaster of *Cophto*. The merchants established themselves there, and commerce flourished a long time, as we learn from Abulfeda "*Cous* (*o*), "says he, situated to the east of the Nile, is the "greatest town in Egypt after *Fostat*. It is the "emporium of the commerce of Aden. The "merchandise is landed at *Cosseir*, from whence "it arrives at Cous, in three days journey, across "the desart."

This town, which like *Cophtos*, was indebted for its consequence to the commerce with India, enjoyed great opulence during the dominion of the Arabs. Since the Turks have got possession of Egypt, and this beautiful country has been laid waste by a Pacha and four and twenty Beys, *Cous* has undergone the fate of her rival. The

(*o*) Abulfeda, description of Egypt. Aden was the most flourishing town of the Yemen, in the thirteenth century; it carried on the commerce of India and Egypt. Gohaa and other writers have placed the ruins of Thebes at *Cous*. This likewise is an error.

vexations

vexations of the Government have ruined her commerce; her glory is eclipsed. In our days we behold nothing but a collection of cottages, inhabited by a few Coptis and Arabs. Giéné, which has succeeded these two cities, has none of their magnificence, because the advantages of its situation and the fertility of its teritory, cannot counterbalance the obstacles which the despotism of the Egyptian government, and the pillage of the Bedouins, oppose to the progress of its commerce.

After making you acquainted with these ancient cities, it is proper to give you some details of this part of Egypt, so interesting, and so little known to Europe. Examine the map of this country, you will see that the Nile, on precipitating itself from its last cataract, bends its course towards Lybia, following the direction of the mountains. Repulsed soon after by these insurmountable barriers, it returns towards the east, and approaches the Red Sea. The interval which separates them being only three and thirty leagues, Strabo has given it the name of an Isthmus. *Giéné* and *Cosseir* are at the two extremities. A deep valley, where at every step we discover traces of the sea, leads from one to the other. It is barren, destitute of verdure, but far from impassable. We find water there, and some acacias called *Naboul*, which produce gum arabic. The Arabs eat it, doubtless, to quench their thirst. The mines of emeralds and precious metals that ancient writers speak of *(p)* and

(p) Pliny, Strabo, Diodorus Siculus.

which conſtituted heretofore the principal ſources of the riches of Egypt, ſtill ſubſiſt in the mountains on the ſide of the road. The fear of being expoſed to the vexations of the Beys, and the ignorance of the modern Egyptians, prevent them from being worked.

The port of *Coſſeir* is very inconſiderable. Large boats enter it, but veſſels are obliged to remain in the road, where they find good anchorage. This advantage made the Greeks and Romans chooſe it as a harbour for their navy. The preſent town, or rather hamlet, contains only about two hundred earthen huts. It is commanded by a caſtle, flanked by four towers, the fire of which would ſuffice for its defence, as well as the ſhips in the harbour; but it is ſuffered to go to ruin, and has at preſent for its whole garriſon, a porter, whoſe buſineſs it is to open and ſhut an antique gate of iron. The inhabitants are a medley of Turks and Arabs, governed by a Cachef, who depends on the Governor of *Giéné*. The enormous duty of ten per cent. laid in kind on the merchandize that arrives at Coſſeir, offers no great encouragement for the merchants. The tyranny of the Beys, the vexations of the Commandant, the fear of the Bedouins, are ſtill more terrible ſhackles. The ſituation of this port, however, for the barter of the productions of Egypt, for thoſe of Arabia and India, is ſo favourable, that its commerce, though greatly diminſhed, ſtill ſubſiſts. It is certain, that a nation, powerful at ſea, might make all theſe obſtacles vaniſh for a very

ſmall

ſmall expence, and ſecure prodigious benefits from this important trade. Every thing depends on the means to be employed.

Mr. Chevalier, Commandant General of the French eſtabliſhments in Bengal, is juſt arrived at Grand Cairo by the way of Coſſeir. I hope, Sir, you will not be ſorry to learn by what means a Frenchman has been able to eſcape from the hands of the Turks and Arabs, who had a great deſire to pillage him. The journal he has communicated to me, will teach you how to travel in theſe deſarts. The veſſel he was on board of, being ſtruck with lightening on the coaſt of Malabar, and afterwards diſmaſted off Gedda, he was obliged to take ſhelter in that port. Theſe accidents had made him loſe the proper ſeaſon for reaching Suez. He muſt either wait for the next monſoon, or riſk himſelf in a ſmall veſſel on this ſtormy ſea. His zeal for the intereſt of his country made him adopt this dangerous alternative. After ſtruggling for three months againſt contrary winds, and being twenty times on the point of periſhing, he reached Coſſeir. From thence he ſet out a few days after, with ſix Europeans mounted on camels. He followed the long valley which traverſes the iſthmus, and whoſe bottom is even, and covered with ſand and petrified ſhells. Sometimes it is ſpacious, and ſometimes very narrow. Here its ſides riſe into mountains, from whence the winter torrents detach huge maſſes of rock, and where the granite, the jaſper, the alabaſter, and the porphyry appear. There it changes into ſandy hillocks, deſtitute of

 a ſingle

a single shrub. These sands and naked rocks, continually smitten by the rays of a burning sun, reflect a light which proves injurious to the eyes, and so great a heat, that neither men nor animals can withstand it. It was in the month of July that Mr Chevalier and his companion crossed this dismal solitude. The night brought them no comfort, because the winds ceasing to blow, the succeeding calm left them exposed to the suffocating exhalations of the burning sands, that served them for a bed; amidst these sufferings, a little paste, half-baked on the ashes, was their only food. They had nothing to quench their thirst but water, which, after remaining some hours in skins, rubbed with stinking oil, was corrupted, and contracted a taste and smell which were insupportable. Add to these evils the continual apprehension of being plundered by the Arabs, the necessity of keeping watch during the night, and you will have an idea of what the man of courage is capable of suffering. Mr. Chevalier had provided for every event. His camels were fastened to each other that they might not separate in case of an attack. One of them carried two small cannon, and the troop, armed with double-barreled guns, sabres, and pistols, never quitted their arms. They encamped every evening at a distance from the camel-drivers, who had orders not to approach under pain of death. Each of the Europeans mounted guard in his turn, whilst the others took a few moments repose. They owed their safety to these wise precautions; for the third day, about sixty Arabs came to attack them.

them. Their guides, who maintained a private correſpondence with the robbers, flew, on the firſt fire, to hide themſelves in the caverns of the rocks. The French, led on by their Chief, advanced in good order, and played off their ſmall artillery with ſucceſs. After a few well-pointed fires, the Bedouins fled behind their mountains. They returned ſeveral times to the charge during the route; but the vigilance, the firm countenance, and the muſquetry of the Europeans, kept at a diſtance the enemy, whoſe buſineſs it was to plunder, not to fight. At length, after a march of four days and a half, they arrived at Giéné, ſcorched by the ſun, dying with thirſt, and exhauſted with hunger and fatigue. After bathing in the waters of the Nile, ſatiating themſelves with the excellent fruits which grow on its banks, and enjoying the various productions of the teeming ſoil it fertilizes, they experienced a comfort, a contentment, a joy, the inexpreſſible delights of which the traveller alone can taſte who has croſſed the deſarts.

A recent diſaſter, proves the prudence of Mr. Chevalier. Nearly at the ſame time that he left Coſſeir, a rich caravan, worth ſeveral millions of livres, loaded for the account of the Engliſh, had been attacked between Suez and Grand Cairo. Several Europeans were with it; but to avoid the fatiguing weight of their arms, they had faſtened them on the camels. Beſides they marched at a great diſtance one from the other, and without caution; this ſecurity, produced by their confidence in the promiſe of the Bey, cauſed their

ruin.

ruin. The Bedouins pouring upon them unexpectedly, did not allow them time to put themſelves on their defence. They pillaged all their wealth, and ſeveral of the travellers periſhed. It is in this fatal affair that Mr. de St. Germain has had the misfortune to loſe a brother whom he loved, and two thirds of his fortune. After wandering, himſelf, for two days and nights in this burning ſolitude, naked, without food, without water, and almoſt without hope, he arrived nearly dead at the tent of an Arab, who waſhed him with freſh water, fed him with milk, cloathed, and conducted him to Grand Cairo. I had theſe particulars from the mouth of this unfortunate gentleman, who is preparing to return to France, where his misfortunes probably will intereſt the beneficence of government.

The route of Coſſeir, Sir, has not the ſame diſadvantages in winter; the heat then is moderate; the fear of robbers alone can ſtop the traveller; but by collecting in a troop, they may put themſelves out of danger of their purſuit. Even during the ſummer, when they take care to provide themſelves with neceſſaries, and to carry the water in earthen jars, or ſkins which are not hardened with rancid oil; men accuſtomed to the temperature of warm climates, take this journey without inconvenience. If the twenty-four tyrants who devour the riches of Egypt, could devote their thoughts for an inſtant to the happineſs of mankind, they would conſtruct three public buildings, where the caravans might find refreſhment and repoſe; but all their ambition conſiſts fiſts in reigning a few days, in giving themſelves up immoderately to their paſſions, intoxicating themſelves with every ſpecies of pleaſure, and mutually deſtroying each other. I have ſeen eleven of them in the ſpace of three years paſs in this manner from the boſomof voluptuouſneſs to death. They periſh by the ſteel of their colleagues, reſerved for the ſame fate. A greater number ſave themſelves by flight. What has agriculture and commerce to expect from ſuch a government? If Egypt fell into the hands of an enlightened people, the route from Coſſeir would be rendered ſafe and commodious. I am of opinion, that it would be poſſible even to turn a branch of the Nile through this deep valley where the ſea formerly has flowed. This canal does not appear to be attended with more difficulties than that which *Amru* executed from Foſtat to Colzoum. It would procure far greater advantages, ſince it would ſave veſſels from India about one hundred leagues dangerous navigation acroſs the narrow extremity of the Red Sea. We ſhould ſoon ſee landed at Coſſeir, the ſtuffs of Bengal, the perfumes of Iemen, and the Abyſſinian gold duſt. The grain, the linens, the various productions of Egypt, would be given in exchange. This beautiful country, in the hands of a nation friendly to the arts, would once more become the centre of the commerce of the world. It would be the point of union between Europe and Aſia. Whilſt one part of its ſhips ſailed from the Arabic gulph towards India, the reſt would cover the Mediterranean; Alexandria would revive from

her

her aſhes. An obſervatory placed under this ſerene ſky would add ſtill farther to the progreſs of aſtronomy. This happy country would be a ſecond time the native country of the ſciences, and the moſt delicious habitation on the globe. A more advantageous ſituation than Egypt cannot be imagined. It communicates with the eaſtern and weſtern ſeas. Nature has done every thing for it, and to reſtore it to that high degree of glory and of power, which once rendered it ſo famous, nothing is wanting but a people worthy of becoming its inhabitants.

I have the honour to be, &c.

LET-

LETTER XXXIV.

JOURNEY FROM COUS TO THEBES. DESCRIPTION OF THE EASTERN PART OF THIS CITY.

Deſcription of Thebes, extracted from Diodorus Siculus and Strabo. State of this city under the Pharaohs, the Romans, and the dominions of the Turks. Porticoes, avenues of the Sphinx, with the ſtructure and ruins of the great temple, near Carnack, *in the eaſtern quarter of Thebes. Its foundations and ruins occupy a circumference of half a league. The plain extending from Carnack to* Luxor, *and anciently covered with buildings, now under agriculture. Deſcription of the remains of the Temple of Luxor, and the ſuperb obeliſks ſituated near it. The The moſt beautiful ſtructures in Egypt, and in the whole world.*

To Mr. L. M.

Grand Cairo.

ON leaving *Coüs*, to aſcend toward Aſſouan, we leave on the right the town of *Nequadé*, the reſidence of a Coptic Biſhop, and where the Mahometans have ſeveral moſques. The Iſle of Matoré is very near, and two leagues beyond it we diſcover the ruins of *Thebes*, whoſe magnificence has been celebrated with emulation by Poets and Hiſtorians. Paſſages from thoſe ancients who ſaw it, will make you acquainted with its former ſplendour. An accurate deſcription of the monuments

numents subsisting in our days, will enable you to judge of the degree of confidence due to their narratives, and the punctuated line on the map, which passes by *Carnak-Luxor*, *Medinet-Abou*, and *Gournou*, will point out to you the extent of this famous city.

" The Great Diospolis, by the Greeks called " Thebes, says Diodorus Siculus (q), was six " leagues in circumference. Busiris, its founder, " erected there superb edifices, which he enrich- " ed with magnificent presents. The fame of " her power, and of her riches, celebrated by " Homer, filled the universe. Her gates, and " the numerous vestibules of her temples, induc- " ed this poet to bestow on her the name of " *Ecatompyle*, or the city with a hundred gates. " Never did a city receive so many offerings in " gold, in silver, in ivory, in colossal statues, and " in obelisks of a single stone. Above all were " to be admired, her four principal temples. " The most ancient was surprisingly grand and " sumptuous. It was half a league round (r), " and was encompassed by walls four and twenty " feet thick, and seventy high. The richness " and finishing of the ornaments corresponded " with its grandeur. Several Kings contributed " to embellish it. It still subsists, but the gold, " the silver, the ivory, and precious stones, were

(q) Diodorus Siculus, l. 1.

(r) Diodorus Siculus comprehends in this circumference, the avenues of Sphinxes, the porticoes, the buildings, and courts which encompassed the temple, properly so called. We shall see that this author is not far from the truth.

" carried

" carried off, when Cambyſes ſet fire to all the
" Egyptian temples."

I have only given you the principal traits of the picture this Hiſtorian delineates of Thebes, in its flouriſhing ſtate, becauſe they are ſufficient to give you an idea of its beauty. Strabo will diſplay it in its fall, that is to ſay, ſuch as it was eighteen centuries before us.

" Thebes or Dioſpolis now preſents only the
" wreck of its former grandeur, diſperſed over a
" ſpace of twenty-five Stadia in length. We ſtill
" remark a great number of temples, partly de-
" ſtroyed by Cambyſes. The inhabitants are
" retired into burghs, ſituated on the eaſt of the
" Nile, where the preſent city is, and on the
" weſtern bank near to Memnonium (*s*). In this
" place we admire two Coloſſuſes of ſtone, plac-
" ed by the ſide of each other. One of them is en-
" tire. The other, it is ſaid, (*t*) was overthrown
" by the ſhock of an earthquake. If we may cre-
" dit the general opinion, that part of the ſtatue
" remaining on its baſis, utters a ſound once a day.
" Curious to examine the truth of this fact, I went
" thither with Ælius Gallus, who was accompa-
" nied by his friends, and followed by a nume-
" rous retinue of ſoldiers. I heard this ſound
" towards ſix o'clock in the morning, but I dare
" not take upon me to determine whether it

(*s*) Strabo calls Memnonium a temple, near to which was the ſtatue of Memnon.

(*t*) Strabo is the only one amongſt the ancients who has attributed the fall of this Coloſſus to an earthquake; all the others agree in telling us that it was overthrown by order of Cambyſes.

pro-

" proceeded from the base of the Colossus, or " was produced by some of the assistants; for, " rather than ascribe it to the effect of an assem- " blage of stones, one is tempted to imagine a " thousand different causes. Above Memnonium " are the tombs of the kings, hewn with the " chisel in the rock. We may reckon about " forty, constructed in a wonderful manner, and " worthy of attracting the attention of travellers. " Some obelisks hewn out near them, bear dif- " ferent inscriptions, which point out the riches, " the power, and the extent of the empire of " these sovereigns who governed Scythia, Bac- " tria, India, and Ionia. They give the detail " also of the greatness of the tributes they im- " posed, and the number of their troops, which " amounted to a million of soldiers."

Previous to laying before you, Sir, what actually remains of the monuments described by these two historians, it is proper to make you acquainted with the distribution of the ornaments, the vestibules, the courts, and edifices, which composed the Egyptian temples, that we may not lose ourselves amongst these ruins.

" *(u)* The temples of Egypt are preceded " by one or more paved avenues, one hundred " feet wide, and three or four hundred long. " Two rows of sphinxes, thirty feet distant " from each other, adorn the sides. These " avenues are terminated by porticoes, the " number of which is indefinite. These porti- " coes lead to a magnificent square in the front

(u) Strabo, l. 17.

" of

" of the temple. Beyond is the ſanctuary, which " is ſmaller, and in which human figures are " never ſculptured, and ſeldom even thoſe of " animals. The ſides of this place are formed " by walls of the ſame height with the temple. " More extenſive at their origin than the width " of its front, they afterwards approach each " other about one hundred feet. They are " covered with large ſculptured figures in the " taſte of the ancient Tuſcan and Grecian works. " A ſpacious edifice, ſupported by a prodigious " number of columns, is the uſual accompani- " ments of theſe temples."

Having nothing to offer you but monuments, mutilated by time or men, I hope this deſcription will ſerve to point out to you what is wanting to their perfection. Guided by this, let us proceed to the ſouthward of Cornack, where we fall in with the remains of one of the four principal temples ſpoken of by Diodorus Siculus. It has eight entries, three of which have ſphinxes before them of an enormous ſize, with two large ſtatues on each ſide. Theſe ſphinxes and coloſſuſes, all of one ſingle block of marble, are hewn in the antique ſtile. After paſſing through theſe majeſtic alleys, we arrive at four porticoes, each of which is thirty feet wide, fifty-two in height, and one hundred and fifty long. Pyramidical gates ſerve by way of entrance, and ſtones of an aſtoniſhing ſize reſt on the two walls, and from the cieling.

The firſt of theſe porticoes is entirely built of red granite, perfectly poliſhed. Four compartments,

compartments, filled with hieroglyphics, occupy the exterior faces. The interior has only three rows, in each of which one remarks two human figures, larger than nature, ſculptured with infinite art. The ſides are decorated with coloſſal figures, elevated fifteen feet above the foundations of the gate. Two ſtatues thirty-three feet high, one of red granite, the other of granite ſpotted with black and grey, are placed without. There is another in the inſide, compoſed of a block of white marble, the head of which is knocked off. Theſe coloſſuſes bear in their hand *a ſort of* CROSS, that is to ſay, the PHALLUS, which, amongſt the Egyptians, was *the ſymbol of fecundity.*

The ſecond portico is half ruined. The gate has only two ranks of hieroglyphics of a gigantic ſize: one to the ſouth, the other to the north. All the faces of the third are covered with hieroglyphics, formed of coloſſal figures. At the entrance of the gate one ſees the remains of a ſtatue of white marble, the trunk of which is fifteen feet in circumference. Its head is covered with a helmet, with a ſerpent entwined round it. In the place of the fourth portico, are walls almoſt entirely overthrown, and heaps of rubbiſh. In the midſt of them one diſtinguiſhes the fragments of a coloſſus of red granite, the body of which is thirty feet round.

At the extremity of theſe porticoes commenced thoſe lofty walls, which formed the firſt court of the temple. The people entered it by twelve gates. Several of them are deſtroyed, and others much decayed. That which has ſuffered the leaſt

leaſt from the injuries of time, and the ravages of the barbarians, looks towards the weſt. There is a long avenue of ſphinxes in the front. It is forty feet wide, about ſixty in height, and forty-eight thick at the foundation. One remarks in the front two rows of ſmall windows, and on the ſides, the ruins of ſtair-caſes, by which they aſcended to the top. This gate, the maſs of which appears immoveable, is in the ruſtic ſtile, without hieroglyphics, and of an awful ſimplicity. It gives an entrance into the great ſquares, the ſides of which are formed by two terraces, elevated ſix feet from the ground, and eighty wide. The traveller admires there two beautiful colonades which extend the whole length of the terraces. Above and in the front of the temple, is a ſecond court, the extent of which correſponds with the majeſty of the building. It is likewiſe decorated with two ranges of columns, which are more than fifty feet high, by eighteen in circumference at the baſe. Their capitals are in the form of vaſes, crowned with large ſquare ſtones, which ſerved probably as pedeſtals for ſtatues. Two coloſſuſes of a prodigious ſize, but mutilated by barbarians, terminate theſe colonades. Arrived at this place, the eye views with aſtoniſhment the immenſity of the temple. It is of a ſurpriſing elevation; its walls built with marble, appear incapable of deſtruction. The roof, of a greater height in the middle than at the ſides, is ſupported by eighteen rows of pillars. Thoſe which ſupport the part the moſt elevated, are thirty feet in circumference, and about eighty in height;

height; the others are one third ſmaller. There is not in the univerſe a building whoſe grandeur bears a more awful character, nor whoſe majeſty ſtrikes more forcibly the feelings. It ſeems conformable with the great idea the Egyptians entertained of the ſupreme Being; and it is impoſſible to enter it without being penetrated with reſpect. All its aſpects, internal and external, are covered with hieroglyphics and extraordinary figures. On the north ſide are ſculptured repreſentations of battles, with horſes and with chariots, one of which is drawn by ſtags. We diſtinguiſh on the ſouth two barks covered with a canopy, at the extremity of which appears a ſun. They are puſhed by mariners with poles. Two men, ſeated at the ſtern, ſeem to direct their courſe, and to receive homage. Theſe deſigns are allegorical. The Greeks, in their poetical language, painted the ſun in a car, drawn by courſers, guided by Apollo. The Egyptians repreſented him borne on a veſſel, conducted by Oſiris and ſeven mariners, emblematical of the planets *(x)*. This entrance, which formed the front of the temple of *Luxor*, is much disfigured, but it muſt have been moſt ſumptuouſly grand if we may judge by the obeliſks which announce it. We ſee two of them ſixty feet high, by one and twenty in circumference at the baſe; and a little farther two others, ſeventy-two feet high, by thirty in circumference. Each of theſe ſuperb monuments, formed of a block of red granite, do honour to

(x) Macrobius dream of Scipio.—Martian Capella, l. 2.

the

the genius and knowledge of the acient Egyptians. Various hieroglyphics are engraved on them, divided into columns. Three of theſe obeliſks are erect; one only is over-thrown.

On quitting this vaſt temple, and proceeding towards the ſouth, we arrive acroſs heaps of rubbiſh, at the building, called by Strabo the Sanctuary. It is not conſiderable; the gate is ornamented with pillars, three of which grouped together, are united under a ſingle capital. The interior is diſtributed into ſeveral halls of granite. It was here they kept the *Virgin*, conſecrated to Jupiter, and *who offered herſelf as a ſacrifice in a very extraordinary manner (y)*.

I have only deſcribed ſuch parts of this temple as are the beſt preſerved. We diſcover in this vaſt encloſure ſeveral buildings, almoſt deſtroyed, which ſerved, doubtleſs, for the Prieſts and the ſacred animals. One remarks alſo a large piece of water, encompaſſed with ruins, and at every ſtep we meet with the trunks of columns, ſphinxes, ſtatues, coloſſuſes, and ſuch magnificent ruins, that one is filled with aſtoniſhment and admiration. If we meaſure with accuracy the ſpace occupied by the veſtibules, the porticoes, and the courts of the temple, we ſhall find that the whole was at leaſt half a league in

(*y*) Jovi quem præcipuè colunt (Thebani) Virgo quædam genere clariſſima, & ſpecie pulcherrima ſacratur; quales Græci pallacas vocant. Ea pellicis more cum quibus vult, coit, uſque ad naturalem corporis purgationem. Poſt purgationem vero viro datur; ſed priuſquam nubat poſt pellicatus tempus in mortuæ morem lugetur. *Strabo.* l. 17.

 circumference,

circumference, and that Diodorus Siculus is not deceived in allowing them that extent.

The plain which extends from *Carnak* to *Luxor* is not leſs than a league in length. This ſpace was covered with the houſes of the Egyptians who inhabited the eaſtern part of Thebes. Although they were, according to Diodorus Siculus (z), five ſtories high, and ſolidly conſtructed, they have not been able to reſiſt the ravages of time and conquerors; they are totally deſtroyed (*a*). Now that the ſoil is greatly raiſed, and that the annual overflowings of the river have covered them with ſeveral feet of mud, the ground is cultivated on their ruins. Corn, flax, and vegetables, grow on theſe ſpots, where three thouſand years ago, were admired public ſquares, palaces, and numerous edifices, inhabited by an enlightened people. At the extremity of this plain ſtands the village of *Luxor*, near to which we behold the avenues and remains of another temple, ſtill more disfigured than the former. It occupied an extenſive ſpace. Large courts, ſurrounded by porticoes, ſupported by columns forty feet high, without including the baſes, buried in the ſand; pyramidal gates, covered with hieroglyphic ſculpture, and of an awful majeſty; the remains of

(*z*) Diodorus Siculus, l. 1.

(*a*) Dr. Pocock, deceived by this total deſtruction, thought that there were formerly no other great edfices at Thebes but the temples; and that the dwellings of the inhabitants were either tents or huts, &c. But the teſtimony of Diodorus refutes this opinion

walls

walls, built with maſſes of granite, and which the barbariſm alone of men has been able to overthrow; whole files of lofty marble coloſſuſes, forty feet high, two thirds of their body buried up; all theſe monuments proclaim what the magnificence of the principal edifice muſt have been, whoſe ſite is marked out by a hill of piled ruins. But nothing gives a greater idea of it than two obeliſks which ſerved it as an ornament, and which ſeem to have been placed there by giants, or the Genii of Fable. Each of them, formed of a ſingle block of granite, is ſeventy-two feet high above ground, and thirty-two in circumference; but as they are greatly ſunk into the ſand and mud, we may fairly imagine them to have been ninety feet from the baſe to the ſummit. One of them is ſplit towards the middle; the other is in perfect preſervation. The hieroglyphics that cover them, divided into columns, and cut in *relievo*, projecting an inch and an half, do honour to the artiſt who was their ſculptor. The hardneſs of the ſtone has preſerved them from the injury of the air; nothing can be more majeſtic than theſe obeliſks. Egypt is the only country where ſuch works have been executed; nor is there a city in the world in which they would not form its nobleſt ornament. Such, Sir, are the moſt remarkable monuments we find in our days in the eaſtern part of Thebes. The very ſight of them alone would be ſufficient to inflame the genius of a poliſhed nation; but the Turks and the Coptis, bending under the iron yoke which lies heavy on their heads, look on them without admiration, and build around them earthen huts which hardly ſhelter them from the ſun. Theſe barbarians when they want a mill-ſtone, do not bluſh to beat down the column that ſupported a temple, or a portico, and to ſaw it into pieces. To this abject ſtate does deſpotiſm degrade men!

I have the honour to be, &c.

LETTER XXXV.

DESCRIPTION OF THE WESTERN PART OF THEBES.

Visit to the tombs of the Theban kings, excavated in the mountain. Description of these subterraneous places, the sepulchres, their galleries and hieroglyphics. Account of a great temple, the roof of which was supported by square pillars, ornamented on the top with statues. Fragments of a prodigious Colossus among its ruins. Ruins of Memnonium, marked out by heaps of marble fragments, and rows of statues, either mutilated, or with a third part of their height buried in the earth; and above all, by the colossal statue of Memnon, famous in ancient times for the sounds which it emitted at sun-rise.

To Mr. L. M.

Grand Cairo.

THE village of *Gournou*, Sir, and that of *Medinet Abou*, situated on the spot occupied by the western part of THEBES, and surrounded by grand ruins; a league to the westward of the former are grottoes, called *Biban El melouk*, the gates of the Kings. It is there we see the tombs of the ancient sovereigns of the Thebais. The road that leads to it is strewed with marbles and with ruins. We arrive there by following the

the windings of a narrow paſs, the ſides of which in many places have been cut with the chiſel. Spacious apartments are cut out of the rock, which muſt have been antecedent to the conſtruction of the houſes and the palaces. At the bottom of this valley, which widens to about two hundred toiſes, we diſcover in the foot of the mountains, openings which lead to theſe tombs. Strabo (*b*) reckons forty, Diodorus Siculus (*c*), forty-ſeven of them; but he adds, that in the reign of Auguſtus there remained but ſeventeen, ſome of which were then greatly damaged. At preſent the greateſt part of them are cloſed up, and there is no getting into above nine of them. The ſubterraneous galleries which are before them are in general ten feet high, by as many wide; the walls and the roof hewn out of a white rock, preſerve the brilliancy and the poliſh of the ſtucco. Four principal alleys, longer and more lofty than the former, terminate at the gate of a large hall, in the middle of which we ſee a marble tomb, with the figure of the prince, ſculptured in *relievo* on the lid. Another figure holding a ſceptre in his hand, adorns one of the ſides of the wall. A third, repreſented on the roof, bears a ſceptre alſo, and wings which deſcend to his heels.

The ſecond grotto, which is ſpacious and well decorated, preſents to the ſight a cieling covered with golden ſtars, birds painted in colours, the freſhneſs and vivacity of which have loſt nothing

(*b*) Strabo, l. 17. (*c*) Diodorus Siculus, l. 1,

of

of their ſplendor, and hieroglyphics divided into columns and cut on the walls. Two men are ſeated by the gate, to which we are conducted by a long flight of ſteps of very gentle deſcent. A block of red granite ſixteen feet high, ten long, and ſix wide, forms the ſarcophagus of the king, whoſe figure cut in *relievo*, adorns the lid. Around it is a hieroglyphic inſcription. The niches formed in the rock, ſerved doubtleſs as the repoſitories of the mummies of the royal family. The tombs depoſited in other apartments have been carried off by violence, as their ruins teſtify. We obſerve here a very handſome grotto, where nothing remains but a lid of marble, ten feet long and ſix wide. At the end of the moſt remote cave, one diſtinguiſhes a human figure ſculptured in *relievo*, the arms croſſed on the breaſt, and two others at its ſide upon their knees.

Theſe galleries, theſe ſubteraneous apartments, which extend very far under the mountains, a ſmall part of which only I have deſcribed, are ornamented with innumerable figures of men, and birds, and different animals, ſome in *relievo*, ſome engraved, and others painted in ineffaceable colours. Theſe unintelligible characters, which compoſe the hiſtory of the time, conceal moſt intereſting ſubjects under their impenetrable veil, as well as the moſt remarkable events of the lives of the Theban monarchs, whoſe power extended even to India. One cannot ſtir in theſe labyrinths but by the light of flambeaux, for that of day never penetrates them. Such

are

are the caverns where the bodies of these kings repose surrounded by darkness and by silence. In surveying them, one is struck with a religious dread, as if the presence of the living could disturb the dead in these asylums of repose and peace.

Returning from these gloomy mansions, and proceeding towards the south-east, the traveller soon discovers the remains of a temple the square pillars of which are crowned by statues, whose heads are all broken. In one hand they hold a scepter, in the other a whip. The building is hardly better than a heap of ruins; on the south is a pyramidal gate which served as an entrance to a portico. The circumference of the courts which encompassed the temple is indicated by remains of columns and stones of an immeasureable size. One of these courts contains the trunks of two statues of black marble, which were thirty feet high. In the other, one stands in a state of stupefaction at the sight of a colossus lying on the earth and broken in the middle; it is one and twenty feet wide from one shoulder to the other; its head is eleven feet long and eighteen in circumference. This gigantick statute is inferior only to that of Memnon. The remains of the buildings which belonged to this temple cover a mile of ground, and leave the mind deeply impressed with its magnificence.

Continuing this route half a league further on, we find the ruins of the *Memnonium* situated near to *Medinet Abou*. There we see the largest colossus of Egypt, which points out the tomb of *Osimondué*;

Osimondué; for Diodorus Siculus marks it as being within that inclosure. Previous to laying before you the remains of this famous monument, permit me to represent you with the account Diodorus gives of it. "Ten stadia from the "tombs of the kings of Thebes *(d)*, says this "historian, one admires that of Osimondué. "The entrance to it is formed by a vestibule "built with various coloured stones. It is two "hundred feet long and sixty-eight in elevation. "On coming thence one enters under a square "perystile, each side of which is four hundred "feet long. Animals formed in blocks of gra-"nite, twenty-four feet high, serve as columns "to it, and support the ceiling which is composed "of squares of marble, of twenty-seven feet "every way. Stars of gold upon an azure "ground, shine there the whole length of it. "Beyond this perystile, opens another entry, "followed by a vestibule built like the former, "but more loaded with all sorts of sculpture. "Before it, are three statues formed of single "stones and hewn by Memnon Sycnite. The "principal one which represents the king, is "seated. It is the largest in Egypt; one of his "feet accurately measured, exceeds seven cubits.

(*d*) Diodorus Siculus, l. 1. The grottoes, where one sees the tombs of the kings of Thebes, are only at three quarters of a league from *Medinet Abou*. Thus Diodorus is pretty exact, since he only is deceived at most in a quarter of a league. Pocock has committed a more considerable error, by placing down the tomb of Osimondué at Luxor, on the other side of the Nile.

"The

" The two others borne on his knees, one on the " right, the other on the left, are thoſe of his " mother and his daughter. The whole work is " leſs remarkable for its enormous ſize, than for " for the beauty of the execution and the choice " of the granite, which in ſo extenſive a ſurface " has neither ſpot or blemiſh. The coloſſus " has this inſcription: *I am Oſimondué the King " of Kings: if any one wiſhes to know how great I " am and where I repoſe, let him deſtroy ſome of " theſe works (e).* Beſides this, we ſee another " ſtatue of his mother, cut out of a ſingle block " of granite and thirty feet high. Three queens " are ſculptured on the head, to ſhew that ſhe " was daughter, wife, and mother of a king. At " the end of this portico, one enters into a pery-" ſtile more beautiful than the former. On a " ſtone is engraved the hiſtory of the war of " Oſimondué, againſt the revolted inhabitants " of Bactria. The facade of the front wall " ſhews this prince attacking ramparts, at the " foot of which runs a river. He combats ad-" vanced troops, having by his ſide a terrible " lion, which defends him with ardour. The " wall on the right preſents captives in chains, " their hands and private parts cut off in order " to ſtigmatize their cowardice. On the wall to " the left, different ſymbolical figures, very well " ſculptured, recal the triumphs and the ſacri-" fices of Oſimondué on his return from this war.

(*e*) I imagine that this inſcription was fatal to this coloſſus, and induced Cambyſes to break it in the middle.

" In

" In the middle of the peryſtile, at the place " where it is expoſed, an altar was prepared, " compoſed of a ſingle ſtone of a marvellous ſize " and of exquiſite workmanſhip. In ſhort, " againſt the bottom wall, two coloſſuſes, each " of them of one block of marble and forty feet " high, are ſeated on their pedeſtals. One " comes out of this admirable periſtyle by three " gates; one of them between two ſtatues, the " two others are on the ſides. They lead to an " edifice two hundred feet long, the roof of " which is ſupported by eight columns. It re- " ſembles a magnificent theatre; ſeveral figures " in wood repreſent a ſenate employed in diſ- " tributing juſtice. On one of the walls one ob- " ſerves thirty ſenators, and in the midſt of them " the preſident of juſtice, having at his feet a " collection of books, and a figure of Truth with " her eyes ſhut, ſuſpended at his neck.

" One paſſed thence into a ſquare ſurrounded " by palaces of different forms, where were ſeen " carved on the table, all ſorts of diſhes which " could flatter the taſte. In one of them, Oſi- " mondué, clad in a magnificent dreſs, was offer- " ing to the gods the gold and ſilver he drew " yearly from the mines of Egypt. Below was " written the value of this revenue, which " amounted to thirty-two millions of ſilver minas. " Another palace contained the ſacred library, at " the entrance of which one read theſe words: " *Remedies for the Soul.* A third contained all the " divinities of Egypt, with the king who offered " to each of them the ſuitable preſents, calling

Oſiris

" Osiris and the princes his predecessors, to wit-" ness that he had exercised piety towards the " gods and justice towards men. By the " side of the library, in one of the most beau-" tiful buildings of the place, were to be seen " twenty tables surrounded by their beds, on " which reposed the statues of Jupiter, Juno, " and Osimondué. His body is thought to be " deposited in this place. Several adjoining " buildings preserved the representations of all " the sacred animals of Egypt. From these " apartments one mounted to the king's tomb, " on the top of which was placed a crown of " gold a cubit wide and three hundred and sixty-" five round. Each cubit answered to one day " of the year, and the rising and setting of the " stars for that day was engraven on each of " them, with such astrological observations as " the superstition of the Egyptians attached to " them. It is said that Cambyses carried off this " circle, when he ravaged Egypt. Such, accord-" ing to historians, was the tomb of *Osimondué*, " which surpassed all others, both by its extent " and by the labour of the able artists employed " on it."

I dare not take upon me to warrant all these facts, advanced by Diodorus Siculus, on the authority of preceding writers; for in his time the principal part of these buildings no longer existed. I admit even that all these wonderful descriptions would pass for pure chimeras in any other country; but in this fruitful land, which seems to have been first honoured with the crea-

tive

tive genius of the arts, they acquire a degree of probability. Let us examine what remains to us of these monuments, and our eyes will compel us to believe in prodigy. Their ruins are in heaps near to *Medinet Abou (f)* in the space of half a league's circumference. The temple, the perystiles, the vestibules, present to the eye nothing put piles of ruins, amongst which rise up some pyramidal gates, whose solidity has preserved them from destruction; but the numerous colossuses, described by Diodorus, are still subsisting, though mutilated. That which is nearest to these ruins, composed of yellow marble, is buried two thirds of its height in the earth. There is another in the same line of black and white marble, the back of which is covered with hieroglyphics, for thirty feet in length. In the space between them, trunks of columns and broken statues cover the ground, and mark the continuation of the vestibules. Farther on, we distinguish two other colossal statues, totally disfigured. A hundred toises from them, the traveller is struck with astonishment at the sight of two colossuses, which, like rocks, are seated by the side of each other. Their pedestals are nearly equal, and formed of blocks of granite, thirty feet long, and eighteen feet wide. The smallest of these colossuses is also of a single block of marble; the other, which is the largest in Egypt, is formed of five courses of granite,

(f) *Medinet Abou* signifies the city of the Father. There is no doubt that *Memnonium* was at this place, since it is called also in the Itinerary *Papa*, Father.

and

and broken in the middle. It appears to have been the ſtatue of Oſimondué *(g)*; for one ſees two figures, cut in *relievo*, the length of his legs, and which are about one third of his height. Theſe are the mother and the daughter of this Prince. The other coloſſus, which is of one ſtone, and which correſponds with the dimenſions of Diodorus Siculus, repreſented alſo the mother of the King. To give you an idea of the gigantic ſtature of the great coloſſus, it is enough to tell you that his foot alone is near eleven feet long, which anſwers exactly to the ſeven cubits of Diodorus. This ſtatue, the half of which remains upon its baſe, and is what Strabo calls the ſtatue of Memnon, uttered a ſound at the riſing of the ſun. It poſſeſſed formerly great renown. Several writers have ſpoken of it with enthuſiaſm, regarding it as one of the ſeven wonders of the world. A multitude of Greek and Latin inſcriptions, that are ſtill legible on the baſe, and the legs of the coloſſus, teſtify that Princes, Generals, Governors and men of every condition, have heard this miraculous ſound. You know, Sir, what the judicious Strabo thinks of it, and I hope you will be of his opinion.

(g) The only objection that can be urged againſt this opinion is, that according to Diodorus Siculus, the ſtatue of Oſimondué, with thoſe of his mother and daughter, were formed of a ſingle block, and that this coloſſus is compoſed of ſeveral; but the firſt layer riſing from the ſole of the feet up to the elbows, includes the two other figures. This is perhaps what our hiſtorian wiſhes to expreſs. In other reſpects, the reſt is conformable to his deſcription.

Such,

Such, Sir, are the remains of Thebes, with her hundred gates, whoſe antiquity is loſt in the obſcurity of ages, and which announces to what a degree of perfection the arts were carried in theſe remote periods. Every thing about it was noble and majeſtic. It ſeems as if the Kings of that city, whoſe glory will never periſh whilſt her obeliſks and her columns remain, laboured only for immortality. They had conſtructed works beyond the injuries of time; but they have proved unable to protect them againſt the barbariſm of conquerors, the moſt dreadful ſcourge of the ſciences, and of the nations, which their inſolence has baniſhed from the earth.

I have the honour to be, &c.

LETTER XXXVI.

ROUTE FROM THEBES TO ESNE.

Description of Armant, *formerly Hermunthis, adorned with two ancient temples, built in honour of Jupiter and Apollo; the latter in good preservation. Account of* Okror, *and its manufactures of earthen ware. An ancient temple situated in the town of Ernè and now used by the Turks as a place of security for their cattle. Another temple in the western part of the town, where the Egyptians worshipped* Neith, *denominated by the Greeks, Minerva. Account of the convent founded by St. Helena, and of the burial-place of the martyrs. Observations on the stone of* Baram, *employed for the making of kitchen utensils.*

To Mr. L. M.

Grand Cairo.

ONE tears oneself with difficulty, Sir, from Thebes, with her hundred gates *(b)*. The monuments

(b) I like this epithet, by which Homer, at a single stroke, paints the greatness of this city. What renders it sublime is, that there is no exaggeration in it. With the smallest attention to the porticoes, the vestibules, the perystiles, the courts belonging to the great temples of Egypt, we must be convinced that Thebes had at least one hundred gates. I should be apt to think, therefore, with Diodorus Siculus, that this epithet, worthy of the pen of Homer, was suggested rather by the gates of her temples, than by those of her boundary. It appears even that this famous city never was encompassed with walls. No historian makes mention of any, nor are there any traces of them.

numents which there ſtrikes the traveller, fill his mind with great ideas. At the ſight of the coloſſuſes and ſuperb obeliſks, which ſeem to ſurpaſs the limits of human nature, he cannot help exclaiming, *This was the work of man*, and this ſentiment ſeems to ennoble his exiſtence. It is true, that when his eyes fall on the huts, placed at the foot of the magnificent works, when he perceives an ignorant people, ſubſtituted for a learned nation, he is afflicted at the annihilation of generations, and at the loſs of the arts; but even this affecting thought has charms for hearts of ſenſibility.

The wind now drives us towards the confines of Egypt. Already the rocks, hewn into coloſſal ſtatues, have diſappeared. Other objects fix the attention. We contemplate with pleaſure the riches which border the two banks of the Nile. We land at the port of *Armant*. This village is built at the foot of the eminence where we view the ruins of *Hermuntis*. This ancient city, which honoured with a particular worſhip, Apollo and Jupiter, had erected two temples to theſe deities. Time has reſpected them. That of Apollo is ſmall, but well preſerved; its walls are formed of granite; a frieze, covered with ſparrow-hawks, conſecrated to the God, runs round it. We mount on a platform by ſtairs formed in one of the ſides. All its aſpects are decorated with hieroglyphics; four rows of human figures are carved without, and three within. The building is divided into ſeveral halls. Five falcons, with their wings ſpread, adorn the cieling of the firſt;

 golden

golden ſtars ſhine upon the roof of the ſecond. Here are two rams which look at each other, with hieroglyphics, ſculptured with an artiſt's hand; two marble oxen *(i)* occupy the extremity of this apartment. Around it we ſee women ſuckling their children. Before this temple was a large building, of which nothing is remaining but the foundations. Beyond, opens out a large baſon deſtined to receive the waters of the Nile. Further on, on the bank of the river, is another edifice, the temple, probably of Jupiter. The Chriſtians had converted it into a church. The plaſter on which the croſſes are painted, covers the Egyptian hieroglyphics and inſcriptions.

Four leagues from Armant, up the country, we meet with the village of *Okſor*. Abulfeda ſays *(k)*, that in his time a great deal of earthen-ware was made here; that manufacture ſtill ſubſiſts. The inhabitants tranſport their vaſes to the banks of the Nile, faſten them on a bed of palm-branches, with their mouths downwards, place a ſecond bed above that, diſpoſed in the ſame manner, and then a third. This ſort of raft floats on the water, ſupported by the air, which, incloſed within the hollow of the vaſes, produces the ſame effect as in the diving-bell. Two men ſeated on it, conduct it from town to town, until they have ſold all their merchandize. I have ſeen ſeveral of theſe rafts deſcend even below Grand Cairo. *El Okſor* is ſituated in the middle of a fertile

(i) The ox in Egypt was the ſymbol of fertility and the inundation.

(k) Abulfeda, deſcription of Egypt.

plain,

plain, producing abundance of grain, and excellent dates.

Aſcending to the ſouthern end, we paſs by *Gebelein*, the two hills; at the firſt of which is the tomb of a Mahometan ſaint. Soon after, we diſcover *Aſſoun*, a pretty conſiderable town, placed on the ruins *Aphroditopolis (l)*. Between Thebes and Sienna one frequently perceives crocodiles, baſking on the ſandy iſlands, left uncovered by the Nile, when it retires. They ſleep in the ſun, but theirs is a very gentle ſlumber; for on the approach of boats they precipitate themſelves into the water. They rarely deſcend into the lower Thebais, and never below Cairo. Theſe voracious animals, though covered with almoſt impenetrable ſcales, fly the places two much frequented by men, and prefer the vicinity of Aſſouan, where there are fewer boats. The ancients have told us that the Ichneumon enters into the maw of this monſter when he is aſleep, and devours his entrails. The Ichneumon, in fact, ſeeks after the eggs which the female crocodile hides in the ſand, and eats them when it finds them. This poſſibly is the origin of that fable.

We land at the port of *Eſné*, a conſiderable town governed by an Arabian prince, and by a Cachef, dependant on the Bey of Girze. The Mahometans have ſeveral moſques here, and the Coptis, a church ſerved by two prieſts. "*Eſne*," ſays

(l) This is the third city of the name. The Greeks called them ſo. In treating of the ancient religion of the country, at the end of this volume, I ſhall give the Egyptian names, which have come down to our time.

Abulfeda *(m)*, " remarkable for its public baths " and its commerce, is built on the weſtward of " the Nile, between *Aſſouan* and *Cous*, but nearer " to this latter. It acknowledges, adds the geo- " grapher of Nubia, the Coptis *(n)* for foun- " ders. Its well cultivated territory abounds in " in grain and palm trees. It is ſurrounded by " gardens filled with fruit trees. One admires " here ſeveral ancient monuments conſtructed " by the Coptis, and ſuperb ruins." This deſcription anſwers to *Eſné* in our time, which is ſituated on the edge of a rich country, and ſhaded by groves of orange trees loaded with fruits and flowers. This town, formerly called *Latopolis*, revered Minerva and the fiſh *Latus (o)*. It contains within its boundary an antique temple; thick walls incloſe it on three ſides. Six large fluted columns, crowned by a capital ornamented with the palm leaf, form the facade of it; eighteen others ſupport the roof, which is compoſed of large ſquares of marble: the building is ſurrounded by a frieze, and innumerable hieroglyphics cover its exterior aſpects. Thoſe of the inſide, executed with much more care, mark the progreſs made by the Egyptians in ſculpture. This temple is ſoiled by the ordure of the cattle kept there by the Turks. Theſe barbarians do not bluſh to convert the moſt beautiful monuments of ancient Egypt into ſtables.

(m) Deſcription of Egypt.

(n) The Arbs call the ancient Egyptians by the name of Coptis or *Cobtis*.

(o) Strabo, l. 17.

A league

A league to the weſt of *Eſné* is another temple, on the walls of which is carved in ſeveral places a woman ſeated *(p)*. It was here that Minerva was worſhiped, and the fiſh *Latus*. The columns of this temple poſſibly gave the Greeks the idea of the Corinthian order. In fact, the capitals are ornamented with a foliage reſembling very much the Acanthus; only it projects leſs, and is ſome times merely perceptible. Several animals painted on the cieling have preſerved all the ſplendor of their colours. The Egyptians often employed in their paintings gold and ultramarine blue; but if we may judge by what remains of their works, they were unacquainted with the art of ſhading, by which the painter, paſſing inſenſibly from one ſhade to the other, knows how to beſtow on objects their ſuitable forms and colours. Their colours are very brilliant, but almoſt always uniform and ſimply laid on.

To the ſouth of *Eſné* we ſee the ruins of a monaſtery founded by Saint Helena, and near it the burying place of the martyrs, adorned with tombs crowned by cupolas, ſupported by arcades. The inhabitants of *Eſné* having revolted againſt the perſecution of Diocleſian, that emperor deſtroyed this town and put them to the ſword. This place, conſecrated by religion, is become a celebrated pilgrimage among the Coptis. They repair thither from the moſt diſtant provinces of the kingdom.

(p) This woman ſeated, was an Egyptian deity called *Neith*. The ancient Greeks gave her the name of Minerva, whom they at firſt painted and engraved in that poſition, in imitation of their preceptors, as we ſhall ſee at the end of theſe letters.

In

In the chain of mountains which ſtretches to the eaſtward of the Nile, and nearly oppoſite *Eſné*, are quarries of a ſoft ſtone, called *Baram* It is made uſe of for kitchen utenſils. It hardens in the fire, and forms excellent kettles and pans, which give no bad taſte to the victuals. I ſhall conclude this letter, by apprizing you, that Father Sicard and Vanſleb have confounded this town with Sienna, ſituated under the tropic, thirty leagues farther to the ſouthward.

I have the honour to be, &c.

LETTER XXXVII.

ROUTE FROM ESNE TO THE LAST CATARACT

Description of Edfou, *famous for a temple erected in honour of Apollo. Dangerous passage of* Hajar Salfalé. *Situation of* Coum Ombo, *anciently Ombos. Observations on the Crocodiles, which are exceedingly numerous in that quarter. Arrival at Siéne, now Assouan. Description of this city, its antiquities, the Solstice-well, the bottom of which reflected the image of the Sun when he reached the tropic of Cancer. Account of the islands of Philé and Elephantine, with their temples and antiquities. Observations on the quarries of granite situated on the west of Cataract. Succinct description of the country lying between Grand Cairo and Siéne.*

To Mr. L. M.

Grand Cairo.

OUR journey, Sir, is almoft finifhed. The heat we begin to feel informs us of our approach to the tropic. The foutherly wind with its burning breath blows in gufts, and raifes up whirlwinds of fands deftructive to man and beaft. The one and the other feek for fhelter in their huts and in the caverns of the rocks. Happily, this dangerous wind feldom continues for two days together; but this fpace of time is fometimes fufficient to make the caravans be fwallowed up in the middle of the deferts

The

The country now aſſumes another aſpect; on ſetting out we left them ſowing their lands in the environs of Cairo. Near Girgé the corn was in ear. Here they reap it at the end of January. Such is Egypt. In travelling through it from one extremity to the other, we ſee it ſenſibly changing its decoration. The verdure, the flowers, the harveſt rapidly ſucceed each other. It is to the progreſſive inundation, and to the heat of the climate, that we are indebted for this diverſity of ſcenery, this variety of produce, which are inceſſantly renewing through a long extent of country.

Above *Eſné*, is the village of *Edfou*, governed by an Arab Scheik, and built on the ruins of the great city of Apollo. It poſſeſſes an ancient temple covered with hieroglyphics; amongſt which we diſtinguiſh men with falcons heads. Its inhabitants were enemies of the crocodile. At ſome leagues from *Edfou*, the bed of the river, hemmed in by rocks which project to the right and left, is only fifty toiſes wide. This place is called *Hajar Salſalé*, the ſtone of the chain, and it is thought that one formerly extended from one ſide to the other. The rocks on the weſtern ſide are hewn in the ſhape of grottoes. We ſee columns, pilaſters, and hieroglyphics, with a chapel cut out of a ſolid ſtone. The water confined between the mountains, precipitates itſelf with great rapidity, and it is impoſſible to aſcend againſt the current without a favourable wind.

After

After paſſing *Hajar Salſalé*, we diſcover to the eaſt of the Nile, *Coum ombo*. The ruins of a temple, ſituated at the foot of this hill, aſcertain the poſition of the ancient *Ombos*, whoſe inhabitants honoured the crocodile. Theſe animals are very common thus high up the Nile. One ſees them deſcend in droves from the iſles of ſand, and ſwim in long ſtrings in the river. It ſeems as if theſe formidable animals had fixed their habitation near to a town where they received homage; but what renders them more numerous here than in the other parts of Egypt, is the ſolitude of the ſituation, the banks of the Nile in this place being almoſt deſerted.

We land, Sir, at the port of *Aſſouan*, formerly Sienna, which will terminate our navigation. Here, as elſewhere, I ſhall follow the plan I have laid down. I ſhall preſent to you the local deſcriptions, as traced out by the beſt writers of antiquity, adding the picture of their preſent ſituation, and the changes which have taken place. No author has deſcribed Sienna and its environs better than Strabo (*q*). Let us hear him: " Sienna is a town of Egypt, on the con-" fines of Ethiopia. It has the iſland of Ele-" phantina before it. One obſerves there a " ſmall town with the temple of Cneph (*r*), " and a Nilometer. It is a well, formed of a " ſingle ſtone, which, placed on the banks of " the Nile, ſerves to meaſure the great, the mo-

(*q*) Strabo, l. 17.

(*r*) An Egyptian Deity, whom I ſhall ſpeak of at the end of theſe letters.

" derate,

" derate, and the ſmalleſt overflowings; for the " water of this well riſes and falls with the ri- " ver. Lines marked on the walls point out the " inſtant of its increaſe, that of attaining its " greateſt height, and other degrees of its eleva- " tion. Men appointed to make this obſervati- " on announce it to all Egypt; ſo that every bo- " dy may know what will be the increaſe of the " year; in fact, they know at a certain period, " from infallible ſymptoms, the height to which " the Nile will riſe, long before it begins even " to overflow its banks. They loſe no time in " acquainting the Governors of the provinces " with it. This knowledge enlightens the coun- " tryman with reſpect to the diſtribution of the " waters, the labour on his dykes, and the " cleanſing of the canals. The officers deputed " to collect the tributes, proportion them to the " degree of the expected inundation (*s*).

" Sienna is immediately under the Tropic; " a well is dug there which marks the ſummer " ſolſtice. This day is diſcovered when the " gnomon of the dial gives no ſhadow at noon. " At that moment the vertical ſun darts his rays " to the bottom of the well, and his whole image " is painted on the water that covers the bottom. " Three cohorts, garriſoned in this town, pre- " ſerve the limits of the Roman empire. At " ſome diſtance above Elephantina the bed of " the river is obſtructed by a rock, and forms a " ſmall cataract. It is levelled in the middle,

(*s*) In our days, when the Nile does not riſe above 16 cubits, Egypt pays no tribute to the Grand Signior.

" that

" that the waters may paſs over it. Perpendi-
" cularly cut at the two extremities, it leaves a
" navigable canal on each ſide, which boats
" mount eaſily. The boatmen venture to allow
" themſelves to drive with the current in flimſy
" ſkiffs, in the middle of the cataract, without
" receiving any damage. The iſle of Philé, ſi-
" tuated above, is the common habitation of
" the Ethiophians and Egyptians. The latter
" occupy a hamlet ſimilar to that of Elephantina
" in point of ſize and conſtruction. It has tem-
" ples, in one of which the ſparrow-hawk of
" Ethiopia is held ſacred."

The iſle of Elephantina, Sir, is half a league long, by a quarter wide. The town deſcribed by Strabo ſubſiſts no longer. A ſmall village is built on its ruins. Near to them we ſee a ſuperb gate of granite which formed the entrance of one of the porticoes of the temple of *Cnept*. A building ſurrounded by thick walls and rubbiſh, formerly made a part of it; an elevated rampart at the point of the iſland ſerved to defend it againſt the inundation. The Nilometer, ſo favourably ſituated in this place, to diſcover the firſt appearance of the increaſe of the waters, and to regulate the labours of the huſbandman, appears no longer. From the deſcription of Strabo, we may imagine that it was a hall ſimilar to that of the *Mekias*, of the iſle of *Raouda*, excepting that it was of a ſingle ſtone, and that inſtead of one column divided into inches and cubits, the inundation was meaſured by lines traced upon the wall. This nilometer, formed of a block of marble, cannot have been deſtroyed; it is probably buried under the ſand and mud of the Nile, whence it may one day be extricated.

The Iſle of Elephantina is ſurrounded by four ſmaller ones, which are only rocks of granite. Enormous maſſes have been detached from them to be employed in the great edifices of Egypt. It is from one of theſe iſlets that the great cube of ſixty feet on each ſide was taken, in the ſolid of which was hewn the ſanctuary of the temple of Latona at Butis *(t)*. Hiſtory informs us, that ſeveral thouſand workmen were employed three years in conveying it to the place of deſtination. This is the moſt enormous weight ever moved by human power.

Aſſouán, ſituated on the eaſt of the river, is only a miſerable hamlet, with a ſmall fort commanded by an Aga of the Janizaries. The remains of Sienna are on the eminence which riſes to the ſouth. Columns and pillars of granite, diſperſed in ſeveral places point out its ſite. One remarks there an ancient edifice, with openings at the top, and windows which look towards the eaſt. Perhaps this was the obſervatory of the Egyptians. The well of the Solſtice might correſpond with one of theſe openings, and the image of the ſun diſplay itſelf on the

(t) See the firſt Vol. of the Letters on Egypt. Mr. Pocock places this large ſtone in the temple of Minerva at Sais; but that is in direct contradiction with Herodotus, who gives the deſcription of it, and who aſſerts that he ſaw it at Butis, in the temple of Latona.

ſur-

ſurface of the water which covered the bottom. This fact, atteſted by all antiquity, cannot be called in queſtion. It proves the aſtronomical knowledge of the Egyptians, and ſhould be regarded as one of the moſt beautiful obſervations of mankind. It is very aſtoniſhing that, for eighteen hundred years, no traveller ſhould have ſtopped at Sienna a few days before the ſummer ſolſtice, to ſearch for this wonderful well, and to eſtabliſh ſo intereſting a diſcovery. Having travelled with a limited fortune, and without the aid of Government, I did not go ſo high up as that town, where it would have been neceſſary to remain at leaſt a week, becauſe theſe journies are very expenſive, and it is impoſſible to be in ſafety from robbers, but by making continual preſents to the Governors, and by keeping the Janizaries in pay. Thus, inſtead of my own obſervations, I have been forced to collect and verify with infinite pains the obſervations of others, in ſome particulars. It is true that I have had private journals, which aided me very much, but it would have been much more deſirable to have ſeen every thing myſelf.

The cataract is ſtill in our days what it is deſcribed by Strabo; the rock which bars the middle of the river is bare for ſix months of the year. Then boats mount and deſcend by the ſides. During the inundation, the waters heaped up between the mountains form one great ſheet, and, breaking down every obſtacle, ſpring from eleven feet height. The boats can no longer aſcend the ſtream, and merchandize muſt be conveyed two leagues over land, above the cataract; they deſcend, however, as uſual, and ſuffer themſelves to be plunged into the gulph. They precipitate themſelves into it with the rapidity of an arrow, and in an inſtant are out of ſight. It is neceſſary for the boats to be moderately laden, and for the boatmen who hold by the ſtern, to be in exact equilibrium, otherwiſe they would infallibly be ſwallowed up in the abyſs.

To the weſt of *Aſſouân*, a road is cut in the mountain that leads to *Philé*. On its ſides are diſcovered immenſe quarries of granite. Mr. Pocock obſerved there obeliſks and columns, half-hewn. They cut them in the flanks of the rock, and when detached, they were drawn to the river, whence they were tranſported on rafts to the place of their deſtination. The granite of theſe quarries, ſpotted with red and grey, reſembles that of the column of Alexander Severus. It is extremely hard, and takes a fine poliſh.

The Iſle of Philé is only half a league round; the Ethiopians and Egyptians inhabited it in common; at preſent it is deſerted, but one admires there two magnificent temples *(u)*. The largeſt has courts ornamented with colonnades. One enters into the firſt by a pyramidal gate, on the ſide of which are two obeliſks of granite. The inſide of the temple is divided into ſeveral apartments. Its walls, formed of

(u) Pocock's travels in the eaſt. Norden's Journey through Egypt.

marble,

marble, present several rows of hieroglyphics, amongst which is distinguishable the sparrow-hawk described by Strabo. To the east of this edifice is another which forms a parallelogram. It is open on all sides. The capitals of the columns which support the roof are sculptured with art.

Now that we are on the confines of Egypt, let us cast an eye on the country we have passed through. In a space of two hundred leagues, we have remarked a narrow valley, bounded on the right and left by two chains of mountains and hills. Except towards the Faioum, the plain is not above ten leagues in its greatest extent, but it is covered throughout by the treasures of abundance. The pyramids, which extend from the environs of *Gisa* as far as *Meidom*, first attracted our attention. These magnificent mausolea, erected by the power of the Pharaohs, have not prevented us from paying our tribute of admiration to the remains of the lake Mœris formed for the happiness of the people. Farther on we have observed porticoes and magnificent temples. The ruins of Thebes, with her hundred gates, have then commanded our attention, and our thoughts have been elevated even to the height of her famous monuments. At length we arrived at Sienna, remarking every where on our route the most beautiful remains of antiquity.

To what event must we attribute the destruction of taste, and of the arts, under the same climate, on the same soil, amidst the same abundance,

dance, if not to the loſs of liberty, and to the government, which beats down or raiſes at its will the genius of nations? Egypt, become a part of the Perſian empire, was ravaged for two hundred years by Cambyſes and his ſucceſſors. This barbarous Prince, by deſtroying the temples and colleges of the Prieſts, extinguiſhed the ſacred fire which they had kindled for ages, under this favourably ſky. Honoured, they cultivated with glory every branch of human knowledge; deſpiſed, they loſt their ſciences and their genius. Under the domination of the Ptolemies knowlegde did not revive, becauſe theſe Kings, fixing the ſeat of Government at Alexandria, beſtowed all their confidence on the Greeks, and diſdained the Egyptians. Become a Roman province under Auguſtus, Egypt was looked upon as the granary of Italy, and agriculture and commerce alone met with encouragement. The monarchs of the lower empire having embraced Chriſtianity, governed it with an iron ſceptre, and overturned ſome of its moſt noble monuments. The Arabs wreſted it from the cowardly Heraclius, too much occupied with theological diſputes to ſend a ſingle veſſel to the ſuccour of the Alexandrians, who implored his aſſiſtance for a whole year. They burnt there that valuable library, the loſs of which will be a ſubject of regret to the learned in all countries, and in every age. The Turks, in ſhort, an ignorant and barbarous people, have been its laſt maſters. They have, as far as they are able, annihilated commerce, agriculture, and the ſciences. After ſo many calamities,

lamities, after the revolution of ſo many ages, behold, Sir, how many glorious ancient monuments this country ſtill poſſeſſes ; ſee if the whole globe combines as many as this little portion of the world. This obſervation alone is ſufficient to give you an idea of its former inhabitants, and of the degree of perfection to which they carried the arts.

I have the honour to be, &c.

LETTER XXXVIII.

DESCRIPTION OF OASIS AND THE TEMPLE OF JUPITER AMMON, WITH THE ROUTES LEADING THITHER.

Situation of Oafis *fixed by Ptolemy and the Arabian geographers. Defcription of the places inhabited in the middle of the Defart. Journey of Alexander to the temple of Jupiter Ammon, traced in the map which is prefixed to this volume. Account of the temple and the people who inhabit its environs. Defeat of the army of Cambyfes, which had been fent to plunder it. Unfortunate expedition of this barbarous invader againft the Ethiopians, followed by the lofs of a part of the troops which he commanded. Oafis a place of exile under the monarchs of the lower empire; and thither St. Athanafius and other perfons were banifhed.*

To Mr. L. M.

Grand Cairo.

THE defcription of Egypt, Sir, would be incomplete, if I paffed over in filence the *Oafis*, dependant on the Thebais *(x)*. Strabo fpeaks of them as follows: " Africa, according to hifto-" rians, and to Cneius Pifo, who governed it, " like to a leopard's fkin, is interfperfed with " fmall habitations, furrounded by defarts, called " by the Egyptians, *Oafis*." Thefe remarkable places

(x) Strabo, l. 17.

places were known by Arabian geographers, who called them *Elouah*. Abulfeda *(y)*, their guide describes them in the following manner: "These " *Elouah* are dependent on the Saïd. They are " islands in the middle of sands. On quitting the " Nile, it takes three days journey across the de- " sart to arrive at them. *Jacout* who reckons " three of them, places them in the west of lower " Egypt, beyond the chain of mountains, pa- " rallel with the river. He adds that the first is " well cultivated; that it possesses abundant rivu- " lets, hot springs, fields covered with harvests, " and other surprising things, but that the peo- " ple there are wretched."

Such, Sir, are the *Oasis* of the Greeks. We are pretty nearly acquainted with their distance from the Nile. Ptolemy determines their latitude *(z)*. He places the large one under the 26th degree, 30 minutes from the latitude of *Abydus*; it is called by the Arabs *Elberbi*, the temple, on account of the monument we find there. The second, in 25 degrees 45 minutes, that is to say, over against *Behnése*; and the most northerly, in 29, 30, under the parallel of Lake Mœris. Let us now enquire, to which of these habitations the temple of Jupiter Ammon was near. The route taken by Alexander, when he undertook this journey, will point it out to us.

(a) " Alexander having pacified the upper " Egypt, without effecting any change in the

(y) Abulfeda, description of Egypt.

(z) Ptolemy, l. 4.

(a) Quintus Curtius, l. 4. chap. 7.

" ancient constitution of government, resolved
" to repair to the temple of Jupiter Ammon.
" The road leading to it is almost impracticable.
" The earth is without wells, and the heavens
" without rain. One discovers on every side
" immense plains of sand, which, struck continu-
" ally by the rays of the sun, emit suffocating va-
" pours. Exhausted by the drought and heat,
" travellers are obliged to cross a deep sand,
" which yielding under their feet, renders the
" march very difficult. The Egyptians exagge-
" rated even these difficulties. But nothing
" could stop Alexander, attracted by an ardent
" desire towards the oracle of Jupiter. His
" soul thirsting for glory, not being satisfied with
" attaining the pinnacle of human greatness, he
" imagined, or wished to be believed, that this
" god was his father *(b)*.

" He descended by the river to Lake Mareotis,
" with the select companions of his journey.
" From thence he set out to accomplish his design.
" The fatigue of the two first days was not great.
" Though they travelled in fact on a barren soil,
" they were not yet entered into the burning so-
" litudes. When they had reached them, they
" perceived nothing around them but prodigi-
" ous heaps of sand, without trees, or plants, or
" the smallest trace of cultivation. From amidst
" this parched desart, their eyes were looking
" out for land, like navigators. The water car-

(b) Callisthenes, according to Strabo, says that Alexander in undertaking this enterprize, wished to imitate Hercules and Perseus who had performed it before him.

" ried

"ried in ſkins upon the camels was ſoon ex-
"hauſted, a loſs which was irreparable, in a
"country deſtitute of ſprings, and where every
"thing was burnt up by the ſun. In this ex-
"tremity, whether by the bounty of the gods,
"or the reſult of chance, the heavens became
"covered with thick clouds, and the rain came
"down in torrents. Life was reſtored to theſe
"unfortunate men, dying with thirſt, and ſinking
"under the exceſſive heat. In ſhort, after four
"days march acroſs this frightful ſolitude, they
"reached the territory ſacred to Jupiter Am-
"mon. With what aſtoniſhment did they be-
"hold in this country, ſurrounded by deſarts,
"foreſts impenetrable to day-light, ſtreams of
"excellent water, and a delicious temperature,
"where the charms of the ſpring reigned
"throughout the year, and beſtowed the precious
"gift of ſalubrity!"

"The inhabitants of theſe woods, called Am-
"monians, dwell in huts diſperſed here and there
"under the ſhade. A triple wall built in the
"middle, ſerves them by way of citadel. The
"firſt incloſure contains the palace of their an-
"cient kings; the ſecond, where the temple
"ſtands, is deſtined for the women, the children
"and the ſlaves; the warriors entruſted with the
"defence of this aſylum, occupy the third.
"The fountain of the Sun flows through another
"thicket, alike conſecrated to the oracle of Am-
"mon. Its water is tepid in the morning, cool
"at noon, warm in the evening, and ſcalding at
"midnight.

"The

"The ſtatue that is worſhipped at this place, "by no means reſembles thoſe uſually fabricat- "ed by ſculptors. Formed of emeralds and pre- "cious ſtones, it is in the ſhape of a ram (c) "from the head to the middle of the body. "When it is to be conſulted, the prieſts carry "it in a gilded boat, on each ſide of which are "ſuſpended cups of ſilver. The matrons and "virgins follow the god, ſinging a hymn in the "language of the country, to make Jupiter "favourable, and to receive from him a certain "oracle, &c."

Alexander ſet out from Lake Mareotis to repair to the temple of Ammon. The two firſt days he proceeded over a barren ſoil, but where he did not ſink in marching, that is to ſay, he followed the ſea ſhore towards the weſt; for had he taken a ſoutherly or ſouth weſterly direction, he muſt have immediately entered the deſart covered with deep ſands. Arrived at ſeven or eight leagues from Panætonium he entered the burning deſart, through which he marched four days; he then bent his courſe directly towards the habitation of the Ammonians, nearly following the line punctuated on the map. I am perſuaded of this from the poſition in which Ptolemy lays down the firſt *Oaſis*, in the parral-

(c) This idol had the form of a ram, becauſe that animal was conſecrated to Jupiter Ammon, a ſymbolical deity, which denoted the ſun entering the ſign of the ram. The boat in which it was carried, repreſented the veſſel in which the Egyptians placed the ſun deſcribing his courſe in the air. Theſe emblems will be explained in the ſucceeding letters.

lel

lel of Lake Mœris, and from Strabo *(d)*, who aſſures us that the temple of Ammon was not far from it. Calliſthenes, who makes Alexander depart from Porætonium, does not vary much from our route. It is poſſible that the conqueror may have advanced as far as that city, and afterwards have aſcended towards the ſouth.

Strabo *(e)* informs us that under the reign of Auguſtus, the verſes of the ſybils, and the Tuſcan divinations had made the oracle of Ammon greatly loſe its credit. In the thirteenth century it was forgotten; but the Arabs aſſert that they ſtill poſſeſſed inhabitants. It appears from their relations, that the fountain of the Sun deſcribed by Quintus Curtius in a wonderful manner, was nothing more than a hot ſpring which ſeemed to be warmer in the night than in the day

Under the ſovereigns of the lower empire, the Oaſis became a place of exile. Theſe princes tainted with theology, a ſcience which ought to be reſerved for thoſe to whom religion has entruſted the ſacred repoſitory, and occupied in promoting the triumph ſometimes of a new ſect, ſometimes of the true doctrine, ſent there alternately both ſectaries, and catholics. Neſtorius and Athanaſius were exiled there. In the digeſt are theſe words *(f)*: "There is a ſort of exile "which conſiſts in baniſhing the criminal into "the Oaſis of Egypt, where he is as if in an "iſland."

(d) Strabo, l. 17.
(e) Strabo, l. 17.
(f) Lib. 48. lit. 22.

" island." Saint Athanasius complains of this cruelty in his apology. " The Arians, says he, " have exceeded the orders of the emperor, " by confining the elders and the bishops in the " middle of frightful desarts; those of Libia in " the great Oasis, those of Thebais, in the Oasis " of Ammon, in order to make them perish in " crossing the burning sands."

These habitations, become famous from the banishment of the most learned personages of the lower empire, were little known by the Persians. Cambyses, after ravaging Egypt, wished to carry off the spoils of the temple of Jupiter Ammon *(g)*. " The troops he sent against the " Ammonians left Thebes, and arrived at the " city of Oasis, inhabited by the Samians of the " tribe of *Escrionia*. This country, distant seven " days march from the capital of Egypt, is cal- " led by the Greeks, *The Isle of the Happy*. It " is reported that the army reached the place of " their destination, but the Ammonians alone " know what became of it, for it has never " since been heard of. It is said also, that be- " ing on their march towards the temple of " Jupiter, and having got half way, it was " swallowed by torrents of burning sand blown " up by the southerly wind."

From the route of this army, it appears that the guides, who abhorred the Persians, led them astray in the middle of the desarts. In fact, to arrive at the temple of a Ammon, they

(g) Herodotus, l. 3.

ought

ought to have taken their departure from the borders of Lake Mareotis, or the environs of Memphis. The Egyptians, who intended to make their enemies perish, conducted them from Thebes to the great Oasis, distant three days journey from *Abydus*. After leading them, doubtless, into the vast solitudes of Lybia, they abandoned them during the night, and gave them up to death.

The Oasis of Ammon is little known by the modern Egyptians. They are better acquainted with the second. Abulfeda *(h)* places a city there, named *Behnése*, and different from that one seen on the canal of Joseph. He marks another higher up, that corresponds with that of *Achmonain*, and around which are admired magnificent remains of antiquity. The great Oasis, the most frequented of the three, being on the road of the caravans of Abyssinia, contains a great number of inhabitants. The Bey of *Girgé* sends a Cachef there as governor; and to collect a tribute. When the Abyssinians who set out from Egypt on their return, have laid in their stock of provisions in this fruitful valley, they mount to the southward, and fall in with another under the tropic, which the geographer of Nubia describes in these terms: " The country of the *Ellouah*, situated to the " west of Assouan, was formerly much peopled.

(h) Abulfeda, description of Egypt. Behnése, says he, is a town situated near Joseph's canal. We find another town of the same name in the country of the *Ellouah*, on the confines of the Negro country, &c.

" At

" At preſent it has no inhabitants. We meet " with abundant ſprings there, and fruit trees, " with cities buried under ruins." It was in paſſing from this valley into Ethiopia that another diviſion of the troops of Cambyſes was deſtroyed.

(i) " Cambyſes being arrived at Thebes, " ſelected fifty thouſand men whom he ordered " to ſack and burn the temple of Jupiter Am- " mon. He marched himſelf againſt the Ethi- " opians with the remainder of his army. But " the proviſions they carried, failed them before " they had proceeded the fifth part of the way. " They ate their horſes, but this reſource was " but of a ſhort duration. Had this prince been " guided by prudence, he would have returned " by the ſame road; but animated by a blind " fury, he went on. As long as the ſoldiers " found herbs and plants they fed on them. " This feeble ſuccour failing them in the midſt " of the ſands, they were *decimated*, and thoſe on " whom the lot fell were devoured by their " companions. At this dreadful news the king " of Perſia abandoned his Ethiopian expedition, " and retreated to Thebes with the loſs of half " his army (k)."

What actually happens in this journey, renders that event very credible. Travellers who ſet out from the fertile valley ſituated under the

(i) Herodotus, l. 3.

(k) It is highly probable that in this as well as the former expedition, the guides purpoſely miſled Cambyſes, who had been ſetting fire to all the temples of Egypt.

tropic,

tropic, march ſeven days journey before they reach the firſt town in Ethiopia. They proceed in the day by eſtabliſhing ſignals, and at night by obſerving the ſtars. The hills of ſand, which have been remarked in the preceding journey hurried along by the winds, frequently deceive the guides. If theſe errors lead them ever ſo little aſtray from their route, the camels after living for five or ſix days without water, ſink under their burden and die. The men ſoon follow the ſame fate, and ſometimes out of a numerous caravan not a ſingle traveller eſcapes. At other times the ſcorching ſoutherly winds lift up whirlwinds of duſt, which ſtifle man and beaſt. The next caravan that paſſes, beholds the earth covered with dead bodies perfectly dried up. This frightful ſpectacle, theſe terrible dangers, do not deter the Abyſſinians, who from the moſt remote antiquity have been the carriers of gold duſt, of muſk, and elephant's teeth into Egypt. Such an empire has habit over men.

I have the honour to be, &c.

LETTER XXXIX.

OBSERVATIONS ON THE INCREASE OF THE NILE.

Remarks on the Nile, its ſources, and the phænomena of its annual inundation. Time when they cut the dyke, at the head of the canal which conducts the waters to Grand Cairo. Deſcription of the public feſtivals and rejoicings at that ſeaſon. Nocturnal recreations on the water in the great ſquares of the capital. The pleaſures thence ariſing. Means of ſecuring to Egypt a regular inundation, and an inexhauſtible abundance.

To Mr. L. M.

Grand Cairo.

THE Nile, Sir, is the moſt celebrated river on the earth. Travellers in all ages have ſpoken with enthuſiaſm of the fecundity of its waters. The poets have ſung its ſeven months, and all hiſtory is filled with the wonders of its inundation. It owed its celebrity to the ancient people who cultivated on its banks the arts and ſciences, and brought them to perfection. Loaded with its bounties, they eſtabliſhed a feſtival in honour of this river, and raiſed altars to it as to a God, or rather as to the moſt exalted gift of the Creator. Had this river nouriſhed only Turks and Arabs, its name, like that of many others, would only have been known on maps and charts of geography; but its glory was connected

nected with that of a celebrated nation, and from the ends of the universe men came to admire the noble works constructed to contain it, and the immortal monuments erected on its borders.

All the ancients, excepting the Egyptians, were ignorant of its origin. A Portuguese Jesuit in the last century pretended to have discovered it. The following is his narrative: "In the pro-" "vince of Sahala, situated to the west of the king-" "dom of Goiam, the inhabitants of which are" "called *Agous*, we discover the sources of the" "Nile. They are two deep fountains in an ele-" "vated situation. The earth around them is" "marshy, and trembles under the feet. The" "water spouts up from the foot of the moun-" "tain, with a noise like that of a cannon. After" "running some time in the valley, it receives a" "second rivulet which comes from the east.—" "Joining together, they direct their course to-" "wards the north. Two other torrents discharge" "themselves into them, and form a river which" "joins the river *Jemam*; and, after long circuits" "to the east and west, throws itself into a great" "lake. On coming out of that lake it forms the" "Nile, which precipitates its course towards the" "Mediterranean."

Whether this account be true or false, this quantity of water would not supply the general inundation, which covers a space of near four hundred leagues; for it is also felt sensibly in Ethiopia. But in the months of March, April, May, and June, the northerly winds drive the clouds towards the lofty mountains on the other side

ſide of the Equator. Stopped by this barrier, they collect in heaps upon their lofty ſummits, diſſolve into rain, which falls in torrents, and fills the vallies. The junction of ſuch an innumerable multitude of ſtreams forms the Nile, and produces the innundation. From the unanimous teſtimony of the Abyſſinians, who bring the gold-duſt to Grand Cairo, we learn that this river on reaching Ethiopia ſeparates itſelf into two branches, one of which, known by the name of *Aſerac*, or the Blue River, ſtrikes off to join the Niger, and, traverſing Africa from eaſt to weſt, throws itſelf into the Atlantic Ocean. The other branch flows towards the north, between two chains of mountains, and, meeting with rocks of granite which obſtruct its bed, forms ſix cataracts, far more frightful than thoſe of Sienna. Theſe tremendous falls abſolutely prevent the navigation of the river. Arrived at the firſt town in Egypt, it falls eleven feet into a gulph it has formed, and the dangers of which are ſurmounted by the boldneſs of navigators.. Deſcended into this beautiful kingdom, it fills the canals and the lakes, overflows the lands, leaving behind it a fruitful mud, and throws itſelf, as formerly, by ſeven mouths, into the Mediterranean.

At the beginning of June the Nile begins to ſwell, but its increaſe is not very ſenſible till the ſolſtice. At this period its waters become troubled, aſſuming a reddiſh tinge, and are then eſteemed unwholeſome. They muſt be purified before they are drinkable. This is done by throwing the powder of bitter almonds, bruiſed,

into

into a jar full of water, and ſtirring them for ſome minutes with your arm plunged in the middle of the veſſel After this operation they are left to ſettle, and at the end of five or ſix hours all the heterogeneous particles are precipitated to the bottom of the veſſel, and the water is clear, limpid, and excellent to drink *(l)*. The inhabitants of Egypt attribute this fermentation of the Nile to the dew which then falls in abundance. Even ſeveral hiſtorians have gravely told us that it contributes to the inundation. But it is much more natural to imagine that the river, overflowing its banks in Abyſſinia and Ethiopia, carries with it a great quantity of ſand, and millions of eggs of inſects, which, hatching towards the ſolſtice, produce the fermentation of the waters, and that reddiſh tinge that renders them unwholeſome.

The Nile continues to ſwell till towards the middle of Auguſt, and often even in September. Formerly the nilometer of Elephantinos ſerved to indicate the future inundation. Particular ſigns, founded on the experience of ſeveral ages, announced it to thoſe who were intruſted with this obſervation. They loſt no time in giving notice to the Prefects of the provinces. According to the nature of this intelligence the huſbandman regulated his labours. When the Arabs

(l) I have tried this proceſs, which I have obſerved throughout all Egypt, with the waters of the Seine, when they were muddy, and I found the ſame reſult. For the operation to ſucceed, the veſſels muſt be large.

con-

conquered Egypt, the nilometer was placed at the Burg of Halouan, oppofite to Memphis. Amrou having overturned that fuperb capital, and built the city of Foftat, the Governors or the Caliphs fixed their refidence there. Some centuries after the *Mekias* was built on the point of the ifland of *Raouda*, and the column for meafuring was placed there, in the middle of a low hall, whofe walls are very folid, and its bottom is on a level with that of the Nile. From that period the Mekias has not changed its place. At this day officers appointed to examine the progrefs of the inundation, communicate it to the public criers, who proclaim it daily in the ftreets of Grand Cairo. The people who are interefted in this event, make them a fmall acknowledgment. It becomes the public topic. Egypt owing no tribute to the Grand Signior, when the waters do not rife to fixteen cubits, they often conceal the truth, and do not publifh their attainment of a certain point, even when they have paffed it.

The moment of this proclamation is a day of rejoicing, and a folemn feftival for the Egyptians. The Pacha defcends from the caftle, accompanied by his whole court, and repairs in pomp to Foftat, where the canal begins that traverfes Grand Cairo. He places himfelf under a magnificent pavillion, prepared at the head of the dyke. The Beys, preceded by their mufic, and followed by their Mamalukes, compofe his retinue. The Chiefs of their religion appear mounted on horfes richly caparifoned.

All

All the inhabitants on horfeback, on foot, and in boats, are anxious to affift at this ceremony. The land and the water are covered by upwards of three hundred thoufand men. The boats in general are agreeably painted, well carved, and ornamented with canopies, and flags of different colours. Thofe of the women are to be diftinguifhed by their elegance, their richnefs, the gilded columns that fupport the canopy, and above all, by the blinds let down over the windows. Every body remains filent until the moment when the Pacha gives the fignal. In an inftant the air is filled with fhouts of joy, the trumpets found a flourifh, and the timbrels and other inftruments refound from every fide. Workmen, collected for the purpofe, throw down a ftatue of earth placed upon the dyke, which is called the *New Bridge*. This is the remains of the ancient worfhip of the Egyptians, who confecrated a virgin to the Nile, and who, in times of calamity, fometimes precipitated her into the river. The dam is foon deftroyed, and the waters having no longer any obftacle, flow towards Grand Cairo. The Viceroy throws into the canal fome pieces of gold and filver, which are immediately picked up by fkilful divers. This tranfaction may be regarded as an homage rendered to the Nile, the fource of the riches of Egypt. During this day's amufement the inhabitants feem in a ftate of intoxication. Mutual compliments and congratulations pafs, and one hears on every fide fongs of thankfgiving. A croud of dancing girls run along the banks of the *Calich*, and enliven the

 fpecſpectators by their laſcivious dances. Every body reſigns himſelf to good cheer and joy, and the poor themſelves have their entertainments. This univerſal gladneſs is not ſurprizing. The fate of the country depends on the inundation. When it arrives, each individual ſees the hope of a good crop, the image of abundance, and anticipates the enjoyment of all its attendant advantages.

The ſucceeding nights afford a ſpectacle ſtill more agreeable. The canal fills with water the great ſquares of the capital. In the evening each family is collected in boats, ornamented with carpets and rich cuſhions, and where voluptuouſneſs has every poſſible accommodation. The ſtreets, the moſques, the minorets, are illuminated. The company go from place to place, carrying with them fruits and refreſhments. The moſt numerous aſſembly is uſually at *Leſbekié*. This ſquare, which is the largeſt in the city, is near half a league in circumference. It forms an immenſe baſon, ſurrounded by the palaces of the Beys, lighted with lamps of various colours. Several thouſand boats with maſts, from which lamps are ſuſpended, produce a moving illumination, the aſpects of which are continually varying. The ſerenity of the ſky ſeldom or ever interrupted by fogs, the golden colour of the ſtars upon a perfect azure, the fire of ſo many lights reflected in the water, make one enjoy in theſe charming parties at once the lightneſs of the day, and the delicious coolneſs of the night. Imagine, Sir, how voluptuous it muſt be for a people, burnt

burnt for twelve hours by an ardent ſun, to come and reſpire on theſe lakes the refreſhing breath of the zephyrs. What adds to the pleaſure of this nocturnal ſcene is, that the calm ſerenity of the air is ſeldom interrupted by the impetuous breath of winds. They fall at the ſetting of the ſun, and the atmoſphere is gently agitated by a ſlight breeze. The ſingularity of the Oriental manners puts an European who aſſiſts at theſe exhibitions a little out of his way. The men accompany the men, and the women the women. It is difficult to procure the charm of their ſociety. The diſguiſe that muſt be aſſumed, the dangers that attend it, alarm the reaſon, and compel to prudence. They are obliged alſo to keep lamps continually burning. The public ſafety requires this precaution, and the *Ouali*, who patrole during the night, enforce a rigid obedience. If the head of the police meets with a boat without light, he has the right to cut off the heads of the perſons who are in it, and without ſuch a preſent as can ſtay the hand of the executioner, who attends him, he executes this rigorous juſtice in a moment.

When the Ramazan falls at the time of the inundation, that month ſo dreaded by the poor, is a continual feſtival for the rich man. He paſſes his night upon the water, and in a conſtant round of entertainments. In the day time he ſleeps in a vaſt ſaloon, in the circulation of pure air, near a marble baſon, from whence plays a *jet d'eau*, quite limpid, the edges of which are ſurrounded by Arabian jeſſamine and odoriferous flowers; a window, always open, placed near the top of the dome, and facing the north, preserves the salubrity with the luxury of the apartment. Whilſt the burnt huſbandman in the country is bedewing the earth with the ſweat of his brow, he enjoys a delicious ſleep, amidſt coolneſs and the exhalations of balſamic plants. To live agreeably, without heeding the affairs of this world, is all the ambition of a Turk out of place; the Beys, on the contrary, a prey to anxieties and fears, make a figure for a moment at the head of the Republic they lay waſte, to periſh at length by the ſabre of their colleagues, or by the poiſon of their ſlaves.

In the courſe of the vaſt number of ages that the Nile have overflowed Egypt, it has prodigiouſly elevated the ſoil. Obeliſks, buried from fifteen to twenty feet, and half-buried porticoes, teſtify this fact. The ancient cities built on artificial mounds, the dykes oppoſed to the impetuoſity of the river, announce that the Egyptians formerly were much more afraid of the great than of the moderate overflowings. At this day, that the ſoil is conſiderably raiſed, the inundation riſes ſo high as to be ſometimes injurious to the cultivation of the country. When it remains below ſixteen cubits, the people are threatened with famine; from eighteen to twenty-two, they may count upon plentiful years. Exceeding this, the waters remaining too long upon the lands, prevent them from ſowing them in time. This event ſeldom or never occurs; too frequently the overflowings are moderate, and all the

the elevated ground is unproductive. If canals were dug, the dykes repaired, and the great reservoirs filled, a much greater extent of country might be watered, and astonishing crops be produced from them.

It is very possible to secure a regular inundation and a constant fertility to Egypt; but Ethiopia must be conquered, or a treaty formed with its inhabitants, by which they would permit dykes to be formed in the places where the waters of the Nile are lost in the sands, and waste themselves to the westward.

" *(m)* In the year 1106, during the reign of " *Elmes Tensor*, Sultan of Egypt, the inundation " totally failed. This Prince sent Michael, Patriarch of the Jacobines, to the Emperor of " Ethiopia with magnificent presents. The " King came to meet him, gave him a favourable reception, and demand the subject of his " mission: the Patriarch answered him, that he " had come thither on account of the deficiency " of the Nile, and that this event, which made " the Egyptians dread a famine, had thrown " them into the greatest consternation. On " these remonstrances, the Emperor made a dyke " be cut which diverted the channel of the river, " and the waters, taking their usual course, rose " three cubits in one day. Michael returned

(m) Elamacin, History of the Arabs. This event happened under the Emperor *Aboulcasem*, the twenty-seventh *Abassid* Caliph, and the eight and fortieth from Mahomet.

" from

"from his embaſſy, and was received with great "honours."

This anecdote demonſtrates the poſſibility of diverting the waters of the Nile, but it proves at the ſame time, that by ſtopping up by a dyke the great arm of it that communicates with the Niger, the volume of its waters would be prodigiouſly augmented. If an enlightened and powerful people poſſeſſed Egypt, it would be no difficult matter to operate miraculous changes, which would render it the richeſt country in the world. In this country there is a certain token of the inundation, and of the height to which it is to riſe. When the north wind, during the month I have mentioned, repulſed by the impetuous winds from the ſouth, is driven back on the northern countries, the clouds retire in a ſmall quantity into the upper Abyſſinia, and the ſwell is then very inconſiderable. The dykes would in that caſe be of the greateſt utility. When, on the contrary, the north wind prevails in that ſeaſon, and drives the hurricanes of the ſouth towards the Equator, it conveys there numerous clouds, and one is ſure of a favourable inundation: under theſe circumſtances, the ſluices of Ethiopia ſhould be opened to give the ſuperfluous waters liberty to eſcape by their ancient drain. One might avail ones-ſelf of this augmentation too, to form a canal from *Cophtos* to *Coſſeir*, a work which would be ranked amongſt the moſt famous and moſt uſeful ever executed in Egypt. Theſe, Sir, are a few ideas thrown into the void of poſſibility. *The ambition of ſeveral*

veral powers is looking with eager eyes on this delightful kingdom, governed by barbarians incapable of defending it. IT WILL INEVITABLY FALL INTO THE HANDS OF THE FIRST NATION THAT ATTACKS IT, *and will undoubtedly assume a new appearance.*

I have the honour to be, &c.

LETTER XL.

GOVERNMENT OF EGYPT.

Egyptian Government from the conqueſt of the Arabs to the preſent time. Changes which it has undergone by the different revolutions of the ſupreme power. Articles of the agreement made in favour of the Circaſſian Mamalukes by the Emperor Selim. Limited power of the Pachas. The great authority of the Beys, and of that which is annexed to the dignities of Scheick Elbalad *and of* Emir Haji. *The manner in which the repreſentatives of the Grand Signior are received in Egypt. Scandalous manner of ſending them back. Obſervations on the ſmall degree of authority which the Ottoman Porte really maintains in Egypt.*

To Mr. L. M.

Grand Cairo.

I PROMISED you, Sir, ſome details on the Government of Egypt, which is almoſt unknown in France; and I flatter myſelf that the obſervations of ſeveral years will enable me to fulfil my engagements; but it will firſt be proper to give you ſome ideas which may throw a light on the objects I am about to ſubmit to your diſcernment.

The Arabs were in poſſeſſion of Egypt from the middle of the ſixth century to the year 1250. During this time it formed a part of the vaſt

vaſt empire of the Caliphs. They ſent thither Viſirs to govern in their name. Inveſted with unlimited powers, theſe Viceroys exerciſed the ſupreme authority. Poſſeſſing the right of life and death, being accountable for their conduct only to the Caliphs, they ruled over this country according to the dictates of their caprice. Whatever may be their tyranny, the voice of the oppreſſed people never could reach the throne, becauſe they took care by rich preſents to gain the perſons who ſurrounded it. This government therefore was deſpotic, and the happineſs or miſery of a nation depended on the virtues or the criminal character of a ſingle man. Several of theſe Viſirs cruſhed this unhappy country with an iron ſceptre; others promoted commerce, agriculture, and the arts. Some, amongſt whom was the famous *Ebn Toulon*, revolted againſt their Sovereigns, and aſſumed the title of Kings; but the crown ſeldom deſcended to their children. After the death of the rebels, this province returned to its maſters.

In the year 982, *Moaz*, King of the weſtern ſide of Africa, and a deſcendant of the Fatimite Caliphs, who had founded a kingdom there for two centuries paſt, conquered Egypt by his Generals, and came and fixed in it the ſeat of his empire. His poſterity reigned over it until 1189, that *Salah Eddin* eſtabliſhed there the dynaſty of the *Aioubites*. This warlike Prince, the terror of the cruſaders, whom he almoſt totally drove out of Paleſtine, was overthrown by *Richard Cœur de Lion*, near the walls of St. John of Acre, and

and the name of the Engliſh Monarch became the ſignal of conſternation throughout the eaſtern world. The Government of *Salah Eddin*, and his ſucceſſors, was monarchical, and Egypt flouriſhed under their dominion. In our days we ſtill ſee the remains of the academies they founded at Grand Cairo, and where they attracted, by large ſalaries, the learned men of the eaſt. In 1250, immediately after the defeat of St. Louis, the Bakarite *(n)* Mamalukes, of Turkiſh origin, murdered *Touran Chah*, the laſt Prince of the family of the *Aioubites*, and the ſon of *Nejim Eddin*, their benefactor. In his perſon terminated the government of the Arabian Princes in Egypt. From that moment it has been always governed by foreigners.

The Baharite Mamalukes changed the form of government for that of the Republican. The principal amongſt them elected a Chief, whom they entruſted with great authority. He had the right of making war or peace, with the advice of his council, of which they were the members. He could appoint Miniſters, Ambaſſadors, Governors, and Generals, provided he choſe them from the Mamalukes. The neceſſity of gaining the ſuffrages of the Chiefs marked the limits of his power. His policy conſiſted in conciliating their favour, ſecuring the moſt powerful party, and in ſtifling in their origin

(n) Mamlouk ſignifies acquired, poſſeſſed. They were called *Baherites*, or maritime, becauſe Nejim Eddin, who created them, gave them the government of the caſtles on the ſea ſhore, and in the iſland of *Racunda*.

the

the plots that might be formed againſt his perſon: for in this ariſtocracy, each of the Mamalukes, on attaining the firſt employments, ſtrove to overthrow the poſſeſſor of the throne, to ſeat himſelf in his place. Though the people were conſidered as nothing, the Prince naturally dreaded their diſcontent, leſt an ambitious Chief might avail himſelf of it to deprive him of the crown. Thus was the Chief of this Republic ſurrounded by precipices, the duration of his empire ſolely depending on his perſonal qualities, nor could he tranſmit his power to his children, unleſs they poſſeſſed diſtinguiſhed talents; accordingly, in the ſpace of one hundred and thirty-ſix years, that the Bahorite Mamalukes governed Egypt, they had twenty-ſeven of theſe Kings, a proof that their reigns were very ſhort, and very turbulent.

Towards the middle of the fourteenth century, the *Circaſſian* Mamalukes dethroned the *Baharites*, retaining the ſame form of government. They kept poſſeſſion of Egypt until the conqueſt of Selim, Emperor of the Turks, who took it from them in 1517. Before I ſpeak of the changes he made in the conſtitution, it is proper to give you a clear and preciſe idea of the Mamalukes. This name, the meaning of which you know, is beſtowed on the children carried off by merchants, or by robbers from Georgia, Circaſſia, Natolia, and the different provinces of the Ottoman empire, and ſold at Conſtantinople, and Grand Cairo. The Grandees of Egypt, who are of a ſimilar origin, bring them up in their

their families, and destine them to succeed to their dignities. The antiquity of this custom is far more remote perhaps than in the time of Joseph, who being sold in this manner to Potiphar *(o)*, High-Priest of Heliopolis, became "Ruler over all the land of Egypt." At present none but these strangers can have the title of Bey, and fill the posts of government. This law is so express, that the son of a Bey can never attain that eminent station. He usually embraces the military life. The Divan assigns him a decent revenue, and calls him *Ebn Elbalad*, child of the country *(p)*.

The Mamalukes are almost all of Christian families. When sold, they are forced to embrace the Mahometan religion, and be circumcised. Language-masters teach them the Turkish and the Arabic. As soon as they can read and write well, they are taught the Coran, which is the code of their religion and their laws. The knowledge of these clear, simple, and precise laws, enables them to judge equitably every affair that

(o) This Egyptian name comes from *Potiphre*, Priest of the Sun.

(p) From what I have said, you, see, Sir, that the word Mamaluke is very different from that of *Abd*, which signifies slave. The former are destined to fill the most distinguished offices; the others are employed in the lowest, and never arrive at dignities. It is improperly, therefore, that historians give the name of slave to the Mamalukes, and that the historians of the lower empire call them *Mammelus*. Writers ought to be scrupulous about disfiguring the names of things and persons, and should give them their real signification; then would history afford distinct ideas and faithful pictures.

happens

happens on the ſpot. The Mahometan, who is perfect maſter of this book, knows all his duties towards God, and towards man. He may then occupy every civil, military, and eccleſiaſtical employment.

From the tendereſt age, the Mamalukes learn to ride, to throw the javelin, to make uſe of the ſabre and fire-arms. They are continually exerciſed in military evolutions, and are taught to ſupport with conſtancy the heat of the climate, and the diſtreſſing thirſt of the deſarts. Theſe exerciſes give them a ſtrong conſtitution, and an unconquerable courage. They want no requiſite to form excellent ſoldiers, but maſters verſed in the European tactics. If this corps were diſciplined by our officers, it would be ſecond in bravery to no nation on the earth; but they fight without order, and are totally ignorant of the art of artillery, brought to ſuch perfection in our days.

At fifteen or eighteen years of age, theſe young men manage with addreſs horſes not broken in, ſpeak and write ſeveral languages, poſſeſs a profound knowledge of the worſhip and the laws of the country, and are capable of filling any employments to which they may be deſtined. They paſs ſucceſſively through the different degrees in the houſehold of the Beys, and their elevation is generally the reſult of merit. Having attained the poſt of *Cachef (q)*, they govern the

(q) The *Cachefs* are the Lieutenants of the Beys; they command in the towns of which their patrons have the government.

towns

towns dependent on their patrons. They are allowed to purchaſe Mamalukes, who follow their fate, and become the companions and inſtruments of their fortunes. There is now only one ſtep to arrive at the dignity of Bey, which gives a ſeat amongſt the twenty-four members of the Divan, or Council of the Republic; but on their attaining it, they do not ceaſe to look upon themſelves as the ſervants of their former maſter, and to preſerve for him the moſt profound ſubmiſſion. Such, Sir, is the origin of the Mamalukes; ſuch is the routine of their career. Let us reſume the thread of our narrative.

The Emperor Selim, having conquered Egypt, and overturned the Circaſſian Mamalukes, unable to reſiſt the innumerable hoſts with which he bore them down, after many bloody battles, hung up *Thomam Bey* at one of the gates of Cairo. This barbarous action alienated their minds, and they waited only for the departure of the Turks to reſume their arms. The fumes of glory with which the Ottoman Emperor was intoxicated being diſſipated, he felt his error, and, to ſecure this important conqueſt, he ſtrove to regain the good opinion of the Mamalukes. To ſucceed in this, he made very little alteration in the conſtitution of their government, and granted them ſpecific privileges in a treaty, of which the following are the principal articles:

"Notwithſtanding our invincible armies have "conquered, with the aid of the Almighty, the "kingdom of Egypt, nevertheleſs, from an effect "of

" of our benevolence, we grant to the twenty-" four Sangiaks *(r)* of that country a republican " government on the following conditions:"

I. The Republic of Egypt ſhall acknowledge our ſovereignty, and that of our ſucceſſors; and as a token of her obedience, ſhe ſhall regard as our repreſentative ſuch Lieutenant as we ſhall think proper to depute, and who ſhall have his reſidence in the caſtle of Cairo. During his adminiſtration he ſhall undertake nothing againſt our will, nor againſt the intereſts of the Republic; but he ſhall concert with the Beys every thing concerning the welfare of the ſtate. Should our Lieutenant make himſelf diſagreeable to the Beys, ſhould he attack their privileges, we authorize them to ſuſpend him from his functions, and to convey their complaints to our Sublime Porte, in order that they may be relieved from his oppreſſion.

II. In time of war, the Republic ſhall be obliged to furniſh us and our ſucceſſors with twelve thouſand troops, commanded by Sangiaks, and to maintain them at her expence until the peace.

III. The Republic ſhall levy annually five hundred and ſixty thouſand *aſlani (s)*, and ſhall ſend them under eſcort of a Bey to our Sublime Porte,

(r) They are called Sangiaks, or Beys.

(s) This ſum has been ſince carried to 800,000 aſlani; but as the Beys make a plea of exceſſive expences for the maintenance of the canals and fortreſſes, they do not ſend the half of it to Conſtantinople. The aſlani is a piece of ſilver coin, worth about three livres French (or half a crown Engliſh money).

Porte, and there ſhall be delivered to him by our *Defterdar* (Treaſurer) a receipt in due form, to which ſhall be affixed our ſeal, and that of our Viſir.

IV. The Republic ſhall levy a ſimilar *Khaſnè* (treaſurer) of five hundred and ſixty thouſand aſlani, deſtined to the ſupport of Medina, and of the *Caaba*, or temple of Mecca. This treaſure ſhall be conveyed annually, under the eſcort of the *Scheik Elbalad (t)* or of the *Emir Haji*, who will deliver it to the Scherif, ſucceſſor of our Prophet, to be employed in the ſervice of the houſe of God, and diſtributed to the perſons reſiding there, in order to obtain their prayers for us and the faithful believers of the Coran *(u)*.

V. The Republic ſhall not keep up, in time of peace, more than fourteen thouſand ſoldiers or Janizaries; but we allow her to augment this army in time of war, that ſhe may be able to oppoſe our enemies and hers.

VI. The Republic ſhall deduct annually from the produce of the country one million of *couffes (x)* of grain, ſix hundred thouſand of wheat, and four hundred thouſand of barley, to be delivered into our magazines.

(t) Scheik Elbalad ſignifies, properly, *the old of the country*. This is the title of the firſt Bey, or Chief of the Republic. *Emir Haji* ſignifies Prince of the Caravan. This is the ſecond dignity of the Republic.

(u) This treaſure is not conveyed in money, but in corn, grain, and other produce of the ſoil of Egypt.

(x) A ſort of oval baſket made of the leaves of the date-tree, which contains 170 pound weight.

VII. In

VII. In virtue of the execution of theſe articles, the Republic ſhall enjoy an abſolute empire over all the inhabitants of Egypt; but in all affairs concerning religion, ſhe ſhall conſult the Mollah, or High-Prieſt, who ſhall be under our authority, and under that of our ſucceſſors.

VIII. The Republic ſhall enjoy as heretofore, the right of coining money, and of ſtriking on it the name of *Maſr (y)*, but ſhe ſhall add thereto our name and that of our ſucceſſors. The Lieutenant we ſhall ſend ſhall have the inſpection of the fabrication of the coin, that the title of it may not be altered.

IX. The Beys ſhall elect from amongſt them a *Scheik Elbalad*, who, confirmed by our Lieutenant, ſhall be their repreſentative, and our officers ſhall acknowledge him for Chief of the Republic. In the caſe where our Lieutenant ſhall render himſelf guilty of tyranny, and exceed the limits of his power, the *Scheik Elbalad* ſhall have the right of repreſenting the grievances of the Republic to our Sublime Porte. If it happens that foreign enemies diſturb her peace, we promiſe for us and our ſucceſſors to protect her with all our might, without claiming any indemnity for the expences incurred on her account.

Done and ſigned by our clemency in favour of the Republic of Egypt, in the year 887 of the Hegira (1517 of our æra).

(*y*) *Maſr* is the name given by the Arabs to Egypt in general, and to Grand Cairo in particular, becauſe they pretend that this country was peopled by *Miſraim*, the grandſon of Noah.

This treaty, Sir, makes you acquainted with the laſt revolution the Egyptian government, become now a mixture of monarchy and ariſtocracy, has undergone. The former is repreſented by the Pacha, the ſecond by the Beys, who compoſe eſſentially the Republic. The Viceroy, properly ſpeaking, is nothing but a phantom, overturned by the ſlighteſt breath. The Sangiaks, at the head of the provinces and the armies, really poſſeſs all the power. The people are abandoned to their mercy. This treaty does not ſay a word in their favour. Is it not the language of a merchant, who for five hundred and ſixty thouſand aſlani, ſells three or four millions of ſlaves, to four and twenty ſtrangers? An abſolute power, in fact, is veſted in their hands; they are permitted to levy arbitrary tributes, and, without any controul whatever, to exercise every ſpecies of tyranny. Is it thus then that deſpots make a traffic of whole nations? and they ſubmit to this diſgrace without vindicating the ſacred rights beſtowed on them by nature!!! It appears as if Selim, through the extent of his vaſt empire, ſaw no *men*, but only a vile herd of *ſlaves*, whom he could diſpoſe of at his pleaſure. The Beys are perfectly ſenſible of their ſituation, and abuſe it to the utmoſt exceſs. A Pacha retains his place no longer than he is ſubſervient to their deſigns. If he dares to lift his voice in defence of the intentions of his maſter, or of the Egyptians, he becomes a ſtate criminal: the Divan aſſembles, and he is ſent off. The following is the manner in which they

they receive and difmifs thefe lieutenants of the Ottoman Emperor.

As foon as the new Pacha has landed at the port of Alexandria, he informs the council of the Republic of his arrival. The *Scheik Elbalad* difpatches the moft artful of the Beys to compliment him. They carry prefents to him, and give tokens of the moft profound fubmiffion. Whilft they furround his perfon, they dexteroufly found his difpofition, ftudy his character, and endeavour to learn from his own mouth, or from his officers, what orders he brings with him. If they find them contrary to their defires, they expedite a courier to the *Scheik Elbalad*, who affembles the Divan, and forbids the Pacha to advance. They write to the Porte, that the new Viceroy comes with hoftile intentions, fit to excite rebellion amongft his faithful fubjects, and they demand his recal, which never is refufed. When the Chiefs of the Republic think that there is nothing to fear from the lieutenant that is fent them, they invite him to repair to Grand Cairo. The deputies place him in a fuperb galley, and efcort him in his journey. All the boats that furround him are agreeably dreffed out, and many of them filled with muficians. He advances flowly at the head of the little fleet, and no boat is permitted to pafs his. Unlucky, the travellers who are mounting the Nile, for they are obliged to fwell his retinue! When he is arrived at the *Hellé* (z), he halts. The *Scheik Elbalad* deputes feveral Sangiaks to receive him,

(z) A fmall village a little below Boulak.

or he comes himſelf. At his landing, the Chiefs of the Republic congratulate him anew, and the Janizary Aga preſents him with the keys of the caſtle, requeſting him to make it his reſidence. He is conducted with pomp into the city. I have ſeen the entry of a Pacha, and can therefore give you a deſcription of it.

Firſt, ſeveral corps of infantry, preceded by their noiſy muſic, filed off in two ranks, with colours flying. Then followed the cavalry. The horſemen, to the number of five or ſix thouſand, advanced in good order. Their cloathing was formed of the moſt ſplendid ſtuffs. Their flowing robes, their enormous whiſkers, and their long lances tipped with glittering iron, gave them a majeſtic and warlike air. After them came the Beys ſuperbly clad, attended by their Mamalukes, mounted on Arabian horſes full of fire, and covered with houſings embroidered with gold and ſilver. The bridles of the horſes of the chiefs were ornamented with fine pearls and precious ſtones. The ſaddles ſparkled with gold. Theſe different retinues, for each Bey had his own, were very elegant. The beauty of the young men, the richneſs of their dreſſes, the addreſs with which they managed their courſers, formed a moſt agreeable coup d'oeil. The Pacha terminated the proceſſion. He advanced ſolemnly, preceded by two hundred horſemen and a band of muſic. Four led horſes, conducted by ſlaves on foot, walked with ſlow ſteps before him. They were covered with embroidery in pearls and gold. The Viceroy was mounted

mounted on a Barb of great beauty, and wore on his turban an aigret of large diamonds, which reflected in flashes the rays of the sun. This entry gives me an idea of the oriental pomp, and of the pageantry which encompassed the ancient Asiatic monarchs, when they shewed themselves in public. The procession commenced at eight in the morning, and lasted till noon.

The next day the Pacha assembles the Divan, and invites the Beys to favour him with their company. The convention is held in a gallery, with a window with iron bars before it, like that of the Grand Signior His Kiaïa, or lieutenant, reads the orders of the Porte, the Sangiaks make a profound reverence, and promise to obey them in every thing not contrary to their privileges. When the reading is finished, a collation is served, and at the breaking up of the assembly, the Viceroy makes a present of a rich fur and a horse magnificently harnessed to the *Scheik Elbalad*, and of a castan to each of the other Beys. Such, Sir, is the installation of the Pacha.

The post he occupies is a sort of exile. He cannot stir out of his palace without the permission of the *Scheik Elbalad*. He is really a state prisoner, who amidst the splendor that surrounds him, cannot but feel the weight of his chains. His revenues arising from the custom-house at Suez, and from the merchandize which arrives by the Arabic gulph, amount to near three millions of livres. The ambition of the Beys too, affords him a fruitful source of wealth. When

the

the knowledge of his ſituation, and a refined policy have taught him to ſow diſſention amongſt the Chiefs of the Republic, and to form a powerful party, each of them ſtrives to avail himſelf of his credit, and he receives gold and ſilver by handfuls. The Sangiaks named by the Divan, purchaſe alſo from the Pacha the confirmation of their dignity. His treaſures are augmented likewiſe by the inheritance of perſons who die without children. It is thus that the repreſentative of the Grand Signior is able to preſerve his place, and to acquire immenſe riches in a very few years; but he muſt uſe the greateſt circumſpection in all his meaſures. In the delicate poſt he fills, the ſlighteſt fault may ruin him. Frequently, even unexpected events overſet all the ſchemes of his politics. If amongſt the Sangiaks, ſome young deſperado deſtroys, by courage and by crimes, the party favoured by the Pacha; if he attains the dignity of *Scheik Elbalad*, he aſſembles the council, and the Viceroy is ignominiouſly diſmiſſed. The order for his departure is entruſted to an officer cloathed in black, who carries it in his boſom, advances into the hall of audience, makes a profound reverence, and taking one of the corners of the carpet that covers the ſopha, ſays to him, in lifting it up, *Inſel Pacha.* Deſcend Pacha: after pronouncing theſe words, he departs. The Viceroy is obliged inſtantly to decamp, and withdraw in four and twenty hours to Boulak, where he waits for his orders from Conſtantinople. In general his perſon is in ſafety, but if the ruling Beys have

any

any complaints againſt him, they make him give an account of his adminiſtration, and of the preſents he has received, and divide his ſpoils amongſt them. During this interregnum, the council of the Republic elect a *Caïmacam* to fill his place, until the arrival of the new Pacha. Theſe are events, Sir, to which I have been a witneſs ſeveral times during my ſtay in Egypt. I hope theſe details will ſerve to make you acquainted with the government of this country. The hiſtory of *Ali Bey*, and of ſome of his ſucceſſors, whoſe picture I ſhall trace out to you in the following letters, will ſhew you the actors on the ſtage, and will furniſh you with the means of making the application of thoſe principles.

I have the honour to be, &c.

LETTER XLI.

HISTORY OF ALI BEY.

Birth-day of Ali Bey. Transportation from his own country, and his change of religion after he had been sold to a Bey of Grand Cairo. His promotion to different offices in the state. Conduct of the Caravan. Defeat of the Arabs, followed by the dignity of Bey, which gave him a seat among the members of the Divan. Death of his patron, who was murdered by the opposite party. Ali obtains the rank of Scheik Elbalad, *and avenges the blood of his protector. Conspiracy formed to make him prisoner. He takes refuge in Jerusalem, and afterwards at St. Jean d'Acre, where* Scheik Daher *receives him with open arms. On being recalled into the capital, he found it impossible to triumph over the hatred of his enemies, and, to save his life, was a second time obliged to take to flight. He visits Arabia, and retires to Jean d'Acre, where* Scheik Daher *treated him with every demonstration of the sincerest friendship. He returns to Cairo, sacrifices his rivals to his resentment, and governs Egypt with wisdom. Treachery of some Beys, and of the Divan at Constantinople. He punishes with death the officers who had been sent to demand his head, and enters into an alliance with the Russians, to revenge the injustice of the Ottomans. He represses the wandering tribes of Arabs, protects commerce, and reduces*

reduces to ſubjection both Arabia and Syria by means of his Generals. He is betrayed by Mahomet Abou Dahab, his ſon-in-law, and obliged to ſave himſelf a third time in Syria. Ali Bey makes himſelf maſter of a number of towns, enters Egypt with the principal part of his forces, intimidates an army much ſuperior to his own, and is conquered by the treachery of his infantry, which went over to Abou Dahab. The death of Ali, of Mahamed, and of Scheik Daher, *baſely aſſaſſinated by order of the Ottoman Porte.*

To Mr. L. M.

Grand Cairo.

ALI BEY was born in Natolia, in 1728, and received at his birth the name of *Jouſeph*, Joſeph. *Daoud (a)*, his father, a Greek Prieſt of one of the moſt diſtinguiſhed families in the country, deſigned him to ſucceed to his dignity, and neglected no part of his education, but fate had otherwiſe ordained. At thirteen years old, Joſeph, hurried on by the ardour of his age, was hunting with other young men in a neighbouring foreſt. Robbers fell upon them, and carried them off in ſpite of their cries and their reſiſtance. The ſon of Daoud being taken to Grand Cairo, was ſold to Ibrahim *Kiaia (b)*, or Lieutenant of the Janizaries, who had him circumciſed, cloathed

(a) Daoud, that is to ſay, David.

(b) The Kiaia and Aga of the Janizaries, that is to ſay, their Lieutenant and their Colonel have the title of Beys, and are in general held in great conſideration.

him

him in the dreſs of the Mamalukes, and called him by the name of *Ali*, under which he has been ſince known. He gave him maſters of the Turkiſh and Arabic languages, and of horſemanſhip. Compelled to give way, he deplored in his heart the loſs of his parents, and his change of religion. Inſenſibly the kind treatment of his patron, the dignities with which his vanity flattered him, and above all, the example of his companions, gave him a reliſh for his new ſituation. The vivacity of his mind afforded him the means of diſtinguiſhing himſelf. In the courſe of a few years he was perfect maſter of the languages that were taught him, and even excelled in all bodily exerciſes. None of the Mamalukes managed a horſe with more addreſs, nor threw the javelin with greater force, nor made uſe of the ſabre and fire-arms with more dexterity than him. His application to ſtudy, and his graceful manners, made him dear to Ibrahim Kiaia. Charmed with his talents, he raiſed him rapidly to the different employments of his houſehold. He ſoon attained the poſt of *Seliƈtar Aga*, Sword-bearer, and of *Kaſnadar*, Treaſurer. The intelligence he diſplayed in theſe employments gained him more and more the good graces of his patron, who created him a *Cachef* at the age of two and twenty.

Become a Governor of towns, he manifeſted his natural equity in the adminiſtration of juſtice, and his diſcernment in the acquiſition of the Mamalukes, to whom he endeavoured to communicate his genius. It was here he laid ſecretly the

the foundation of his future greatneſs. Not only had he gained the affection of Ibrahim, but judging that the favour of the Pacha might be made ſubſervient to his ambitious views, he made a point of pleaſing him. This Viceroy was called *Rahiph*; he was a man of real merit. Diſcovering in the young Cachef an upright and elevated mind, he granted him his friendſhip, and declared himſelf his protector. He would have raiſed him in a ſhort time to the dignity of Bey, had not an unforeſeen cataſtrophe unhinged his projects. *Rahiph*, endowed with one of thoſe happy characters, which carry with them an irreſiſtible charm, had gained the confidence of the Chiefs of the Republic. Far from imitating his predeceſſors, who had uniformly built their authority on the diſſentions they fomented againſt the Sangiaks, he was indefatigable in promoting peace and union. For the firſt time, the repreſentative of the Grand Signior and the leaders of the Government united together, to promote the general good. The people enjoyed a peaceable adminiſtration, and wiſhed for its continuance. The Beys themſelves loved the Pacha, and dreaded his recal. This was ample food for envy, that monſter which is continually on the watch for the misfortunes of mankind, and breathes its poiſon from one end of the world to the other. The Members of the Divan at Conſtantinople repreſented to Sultan Mahmoud the good underſtanding that prevailed between his Lieutenant and the Chiefs of the Republic, as a conſpiracy formed to withdraw the country from

from its obedience. They coloured their calumnies with these specious reasons, which in Courts too frequently appear convincing proofs. Without farther enquiry the Grand Signior was determined to put the fidelity of *Rabiph* to the test. He sent him a Firman, commanding him to put to death immediately as many of the Beys as he could. This iniquitous order shocked the Pacha; but he must either obey or lose his head. He hesitated for three days. At length he adopted the first measure. Having sent for the most faithful of his slaves, he shewed them the Firman, and ordered each of them to kill a Bey, at the moment of their assembling in the hall of audience. Accordingly when they were holding the Divan, these Satellites, who had swords concealed under their robes, ponyarded the unhappy victims of calumny. Four of them lay dead on the spot; the rest, being only wounded, defended themselves courageously, and made their escape. Even at this day the marble of the hall where they were assassinated is red with their blood. I have frequently shuddered on beholding the marks of this barbarous execution, commanded on a bare suspicion, by a despotic Government.

The astonishment of the Sangiaks who escaped from this butchery was extreme. They could not reconcile this atrocious action with the past conduct of *Rabiph*. The Council was assembled; they resolved to punish the traitor, and to expiate by his death the outrage committed on the Republic. But when they wanted to make sure of

the

the criminal, he produced the Firman of the Porte, and they contented themſelves with baniſhing him on the ſpot. The Pachalick of Natolia, that of Damaſcus, and at length the brilliant ſtation of Grand Viſir, became the recompence of his crime.

This painful event retarded the elevation of *Ali*. He remained ſeveral years a Cachef. His patron, Ibrahim, being elected *Emir Haji*, or Prince of the Caravan, which is the ſecond dignity in Egypt, he took him with him to eſcort the pilgrims. In their march they were attacked by the Arabs. *Ali* fell upon them at the head of the Mamalukes he commanded, and behaved with ſo much valour, that he repulſed the enemy, and killed a great number on the ſpot. On his return, ſeveral tribes being collected, were determined to avenge their defeat. The young Cachef gave them battle. He precipitated himſelf like lightning amidſt their ſquadrons, and, overturning every thing that oppoſed his paſſage, he obtained a ſignal victory. The Arabs appeared no more. Ibrahim did juſtice to the ſervices of his Lieutenant in full council, and propoſed to create him a Sangiak. Ibrahim, the *Circaſſian*, an enemy to the former, oppoſed it with all his might, and employed all his eloquence to prevent a nomination which diſpleaſed him. The *Emir Haji* prevailed. *Ali* was nominated by the Divan ; Eddin Mohamed, the Pacha, confirmed this choice, cloathed him with a caftan, and gave him, agreeable to cuſtom, the Firman of *Bey*.

Become now one of the 24 members of the Republic, he never forgot his obligations to his patron,

patron, and defended his interests with an admirable constancy. In 1758 the *Emir Haji* was murdered by the party of Ibrahim, the *Circassian*. From this moment *Ali* meditated vengeance. For three years he concealed in his heart his resentment for this murder, and employed all the resources of his mind to arrive at the post of *Scheik Elbalad*, the first dignity of the Republic. In 1763 he attained that dangerous title, the summit of his ambition. Soon after, he revenged the blood of his protector, by sacrificing Ibrahim, the Circassian, with his own hand. In committing this desperate action, he followed the impulse of hatred, rather than of prudence; for it raised up numerous enemies against him. All the Sangiaks attached to the party of the Circassian, conspired against him. Exposed to their intrigues, and on the point of being murdered, he saved himself by flight. After rapidly crossing the desarts of the isthmus of Suez, he repaired to Jerusalem. Having gained the good graces of the Governor of that city, he thought himself in safety. But friendship has no sacred asylum amongst the Turks, when opposed to the commands of the despot. His enemies were afraid of him even in his exile. They wrote to the Porte to demand his death, and orders were immediately sent to the Governor to strike off his head. Fortunately, *Rabiph*, his old friend, now one of the members of the Divan, gave him timely warning, and advised him to fly Jerusalem. *Ali* therefore anticipated the

the arrival of the Capigi Bachi *(d)*, and took refuge with *Scheik Daher*, Prince of St. John of Acre. This respectable old man, who for fifty years had defended his little principality against the whole forces of the Ottoman empire, received with open arms the unfortunate *Scheik Elbalad*, and afforded him *hospitality*, that sacred pledge of the safety of mankind, whose holy ties are never violated by the Arabs. He was not long in discovering the merit of his guest, and from that moment loaded him with caresses, and called him his son. He exhorted him to support adversity with courage, flattered his hopes, soothed his sorrows, and made him taste of pleasures in the bosom even of his disgrace. *Ali Bey* might have passed his days happily with *Scheik Daher*, but ambition, that preyed upon him, would not suffer him to remain inactive. He carried on a secret correspondence with some of the Sangiaks attached to his interest. He inflamed their zeal by the temptation of better governments. The Prince of Acre on his part, wrote to his friends at Grand Cairo, and urged them to hasten the recal of the *Scheik Elbalad*. While this was going on, *Rahiph*, now Grand Visir, openly espoused the interest of his old friend, and employed all his credit to obtain his re-establishment. These different means succeeded to the wishes of *Ali*. The Beys invited him to return to Grand Cairo, and to resume his dignity. He set off imme-

(d) Messengers of the Grand Signior, who, provided with a Firman, are sent to take off the heads of the disgraced Grandees.

diately,

diately, and was received with the acclamations of the people.

The *Scheik Elbalad* reſtored, was nevertheleſs perfectly acquainted with the precariouſneſs of his ſituation. He could never reckon upon a tranquil adminiſtration. Hatreds were ſtifled, but not extinguiſhed. On all ſides the ſtorm was gathering around him. All thoſe whom the murder of Ibrahim, the Circaſſian, had offended, were conſtantly ſpreading ſnares for him. All his penetration was neceſſary to avoid them. They waited only for a favourable occaſion to let their reſentment break out. The death of *Rabiph*, which happened in 1763, furniſhed them this opportunity. They threw off the maſk, and declared open war againſt him. On the point of periſhing, he eſcaped into Arabia Felix, viſiting the coaſts of the Red Sea, and once more took refuge with the *Scheik Daher*, who received him with the ſame tenderneſs. This wiſe old man, taught by the experience of fourſcore years, had gone through every reverſe of fortune. He was calculated to furniſh conſolation to the wretched. He charmed by the wiſdom of his converſation the liſtleſſneſs of his gueſt; he revived his courage by the hope of a happier hereafter, and endeavoured to make him forget his misfortunes. Whilſt he was alleviating his deſtiny, the Sangiaks of the party of Ibrahim, the Circaſſian, truſting in the total deſtruction of their enemy, abandoned themſelves to all ſorts of vexations, and perſecuted thoſe who were devoted to the intereſts of *Ali*. This imprudence

opened

opened the eyes of the majority. They perceived that they were the dupes of a few ambitious men, and to ſtrengthen their party, recalled the *Scheik Elbalad*, and promiſed to ſupport him with all their power. He ſet off immediately, with the embraces of the *Scheik Daher*, who proffered the ſincereſt wiſhes for his proſperity.

On his return to Grand Cairo in 1766, *Ali* held a council with his partizans. He repreſented to them, that moderation had only excited to revenge the friends of Ibrahim; that nothing but flight would have ſaved him from their plots; and that to ſecure the common ſafety, theſe turbulent ſpirits muſt be ſacrificed. The whole aſſembly applauded this reſolution, and the next day they took off the heads of four of them. This execution inſured the tranquillity of *Ali*. He ſaw himſelf at the head of the government, and in the ſpace of ſix years he raiſed ſixteen of his Mamalukes to the dignity of Beys, and one of them to that of Janizary Aga. The principals were *Mahamed Abou Dahab*, *Iſmael*, *Mourad*, *Haſſan*, *Tentaoui*, and *Ibrahim*. The firſt was his countryman. He purchaſed him in 1758, and had a particular affection for him.

Supreme chief of the Republic, he adopted every meaſure to render her power durable. Not content with increaſing his Mamalukes to the number of ſix thouſand, he took into pay ten thouſand *Mograbi* (*e*). He made his troops

(*e*) Mograbi ſignifies weſtern people. The Egyptians beſtow this name on the inhabitants of the coaſt of Barbary.

obſerve the moſt rigid diſcipline, and by continually exerciſing them in the handling of arms, formed excellent ſoldiers. He attached to himſelf the young men who compoſed his houſehold, by the paternal attention he paid to their education, and above all by beſtowing favours and rewards on thoſe who were the moſt worthy. His party became ſo powerful, that ſuch of his colleagues as were not his friends, dreaded his power, and did not dare to thwart his projects. Believing his authority eſtabliſhed on a ſolid baſis, he turned his attention to the welfare of the people. The Arabs, diſperſed over the deſarts, and on the frontiers of Egypt, committed ravages not to be ſuppreſſed by a fluctuating government. He declared war, and ſent againſt them bodies of cavalry which beat them every where, and drove them back into the depth of their ſolitudes. Egypt began to reſpire, and agriculture encouraged, flouriſhed once more in that country. Having rendered the chiefs of each village reſponſible for the crimes of the inhabitants, he puniſhed them until the authors of the offence were delivered into the hands of juſtice. In this manner, the principal citizens looked after the public ſafety, and for the firſt time, ſince the commencement of the Turkiſh empire, the traveller and the merchant could paſs through the whole extent of the kingdom, without the apprehenſion of an inſult. Acquainted with the exceſſes of mercenary ſoldiers, both in the capital and in the provinces, he ordered the perſons injured to addreſs their com-

plaints

plaints immediately to him, and he never failed to do them juſtice. Amongſt the numerous anecdotes that are cited of his impartial equity, I ſhall relate only one. A Sangiak meeting with a Venetian merchant, near to old Cairo, made him diſmount, and tore from him his *ſhawl*. *Ali* being informed of it, ſent for the offender, (*though a Sangiak*) reprimanded him ſeverely in the preſence of the foreigner, forced him to make a public apology, and was very near taking off his head. This integrity, which he obſerved in every part of his adminiſtration, rendered the Egyptians happy. They thought they ſaw the revival of the golden age. Even at this day, they never ceaſe to bleſs his memory, and ſing to his praiſes.

Ali Bey had purchaſed a female ſlave, who had been carried off from the Red Ruſſia. She was beautiful. Her white locks flowing to the ground, a noble ſtature, a complexion of the moſt dazzling fairneſs, blue eyes arched over with black eyebrows; theſe were amongſt the ſmalleſt treaſures with which nature had adorned the young *Marta*. She had a ſoul far ſuperior to her beauty. Never could the misfortune of her deſtiny prevail on her to comply with the deſires of her maſter. He ſpoke of his power, but ſhe ſhewed him that ſhe was free even in her chains. He tried to dazzle her with the ſplendor that ſurrounded him. She appeared inſenſible to the allurements of grandeur. Charmed with the loftineſs of her character, a ſentiment was deeply impreſſed in his own mind; he addressed her with the ardour of a lover, and offered her his hand, on condition of her renouncing christianity. Maria, though she felt an inclination for a man who had treated her with all the respect due to her sex, had the courage to refuse. At length, he permitted her to remain in the religion of her fathers, provided she gave no exterior marks of it, and he obtained her consent. He loved her tenderly, and as long as he lived he had no other wife.

Having attained the pinnacle of greatness, *Ali* did not forget the authors of his being. On his reconciliation with the Porte, he entrusted to *Tentaoui* the escort of the *Khasné*, sent annually to Constantinople, charging him to pass into Natolia, and to bring to him his father and his family. On hearing of their arrival at Boulak, he went to meet them, followed by a numerous retinue. As soon as he perceived the aged *Daoud*, he dismounted from his horse, flew to meet him, and throwing himself on his knees, kissed his feet, calling him his father. The old man shed tears of joy, and this was the happiest day of his life. He embraced his sister, and a nephew he presented him. After this tender acknowledgment, he conducted them to his palace which looked upon the square of the *Esbekié (f)*. The Mamalukes eagerly pressed forward to wash the feet of the father of their master, and after cloathing him in a magnificent dress, he was introduced into the Haram, where the wife of *Ali* loaded him with caresses.

(f) The name of the largest square of Cairo. The Beys in general have their palaces here.

Daoud,

Daoud, mounted on a ſuperb horſe, was conducted to the hall of the Divan. The Beys, the Pacha himſelf, complimented him, and made him preſents. After ſeven months ſtay in Egypt, he was deſirous of returning into his own country, and Ali ſent him back to his native place laden with riches. You ſee, Sir, that events ſimilar to the hiſtory of Joſeph frequently occur in Egypt *(g)*.

The *Scheik Elbalad*, wiſhing to give a freſh proof of his friendſhip to Mahomed *Abou-Dahab*, and to attach him by an indiſſoluble tie, beſtowed his ſiſter in marriage on him. For three days their nuptials were celebrated by illuminations, by horſe races, and brilliant entertainments.— But this was only accumulating favours on a traitor, who was meditating in ſilence the ruin of his benefactor. Connected ſecretly with the remains of Ibrahim's family, he aſpired to the ſovereign power. Ambition and thirſt of gold *(h)* had corrupted his heart. Every method by which he might poſſibly attain the dignity of *Scheik Elbalad* appeared to him legitimate. The Sangiaks, with whom he had an underſtanding, being no ſtrangers to his avarice, gave him conſiderable ſums to engage him to put *Ali* out of the way. Knowing how difficult his own vigilance, and the

(g) Jacob being arrived in Egypt, Joſeph mounted on his chariot, and went to meet his father. On perceiving him, he immediately deſcended, and "fell on his neck and wept." Geneſis, chap. 46. This new Joſeph ſhewed no leſs tenderneſs for his relations.

(h) He was called *Abou Dahab*, Father of gold, on account of his avarice.

love

love of those about him, rendered the execution of this plot, and fearing for his life, he deferred it to a more favourable moment, and kept the gold. But to encrease the confidence of his friend, and still more to blind him, he discovered the conspiracy. This confession succeeded beyond his expectation. The tenderness of *Ali* for a brother-in-law, to whom he thought himself indebted for his life, became excessive. *Abou Dahab* never lost sight of his infamous project. He attempted the fidelity of *Tentaoui*, and offered him 300,000 livres to murder his patron, whilst he played at chess with him. This brave chief flew immediately to acquaint *Ali* with the proposal. The *Scheik Elbalad*, too much prejudiced in favour of Mahomed, only laughed at it. The traitor, defeated in this, tried another method. He endeavoured to force his wife to poison a brother she loved, by presenting him a dish of coffee. She rejected the proposition with horror, and sent af aithful slave to conjure *Ali* to be upon his guard, and to fear every thing from Abou Dahab, as his most dangerous enemy. So many warnings ought to have opened his eyes, but his tenderness for him was excessive. He could not believe in crimes his own heart revolted at, and the consciousness of his bounties removed every apprehension.

In 1768, the Russians declared war against the Porte, and their fleets penetrated into the Mediterranean. The *Scheik Elbalad*, according to custom, levied twelve thousand men to send to the assistance of the Grand Signior. His

enemies

enemies availed themſelves of this circumſtance to ruin him. They wrote to the Divan of Conſtantinople, that the troops he was collecting were deſtined to ſerve in the Ruſſian armies, with which court he had formed a treaty of alliance. The letter was ſigned by ſeveral Beys. The calumny was credited without further examination, and the Sultan immediately diſpatched a Capigi Bachi, with four Satellites, to take off his head. Fortunately for *Ali*, he had a truſty agent in the council. He ſent off without loſs of time two couriers, one by ſea, the other by land, to acquaint him with this treachery. They arrived before the Grand Signior's meſſengers. The *Scheik Elbalad* kept the matter ſecret. He ſent to *Tentaoui*, in whom he placed great confidence, and diſcovering to him the myſtery, commanded him to diſguiſe himſelf like an Arab, and to go with twelve Mamalukes, twenty miles diſtant from Cairo, and wait for the Grand Signior's emiſſaries. You will take from them, added he, their diſpatches, and you will put them to death.

Tentaoui acquitted himſelf perfectly well of his commiſſion. After waiting ſome time in the ſtation aſſigned him, the Capigi Bachi and his Satellites made their appearance. He laid hold of their perſons, wreſted from them the fatal order, ſlew them all, and buried them in the ſand. Poſſeſſed of the Firman the *Scheik Elbalad* aſſembled the chiefs of the republic, and after communicating it, he addreſſed them: "How long ſhall we "ſubmit to be the victims of the deſpotiſm of "the Ottoman Porte? What confidence can we "have

"have in treaties with her? A few years ſince, "ſhe made a part of the chiefs of this republic "periſh, contrary to all juſtice. Several amongſt "you witneſſed that bloody execution, and ſtill "bear the marks of it. Behold the blood of "four of your colleagues, with which this mar-"ble we are this moment treading on is ſtill red. "To-day my death is ordered. To-morrow "will be demanded the head of him who ſhall "fill my place. This is the moment to ſhake off "the yoke of a deſpot, who, violating our pri-"vileges and our laws, ſeems to diſpoſe of our "lives as he thinks proper. Let us join our "arms to thoſe of Ruſſia. Let us free this re-"public from the domination of a barbarous "maſter. Aid me with your efforts, and I will "anſwer for the liberty of Egypt." This diſcourſe produced all the effect that *Ali* had a right to expect from it. The ſixteen Beys of his party exclaimed with one voice, that war muſt be declared againſt the Grand Signior. Such as were of a contrary opinion, unable to oppoſe the project, promiſed to ſecond it with all their power. The Pacha received an order to quit Egypt in four and twenty hours. The *Scheik Elbalad* communicated this reſolution to the Prince of Acre, promiſing to join his troops with thoſe of Egypt, in order to conquer Syria.

As ſoon as the Divan of Conſtantinople heard of the rebellion of the Beys, and of the ſtorm that menaced Syria, they commanded the Pacha of Damaſcus to attack *Scheik Dahar* before this junction took place This Viceroy marched immediately

mediately at the head of twenty thouſand men, haſtily collected, to ſurprize St. John of Acre. The old Prince, who all his life had made war againſt the Turks, was not at all alarmed at their approach. He mounts on horſe-back, calls together his ſeven ſons, who all commanded fortified caſtles, and putting himſelf at the head of nine thouſand horſemen, marches ſtrait towards the enemy. Whilſt one of his ſons harraſſed them with a body of light cavalry, *Scheik Daher* went and took poſt near Lake Tyberias. He was informed of all their motions. When he knew for certain that the Turks were near at hand, he ſeparated his troops into three diviſions. He ordered the two firſt to conceal themſelves in the mountains until he gave the ſignal. As for himſelf, abandoning his camp full of proviſions, he retreated to ſome diſtance. At the beginning of the night, the Pacha, thinking to ſurprize the Arabs, advanced in ſilence, under favour of the darkneſs. He reaches the camp, and the few troops he left in it fled precipitately after a ſlight ſkirmiſh. Their flight he attributed to fear, and his ſoldiers, heated by a forced march, looked upon the abundant proviſions they found there as a conqueſt, and drank greedily of the wine. At the break of day *Scheik Daher* gave the appointed ſignal, and the three corps of cavalry poured together into the camp, ſabre in hand. Finding nothing but drunken men, they had no trouble but to ſlay them. They killed eight thouſand of them, made a great number of priſoners, and took all the tents, arms, and baggage of the Pacha,

Pacha, who eſcaped during the tumult, and hid himſelf within the walls of Damaſcus. The *Scheik* diſpatched a courier to Grand Cairo with the news of his victory, and returned into his principality.

Ali, ſeeing his ally in ſafety, turned his arms to another quarter. He had formerly, as we have ſeen, ſurveyed the Jemen, and the eaſtern coaſt of the Red Sea. Judging what advantages he might derive from the commerce and productions of thoſe countries, if he could ſubject them to his government, he levied two armies, the one of twenty-ſix thouſand cavalry, the other of nine. The command of the former he gave to his brother-in-law, and that of the ſecond to Iſmael Bey. *Abou Dahab* was to attack Arabia Felix, and the interior provinces; Iſmael the maritime towns, and the ſeaports. He gave the Generals the plans they were to follow, and equipped a fleet to coaſt along the Red Sea, and ſupply them with proviſions. He had calcutated, like an able warrior, the obſtacles they had to ſurmount, and ſucceſs depended on their fidelity in carrying his orders into execution. The Egyptian Cohorts left Egypt in 1770. Whilſt they were on their march to the conqueſt of Arabia, the *Scheik El-balad* remained in the capital, where he gave up his whole attention to the internal police of the kingdom, and to the happineſs of the people.

The cuſtom-houſes of Egypt had long been in the hands of Jews, who committed horrid depredations, and harraſſed foreigners with impunity. He removed them, and entruſted their adminiſtration

ſtration to Chriſtians of Syria, with a particular recommendation to favour the European merchants. He was ſenſible how flouriſhing Egypt might become by commerce. His project was to open it to all the nations of the world, and to render it the emporium of the merchandize of Europe, India, and Africa. To effect this, it was only neceſſary to provide for the ſecurity of the caravans, and put the merchants under the protection of the laws; which he did, by checking on every ſide the vagabond Arabs, and by eſtabliſhing at Grand Cairo, Selim, Aga, and Soliman, Kiaia of the Janizaries to protect the merchants, and to ſee juſtice done them. With the ſame view he ordered his Generals to leave officers in the ſea-ports they might take, to receive the veſſels from India, and to defend them againſt the natives of the country. He was not long in reaping the fruits of his wiſe adminiſtration.—He had the happineſs to ſee the Egyptians relieved, ſtrangers favourably received, the public ſafety eſtabliſhed, agriculture encouraged, and the Republic raiſed to a pitch of ſplendor ſhe never had attained from the firſt hour of her exiſtence.

Whilſt he was thus glorioully employed, his Generals triumphed in Arabia. *Abou Dabab* conquered the Jemen in one campaign, deſtroyed the Scherif of Mecca, and ſubſtituted in his place the Emir Abdalla, who, to pay his court to Ali, gratified him with the pompous title of Sultan of Egypt and the two ſeas. Iſmael, on his ſide, made himſelf maſter of all the towns bordering

on

on the eaſtern ſhore of the Arabic Gulph. They returned to Cairo covered with laurels. The inhabitants received them with loud acclamations, and their triumphs were celebrated by ſplendid feſtivals.

Ali had not laid aſide the expedition againſt Syria. In 1771 he ſent Mahamed *Abou Dahab* to attempt that conqueſt, at the head of forty thouſand men. Whilſt theſe troops were traverſing the deſart, veſſels equipped at Damietta, tranſported to St. John of Acre the neceſſary ſupplies for them. Availing himſelf, like an able politician, of the preſent circumſtances, the *Scheik Elbalad* wrote to Count Alexis Orlow, then at Leghorn, to form a treaty of alliance with the Empreſs of Ruſſia. He offered the Admiral on his part, money, proviſions, and ſoldiers; requiring only a few engineers, and engaged to unite his forces with thoſe of the Ruſſians to overthrow the Ottoman throne. The Count thanked *Ali*, encouraged him in his glorious enterprize, made him great promiſes, which were never realized, and aſſured him that he ſhould loſe no time in laying his diſpatches before his ſovereign.

He had deputed the year before a Venetian merchant called Roſetti, to propoſe an alliance with the Republic of Venice, and to enconrage her to retake from the Turks thoſe iſlands and delightful provinces ſhe had formerly poſſeſſed in the Mediterranean. He promiſed to aid her with all the forces of Egypt, and to re-eſtabliſh there her ancient commerce; but the Republic declined this hardy enterprize.

During

During these negotiations, *Abou Dahab*, assisted by the counsels and the succours of the Prince of Acre, took all the towns of Syria from the Ottomans, and drove them before him like a flock of sheep. Arriving on the 9th of March, near the walls of Gaza, which was provided with a strong garrison, he carried it by storm in three days. Rama cost him more time and trouble. The besieged defended themselves with such intrepidity, that he could not become master of it by force. He formed a blockade, and, after a month's resistance, it capitulated. The Governor had made his escape, dreading the fate that awaited him. The Turks durst not appear in the field, and defended themselves only under shelter of their walls. After these two conquests the victor laid siege to *Naplous*, formerly Neapolis. The obstinate resistance of the besieged, joined to the inexperience of the Egyptians in the use of artillery, protracted the siege. Various encounters took place round the walls, but without any decisive success. *Abou Dahab*, despairing of carrying the place by storm, contracted his lines of circumvallation, and carried it by famine. He then turned his arms against Jerusalem, called by the Mahometans, as well as the Christians, the Holy City, and which they held in great veneration, pretending that Mahomet was miraculously transported thither, where he prayed in the company of the Prophets *(i)*.—

(i) "Praise to God! who has transported, during the night, "his servant of the Temple of Mecca to the Temple of Jerusa-"lem, the enclosure of which we have blessed in order to leave "the marks of our power." Coran, chap. 17.

Having

Having ſummoned it to ſurrender, the Governor and the High-Prieſt ſent a deputation to him with preſents. They conjured him to avert the ſtorm from the walls of Jeruſalem, to reſpect the place where the Prophet had offered up his prayers, aſſuring him that if he ſucceeded in reducing Damaſcus, they would ſubmit to follow the fate of the capital, and open their gates to him. The Egyptian General acquieſced in their requeſt, and led his troops to *Jaffa*, the ancient Joppa. It is built on a rock that projects into the ſea. Its fortifications and advantageous poſition rendered the ſiege long and bloody. For two months, *Abou Dahab* battered the walls with all his artillery ; but as it neither was conſiderable, nor directed by ſkilful engineers, he could not make any breach in them. The Egyptians made many aſſaults, and the intrepid Mamalukes mounted to the top of the ramparts, but they were repulſed with loſs. A part of the beſieged, however, had periſhed. Such as remained, fearing to be put to the ſword, ſhould the place be carried by ſtorm, at length capitulated. The General, after leaving a ſtrong garriſon, repaired to St. John of Acre at the beginning of September. The Arab Prince received him with joy, congratulated him on his ſucceſs, and ſupplied him with proviſions and ammunition.

Mahomed, after giving his troops a fortnight's repoſe, marched to attack *Seide*, the ancient Sidon, near which flouriſhed in former days the city of Tyre, ſo celebrated for her commerce, her arts, and her navy. The peninſula on which it it ſtands preſents nothing but ruins. *Seide* ſurrendered on the firſt ſummons. Maſter of the moſt important towns in Syria, *Abou Dahab* proceeded to the capital. *Damaſcus*, ſituated in a rich plain, is ſurrounded by rivulets, and gardens filled with orange, piſtachio, and pomegranate, and a multitude of other fruit-trees, bearing the moſt delicious fruits. Exquiſite ſweetmeats are made of them, which ſerve in the *Sorbet*, or *Sherbet*, and which are ſold throughout the eaſt. Nothing can be more beautiful, gayer, or more freſh than the environs of this city. Nothing is to be ſeen on every ſide but groves, rivulets, and charming pavillions, where Turkiſh effeminacy is lulled aſleep on cuſhions of velvet and of ſattin. The Arabs call it *Echchams*, the City of the Sun. The water is of an admirable quality for the tempering of ſteel; and the arms, the poniards, the ſabres, fabricated here, are renowned throughout the world. The Pacha was ſhut up there with a numerous garriſon. For two months he defended it with courage. At the end of November, ſeeing the walls overthrown, the advanced works deſtroyed, and the enemy ready to mount to the aſſault, he fled during the night, and the city ſurrendered. The garriſon had retired into the citadel. It was neceſſary to form a ſecond ſiege, and it coſt the Egyptians many efforts to get poſſeſſion of it.

The Turks had now no conſiderable place remaining but Aleppo. The capture of that city would have ſecured to the Republic of Egypt the entire poſſeſſion of Syria; but *Abou*

Dahab

Dabab feared lest this conquest might retard his designs. He had long meditated the ruin of *Ali*, his patron, his brother in law, his friend. The desiring of gaining the soldiery, by making them the companions of his victories, had alone induced him to take arms, and influenced all his measures. The interest of Egypt, which the union with Syria would have rendered independent of the Porte, had no part in his projects. No sooner was he sure of his officers and soldiers, than after making them take an oath of fidelity, he hoisted the standard of rebellion. He withdrew all his garrisons from the conquered places, and rendering abortive the fruit of so much blood spilt, and of a whole year of conquests, he re-entered Egypt. On his departure the Turks retook, without a struggle, the cities he had taken from them, raised their walls, and added new fortifications. *Abou Dabab*, thus elated with success, did not dare at first to attack the capital, where his rival was too powerful. He kept along the western coast of the Red Sea, crossed the desart, and marched into upper Egypt. It was then he made an open display of his criminal intentions. He took Girgé, and other important towns. By force, or by address, he gained the Beys who commanded there, and descended towards Cairo.

Ali Bey repented, but too late, having followed the emotions of his heart, rather than the dictates of prudence, by placing in the hand of a traitor a command with which he should never have entrusted him. He still had resources, and he he haſtened to oppoſe them to his enemy. Having collected twenty thouſand men, he put at their head *Iſmael Bey*, on whoſe experience and fidelity he thought he could ſafely reckon. *Abou Dahab* was incamped near Gaza; *Ali* ordered his General to take poſt near to Old Cairo, and prevent the enemy from paſſing the river. Nothing was more eaſy; but the perfidious *Iſmael*, baſely betraying the intereſts of his patron, formed a treaty of alliance with *Abou Dahab*, and paſſed over to his camp. The junction of the two armies was a thunderſtroke for the generous *Ali*. In the firſt emotions of deſpair, he determined to ſhut himſelf up in the caſtle of Grand Cairo with his few brave adherents, and to bury himſelf under its ruins. The ſons of *Scheik Daher*, who loved him, repreſented to him the folly of this reſolution, and conjured him once more to eſcape with them to St. John of Acre. He felt the wiſdom of their counſel, and followed it. He wrote inſtantly to *Count Orlow*, requeſting him to ſend ſome warlike ſtores, and ſome officers, to him into Syria. He entruſted theſe diſpatches to the Armenian Jacob, who had already acquitted himſelf of a ſimilar commiſſion, collected his treaſures, and loaded them on twenty camels. He ſent to demand from *Mallem Reiſk*, whom he had made Intendant of the revenues of Egypt, all the money he had collected; but the knave had hid himſelf, and it was impoſſible to find him. In the middle of the night, *Ali Bey*, accompanied by the ſons of *Scheik Daher*, by Tentaoui, Roſſuan, Haſſan, Kalil, Mourad, Abd

 Errohman,

Errohman, Latif, Moustafa, Ibrahim, Zoulficar, Hacheph, Osman, Selim, Aga, and Soliman, Kiaia of the Janizaries, all Beys of his creation, and about 7000 troops, left Cairo for the third time, and fled across the desarts. He carried with him twenty-four millions of livres (about one million sterling) in gold and silver. After five days forced march, he arrived on the 16th of April, 1772, at the gates of Gaza, and his troops began to breathe. The treason of two men, on whose friendship he had the strictest claims, rent his heart with sorrow. He shuddered at the very name of *Abou Dahab*, and his blood boiled in his veins. This agitation, added to the fatigue of so difficult a route, brought on a serious malady. A prey to the most gloomy melancholy, he looked for death with a sort of consolation. Liberty procured to Egypt, Arabia submitted to his sway, justice established in the cities, commerce flourishing, the good he had already done the people; all those advantages, which it was the wish of his heart still further to procure them, he saw for ever vanished, and this bitter reflection filled the measure of his misfortunes. Whilst he was cruelly suffering under these poignant cares, the *Scheik Daher*, that respectable old man, his faithful friend, his protector in adversity, came to visit him in his tent. After mingling his tears with those of *Ali*, he called him his son, and tried, by exhortations full of sense and tenderness, to communicate some comfort to his sorrows. He represented to him that his situation was not desperate, that the Russian

ſian ſquadron was at hand, and that, with this ſuccour, he might ſtill regain the dignity from which he had been precipitated by treaſon. How powerful are the tender conſolations of friendſhip on ſenſible hearts! It is a ſalutary balm that penetrates all our ſenſes, and heals, as if by enchantment, the wounds both of the ſoul and of the body. *Ali* experienced its effects, and hope once more appeared to renew the lamp of life. The Arab Prince had brought with him a phyſician, whom he left with his ſick friend, and he recovered his health in a few weeks.

A detachment of the Ruſſian ſquadron appearing before Acre, *Ali* took the advantage of this opportunity to write to *Count Orlow*. He made the ſame requeſt as before, deſiring him to ſend him ſome cannon and engineers, and a corps of three thouſand Albanians. He aſſured him, that immediately after his reinſtatement, all the forces of Egypt ſhould be at his diſpoſal. Beſides this, he addreſſed a letter to the Czarina, in which he ſollicited her alliance, and propoſed to her a commercial treaty with Egypt. Zulficar Bey, the bearer of theſe diſpatches, was commiſſioned to preſent to the Ruſſian Admiral three fine horſes, richly capariſoned. *It is certain that if Ruſſia had only ſent this feeble ſuccour to the* SCHEIK ELBALAD, *he would have triumphed over his enemies, and have been proclaimed King of Egypt.* Nor can it be doubted from his character, and every concurrent circumſtance, that he would have delivered *into the hands of the Ruſſians the commerce of the eaſtern world*, and have granted them *ports in the Red Sea and the Mediterranean.* This alliance might have operated a total change of affairs in the east. The Russian ships set sail for Paros the 18th of May, 1772, and conducted the Ambassador of *Ali*.

The precipitate retreat of *Abou Dahab* had given the Turks time to regain their possessions, and to fortify them. *Ali* endeavoured to expel them a second time. Having formed a corps of six thousand men, he gave the command of it to the brave *Tentaoui*, and ordered him to attack Seide. *Scheik Lebi*, and *Scheik Crim*, one the son, the other the son-in-law of the Prince of Acre, joined the Egyptian Chief, and marched in concert with him. In their route they fell in with the celebrated *Hassan Pacha*, who was expecting them, in the advantageous post, at the head of thirteen thousand men. Notwithstanding their inferiority, they did not hesitate to give him battle. Their cavalry was excellent. They rushed in a body on the Turks, broke through their ranks, cut a great number of them in pieces, and put the rest to flight. The fugitives conveyed the alarm to Seide, which instantly opened her gates to the conquerors. *Tentaoui* leaving a garrison in the town, under the orders of Hassan Bey, returned to the camp, where he received the compliments of *Ali*, and of the Prince of Acre.

On the 13th of August in the same year, *Ali* marched again Jaffa, accompanied by the valiant sons of the *ScbeikDabar*. This prince equipped two vessels to carry ammunition and provisions to the assailants. As soon as the troops were assembled

aſſembled before the place, the general ſummoned the commandant to ſurrender, and on his refuſal laid ſiege to it. He battered the walls for forty days, but his artillery was too weak to form any conſiderable breach. Nevertheleſs he gave the ſignal for the aſſault, and his ſoldiers went to it with intrepidity. The difficulty of ſtoring the place, and the valour of the beſieged, compelled him to retreat. Deſpairing of being able to carry it by force, he formed a blockade, and determined to take it by famine. During the blockade, he ſent *Tentaoui* with a detachment of cavalry to ſurprize Gaza. This brave captain ſet off like lightening, carried the place on the firſt onſet, and after leaving a garriſon, returned to the camp covered with laurels. The inhabitants of Jaffa, receiving ſuccours by ſea, defended themſelves with reſolution. They were in want of nothing but wood. The adjacent country is delightful; it is interſected with gardens deliciouſly ſhaded by orange and lemon trees. They are ſupplied by copious ſprings, which gliding from the foot of the mountains ſerves to water them, and preſerve their perpetual verdure. Theſe beautiful trees are at one ſeaſon of the year loaded both with flowers and fruit. *Ali* had ſpared them. Perceiving however that the beſieged came and cut them down, and carried them off under favour of the night, he made them all ſuffer the ſame fate, and deſtroyed theſe charming plantations.

Whilſt all this was going on, *Ali's* ambaſſador, and the American Jacob returned from their miſſion

miſſion on board of an Engliſh veſſel commanded by *Captain Browne*. *Count Orlow* ſent him two Ruſſian officers with diſpatches, in which he aſſured him of his friendſhip, and promiſed him powerful ſuccours. Theſe officers preſented him, on the part of the admiral, with *three* braſs field pieces, four pounders, 500 balls, and *ſeven* barrels of powder. This was all the aſſiſtance he derived from the magnificent promiſes of *Count Alexis*!!

The ſiege ſtill continued. *Clinginoff*, a Ruſſian captain, raiſed a new battery of three cannon, twelve pounders, with which he did great damage to the town. He had already beat down a part of the wall, when, deſirous of obſerving the effect of the artillery, and looking through an embraſure, he was killed by a muſket ſhot. A ſhort time before, this brave officer embarked with one ſingle man during the night, to burn the Turkiſh ſhips at anchor in the harbour. Being diſcovered, before he could put his deſign in execution, the fire from the ramparts obliged him to make a precipitate retreat.

Captain Browne made an addition of ſix cannon to thoſe which were already playing on the town. Theſe various batteries at length formed practicable breaches. *Ali* ſounded the charge, and his troops mounted to the aſſault. In ſpight of their ardour, they were obliged to give way to the valour of a numerous garriſon, who were continually receiving freſh reinforcements by ſea. Several Ruſſian ſhips, at the requeſt of *Ali*, approached Jaffa, bumbarded the town for two days

days, and beat down a part of the houſes; but fearing to be thrown upon the coaſt, if the weſterly winds ſhould blow with violence, they quitted this dangerous road. Theſe multiplied attacks had reduced the beſieged to great extremity. They ſaw nothing around them but heaps of ruins. The governor, terrified, eſcaped during the night, and eluding the vigilance of the enemy, gained *Naplous* where his brother commanded. The next day, the thirty-firſt of January, 1773, *Ali* entered the town. This bloody ſiege coſt him three Beys, and a great number of Mamalukes. He delivered the place to the Prince of Acre who had ſupplied his army with ſtores and proviſions.

Whilſt he lay encamped before Jaffa, *Mallem Reiſk*, the intendant of the Cuſtom-houſe of Egypt, came and found him in his tent, in the diſguiſe of a Derviſe. His ſun-burnt viſage, his meagre appearance, his dirty and torn garments, rendered him difficult to be known. He pleaded in his excuſe, that as ſoon as he learnt the elevation of *Abou Dahab*, dreading the avarice of that traitor, he had buried his riches, and eſcaped into the deſarts, where for above a year he had led a miſerable life. *Ali* ſeeing him wretched, took pity on his hard fortune, forgot his perfidy, and ſupplied him with cloaths and money. At the ſame period, the camp witneſſed another example of the the viciſſitude of human affairs. The *Emir Abdalla*, who by *Ali*'s orders had been elevated to the principality of Mecca, in the place of the *Scherif*, came likewiſe to implore,

plore his aſſiſtance. The enemy had reſtored his rival, and he was obliged to fly. *Ali* conſoled him, loaded him with preſents, and he returned to Medina. It is thus that the misfortune of the Chief of the Egyptian Republic involves the downfall of every perſon attached to his party.

After the capture of Jaffa, the *Scheik Elbalad* led his troops to Rama, which was carried ſword in hand. Theſe ſucceſſes raiſed the hopes of his partizans, and inſpired him with the confidence of returning triumphant to Grand Cairo. *Ali* had conſtantly maintained a correſpondence with the chiefs of the Janizaries, who have great power in the capital. The promiſes with which he flattered them, and the averſion with which *Abou Dahab's* avarice inſpired them, determined them openly to eſpouſe his party, and to demand his recal. They wrote to him, that he might return, and that they would defend his intereſts. This news overwhelmed him with joy; he imparted it to his friends, and prepared for his return to Egypt. *Scheik Daher* was of a different opinion. He adviſes him to wait the promiſed ſuccours of the Ruſſians, to foment diviſions amongſt the chiefs of the Republic, to be previouſly well aſſured of the diſpoſition of the troops in his favour, and not raſhly riſk his fortune and his life. Theſe councils, dictated by prudence, were not followed. *Ali*, impatient to return to Grand Cairo, and humble his enemies, fondly imagined he was marching to victory. He collected the garriſons of the conquered

quered towns, raiſed contributions in them, arrived at Gaza the 21ſt of March, and left it on the 4th of April, 1773.

His whole cavalry conſiſted of two thouſand men, and two hundred and fifty Mamalukes. Three thouſand four hundred Mograbi compoſed his infantry. *Tentaoui*, *Kalil*, *Latif*, *Haſſan*, *Abd Errohman*, *Mourad*, *Selim* the Aga, and *Soliman* Kiaïa of the Janizaries, were all his reremaining Beys. Six hundred and fifty horſe, commanded by the ſon and ſon-in-law of *Scheik Daher*, accompanied this little army, which formed in all ſix thouſand three hundred and ten combatants.

Abou Dahab had ſent twelve thouſand men to Salakia, a town ſituated on the Iſthmus of Suez, to oppoſe *Ali*'s paſſage. As ſoon therefore as he approached this place, theſe troops advanced to meet him, and ranged themſelves in line of battle The *Scheik Elbalad* without heſitation, accepted the challenge. He ruſhed upon him with the rapidity of lightning. He fought ſabre in hand at the head of his Mamalukes, who, encouraged by his preſence, carried deſtruction through the ranks. The enemy ſuſtained this terrible ſhock for four hours. At length, penetrated in all parts, they fled into the deſart, leaving a great number of dead upon the field of battle. This glorious victory encouraged the little troop of *Ali*, who thought themſelves invincible under ſo brave a leader. Profiting by the ardour of his warriors, he advanced directly to Grand Cairo. The fugitives carried the news

of

of their defeat, and of his approach. *Abou Dahab* assembled the Beys brought over to his interest, and the principal people, and addressed them in these terms: " Brave chiefs of the Re-" public, and you Egyptians, who cherish the " law of our Prophet, you know *Ali*. He is a " christian in his heart, and has contracted alli-" ances with the infidels. He wishes to subject " this country, that he may abolish the religion " of Mahomet, and force you to adopt chris-" tianity. REMEMBER WHAT THE EUROPEANS " HAVE DONE IN INDIA; the Mussulmen of " those rich countries received them with kind-" ness, admitted them into their ports, granted " them factories, and made commercial treaties " with them. What was the consequence? The " *Christians* have *ravaged their provinces*, *destroyed* " *their cities*, *conquered their kingdoms*, and after " *reducing them to slavery*, have established ido-" latry *(k)* on the ruins of the true religion. " Faithful Mussulmen, a similar fate awaits you. " *Ali*, the ally of these Europeans, is about to " overturn the constitution of your empire, to " throw open Egypt to the infidels, and force " you to become christians. Aid me to repulse " the enemy of the Republic, of your laws, of " Islamism; or prepare yourselves for all *the* " *miseries your* BRETHREN OF BENGAL have suf-" fered.—Chuse between him and me." At the

(k) The Mahometans call us idolators, because being *unable to comprehend our mysteries*—they say we worship *several gods*.

conclu-

couclufion of this harangue, *Abou Dahab* pretended a defire to abdicate the dignity of *Scheik Elbalad* and to withdraw. But the whole audience pronounced with one unanimous cry, anathemas againft *Ali*, and promifed to fpill the laft drop of their blood in defence of the common caufe. Availing himfelf adroitly of this moment of enthuftafm, *Abou Dahab* publifhed a manifefto in the city, by which every man who loved his religion and his country was invited to take arms, and before the clofe of day, twenty thoufand men were ranged under his banners. He fet out immediately at the head of this army, to attack the enemy. The Janizaries, faithful to their promife, refufed to follow him, and waited with tranquility the refult of the combat.

Ali was unprepared for this event. He no fooner heard that *Abou Dahab* was approaching with troops, three time fuperior to his in number, than he abandoned himfelf to defpair, and fell dangeroufly ill. His friends advifed him to return to Acre, but he declared he would fooner perifh than retreat an inch.

The 13th of April, 1773, the army of Grand Cairo appeared in the prefence of his camp. He immediately ranged his troops in order of battle. *Scheik Lebi* and *Scheik Crim* had the command of the left wing. The right he gave to *Tentaoui*, and placed his infantry in the centre. Having made thefe able difpofitions, and exhorted the Chiefs to fight valiantly, he made them convey him to his tent, for he was too weak to fit on horfeback. The battle began at eleven in the

the morning. Both parties charged with fury, and, in ſpite of the inferiority of *Ali*'s troops, they at firſt had the advantage. *Scheik Lebi* and *Scheik Crim* glorioufly repulſed the Egyptian cavalry. *Tentaoui*, at the head of the brave Mamalukes, overthrew every thing before him. Victory was declaring for *Ali*, when the *Mograbi*, thoſe mercenary troops, invariably led by the allurement of gain, ſuffered themſelves to be corrupted by the ſplendid promiſes of *Abou Dahab*, and paſſed over to his ſide. The fortune of the day was changed. The fugitives rallied, and having now but three thouſand men to contend with, the environed them on every ſide, and ſlew a great number of them. The generous *Tentaoui* could not ſurvive his defeat. He precipitated himſelf into the middle of their ſquadrons, and fell, covered with wounds, on a heap of dead, whom he had ſacrificed. *Scheik Lebi*, the valiant ſon of the Prince of Acre, defended himſelf for a long time with his Arabs, and died combating. *Scheik Crim*, opening himſelf a paſſage through the Egyptian ranks, rode full ſpeed to the tent of *Ali*, and conjured him to take refuge with him at St. John of Acre. *Mourad*, *Ibrahim*, *Soliman*, and *Abd Errohman*, arrived there alſo, and made the ſame remonſtrances. My friends, replied he, fly, I command you; as for me, my hour is come. Scarcely had they quitted him before he was ſurrounded by the victorious troops. The Mamalukes, who was near his tent, defended their maſter to the laſt drop of their blood, and all periſhed with

with their arms in their hands. Deſpair having given new force to the unhappy *Scheik Elbalad*, he roſe up, and ſlew the firſt two ſoldiers who attempted to ſeize him. He was fired upon, and wounded with two balls. At this moment the Lieutenant of *Abou Dahab* appearing, ſabre in hand, *Ali* ſhot him with a piſtol. Swimming in his blood, he fought like a lion, but a ſoldier having beat him down by the back ſtroke of a ſabre, they threw themſelves upon him, and carried him to the tent of the conqueror. The traitor carrying his perfidy to its greateſt height, ſhed feigned tears on ſeeing him in this condition, and tried to conſole him for his diſgrace. *Ali* turned away his eyes, and uttered not a word. He died of his wounds eight days after. Others have aſſured me that they were not mortal, and that he was poiſoned by his infamous brother-in-law. This was to complete his enormities; nor can we reflect, without ſhuddering, on the horrors to which men are hurried by ambition.

Ali was of the middle ſize; he had large eyes, full of fire; his carriage was graceful and noble, and his character frank and generous. Nature had endowed him with an unſurmountable courage, and a lofty genius. Far removed from that barbarous pride which leads the Turks to deſpiſe ſtrangers, he loved them for their talents, and generouſly repaid their ſervices. He wiſhed ardently for officers to diſcipline his troops, and teach them the European tactics. He died the victim of his friendſhip. His misfortune aroſe from

from nourishing and bringing up a traitor, who took advantage of his bounty to imbitter his days, and to conduct him to his grave. Had *Russia* availed herself of his offers, had she but granted him some engineers, and three or four thousand men, he would have made himself Sovereign of Syria and Egypt, and have transferred to his ally the commerce of Arabia and India. He perished at 45 years of age. The Egyptians long wept his loss, and saw themselves again plunged into all the miseries from which he had delivered them.

As soon as *Scheik Daher* heard of the death of *Ali*, and that of his son, he abandoned himself to sorrow and regret. The wretched old man threw himself on his face upon the earth, covered himself with dust, and shed torrents of tears. But he must soon think of defending his life and his principality, *Abou Dahab*, elated with his triumph, determined to take revenge for the protection afforded by the Arabian Prince to *Ali*. He marched against Syria with the whole force of Egypt, leaving Ismael to govern in his absence. Jaffa was the first city he attacked. *Scheik Crim* defended it with courage, and the siege was protracted for some time. Unfortunately an European, gained by the promise of *Abou Dahab*, sprung a mine, which overthrew a considerable part of the walls. The Egyptians entered by the breach, and put *all the inhabitants to death* *. After

* *Baron de Tott* has the following passage in his *Memoirs*:—"On approaching the coast, they shewed me the horrid pyramid erected by Mahomed Bey. This monster had formed it of *fifteen*

ter this barbarous execution they marched towards St. John of Acre. *Scheik Daher*, who loved his people, and who was afraid of expoſſing them to the ſame cruel fate, adviſed them to open their gates to the conquerors, and retired himſelf into the mountains with his children. *Abou Dahab* meeting with no reſiſtance, ſpared their blood. But imagining that the Monks of Nazareth concealed the treaſures of the Prince, he ſent for them, and commanded them to deliver them upon the ſpot. Theſe unhappy men in vain aſſured him that they knew nothing of them. He took off the heads of three of them. Not content with this cruelty, he put to death by torture *Mallem Ibrahim Saba*, the Intendant of *Scheik Daher*, to force him to diſcover theſe imaginary treaſures. Some of the ſons of the Arabian Prince underwent the ſame fate, but with no more ſucceſs.

Here finiſhed the crimes of *Abou Dahab*. One morning he was found dead in his bed. It was pretended that he was poiſoned by one of his ſlaves, but this fact is uncertain. On this news, the Egyptian troops took the route of Grand Cairo, and the traitor *Iſmael* was erected *Scheik Elbalad*. The Prince of Acre immediately deſcended from the mountains, and re entered his principality. The people celebrated his return by ſhouts of joy and ſolemn feſtivals §.

During

fifteen hundred heads he had ordered to be cut off, after taking of this town" (*Joppa*). P. 113, 4th part, 2d vol. edit. by Jarvis.

§ The ſame *enlighten author* bears his teſtimony to the virtues of this good Prince. In ſpeaking of *Acre*, he ſays, "It was only,

During theſe tranſactions, a Turkiſh ſquadron came to anchor on the coaſt of Syria. The *Captain Pacha* (that too celebrated tyrant) having obtained permiſſion from *Scheik Daher* to pay him a viſit, brought him a Firman of the Grand Signior, granting to him and his deſcendants the ſovereignty of Acre, and the pardon of what was paſt. The old man was overcome with joy. Ready to drop into the grave, he ſaid that he ſhould die without regret, now that he ſaw that power rendered legitimate which he had purchaſed by ſixty years war and trouble. The *Captain Pacha* teſtified his thanks, and before he quitted him, preſſed him to come and dine on board his veſſel. The Arabian Prince, after the Firman he had received, had not the ſmalleſt ſuſpicion of the treachery intended him, and accepted of the invitation. On entering the ſhip, he was ſaluted by a diſcharge of artillery, and the next moment the Admiral drew from his boſom another Firman, ordering his death, and inſtantly took off his head. This reſpectable old man, ſo baſely betrayed, was 86 years of age. He was adored by his people, whom he had all his life defended againſt the tyranny of the *Pacha*. It is thus that the Divan of Conſtantinople treats the great men under its dominion! But any Government that employs ſuch means to reduce Princes and Governors to their duty, betrays its weakneſs; and an empire which has no other arms to pre-

only, therefore, under the *quiet* and *beneficient* reign of *Scheik Daher* that the plentiful corps multiplied our eſtabliſhments in Syria; and it is ſince the tragical end of that Prince that commerce has begun to decline. P. 319, 4th part, 2d vol. edit. by Jarvis.

ſerve

ſerve its provinces with than perfidy, is *on the brink of ruin.* When the Greek Emperors, corrupted by effeminacy, flattery, and the ſpirit of ſect, deſtroyed by poiſon and the dagger every perſon who gave them umbrage in the whole extent of their dominions, they were ſoon dethroned, and Conſtantinople paſſed into the hands of a more generous people. At this day, when the degraded Ottomans make uſe of ſimilar expedients, a ſimilar deſtiny awaits them. I believe theſe reflections to be juſt; for on peruſing with attention the annals of all hiſtory, we ſee kingdoms fall with the virtue and manners of the nations.

LETTER XLII.

SEQUEL OF THE HISTORY OF ALI.

History of Ismael Bey become Scheik Elbalad. *Passage of Moura and Ibrahim, Beys in upper Egypt. Their connections with the Arabs. Ismael dispatches a body of troops against them, and they retreat into the Desart. They fortify themselves, take possession of some of the principal towns in the district of Said, penetrate as far as Gaza, and enter into a treaty of alliance with Ismael. Re-entering Grand Cairo, and on the point of being massacred, they betake themselves to flight, retire precipitately to Girgé, call to their assistance the Arabians, and defeat the army which was sent by Ismael to oppose them. He arrives in person at the head of a body of troops. The associated Beys contrive means to corrupt their fidelity; and the* Scheik Elbalad *retires into Syria with his treasures. On their return to the capital, they promote their creatures to the rank of Bey, and assume the government of Egypt. Engagement with Hassan Bey abandoned in the streets of Grand Cairo, and its consequences. Mourad conducts the caravan of Mecca; and the usual tribute being demanded of him by the Arabs, he orders them to be beheaded. Attacked and wounded on his return, he obliges the enemy to retreat. His quarrels with Ibrahim.*

To Mr. L. M.

Grand Cairo.

I Hope, Sir, it will not be disagreeable to you to be informed of such events as may serve as a continuation

tinuation of the hiſtory of *Ali*, of the greateſt part of which I was myſelf a ſpectator. After the death of this valiant chief, and that of Mahamed *Abou Dahab*, *Iſmael* enjoyed quietly the fruits of his treachery. Elected *Scheik Elbalad*, he governed Egypt as a ſovereign. Having diſtributed the provinces amongſt his creatures, he was ſurrounded by perſons he had protected, and reigned at *Grand Cairo*. To ſecure his power, he availed himſelf of the credit of the *Pacha*, an artful and enterpriſing man. As ſoon as he had gained the Viceroy, and the officers of the *Janizaries*, he iſſued his commands from one end of Egypt to the other, and his will became a law. Educated by *Ali*, he was exerciſed in the profeſſion of arms, was courageous, and had a thorough knowledge of buſineſs. But all theſe qualities were tarniſhed by avarice. He collected gold from every part, and inſtead of occupying himſelf with the welfare of his people, and the glory of the ſtate, he thought of nothing but ſwelling his treaſures. Whilſt he imagined he had nothing to apprehend, *Mourad* and *Ibrahim* were burning with the deſire of avenging the defeat of their patron. The former, full of fire and ardour, was courageous and frank, but inconſiderate; the latter united to moderation of character, an acute underſtanding, well adapted to form a party. Having vowed perpetual friendſhip, they ſet out from Syria with a ſmall body of Mamalukes attached to their fortune, croſſed the deſarts, and proceeded into the Saïd. Before they had time to form partizans there, *Iſmael* ſent an army against them. *Mourad* wished to engage with their handful of men, but was prevented by the prudence of *Ibrahim*, and they retired into the depths of those solitudes where the enemy did not dare to follow them. During their abode here, they brought over to their interest an independent *Arab* prince, promising to augment his dominions if, by his means, they might regain the capital. The *Emir*, charmed with the opportunity of affording protection to disgraced *Beys*, against *Ismael* who had attempted to levy contributions within his jurisdiction, vowed that he would aid them with all his power. He gave orders for his *Arabs* to take arms, and six thousand horsemen ranged themselves in an instant under his banners. With this little army they kept along the Nile, took possession of the principal towns situated on its banks, and descended towards Cairo. After defeating several parties *Ismael* had sent against them, they encamped near *Gaza* in 1777. The *Scheik Elbalad* set out from the castle at the head of a numerous army, to stop them at the passage of the Nile. Whilst the armies were in presence of each other, deputies reciprocally passed between the two generals, and treated of an accommodation. *Ismael*, who dreaded the impetuous valour of *Mourad*, and the wisdom of *Ibrahim*, was unwilling to risk his fortune on the event of a battle, and offered to suffer them to resume their station as members of the Republic. Peace was signed on this condition. They entered the capital therefore, preceded by the Arabian prince, who, mounted on a superb horse,

marched

marched at the head of cavaliers, armed with ſabres and with lances. After three days ſtay at Grand Cairo, ſeeing the completion of his deſigns, he returned into his principality, loaded with preſents and flattering promiſes. The reconciliation was not ſincere. *Iſmael* had ſeduced his enemies to deſtroy them without fighting. Poſſeſſed of the treaſures and the power, he imagined he ſhould find no difficulty in accompliſhing his project. The new Beys therefore were ſurrounded by precipices on every ſide. Great addreſs was neceſſary to avoid the ſnares that were laid for them. In 1778, rhe *Scheik Elbalad* fearing, leſt if he attacked them in their palaces, where they were always on their guard, the people might take part with the remains of the houſe of *Ali*, formed in concert with the Pacha and his partizans, the reſolution to maſſacre them the firſt time they appeared at the Divan. They were apprized of this plot, and eſcaped in the night into upper Egypt. They fortified themſelves in Girgé, called the Arabs to their ſuccour, and waited boldly for the enemy. *Iſmael* ſent a body of cavalry to purſue them. The fugitives gave them battle and diſcomfited them. He then marched himſelf at the head of thirty thouſand men. Full of confidence in his forces, he reckoned on a certain victory. But the dexterous *Ibrahim* employed againſt him the ſame arts which had proved of ſuch ſervice to *Abou Dahab*. Acquainted with his avarice, and knowing that his ſoldiers were ill paid, he offered them more conſiderable pay, and promiſed to promote

promote the officers. No more was neceſſary to debauch a part of theſe mercenary troops, always ready to ſell themſelves to the beſt bidder. *Iſmael* no ſooner perceived himſelf abandoned, than he fled precipitately towards Cairo, loaded fifty camels with gold and ſilver, and traverſing the Iſthmus, he took refuge in Syria. This villain, juſtly puniſhed for having betrayed his friend and maſter, from that moment led a wretched life, in the different provinces of the Ottoman empire. I have been aſſured that he afterwards repaired to Conſtantinople, on the faith of the promiſes of the Porte, whoſe authority he had reſtored in Egypt, and that the Divan, after ſtripping him of wealth, had given him up to his unhappy deſtiny.

The retreat of *Iſmael* rendered *Mourad* and *Ibrahim* maſters of the kingdom. They entered in triumph into Grand Cairo, where they were received with the acclamations of the people. The latter was appointed *Scheik Elbalad*, and the former *Emir Haji*. Their firſt ſtep was to depoſe the Pacha, who had been imprudent enough to take part againſt them, by declaring them enemies of the Grand Signior. The *Caracoulouck*, or emiſſary dreſſed in black, repaired to his apartment, folded up the corner of the carpet, and the Viceroy immediately retired to Boulak, where he waited his orders from Conſtantinople. As ſoon as a new Pacha was ſent, they thought of raiſing their Mamalukes to the dignity of Beys. *I aſſiſted* at this nomination, by means of my Turkiſh habit. The Sangiaks were

were ſeated at the extremity of the hall of council, near to the grating where the Pacha was. After delivering to the *Kiaïa* the names of thoſe they wiſhed to create, he read them with a loud voice, cloathed them with a Caftan, gave them the Firman of Sangiak, and they were proclaimed Beys. This ceremony finiſhed, they conducted the *Scheik* and the *Emir Haji* back to their palaces with pomp. The proceſſion was very brilliant. *Ibrahim* and *Mourad*, mounted on horſes covered with gold and diamonds, ſaluted, to the right and left, the people ranged on each ſide, who repeated their names with ſhouts of joy, wiſhing them all ſort of proſperity. Theſe two chiefs threw amongſt them every inſtant, handfuls of Medinas, of Piaſters, and Sequins, which were greedily picked up by the Egyptians. They were preceded by ſix hundred Mamalukes magnificently clad, and mounted on courſers richly capariſoned. The Janizaries, the Arabs, and the different bodies of troops followed in good order. This pompous ſpectacle laſted two hours. Upwards of four hundred thouſand perſons were ſpectators. I could not help being ſurprized at ſeeing ſo numerous a body of men voluntarily ſubmitting themſelves to ſeven or eight thouſand foreigners, who have no other employment than their deſtruction. But the natives of Egypt, gentle and peaceable, without force, and without energy, ſeemed deſtined to eternal bondage. Bent for ages under the yoke of deſpotiſm, they ſuffer every ſort of miſery, without lifting up their

their heads. Were they ſubjects of a mild government, there would not be a happier people upon earth. In ſpight of their wretched deſtiny, they paſſionately love their country, and nothing can tear them from it *.

Ibrahim and *Mourad*, having expelled *Iſmael* from Grand Cairo, reſolved to exterminate, root and branch, every perſon belonging to his houſehold. Above all, they dreaded *Haſſan Bey*, who, by his generoſity, his juſtice, and his valour, had gained the favour of the people and the Grandees. Not ſucceeding by ſtratagem, they determined to make uſe of open violence. Retiring into the caſtle, they directed a battery of ſix cannon againſt his palace, and diſtributed bodies of troops in the environs to attack it in parts. *Haſſan* defended himſelf valiantly with

* *Colonel Capper*, in the admirable account he gives in his *Voyage*, and *Journey from India*, ſpeaks as follows of the Egyptians: "The preſent Egyptians are an heterogeneous mixture "of all nations, and having unfortunately retained only the "worſt features both of the minds and perſons of their anceſ-"tors, in my opinion they are now become the moſt diſagree-"able nation on earth, bearing no more reſemblance to the "former Egyptians than the preſent ruins do to their once mag-"nificent buildings." The tranſlator takes the liberty to remark, that Mr. *Savary* paſſed three years *in*, the Colonel only paſſed *through* the country. The *Engliſhman*, conſtitutionally the advocate for freedom, contents himſelf with abuſing and contemning this unhappy people. The *French* writer acknowledges their degraded character, ſpares his invective, benevolently deplores their fate, and philoſophically aſſigns the cauſe of it. A citizen of the world prefers the latter mode of ſeeing things, and of expreſſing them. Do not Engliſhmen too often travel thus ?——*Tranſlator*.

his

his Mamalukes, and repulſed every aſſault. The noiſe of the artillery ſpread conſternation amongſt the inhabitants. War was made in the middle of the ſtreets, and from the tops of the roofs. On all ſides was heard the tumult of the combatants, horſes falling, and the cries of the unhappy victims of the diſſention. Bands of villains, taking advantage of the confuſion, ran through every quarter of the city, breaking open doors, entering into houſes, and putting all to fire and ſword. The French merchants were diſmayed. They expected at every inſtant to ſee the gate of their diſtrict forced, their fortune deſtroyed, and to periſh amidſt their wives and children. I was preſent at this tragedy, determined with ſome other young men to defend the entrance of the ſtreet to the laſt drop of blood, and to die at leaſt in combating. Our alarms were not ill-founded. About two hundred robbers came with axes and arms of every kind, to beat down the only gate we had to ſhelter us; but as it was very ſtrong, and they expected to meet with ſome reſiſtance, they went off another way, and pillaged the neighbouring houſes. Two days and two nights did the ſcene of horror laſt, during which the noiſe of cannon and muſketry, and the ſhrieks of deſpair were concontinually heard. We were well able to judge of this, for not one amongſt us had the leaſt deſire to go to ſleep. At length, on the third day of the combat, we perceived, from the top of our terraces, *Haſſan Bey*, who, accompanied by two hundred Mamalukes, ſabre in hand,

hand, opened a paſſage through his enemies, and made his eſcape from Grand Cairo. In his attempt to reach Syria, he fell in with a body of three thouſand Arabs of the enemy's party in the deſert, who cut off his retreat. He ſtrove to cut his way through their ſquadrons, and fought moſt deſperately. All his Mamalukes periſhed by his ſide. Though covered with blood, he defended himſelf for an hour. Being taken, the Arabs brought him back towards the capital. On his arrival at Boulak, he conjured them to permit him for an inſtant to enter the houſe of a *Scheik*, his friend, to take a laſt farewell of him. They complied with his requeſt, and diſpatched a courier to acquaint *Mourad* that they were bringing his enemy a priſoner. On this news the *Emir Haji* ſent two hundred Satellites to cut off his head. They ſurrounded the houſe, and loudly demanded him. The *Scheik* refuſed, and declared that he never would violate the laws of hoſpitality delivering up his friend. They were preparing to carry him off by force. "I will not ſuffer you, "ſays *Haſſan*, to expoſe yourſelf to the violence "of theſe madmen, who would murder you, "your wife, and children. Let me go out." Saying this, he tears himſelf from the arms of the *Scheik*, mounts upon the terrace, paſſes over to another, and perceiving that the gate of that houſe was only guarded by one ſoldier, he deſcends without making any noiſe, opens it, ſeizes the arm that was about to ſtrike him, knocks the Cavalier from his horſe, wreſts from him

his

his ſabre, and ſets off full ſpeed to Cairo. At this ſpectacle the Satellites were ſtruck motionleſs with ſurprize. Recovering themſelves, they fired upon the fugitive, and purſued him with all their might. Two horſemen had already overtaken him; but he overſet them with blows of his ſabre, and continued his courſe. All the ſtreets of Grand Cairo have gates for the public ſafety. In paſſing, he made ſeveral of them be ſhut, and carrying the keys with him, they ſtopped the progreſs of his enemies. Repairing to the palace of *Ibrahim*, he entered by the Court of the *Haram*, covering his viſage with his ſhawl, that he might not be diſcovered. The wife of the *Scheik Elbalad* was his relation: he prayed her to intercede for him with her huſband. She went and threw herſelf on her knees, imploring the life of her couſin. *Ibrahim* gave way, took *Haſſan* under his protection, had him cured of his wounds, and, for a long time, reſiſted *Mourad*, who ſolicited his death. Seeing that the *Emir Haji* was preparing to go to war with him, unleſs he obtained his demand, he became reconciled to him, on conſenting that the priſoner ſhould be baniſhed to Gedda. He was conducted to Suez, and delivered to the Captain of a ſmall veſſel, who received orders to tranſport him to the place of his exile. Two of his ſlaves, the voluntary companions of his misfortunes, followed him from attachment. They were apprized that the Captain was poſſeſſed of a Firman, ſigned by *Mourad*, which condemned the head of their maſter on their landing,

landing, and lost no time in acquainting him with it. *Hassan*, feigning ignorance of his destiny, begged the Captain to put him on shore on the coast of Egypt, instead of conveying him to Gedda. Neither promises nor menaces could prevail upon him. On his refusal, he seized on the arms which were on board, during the night, and, assisted by his two slaves, cut off the head of the Captain, and of three sailors, threw them into the sea, and taking the helm, conducted the vessel to Cosseir, whence he repaired into the Sayde, carrying with him the sum of 400,000 livres which he found in the vessel. From that moment he is labouring to procure himself partizans, and he may one day, perhaps, re-enter Cairo, where he is looked for by the wishes of the people.

The death of six Beys of *Ismael's* party, and the flight of the others, rendered *Ibrahim* and *Mourad* absolute masters at Grand Cairo. Having now nothing to disturb them, the *Emir Haji* prepared, according to custom, to conduct the caravan of Mecca. The pilgrims gathered together from all parts in the plain of *Hellé*, in the neighbourhood of the city. About ten thousand tents were pitched; they covered a great extent of ground. Those of the officers and chiefs were composed of painted linen, lined on the inside with sattin, and adorned with cushions embroidered in gold and silver. During the night, a great number of lamps of coloured glass were lighted around each tent, which produced a brilliant and variegated illumination.

The

The reflections of the light, gilding the foliage of the orange and date-trees spread over the plain, formed a charming spectacle. The relations and friends of the pilgrims came to pass the night with them. At the break of day the *Emir Haji* gave the signal with the drum and trumpets. Every man struck his tent, and putting his baggage and provisions on camels, began the journey.—First went the van guard, escorted by a corps of cavalry, well mounted. Next appeared the camel bearing the tapestry destined to cover the *Caaba*, or house of God. His head was decorated with a magnificent plume of feathers, and his back covered with a cloth of gold. He was environed by Priests, singing the hymns of the Coran. About twenty thousand pilgrims followed on foot, on horseback, and on camels. A body of five thousand cavalry, distributed in different troops, under the command of the *Emir Haji*, marched on the flanks of the caravan. A few ladies also, borne in litters, were making the pilgrimage. Nothing can be more magnificent than the departure of this caravan. The men, neatly clad, seem full of health and vigour; the horses, of fire and ardour. On their return every thing is changed; the animals meagre and languid, and the pilgrims pale, lank, and sun-burnt, appear like skeletons. In fact, this journey, which is extremely difficult, lasts forty days across the desarts, where they are obliged sometimes to travel fifty leagues without finding a single drop of water that is drinkable. The heat of the sun is excessive, and the duſt raiſed by the feet of ſuch a multitude of men and animals, darkens the air, fills the eyes and mouth, and prevents reſpiration. Sometimes the peſtiferous winds from the ſouth-eaſt roll it along in ſuch terrible whirls, that three or four hundred men periſh in a day. This calamity is highly advantageous to the *Emir Haji*, who is entitled to the baggage and commercial effects of all thoſe who die upon the way. Accordingly he frequently returns to Cairo poſſeſſed of the third of the property that went from it.

The caravan under the convoy of *Mourad*, after turning the extremity of the Red Sea, entered Arabia Deſerta. The Arabs preſented themſelves, and attempted to exact the cuſtomary tribute. He cut off the headsof their Chiefs, and the others, unable to diſpute the paſſage with him returned totheir tents, breathing vengance. The caravan arrived ſafely at *Bedder*, where according to cuſtom,it joined that of Damaſcus, and ſix days after they reached Mecca. During the fourteen days that the Mahometans, collected from all parts of the world, remain in this city, to perform the duties of religion, an imenſe commerce is carried on. Part of the pilgrims repair thither to fulfil the precept which commands every Muſſulman once in his life to viſit the houſe of God. The reſt are drawn by the allurement of intereſt, and carry with them the rareſt produce of their reſpective countries. Here the pilgrim meets with abundance of the precious ſtuffs, and of the diamonds of India; the beautiful pearls of the Perſian Gulph, the balſam, in ſuch requeſt

amongſt

amongſt the Orientals, the ſteel weapons of Damaſcus, Moka coffee, the gold-duſt of Africa, and the ſequins of Grand Cairo. It is perhaps the richeſt fair in the whole world. Upwards of one hundred thouſand merchants are collected here; and as the time is ſhort, one cannot calculate the number of millions that are bartered for in the ſpace of fourteen days. It were to be wiſhed, that ſome European, verſed in the Arabic tongue, and diſguiſed as a merchant, could aſſiſt at this ſolemnity, and give us ſuch details of it, as we are now forced to receive from the mouth of thoſe in whom we cannot place perfect confidence, the Muſſulmen never willingly converſing with Infidels on ſubjects reſpecting their religion. Veſſels which could at this time reach Gedda, laden with certain European and Indian merchandize, *would be ſure of ſelling their cargoes in a few hours, and of being paid for them immediately in gold. The Engliſh* have made ſome ſucceſsful adventures of this ſort, which, no doubt, they would have continued, had not political views, and diſputes between them and the natives of the country, prevented their proſecution*.

Mou-

* *Colonel Capper* ſtates this matter in his voyage and journey from India. "*It is much to be lamented,*" ſays he "that the "*Coventry frigate,* which lately went up the Red Sea, was "*inadvertantly betrayed* into a quarrel with the inhabitants of "*Coſſeir,* a place about ſix degrees north of *Geddo,* on the "weſtern ſhore, and only one hundred and twenty miles from "the banks of the Nile.——It is ſaid, that not only the fort "and a number of houſes were deſtroyed, but that alſo near "*ſix hundred of the inhabitants were killed.* This account is "probably much exaggerated; but *it is much to be feared* as a "heavy

Mourad Bey was not ſo proſperous in his return as he had been in going to Mecca. Several Arab tribes combined their forces to avenge the blood of their chiefs. They waited the moment when the caravan muſt paſs betwen the mountains, and attacked it with advantage. At firſt, there was nothing but confuſion amongſt this vaſt multitude who overturned each other in endeavouring to take to flight. A great number of them was cruſhed to death, and many killed by the continual fire of the enemy. The *Emir Haji*, collecting his troops, put himſelf in a poſture to repulſe them. He marched at the head of his Mamalukes, and in ſpight of the fire of the Arabian artillery, climbed up the mountains and gave them a bloody battle. He loſt a great number of men, and was himſelf wounded in the thigh and arm by two balls. Theſe wounds however did not prevent him from vanquiſhing

" heavy fire was kept up on the town for upwards of two hours; " *many of the people* muſt have fallen, (and conſidering the po- " pulation, *why not* ſix hundred?) and therefore at preſent it is " unneceſſary to examine more minutely into this route. I can- " not however conclude this digreſſion without expreſſing a " hope (*ſpes vana!*) that ſome atonement will be made to " them for their loſſes, (*the loſs of life!*) which, whether they " were attacked juſtly or not, is abſolutely neceſſary before *any* " *European* ought to venture to paſs that way." There is abundant matter for reflection in this extract from the work of a good citizen as well as excellent ſoldier; but if England will perſiſt in her domineering ſpirit every where, though marked with blood, let her remember ſhe is a *commercial* nation, and obſerve the above paſſage of *Mr. Savary*, and above all let her attend to the example of her rival nation, who is ſeldom or never engaged in ſuch ill-judged or dangerous diſputes.

Tranſlator.

quiſhing the Arabs, and obliging them to fly in confuſion. They appeared no more during the remainder of his route. He arrived at Grand Cairo, ſpent with fatigue, and almoſt dying. Mr. Grace, phyſician of the French, was called, and cured him, but not without very ſerious anxiety, *for his life was to anſwer for that of the ſick Bey.* All the inhabitants of Grand Cairo went out to meet their friends and relations. Some of them had to lament the loſs of a brother, a father, a huſband, and gave way to bitter lamentations. Mothers in deſpair were ſeen tearing their clothes, and covering their faces with the duſt. Others, joyful at the return of the perſons who were dear to them, filled the air with ſhouts of gladneſs, and returned thanks to heaven. It is impoſſible to expreſs the various ſentiments this ſpectacle inſpired. One was a witneſs alternately to the exceſs of grief, and the intoxication of joy. On returning to his houſe, each pilgrim found an apartment prepared according to his ſitnation. The walls were newly painted, all the furniture, the carpets, the ſophas, the cuſhions were new, as if any thing ancient were unworhy of belonging to a man returned from the holy pilgrimage. Theſe traits teſtify at once, Sir, the filial tenderneſs, and the piety of the Egyptians; and the ſublime idea they entertain of their religion. The perſons returned from Mecca aſſume for the remainder of their lives the ſurname of *Hajji* (1), and bear it as an honourable title. The rich who dread the fatigues of the journey, imagine they fulfil the precept, by

(1) Pilgrim

ſending a ſubſtitute in their place, and by defraying his expences.

Having quitted Egypt at the end of 1776, I am unable to give a circumſtantial detail of the ſubſequent events. I have only learnt by letters from Grand Cairo, that the impetuous *Mourad*, wiſhing to attain to the dignity of *Scheik Elbalad*, had declared war againſt his rival; that they had fought and been reconciled; and that in 1784, being embroiled anew, they were, each of them, at the head of an army, and ready to come to blows. I am ignorant of the ſucceſs of the battle; but whoever be the victor, he will ſtrive to elevate his creatures, and to exterminate all the Beys of the oppoſite party, until treaſon or defeat ſhall have made him experience a ſimilar deſtiny.

You will readily conceive, Sir, what muſt be the fate of Egypt, reſigned to the robbery of eight thouſand foreigners, who devour the produce of her rich provinces, and make her inceſſantly ſuffer all the horrors of war. But whatever ideas you may form of her misfortunes, they will be much below the reality. Agriculture deſtroyed; the canals, which circulated abundance through every part of it, choaked up; arbitrary tributes levied by violence; men of property ſtripped and maſſacred; rogues employed in every department; war, peſtilence and famine, the uſual reſult of the diſcord of her chiefs; ſuch are the miſeries to which the people of Egypt are condemned.

I have the honour to be, &c.

LET-

LETTER XLIII.

OBSERVATIONS ON THE AGRICULTURE OF THE COUNTRY.

Agriculture anciently flouriſhing in Egypt. The immenſe labour which has been beſtowed on confining the river, and on watering the land. The decay of thoſe uſeful monuments. Productions of the ſoil. The ſeaſons of ſowing and reaping different according to the ſituation of the lands. Their prodigious fertility in ancient times. The means neceſſary to be employed for procuring much fertility. The method of raiſing the bees which the Egyptians carry in a boat from one extremity of the kingdom to the other.

To Mr. L. M.

Grand Cairo.

AGRICULTURE, Sir, was in great eſteem amongſt the ancient Egyptians. They had rendered it very flouriſhing in the whole extent of their empire; witneſs the immenſe works they have made, in the diſtribution of the canals and for watering the land. At preſent we reckon eighty canals like rivers, all dug by the hand of man, ſeveral of which are twenty, thirty, and forty leagues in length. They receive the inundation, and circulate the waters through the country. Six only have water in them the whole year. The others nearly choaked up, are dry upon the fall of the Nile. The great lakes of *Mœris*, of *Behiré*, and *Marcotis* form vaſt reſervoirs calculated to contain the ſuperfluous waters and at length to ſpread them over the adjacent plains. They raiſed them upon the elevated grounds by means of vertical wheels, the invention of which is due to the Egyptians. One ox was ſufficient to turn them, and to water a vaſt field. Theſe wheels gave to Archimedes, in his journey into Egypt, the idea of the ingenious chain, or *chapelet*, ſtill made uſe of in our days. Beſides theſe reſervoirs, all the towns at ſome diſtance from the Nile are ſurrounded by ſpacious ponds to ſupply the wants of the inhabitants, and for the advantage of cultivation. Some great dykes, the ruins of which are ſtill to be ſeen, ſerved to keep in the river; others were oppoſed to the torrents of ſand which have a continual tendency to cover the face of Egypt. The waters are conveyed by aqueducts to the very ſummit of the hills. They were received there in immenſe baſons hewn out of the rocks, from whence flowing into the midſt of deſarts, they converted them into fruitful fields. Near to to *Babain* we diſcover the ruins of one of theſe aqueducts, which bends its courſe towards Lybia. It bears the character of majeſty, peculiar to all the Egyptian monuments. Theſe works, not leſs marvellous than the pyramids and coloſſuſes of the Thebais, had infinitely more utility. They prevented the ravages of extra-

ordinary

ordinary overflows, supplied the deficiency of moderate ones, and gave food to millions of inhabitants,

In the period of 1200 years that this country has been subject to nations who are not cultivators, they have suffered the greatest part of these noble works to go to ruin. The barbarism of the present government will put the finishing hand to their destruction. Every year, the limits of cultivated Egypt are encroached upon, and barren sands accumulate from all parts. In 1517, the æra of the Turkish conquest, Lake Mareotis was at no distance from the walls of Alexandria, and the canal which conveyed the waters into that city was still navigable. At this day the lake has disappeared, and the lands it watered, and which, according to historians, produced abundance of corn, wine, and various fruits, are changed into desarts, where the sorrowful traveller finds neither shrub, nor plant, nor verdure. The canal itself, the work of Alexander, necessary even to the subsistence of the inhabitants of the city he built, is nearly choaked up. It only receives the waters when the inundation is at its highest point, and preserves them but for a short time. Forty years ago, a part of the mud deposited by the river was cleared out of it, and it retained the water three months longer. By compleating this operation, it would resume its ancient utility. The Pelusiac branch which discharges itself into the eastern part of the lake of *Tanis* or *Menzalé*, is totally destroyed. With it perished the beauti-

ful

ful province it fertilized, and the famous canal begun by Necos *(m)*, and finifhed by Ptolemy Philadelphus. It was drawn from this branch to Aggeroud *(n)*, the ancient Arfinoé, fituated at the extremity of the Red Sea. As they were apprehenfive left by opening this communition, the Arabic gulph which was thought to be eleven feet higher than the Mediterranean might overflow the country, they had placed large fluices at the entrance. But I am of opinion that this fuppofition was ill founded, fince other canals drawn from the Nile to the Arabic gulph, have produced no inconvenience. Thefe immortal works, executed by kings who made the profperity of the people their happinefs and the glory of their empire, have not been able to refift the ravages of conquerors, and that defpotifm which deftroys every thing, until it buries itfelf under the wreck of the kingdoms, whofe foundations it has fapped. The canal of *Amrou*, the laft of the great works of Egypt, and which communicated Foftat to Colzoum, reaches no farther at prefent than to four leagues beyond Cairo, and lofes itfelf in the Lake of Pilgrims. Such, Sir, is the prefent ftate of this country. We may confidently affert that upwards of one third of the lands formerly in cultivation, are metamorphofed into defarts whofe horrid afpect frights the traveller.

(m) Strabo and Pliny atteft this fact, as well as Diodorus Siculus; *fee alfo the Memoirs of Baron de Tott*, 2d vol. edit. by Jarvis.

(n) Between the time of Ptolemy and our days, the Red Sea has retired *two leagues*, for Aggeroud is at that diftance from Suez.

It

It is the ſame with reſpect to population.—— Ancient Egypt furniſhed ſubſiſtence for about eight millions of inhabitants, and ſupplied Italy and the neighbouring provinces with proviſions. At this day we do not reckon half the number. I will not believe with Herodotus and Pliny that there were twenty thouſand cities in this kingdom in the time of Pharaoh Amaſis, but the aſtoniſhing ruins we meet with at every ſtep, and uninhabited places, announce that they muſt have been three times more numerous than in our days. If you have deigned to read with attention the picture I have traced out to you of the preſent Government, you will ceaſe your ſurprize at the downfal of this country. The population of a ſtate is never beyond the proportion of the means of ſubſiſtence. It increaſes, diminiſhes, and terminates with them. Now that the merchant and the huſbandman is deſpoiled at the pleaſure of eight thouſand foreigners, one abandons his commercial ſpeculations, the other the labours of agriculture, and the country is ſenſibly depopulating every day.

All the lands belong to the Chiefs. They ſell them to individuals. At the death of the proprietors they revert to the public Exchequer.— The ſon is obliged to purchaſe the inheritance of his father, but without being always ſure of obtaining it. The beſt bidder, or he who has the moſt credit, obtains the inveſtiture. What can a huſbandman be expected to perform for the improvement of lands, who is not certain of tranſmitting his poſſeſſions to his children? His cares

are

are limited to a preſent livelihood, and he leaves part of his lands untilled. The Cachefs and the Sangiaks, authorized by the treaty with the Grand Signior to levy arbitrary tributes, commit unheard-of vexations. Frequently the wretched countryman wants common neceſſaries in the midſt of the abundance that ſurrounds him, and is obliged to ſell his inſtruments of huſbandry to pay the impoſts. This tyranny diſables them from cultivating the richeſt ſpot of ground on earth.

Another evil, not leſs fatal, reſults from the viciſſitudes of the Government. When the Beys go to war, the people take part in their quarrels, and employ fire and ſword mutually to deſtroy each other. I have more than once ſeen villages burnt, all the inhabitants murdered by their neighbours, and the fruit of their harveſt periſh in the flames.

The Chiefs of the Republic retain from the tribute ſent annually to Conſtantinople, conſiderable ſums, which ought to be employed in the ſupport of the public buildings and the canals. Their continual diſſentions, the neceſſity they are under of amaſſing gold to purchaſe the Mamalukes, to pay troops, and to encreaſe their party, prevents them from attending to this indiſpenſable labour. This negligence gives a mortal ſtab to agriculture; a whole diſtrict, which owed its fertility and its riches to the waters of a canal, no longer receiving a ſufficient quantity, becomes uncultivated and abandoned. The Nile, in the courſe of 900 leagues, traverſing deſarts and

and barren mountains, brings with it a prodigious quantity of ſand and mud. I have ſeen rivulets dug, where, after remaining a year, it had depoſited three feet of ooze. Judge with what rapidity it muſt fill up the moſt uſeful canals, did not human ſkill conſtantly look after their preſervation. This fact alone will explain to you why immenſe lakes are at this day dried up, and once-fruitful provinces are become ſervile and uninhabited.

How culpable are they who thus ſuffer the ſprings of plently to dry up? for wherever the waters of the Nile are conveyed, there is the earth covered with treaſures; it only ſeeks to be productive. In the Delta, as in the Saïd, the plough is made uſe of in cultivation. When the ox has traced out a ſlight furrow, the clods are broken with the hoe, and the ground is made as level as a garden. After it is ſown, it undergoes a ſlight harrowing. Here finiſh the labours of the huſbandman till the harveſt, which is extremely plentiful, and never fails, but with the failure of the inundation. When the barley and the corn are ripe, they are reaped and ſpread out on the barn floor. A peaſant ſeated on a cart, the wheels of which are very ſharp, and drawn by oxen with a bandage over their eyes, drives over the ſtraw, and haſhes it in pieces. The corn is then ſeparated from the chaff. The grain is yellow, large, and of an excellent quality. The Egyptians make a ſort of red bread of it, half baked, and bad; becauſe, inſtead of employing wind and water-mills, they make uſe only of hand-mills, and

do

do not sufficiently bolt the flour. The French baker here, with the same corn, made bread as white as snow, and admirably well tasted. The rice, as I have already observed to you, requires a little more attention. The field designed for it must be overflowed, all other herbs rooted out, and must be watered every day after it is planted, which is done by *roses à chapelet*. At the end of five months they cut it, and usually reap eighty bushels for one. Besides these grains, Egypt produces in abundanae, dourra, or Indian millet, flax, formerly so famous, hemp, chartame, or *safranum*, and innumerable sorts of exquisite melons and vegetables, which the people feed on during the heats.

The seed time is different in different provinces, and according to the exposure of the lands. Near to Sienna they sow the barley and the corn in October, and reap it in January. Towards Girgé they cut it in February, and in the month of March in the neighbourhood of Cairo. This is the usual progress of the harvest in the Saïd. There are also a number of partial harvests, according as the lands are nearer or at a greater distance from the river, lower or more elevated. In the lower Egypt they are sowing and reaping all the year. Wherever the waters of the river can be procured, the earth is never idle, and furnishes three crops annually. It is there that the traveller has constantly before his eyes the charming spectacle of flowers, fruits, and harvests, and that the spring, the summer, and the autumn, present all their treasures at a time. In descend-

ing

ing from the cataracts at the beginning of January, one perceives the corn almoſt ripe; lower down it is in ear, and, advancing farther, the plains are covered with verdure.

The Lucern, which they cut three times between the months of March and November, is the only hay of the Egyptians. Their flocks are principally fed with it. The horſes, aſſes, mules, and camels, graze in the meadows during the winter; the reſt of the year they eat cut ſtraw, barley, and beans. This food contributes to their health, and gives them great force and ardour. The Arabs accuſtom their horſes to the greateſt abſtinence, leading them only once a day to water, and feeding them with a little barley and milk.

The Egyptians rarely cultivating the olive-tree, they purchaſe their oil in Crete and Syria. But as they derived from their anceſtors a taſte for illuminations, they extract oil from different plants. The moſt common is the produce of the Seſame, called by them, *Sireg*, oil for burning. They make oil alſo of the ſeed of the chartame, of flax, of the poppy, and the lettuce. The people eat that made of chartame.

I have already ſpoken to you, Sir, of the art with which the Egyptians hatch chickens, an art peculiar to themſelves. Their manner of bringing up bees is not leſs extraordinary, and announces a great deal of underſtanding.

As upper Egypt only retains its verdure for four or five months, and the flowers and harveſts are earlier there, the inhabitants of the Lower profit

profit by these precious moments. They collect the bees of different villages in large boats. Each proprietor trusts to them his hives, which have a particular mark. When the bark is loaded, the men who have the management of them, gradually mount the river, and stop at every place where they find flowers and verdure. The bees, at the break of day, quit their cells by thousands, and go in search of the treasures with which they compose their nectar. They go and come several times laden with their booty. In the evening these ingenious labourers return to their habitations, without ever mistaking their dwelling. After travelling three months in this manner on the Nile, the bees having culled the perfumes of the orange flower of the Saïd, the essence of roses of the Faioum, the treasures of the Arabian Jessamine, and a variety of flowers, are brought back to the places they had been carried from, where they now find new riches to partake of. This industry procures the Egyptians delicious honey, and bees-wax in abundance. The proprietors, in return, pay the boatmen a recompence proportioned to the number of hives he has been thus carrying about from one end of Egypt to the other.

I have the honour to be, &c.

LETTER XLIV.

ACCOUNT OF THE TEMPERATURE OF THE CLIMATE.

The heats excessive in Upper Egypt, and moderate in the Lower. The small number of diseases which prevail among the Egyptians. The means they use for curing a fever, and preserving their health. During a part of the winter and spring, the wind blows from the South, and proves prejudicial. Through the remaining part of the year, the North wind produces salutary effects. The leprosy unknown in the country. The plague not a native disease of the climate. The Europeans avoid this terrible scourge by shutting themselves up.

To Mr. L. M.

Grand Cairo.

YOU are now, Sir, well acquainted with Egypt and its productions; but you must have still some doubts remaining on the salubrity of the climate. The overflowings of the Nile, the stagnant waters in many parts of it, will naturally have induced you to imagine that this country is unhealthy, and its inhabitants subject to a great many disorders. A pretty long experience, and information obtained upon the spot, will furnish you

you with materials calculated to calm your fears, and to form your opinion.

This kingdom begins at the Torrid, and extends itself nine degrees into the Temperate Zone. It is true that the heats of the Thebais exceed those we experience in many countries directly under the Equator. While the fiery breath of the south wind continues, Reaumur's thermometer sometimes rises to 38 degrees above the freezing point, and frequently to 36 degrees. This phenomenon must be attributed to the arid nature of the sandy plains with which Upper Egypt is environed, and to the reverberation from the mountains which hem it in, in its whole length. If heat were the source of the disorders, the Saïd would be uninhabitable. The burning fever is the only one it seems to give rise to, and to which the inhabitants are subject. They soon get rid of it by regimen, drinking a great deal of water, and bathing themselves in the river. In other respects they are a robust and healthy race of people. They have a great many old men amongst them several of whom mount on horseback at fourscore years of age. The regimen they observe during the hot season, greatly contributes to the preservation of their health. They scarcely take any thing but vegetables, pulse, and milk. They make frequent use of the bath, eat little, rarely drink fermented liquors, and mix a great deal of lemon-juice in their aliment. This sobriety preserves their vigour to a very advanced age.

Soon after the inundation, the fields are cloathed with harvests. The exhalations of the waters

ters, attracted by the ſun in the day-time, are condenſed by the coolneſs of the nights, and fall in copious dews. The north wind which prevails conſtantly during the ſummer, meeting with no obſtacle in its current in the extent of Egypt, the mountains of which are of no conſiderable height, drives the vapours of the lakes and marſhes towards Abyſſinia, and perpetually renews the atmoſphere. Perhaps, too, the balſamic emanations from the orange-flower, the roſes, the Arabian jeſſamine, and other odoriferous plants, contribute to the ſalubrity of the air. Undoubtedly the water of the Nile alſo, which is lighter, ſweeter, and more agreeable to the palate than any I ever taſted has a great influence on the health of the inhabitants. Its excellence is acknowledged by all antiquity *(a)*. It is very certain at leaſt, that one drinks it with a ſort of voluptuouſneſs, and that no bad conſequence ever follows from taking any quantity of it. But as it is ſlightly impregnated with nitre, it poſſeſſes a gentle laxative quality when uſed to exceſs. I ſhall not ſay, with many writers, that theſe waters procure fecundity to women, and beſtow vigour and good plight of body on the men. The faithful hiſtorian ſhould ſtop where the marvellous begins, and cite no facts beyond the reach of teſtimony.

(a) Ptolemy Philadelphus, having married his daughter Berenice, to Antiochus, King of Syria, ſent her Nile water, as the only water ſhe could drink. *Athenæus*, The Kings of Perſia ſent for Nile water, with ſal-ammoniac. *Hiſtory of Perſia.*

The Egyptians alone of all people preſerved the Nile water in ſealed vaſes, and drank it when old, with the ſame pleaſure that we drink old wine. *Ariſtides*, the *Rhetorician.*

In

In Lower Egypt, the neighbourhood of the ſea, the immenſity of the lakes, the abundance of the waters, deaden the fires of the ſun, and maintain there a delightful temperature. Neither Strabo nor Diodorus Siculus, who long reſided in this country, looked upon it as unhealthy.

They have praiſed the fertility of its ſoil, the excellence of its productions, the grandeur of its monuments, and its numerous population, without ſo much as mentioning thoſe frightful maladies, of which the moderns make this country the focus. Heroditus expreſsly ſays, "The "Egyptians are the moſt healthy people in the "world, an advantage they owe to the ſolubrity "of the air, and the temperature of their cli- "mate, which varies very little; for moſt of "the diſorders of men are to be attributed to "the rapid viciſſitudes of the ſeaſons." It was reſerved for ſome moderns, who have never travelled in this beautiful country, and above all to Mr. Paw, to lay down a contrary doctrine. He pretends, that in our days, "it is become, by the "negligence of the Turks and Arabs, the cradle "of the plague (*b*): that another epidemic diſ- "temper, as terrible as that brought to Cairo by "the caravans from Nubia, manifeſts itſelf there "from time to time; that the culture of rice "alone is ſufficient to engender numerous ma- "ladies; that the want of rain and thunder "makes the air of the Thebais acquire violence "enough to occaſion a fermentation of the hu- "mours of the human body, &c." Theſe aſſer-

(*b*) Recherches ſur les Egyptiens & les Cinois.

tions

tions carry with them an air of probability, calculated to impose on persons who have not dwelt in Egypt. But Mr. Paw has hazarded them from his closet, without being guided by experience. Had he lived at any time on the spot, facts would have convinced him of his error *.

In the vallies hemmed in by lofty mountains, where the atmosphere cannot be perpetually renewed by a current of air, the culture of rice is unwholesome, and the husbandmen often pay with their lives the rich harvest they are seeking from the earth. It is not the same in the environs of Damietta and Rosetta. The plains are almost always on a level with the sea. There is neither eminence nor hill to divert the refreshing breeze of the north wind. It drives towards the south the clouds and exhalations of the deluged fields. It continually purifies the atmosphere and preserves the health of the inhabitants. Whether it be owing to this cause or to others of which I am ignorant, it is at least certain, that the country-

* Baron de Tott, in his ingenuous Memoirs, Vol. XI. p. 288, fully confirms this. "The inquiries I carefully made, "says he, respecting the plague, which I had always imagined "to be of Egyptian oirgin, convinced me that *it would not eaen* "*be known in that country*, were not the infection conveyed to "*Alexandria* by its commerce with *Constantinople*. It is in the "former town it always begins to shew itself. It is but very "seldom too that it reaches Cairo, although no precaution is "taken to prevent it; and when it does, the great heats soon "put a stop to it, and hinder it from penetrating into that city; "besides, it is well known that the piercing dews which fall in "Egypt towards midsummer, destroy *even at Alexandria*, the "very seeds of this disorder."

Translator.

men employed in the cultivation of rice are no more subject to illness than those of the Thebais, who do not cultivate it. I passed a whole year amongst the rice grounds, which I went to see them water evey day, without suffering the slightest inconvenience. An old surgeon, a native of Nice, and who had practised physic thirty years at Damietta, has a hundred times confirmed to me, every thing I have advanced on the salubrity of the country. What torments the inhabitants the most are the gnats and innumerable swarms of musquetoes, which rising by millions from the morasses, fill the air and the houses. One must never be without a fly-flap in one's hand in the day time, which indeed is the first thing you are presented with on a visit; and at night you are obliged te sleep under musquetonets.

Disorders of the eyes are the most common in Egypt. Persons blind of one eye or of both eyes, are met with here in great numbers. This calamity must not be wholly attributed to the reverberation of a burning sun, for the Arabs who live in the midst of sands, have in general strong eyes and a piercing sight. Nor must we give more credit to Mr. Hasselquest *(c)*, who resided a short time in this country, when he says, that this disorder proceeds from the vapours which exhale from the stagnant waters, for the French merchants whose houses line the canal of Grand Cairo, which for six months of the year contains standing water of an insupportable odour, would

(*c*) Voyage d'Egypte.

be

be all blind, and for fifty years paſt not one of them has loſt his ſight (*d*). The cuſtom the Egyptians have of ſleeping in the open air in the ſummer, either on the terraces of their houſes, or near their huts, is doubtleſs the origin of this infirmity. The nitre generally diffuſed throughout the air, and the heavy dews of the night, attack the delicate organ of ſight, and deprives them either of one or both eyes. Eight thouſand of theſe unhappy people are kept in the great moſque of Cairo, and they are provided with a decent ſubſiſtence.

The ſmall-pox and hernias are alſo very common, but without making any great ravages in Egypt. As to the phthiſic aud fluxions of the breaſt, which in cold countries carry off ſo many perſons in the flower of their age, they are ſtrangers to this happy climate. Pains of the breaſt are never felt here. I am perſuaded that perſons attacked by thoſe cruel maladies, would recover their health in a country where the air, denſe, warm, and moiſt, impregnated with the perfume of plants and the oily quality of the earth, appears highly favourable to the lungs (*e*).

(*d*) One only of theſe merchants loſt his ſight, but he lived within the city, and not on the banks of the canal. This fact therefore proves nothing in favour of Mr. Haſſelqueſt's opinion.

(*e*) Mr. Paw pretends that the Egyptians have been at all times afflicted by the leproſy. Herodotus, Strabo, Diodorus Siculus, who were well acquainted with this country, do not however mention this malady, a proof that it was unknown there, in their time. I have ſeen lepers in the iſlands of the Archipelago, ſequeſtered from ſociety, as among the Jews: they inhabit

It muſt be admitted, however, that there is an unhealthy ſeaſon in Egypt. From February to the month of May, the ſoutherly winds blow at intervals. They fill the atmoſphere with a ſubtle duſt which impedes reſpiration, and bring with them pernicious vapours. The heat becomes ſometimes inſupportable, and the thermometer riſes ſuddenly twelve degrees. During this ſeaſon, called *khamſin* or *fifty* by the inhabitants, from the period in which this wind is more peculiarly felt, from Eaſter to Whitſuntide, they feed on rice, vegetables, freſh fiſh, and fruits. They bathe frequently, and make great uſe of lemon juice and perfumes. With this regimen they guard themſelves againſt the dangerous effects of the *khamſin*.

It muſt not be imagined that this wind, which corrupts in a few hours fleſh meat, and all animal ſubſtance, laſts fifty days together; it would make Egypt a deſart. But it rarely blows three days ſucceſſively. Sometimes it appears only in the ſhape of an impetuous whirlwind, which paſſes rapidly, and is fatal only to the traveller ſurprized in the middle of the deſarts. A hurricane of this ſort ſuddenly aroſe whilſt I was at Alexandria, in the month of May, rolling before it torrents of burning ſand. The firmament was enveloped in a thick veil; the ſun appeared of the colour of blood. The duſt penetrated into the very apartments, and burnt the face and eyes.

inhabit cottages on the ſide of the highway, and beg alms of paſſengers. But in Egypt, where I have travelled a great deal, I never met with one of theſe unfortunate perſons.

eyes. At the end of four hours the tempeſt calmed, and the ſky reſumed its ſerenity. Some wretched travellers who happened to be in the deſart were ſuffocated. I ſaw ſeveral dead brought in, and ſome who were thought to be of the number, reſtored to life by bathing them in cold water. The inhabitants of Grand Cairo, ſituated farther up the country, ſuffer more from this calamity, and a French merchant who was very luſty, died there, ſuffocated by the heat. Similar phenomena have buried whole armies and caravans.

Several modern authors, at the head of whom appears Mr. Paw, have aſſerted that the plague is of Egyptian origin. Were this a fact, it would certainly greatly diminiſh the advantages of this country, for no fertility or riches can ever balance the miſeries inflicted by this ſcourge upon humanity. The information I have acquired, both from the natives of the country, and from foreign phyſicians who have reſided here from twenty to thirty years, tends to prove the contrary. They have all aſſured me that this epidemical diſeaſe was brought there by the Turks, and that it afterwards committed great havock. The following circumſtanee has fallen within my own obſervation. In 1778, the Grand Signior's Caravelles arrived at Damietta, and landed according to cuſtom, the ſilks of Syria. The plague is almoſt always on board of theſe veſſels. They put on ſhore without oppoſition their merchandize and the perſons ſick of the plague. This was in the month of Auguſt, and as the epidemic ceaſes in Egypt at that ſeaſon, it did not com-

communicate. The veſſels ſet ſail, and proceeded to poiſon other places. The ſummer following, ſome ſhips from Conſtantinople infected with this diſorder, arrived at the port of Alexandria. They landed their ſick without doing any miſchief to the inhabitants. Since that period ſome ſhips from Smyrna have brought this contagion at the beginning of winter. It has ſpread throughout the country, and has deſtroyed a number of the Egyptians.

The following is an obſervation made for ages paſt. During the months of June, July, and Auguſt, if merchandize infected with this poiſon be introduced into Egypt, it dies of itſelf, and the people are under no alarm. If it has been conveyed into the country at any other ſeaſon, and has been communicated, it invariably ceaſes at that period. But what nearly amounts to a demonſtration of its being a ſtranger to this country, is, that except in times of great famine, it never breaks out firſt in Grand Cairo, nor in the interior cities. It always begins in the ſea-port towns, on the arrival of Turkiſh veſſels, makes a gradual progreſs to the capital, from whence it aſcends as far as Sienna. When it has attained its period at Grand Cairo, and is afterwards introduced anew by the inhabitants of the Thebais, it rages with redoubled fury, ſometimes deſtroying two or three hundred thouſand men; but it always ceaſes in the month of June, and thoſe who then catch the infection, recover. Muſt its ceſſation then be attributed to its great heats, to the ſalubrious north winds which reign during the ſummer, or to the abundant dews which fall in that ſeaſon? Perhaps all theſe different cauſes contribute towards it (*f*). Another remark deſerving our particular attention, is, that the extremes of heat and cold are alike enemies to this terrible contagion. The winter puts an end to it at Conſtantinople; the ſummer deſtroys it in Egypt. It ſcarcely ever reaches to the polar circle, and never paſſes the tropic. The caravans of Grand Cairo, Damaſcus, and Iſpahan, which are ſometimes infected with it, never propagate the diſorder at Mecca, and the yemen is wholly free from this calamity.

In reading hiſtory we ſeldom find the plague at Lacedæmon Athens, or Byzantium. When it ſpread itſelf in Greece, the people ſoon put a

(*f*) I muſt lay before you a fact, Sir, which was related to me by a captain worthy of credit, ſince it may furniſh ſome light to phyſicians who are ſeeking for an antidote againſt this deſtructive ſcourge. "I left Conſtantinople where the plague "was raging. My ſailors had contracted this epidemic diſor-"der. Two of them died ſuddenly. In taking care of "them, I caught the infection. I felt an exceſſive heat which "made my blood boil. My head was very ſoon attacked, and "I perceived that I had but a few moments to live. I employ-"ed the little judgment I had remaining to make an experi-"ment. I ſtripped quite naked, and laid myſelf for the re-"mainder of the night on the deck. The copious dew that "fell, pierced me to the very bones. In a few hours it ren-"dered my reſpiration freer, and my head more compoſed. "The agitation of my blood was calmed, and after bathing "myſelf in ſea water in the morning, I was completely "cured." I do not know, Sir, whether this be an infallible remedy, but I am certain, that all infected ſubſtances that have paſſed through water, no longer communicate the poiſon.

ſtop

ſtop to it by keeping great fires lighted in the public places, by cleaning the canals, by cutting the hills which intercepted the vapours, and by ſtopping the communication. There is no change in the air, the water, the ſun of theſe beautiful countries; and the ſame ſalubrity would reign there, were they ſtill inhabited by natives whoſe government was attentive to the public welfare, and the health of the citizens. In our days, Smyrna and Conſtantinople are the foci of this frightful malady. The cauſe of this muſt be attributed to the little value the Turkiſh government ſets on the lives of men, and to their abſurd ideas of predeſtination. What ſignifies it to the deſpot whether one half of his people periſh, provided he can himſelf brave death, ſhut up in the receſſes of his Seraglio? what matters it to the Mahometan to ſee thouſands of his fellow creatures ſwept away from his ſide by the plague, ſince he can only ceaſe to live when his hour is come? He will make no attempt therefore to retard it?

When the contagion reaches the houſes of the Europeans and Greeks, they purify them by fumigations; they leave the windows open to give a free circulation to the air, and burn every thing that has belonged to infected perſons. Not ſo with the Armenians and Turks; they neither burn nor purify any thing. When the principal members of a family are extinguiſhed, the Jews purchaſe at a low price the furniture and other effects belonging to them, and ſhut them up in their magazines. As ſoon as the calamity has ceaſ-

ceaſed, they ſell them very dear to ſuch perſons as ſtand in need of them, and with them communicate the peſtilential poiſon *(g)*. It ſoon breaks out afreſh and cauſes new ravages. It is thus that this nation covered with opprobrium, valuing gold beyond life, ſells the plague to the muſſulmen, who purchaſe it without fear, and go to ſleep with it until the fatal moment, when reſuming its activity, it precipitates them to the grave *.

The ſpectacle this calamity preſents, eſpecially at Grand Cairo, chills an European with horror. This immenſe city, from there port of the Intendants of the cuſtom-houſes, contains from eight to nine hundred thouſand inhabitants. They are heaped together by thouſands. Two hundred citizens there occupy leſs ſpace than thirty at Paris §. The ſtreets are very narrow, and always crouded with people. They preſs forward, they run againſt each other, and one is ſometimes obliged to wait ſeveral minutes without being able to get through the crowd. A ſingle infected perſon communicates the poiſon to a hundred wretches. The diſorder makes a rapid progreſs, and ſpreads with the violence of a conflagration, aided by the wind. The Mahometans die in their houſes, in the public ſquares,

(g) The laſt plague at Moſcow, which carried off 200,000 inhabitants, was conveyed thither by peſtiferous merchandize out of the warehouſes of the Jews.

* See De Tott's Memoirs, p. 75, vol. I. T.

§ And thirty citizens of Paris occupy leſs ſpace than ten in London. [Tranſlator.]

in the ſtreets, without affording any uſeful example of terror to the ſurvivors. *Ell moukaddar*, ſay they, *it is their deſtiny*; yet they have before their eyes the example of the Europeans, who alone eſcape the general diſaſter.

As ſoon as the epidemy is declared, the French ſhut up their quarter, and cut off all communication with the city. Arab ſervants who live without, bring them every day their neceſſary proviſions. Except *bread, which does not communicate the poiſon*, they throw every thing elſe through a wicket in each gate, into a bucket of water. *This fluid puriſies them*, and they are taken out without any danger. By means of theſe precautions, the French merchants preſerve their health and their lives, environed as they are with all the horrors of death. The ſtreets are continually filled with funeral proceſſions, followed by mourning and by tears. When the Egyptians carry to the grave their relations and their friends, hired female mourners make the air reſound with their groans *(b)*; deſolated mothers abandon themſelves to lamentations, cover their faces with duſt, tear their

(b) In the time of Herodotus, the mourning was the ſame. He ſpeaks of it as follows: "When a perſon of any importance dies, all the women of the family cover their faces with "mud. They run through the city with their hair diſhevelled, "their boſoms expoſed, their clothes tucked up, and, making "loud cries, beat their breaſts!" *Euterpe.*——The inhabitants of the South Sea Iſlands carry ſtill farther their filial piety, their maternal tenderneſs; for at the death of their relations they make deep ſcars upon their faces, and ſignalize their ſorrow by ſhedding ſtreams of blood.

garments, and conduct to the very edge of the tomb the child they have been clasping in their arms, and whom they are to follow probably a few moments after; for the Orientals, more pious than we are, never abandon their infected relations. They bestow their cares on them to the last moment, though morally certain that this act of tenderness will cost them their lives. These cries of despair, these funeral processions, spread universal consternation, and the French tremble in the bosom of their sanctuaries; and who could without grief and horror behold humanity groaning under the rigour of so severe a scourge. They do not all perish who are attacked with it; several are cured, but I have been assured, that the plague carries off sometimes at Grand Cairo, three hundred thousand inhabitants. Can you conceive it possible that the example of the French, who come out of their houses after the contagion is at an end, safe and healthy, furnishes the Turks with not the smallest idea of making use of similar precautions? Can you imagine that, in the vast extent of the Ottoman empire, there is not a single port for performing quarantine? Does such a nation deserve to occupy the country of the ancient Greeks, and the Egyptians, their masters? It has destroyed the arts, liberty, and commerce. It leaves the wretches it has reduced to slavery to perish for want of Government. It perpetuates amongst them the most destructive of calamites, and converts kingdoms, celebrated islands, and flourishing cities, into desarts.

I have the honour to be, &c,

LETTER XLV.

OBSERVATIONS ON THE DIFFERENT INHABITANTS OF EGYPT.

The Coptis, descendants of the Egyptians, have lost the genius and knowledge of their ancestors. Next to them the Arabians, the most ancient inhabitants of the country. Their dominion twice extended over it. Those who, under the government of the Beys, cultivate the lands, have entirely lost the good faith natural to the nation, while those who live under their Scheiks have preserved their honesty and virtues. The Bedouins inhabit the desarts, and declare war against all the caravans; but they are generous, hospitable, and pay a sacred regard to their oaths. The Christians of Syria, the Greeks, and the Jews, practise the mechanical arts. Real Turks not numerous in Egypt.

To Mr. L. M.

Grand Cairo.

I Have hitherto only spoken vaguely to you, Sir, of the different races of people who inhabit Egypt. It is proper to make you more particularly acquainted with their character, their customs, and their arts. The Arabs, especially those who environ this kingdom, and who partly occupy it, merit a peculiar attention. The de-

details I am now about to offer you will explain how poſſible it is for four millions of men to ſubmit to the yoke of eight thouſand foreigners, and in what manner a wandering nation has been able to preſerve its liberties and laws, amidſt the formidable powers that ſurround it.

The genuine natives of Egypt are the Cophts, or Coptis, who, according to ſome authors, derive their name from *Cophtos*, that once celebrated city of the Thebais, and, according to others, from *Coptos*, *Cut*, becauſe they have always preſerved the cuſtom of circumciſion. Theſe are the ſole deſcendants of the Egyptians. Subjected for upwards of two thouſand years to foreign Princes, they have loſt the genius and the ſciences of their anceſtors; but they have preſerved many of their cuſtoms, and the ancient vulgar language of the country. The knowledge tranſmited to them from father to ſon, of all the cultivated lands, of their value and extent, makes them be ſelected as Secretaries to the Beys, and Intendants of all the Governors. In order to prevent theſe great men from becoming acquainted with their books of account, they write them in general in Coptic. They do not, however, perfectly underſtand the language they make uſe of; but as their maſs-books, the Pentateuch, and many of the works they are poſſeſſed of, are accompanied with an Arabian tranſlation, the ancient vulgar tongue of the Egyptians is not loſt. It will furniſh the learned poſſibly ſome day with the means of throw-

throwing a light on the darkneſs ſpread over the firſt ages of the monarchy of the Pharaohs, and of lifting up the veil which covers the hieroglyphic myſteries.

The Cophts embraced Chriſtianity in its origin. After Amrou conquered Egypt, he permitted them the free exerciſe of the Chriſtian religion. They have ever ſince had Churches, Prieſts, Biſhops, and a Patriarch, who fixed his ſeat of reſidence at Grand Cairo, when that city became the capital. Devoted to the errors of Monothe-liſm, their ignorance will not allow them to diſcover the blindneſs into which they are plunged. They are enchained by obſtinacy and the ſpirit of ſect, and nothing can alter their belief. They mix in their worſhip a number of ſuperſtitious cuſtoms, which they have received from their anceſtors. In other reſpects, the Cophts are gentle, humane and hoſpitable. Paternal tendeneſs and filial love conſtitute the happineſs of their families. They honour and cheriſh all the ties of blood. The internal commerce, the art of hatching chickens, and of bringing up bees, form almoſt their only ſcience. They often acquire prodigious wealth in the management of the affairs entruſted to them, but they never enjoy the fruit of their labours in tranquillity. The Bey, who ſees them in opulence, ſtrips them of their riches without pity; too happy if they can purchaſe their lives by the loſs of their fortune. Theſe vexations never excite them to revolt. Their want of energy holds them chained down to ſervitude and miſery

ſery, and they ſupport them without murmuring

After the Cophts, the Arabs are the moſt ancient people of Egypt. Twice have they reigned over that country. The firſt epocha of their dominion goes back to the remoteſt antiquity, and, according to grave writers, precedes the arrival of Joſeph in the country. The ſecond commences with the ſeventh century, and finiſhes with the twelfth. They ſtill compoſe two thirds of the inhabitants. Their manners vary with their ſituation. Such as have become huſbandmen, and live under the government of the foreigners who rule the country, afford to the philoſopher a ſtriking example of the influence of laws on men. In ſubjection to a tyrannical government, they have loſt the good faith, the uprightneſs, which characterize their nation. They take part in the quarrels of their maſters. Villages riſe up in arms againſt villages, cities againſt cities. During the perpetual revolutions at Grand Cairo, the country preſents a frightful ſcene of carnage and of horror. The harveſts are devoured by the flames, and the blood of the peaſants bathes thoſe fields from which they heretofore produced abundance. As hatreds are unextinguiſhable amongſt theſe people, as the mother infuſes the deſire of vengeance with her milk, into her infant, men are only born to be mutual deſtroyers. Theſe degenerate Arabs, known by the name of *Fellah*, render the navigation of the Nile very dangerous. They attack boats under cover of the darkneſs, murder the

the travellers, take possession of their merchandize, and commit all sorts of robberies.

Another part of the Arabs, who may be also called cultivators, live under the government of their *Scheiks*, who possess several principalities in the Thebais. This word, which signifies *old man*, is the most illustrious token of their power. They are still, as heretofore, the Judges, the Pontiffs, and the Sovereigns of their people. They govern more like fathers of families than Kings. These venerable patriarchs usually take their repasts at the doors of their houses, or their tents, and invite all who present themselves. On rising from table they cry with a loud voice, *In the name of God, let him that is hungry come near, and eat*; nor is this invitation a barren compliment. Every man, whoever he be, has a right to seat himself, and to partake of the food he finds there. Permit me to quote the passage of Genesis *(i)*, where Abraham receives the angels, that you may compare their present manners with those of the same people in such distant ages. " And Abraham sat in the tent " door, in the plains of Mamre, in the heat of " day. And he lift up his eyes, and looked, and " lo! three men stood by him; and when he saw " them, he ran to meet them from the tent door, " and bowed himself towards the ground, and " said, *My Lord* *, if now I have found favour

(*i*) Genesis, chap. 18.

* The version of the Bible has it, My Lords, *Seigneurs*, which certainly appears most accurate—but this with humility.——*Translator*.

" in

"in thy ſight, paſs not away, I pray thee, from "thy ſervant. Let a little water I pray you be "fetched, and waſh your feet, and reſt your- "ſelves under the tree, and I will fetch a morſel "of bread, and comfort ye your hearts; after "that you ſhall paſs on, for therefore are ye come "to your ſervant. And they ſaid, ſo do as thou haſt "ſaid. And Abraham haſtened into the tent unto "Sarah, and ſaid, make ready quickly three mea- "ſures of fine meal, knead it, and make cakes "upon the hearth. And Abraham ran into the "herd, and fetched a calf, tender and good, and "gave it unto a young man, and he haſted to dreſs "it; and he took butter, and milk, and the calf "which he had dreſſed, and ſet it before them, "and he ſtood by them under the tree."

The Arabs give the ſame reception to ſtrangers and travellers who come near their tents. Ser- vants waſh their feet. The women knead unlea- vened bread, which they bake upon the aſhes, and they are ſerved with roaſted ſheep, milk and honey, and the beſt of every thing they are poſ- ſeſſed of. The ſlight impoſitions levied by the Scheiks through their territories, do not oppreſs their ſubjects. They enjoy their affection. The Arab comes and expoſes his affairs at their tribunal. They are not complicated, and the light of natural reaſon, aided by the ſimple and clear laws of the Coran, ſuffice to terminate them on the ſpot. Their judgments are almoſt always dictated by equity. Under this paternal government, man poſſeſſes all his liberty, and is no further attached to his Prince than by the ties of respect and gratitude. He may speak freely to him, therefore, and censure or commend him according to the circumstances. I shall cite you a trait to prove how far the Arabs carry this spirit of frankness.

"Elmansor, the second Abassid Calif, laid the "foundation of Bagdad in 769. He made him-"self famous by his victories, his power, and the "art by which he knew how to govern im-"mense states. His affability was extreme: but "so many good qualities were sullied by un-"bounded avarice. An Arab accosted him one "day, and said to him, Health to the father "of Jafar! Health to thee, replied Elmansor. "Thou art the descendant of the generous race "of Haschem; grant me a small part of the "treasures thou art master of.—It is not to me, "it is to the Apostle of God thou shouldst address "thy wishes.—My clothes are tatters; years "have worn out my strength.—Let us ex-"change; take mine. He pulled his clothes "off on the spot, and gave them to him. The "Arab, perceiving that they were worn and "pieced, says to him, Prince, art thou ignorant "of this sentence of the son of Harima: *The "rich who covers himself with rags, is not less subject "to death.*"

It is with this sort of liberty that the Arabs speak to their Chiefs. Wholly devoted to their interests, on the least sign of their will, they arm to repulse the oppression of the Turks, who have never been able to reduce them. If victory declares in their favour, they remain in possession of their territories. If conquered, they abandon them, and,

and, carrying with them their wives, their children, and their flocks, they retire into the depth of the desarts. There they wait to avail themselves of the times of trouble and confusion, when they return, full armed, to attack the enemy, and resume their possessions. Were these Chiefs to unite their forces, and form a league against the Turks, they would expel them without difficulty, and make themselves sovereigns of Egypt. The policy of the Beys prevents these alliances, by sowing dissentions amongst them, by aiding the weak against the strong, by confirming the authority of those only who appear favourable to their designs; and above all, by destroying, by stratagem, or poison, the Emirs, whose power, talents, and ambition, they greatly fear.

These Arabs are the best people in the world. They are ignorant of the vices of polished nations. Incapable of concealment, they are strangers to trick and falsehood. Lofty and generous they openly repulse an insult with an armed hand, and never revenge themselves by treachery. Hospitality amongst them is sacred. Their houses and their tents are open to all travellers of every religion. They treat their guests with as much respect and affection as their own relations. This honourable virtue is carried so far amongst them, that if the enemy, whose death they have vowed, can submit to come and take coffee with them, he has no longer any thing to fear for his life. This is the only circumstance wherein they forget their resentment, and renounce the pleasure of revenge. The following fact, to which I was a witness, will give you some idea of their uprightness. An Arab Scheik has long paid an annual visit to the French quarter. He takes such goods as he wants of a merchant, without any other security than his word. The following year he returns at the same period with the price of his former purchase, and to buy new stuffs. One year he was prevented by illness from attending at the usual time, but he sent his son with the gold, and likewise to continue this commerce, a circumstance which does equal honour to the two nations.

The third species of Arabs is comprehended under the general denomination of *Bedaoui*, inhabitants of the desart. These pastoral people occupy those burning solitudes, which extend to the east and west of Egypt. Separated into tribes, they do not cultivate the earth, and feed on barley, the fruit of the date-tree, the flesh and milk of their herds. These they conduct into the vallies, where they find pasturage and water. When every thing is exhausted in one spot, they place their tents, their wives, and children, on camels, mount on horseback themselves, and the whole tribe sets off in search of another habitation. These sovereigns of the desarts, declared enemies of all the caravans, attack them wherever they fall in with them, and compel them either to pay a tribute or to fight. If they meet with too sharp a resistance, they retire without apprehending the pursuit of their enemies. If they couquer, they strip every body, and divide the booty; but they never kill any one unless

to

to avenge the blood of their companions. The traveller who puts himſelf under their protection has nothing to fear either for his life or his riches, for their word is ſacred. I have never read in hiſtory, I have never heard upon the ſpot, that an Arab ever violated his plighted faith. This is a trait which characterizes at once, and ſeparates this from all other nations on the earth. Their eagerneſs for plunder has not made them renounce the laws of hoſpitality. This virtue is not leſs honoured amongſt them than amongſt the Arab cultivators. Mr. de St. Germain, after his misfortunes in paſſing the iſthmus of Suez, arriving at the tent of a Bedouin, almoſt dead, owed his life to the generous attention of his hoſt, who conducted him to Grand Cairo as ſoon as his health was reſtored. Mr. Pagès, flying acroſs the ſands of Deſart Arabia, with ſeven Arabs, loſt his water and his proviſions. Falling from his camel, he was on the point of being ſacrificed to the reſentment of a tribe which had been inſulted. One of his companions diſmounted at the hazard of his life, made the Frenchman mount behind him, and carried him off to a place of ſafety. On the journey, the Arabs, who had only a ſmall barley cake for their daily nouriſhment, divided it into eight ſhares, of which they always gave a double portion to the ſtranger.

Their exceſſive love of liberty makes them prefer theſe frightful deſarts, where they live independent, to the rich plains of Egypt, which would enſlave them. That Government has more than once offered them lands, which they have

have refused rather than submit to be governed by despots. This spirit of independence, so well painted in the scriptures, they have inviolably preserved from Ismael, their ancestor. Herodotus, the most ancient historian, thus represents them: "Cambyses (k), desirous of leading an army into Egypt, sent Ambassadors to the King of the Arabs to demand a safe passage of him. He obtained his demand, and the two nations pledged their mutual faith. The Arabs, of all people, preserve their oaths with the most fidelity. The following is their method of concluding treaties. One of them, standing up between the contracting parties, cuts the palm of his hand with a sharp stone; he then takes the border of their robes, tinges them with blood, and rubs seven stones with it, which he places in the midst of them, invoking Bacchus and Urania. If he who has solicited the alliance be a stranger, he becomes after this ceremony their sacred guest, and if a native of the country, he is looked upon as a citizen of the tribe with whom the treaty is formed. This compact is inviolable for ever." These ceremonies are no longer observed amongst the Arabs. On occasion of treaties, they content themselves with mutually squeezing the hand, and swearing by the head, that they will faithfully observe the conditions agreed upon, and they are never perjured.

Diodorus Siculus, who wrote several ages after Herodotus, paints them in the same colours. I

(k) Heroditus, *Thalia*.

shall

ſhall add this paſſage, becauſe it will demonſtrate to you how little this people are changed, and as it is perhaps the only hiſtorical portrait which, at the end of eighteen hundred years, will ſerve for the ſame nation (*l*). " The wandering " Arabs dwell in the open country, without any " roof. They themſelves call their country a " ſolitude. They do not chooſe for their " abode places abounding in rivers and in foun- " tains, leſt that allurement alone ſhould draw " enemies into their neighbourhood. Their law " or their cuſtom forbids them to ſow corn, to " plant fruit-trees, to make uſe of wine, or to " inhabit houſes. He who ſhould violate theſe " uſages would be puniſhed infallibly with " death, becauſe they are perſuaded that who- " ever is capable of ſubjecting himſelf to ſuch " conveniencies, would ſoon ſubmit to maſters " in order to preſerve them. Some lead their " camels to graze, ſome their ſheep. The lat- " ter are the wealthieſt; for beſides the advan- " tages they derive from their flocks, they go to " ſell in the ſea-ports, frankincenſe, myrrh, " and other precious aromatics, which they " have received in exchange from the inhabi- " tants of Arabia Felix. Extremely jealous of " their liberty, at the news of the approach " of an army they take refuge in the depth of " the deſarts, the extent of which ſerves them " as a rampart. The enemy, in fact, perceiv- " ing no water, could not dare to traverſe them, " whilſt the Arabs being furniſhed with it by " means of veſſels concealed in the earth, with

(*l*) Diodorus Siculus, lib. 19.

" which they are acquainted, are in no danger " of this want. The whole ſoil being compoſ- " ed of clayey and ſoft earth, they find means " to dig deep and vaſt ciſterns, of a ſquare " form each ſide of which is the length of an " acre. Having filled them with rain-water, " they cloſe up the entrance, which they make " uniform with the neighbouring ground, leav- " ing ſome imperceptible token, known only to " themſelves. They accuſtom their flocks to " drink only once in three days *(m)*, ſo that " when they are obliged to fly acroſs theſe " parched ſands, they may be habituated to ſup- " port thirſt. As for themſelves, they live on " fleſh and milk, and common and ordinary " fruits. They have in their fields the tree " which bears pepper *(n)*, and a great deal of " wild honey, which they drink with water. " There are other Arabs who cultivate the earth. " They are tributary like the Syrians, and re- " ſemble them in other reſpects, except that " they do not dwell in houſes. Such are pretty " nearly the manners of this people.

This picture, drawn by the hand of an enligh- tened hiſtorian, is of a very ſtriking accuracy. We diſcover it in the Bedouins of our days. May I be permitted to extract from the ſame author a paſſage which wonderfully paints at once

(m) The Abyſinians, who ſet out from Girgé to their own country, having a deſart of ſeven days journey to paſs, accuſtom their camels to perform it without drinking.

(n) I imagine Diodorus was deceived here, and that the pepper was brought into Arabia by ſhips from India.

once their uprightneſs of character, and the treachery of the Greeks. " The Nabathean Arabs " had quitted their deſarts, to repair to a place " of commerce, where a celebrated fair was " held. Before their departure they had depo- " ſited in the caverns of a mountain, their wives, " their children, and their riches. This rock, " ſituated at two days journey from every ha- " bitation, and protected both by its poſition, " and by the burning ſolitudes, appeared to them " out of the reach of the enemy; but the Greeks, " thirſting after gold, availed themſelves of this " moment to attack it. Athenæus, one of the " captains of Antigonus, ſet out from Idumea " with a body of light armed troops, marched " ninety-one leagues in three days and nights, " and reached the aſylum of the Nabatheans. " He entered it by force, ſlew a part of the " wretches ſhut up in it, made a great many " priſoners, carried off the frankincenſe, the " myrrh, and four hundred talents of ſilver which " were depoſited there. He only remained " there three hours, and fled acroſs the deſart with " his booty. When he had got ten leagues from " the rock, the heat and fatigue obliged him to " repoſe. A camp was haſtily prepared. The " ſoldiers, worn down with laſſitude, and ima- " gining they had nothing to fear, reſigned them- " ſelves to ſleep. But the Nabatheans had been " apprized by meſſengers of the invaſion of the " Greeks. Setting off immediately they repair- " ed to their habitation. The blood of their old " men; the lamentations of the wounded, filled

" them

" them with horror. They flew to vengeance; " and in a few hours came up with their ene- " mies. Some of the priſoners, taking advan- " tage of the negligence of the Greeks, broke " their chains, and gave information of the ſtate " they were then in. On this intelligence, the " Arabs attacked the camp on all ſides, and en- " tered under cover of the darkneſs. They put " to death the ſoldiers that were aſleep, and " pierced with their darts thoſe who were riſing " to take arms. The maſſacre was general. " Fifty horſemen only eſcaped, and they were " moſtly wounded. The Nabatheans, having " recovered their priſoners and their treaſure, " conveyed them back to their habitation. After " giving this leſſon to the Greeks, they wrote to " Antigonus, to complain of Athenæus, and to " juſtify their conduct. That prince diſavowed " the expedition of his general, declared that he " had undertaken it without his participation, " and that their defence was ſtrictly juſt. He " made uſe of this diſſimulation to put them off " their guard, by removing every cauſe of miſ- " truſt, hoping to avail himſelf of ſome favour- " able moment to revenge the defeat of his " troops; but the Arabs reckoning little on the " good faith of the Greeks, kept upon their " guard, and placed centinels on elevated ſitua- " tions to give notice of the appearance of an " enemy. They ſoon diſcovered the wiſdom of " this precaution. After ſome months had elapſ- " ed, Antigonus ſent eight thouſand picked men " againſt them, commanded by his ſon Deme-

" trius.

" trius. This corps marched by indirect routes " in order to surprize them. The Nabatheans, " apprized by their spies, withdrew their flocks " towards the extremity of the desart, and for- " tified themselves in the mountain. Demetrius " found it guarded by a body of brave youth, " who made a vigorous resistance. After mak- " ing a fruitless attack on it with all his forces, " he retreated and pretended to take flight. The " next day he renewed the attack with no greater " success. Then an Arab cried to him with a " loud voice: King Demetrius, what can induce " you to make war against a people who dwell " in a desart, without water, wine, and provi- " sions; in a word, destitute of every thing " which forms the object of your cupidity and " your quarrels? The horror of slavery has con- " ducted us into this solitude, deprived of all the " good things so greedily sought after by men. " This it is which has reduced us to such a soli- " tary and savage life as disables us from doing " you any injury. We supplicate you there- " fore, and the King your father, to leave us in " repose. We will even make you presents to " engage you to withdraw your army, and to " receive the Nabatheans amongst the number " of your friends. If these reasons cannot pre- " vail upon you, necessity will oblige you to " quit a desart, where you will soon want water " and provisions. Never will you subject us to " other customs. What do you hope for then " from this expedition? It will terminate at the " worst by carrying off from us some slaves,

" who

"who will only ſerve you againſt their inclina-"tion, and whom you will not be able to bend "to your manners, and your uſages. Struck "with this diſcourſe, Demetrius made peace "with the Nabatheans."

Such, Sir, were the Arabs before and after Alexander; ſuch are they in our days. The love of independance ſtill glows in their hearts. Their averſion for all foreign dominion, makes them prefer the horror of theſe deſarts to the moſt advantagous eſtabliſhments. Liberty has ſo many charms for them, that ſupported by her they boldly brave hunger, thirſt, and the conſuming ardour of the ſun. Humbled ſometimes, but never ſubjected, they have bid defiance to all the powers of the earth, and have repulſed thoſe chains which have alternately been borne by the other nations. The Romans, thoſe maſters of the world, loſt whole armies which they ſent to the conqueſt of this country. The Egyptians, the Perſians, the Ottomans, have never been able to reduce them. This lofty people alone, therefore, have preſerved that elevation of character, that generoſity, that inviolable fidelity which do honour to humanity. Treachery and perjury are unknown amongſt them. Ignorant, without deſpiſing the ſciences, a ſound reaſon, a rectitude of underſtanding, an elevated mind, diſtinguiſh them from all the Orientals. Before ſtrangers, as in the preſence of their princes, they invariably maintain the dignity of man, and never deſcend to low flatteries. Serious without moroſeneſs, witty without oſten-

ostentation, frank without imprudence, they are well acquainted with the charms of a conversation intermixed with gaity and wisdom. Friendship is sacred amongst them, and friends are brothers. Nor are they strangers to delicacy of sentiment. Their poems afford a description of that burning love which they respire with the ardour of the sun, and not unfrequently of that gallantry, which seems peculiar to polished nations. Such, Sir, are these Arabs whom the powerful genius of one man knew how to unite in overthrowing the neighbouring thrones, in conquering kingdoms, and giving laws to two thirds of the habitable globe. They have lost their conquests, but they have retained their character, their religion, and their manners. Could another Mahomet be found in the east capable of collecting their different tribes under one banner, he might once more subject Asia and Africa to their dominion. It is amongst the Arabs the philosopher should go to study primitive man, and not amongst nations, whose minds and hearts, and affections, are corrupted by despotism and servitude.

After the Coptis and the Arabs, the Mograbians, or Western Mahometans, are the most numerous inhabitants of Egypt. Some dedicate themselves to commerce, others serve in the armies. Their nation must not be judged from the specimen of those individuals we see at Grand Cairo. Such as embrace the military line are, almost all adventurers, guilty of great crimes,

crimes, and whom the dread of juſtice has baniſhed from their country. Theſe mercenary ſoldiers, lawleſs, and without faith, abandon themſelves to every exceſs, and invariably ſell themſelves to the Bey who promiſes them the higheſt pay.

The real Turks are by no means numerous in this country. The corps of Janizaries and of Arabs are compoſed of them. They abuſe their power, to pillage the Egyptians, and ſtrangers, and employ every method to amaſs great wealth. Sometimes they make themſelves formidable to the Pacha and the Beys, and ſell their ſuffrages for gold. Theſe troops, as well as the Mograbians, have no diſcipline, and are totally ignorant of the uſe of artillery. It would be impoſſible for them to reſiſt European tactics.

The Chriſtians of Syria, the Greeks, and the Jews, devote themſelves wholly to commerce, to the exchange, and to the arts. The ſubtlety of their underſtanding has rendered them alternately Directors of the Cuſtom-Houſes, and Intendants of the revenues of Egypt. There is no depending on their integrity. One ſhould be always on one's guard againſt their artifices. When they get into credit, they make uſe of every ſtratagem to oppreſs the European merchant, to ſtir up injuries againſt him, and to put ſhakles on his trade. The principal part of them are goldſmiths, and work in gold, ſilver, and precious ſtones, with a tolerable degree of perfection. Their works in fillagree merit the approbation of connoiſſeurs. Several of them have eſtabliſhed manufactures of light

ſtuffs,

ſtuffs, which they fabricate with Bengal cotton, and Syrian ſilk. The natives purchaſe it for their uſe. Theſe ſtuffs, though well woven, are but of an indifferent dye. Their colours have neither the brilliancy nor the duration of thoſe of India. This is entirely owing to the ignorance of the artiſts, for Egypt produces excellent indigo carthamum; and various ſubſtances for colours. It is the ſame with their linens. The Egyptians flax, heretofore ſo celebrated, has loſt nothing of its quality. It is long, ſoft, and ſilky, and would make ſumptuous linen; but from the fault of the ſpinners, who know not how to employ it, coarſe linens only are manufactured from it.

All theſe inhabitants, Sir, of different manners, nations and religions, amount to near four millions. They are governed by eight thouſand Mamalukes. If you are ſurprized that ſo ſmall a number of foreigners can keep this vaſt herd under the yoke, you will ceaſe your aſtoniſhment on being informed, that in the time of Auguſtus, three cohorts were ſufficient to guard the Thebais. Strabo, an ocular witneſs, and one of the wiſeſt hiſtorians of antiquity, relates the following intereſting facts.

" The Egyptian nation is extremely numerous, but it is by no means warlike, nor " are the neighbouring people more ſo. Cornelius Gallus, the firſt Roman governor ſent " into Egypt, marched againſt the inhabitants of " Hieropolis (o), who had revolted, and made

(o) This city is totally deſtroyed. Its ruins are buried under the ſands of the Iſthmus of Suez.

" them

" them return to their duty with a ſmall body " of ſoldiers. The rigour of the impoſitions " having cauſed a general revolt in the Thebais, " he appeared, and the rebellion was immedi- " ately calmed. After him, Petronius, at the head " of ſome cohorts, ſtopped the impetuoſity of " many thouſand Alexandrians who had attack- " ed him, and left a great number of them " dead on the field of battle. Elius Gallus, " having entered Arabia with a part of the " troops which guarded Egypt, proved by his " victories how unwarlike theſe people are, " and would have conquered Yemen but for the " treachery of Syllæus. The Ethiopians, tak- " ing advantage of his abſence, made an irrup- " tion into the Thebais, overturned the ſtatues " of Cæſar, carried off a rich booty, and led away " priſoners the feeble garriſons of Philé and " Elephantinos. Patronius purſued them with " ten thouſand infantry and eight thouſand " horſe; and though their army was compoſed " of thirty thouſand ſoldiers, he forced it to " retire to *Pſelcha*, a city of Ethiopia. Unable " to obtain by his ambaſſadors the reſtitution " of the captives, he penetrated into the coun- " try and gave them battle. Theſe troops, " badly armed and without diſcipline, could not " ſtand againſt the valour of the Romans. " Some fled into the deſarts, others took ſhelter " within the walls of the capital, and the greateſt " number eſcaped by ſwimming to an iſland in " the river. Amongſt the latter were ſeveral " generals of Candace, a warlike woman, then

Queen

"Queen of Ethiopia. Petronius crossed the "Nile in boats, made them all prisoners, and "sent them to the city of Alexandria. He "then laid siege to Pselcha and took it. A part "of the inhabitants perished in this attack. After this conquest he marched towards Premnin, a town fortified by nature, and to arrive "at it, crossed these vast sandy desarts, where "the army of Cambyses was suffocated by the "winds *(p)*. Having carried it by storm, he "went to lay siege to Napata, where was the "palace of Candace with her son. The queen "shut up in a neighbouring fortress, sent ambassadors to the Roman general to treat of "peace, and to offer restitution of the captives, and the statues carried off. Without "hearkening to these propositions, he attacked "the place and became master of it, but the "young prince saved himself by flight. Imagining that it would be difficult to penetrate "any farther, he returned by the same route, "carrying back with him vast riches. He left "four hundred men in garrison at Premnin with "provisions and ammunition for two years, and "returned into Egypt."

This passage, Sir, compleatly exposes the weakness of the Egyptians and Ethiopians in the time of the Romans. They have not since changed. A long slavery has served to extinguish the little energy they then displayed. Their ignorance in the profession of arms still

(p) This passage confirms what I have told you of this disaster, on the credit of Herodotus.

 fur-ſurpaſſes their cowardice. During thoſe calamitous days when war ranged in Grand Cairo, we heard the ſix pieces of cannon belonging to the caſtle fire againſt the town. We obſerved that it took the artillery men half an hour to charge them, for there was, that interval between every volley. Judge, Sir, if ſuch troops could ſtand an inſtant againſt a few European regiments. Any warlike nation which ſhould attack Egypt, would take it without an obſtacle; ſhe might alſo eaſily conquer Ethiopia, get poſſeſſion of the gold of thoſe countries; and miſtreſs of the waters of the Nile, divert them at pleaſure throughout Egypt, and preſerve an inexhauſtible abundance.

I have the honour to be, &c.

LETTER XLVI.

OBSERVATIONS ON MARRIAGE AMONG THE EGYPTIANS.

Dignified with the title of ſacrament, marriage among the Chriſtians indiſſoluble. The Legiſlator of Arabia, copying the authority of the patriarchs, and influenced by the force of cuſtom, has permitted repudiation, but at the ſame time endeavoured to reſtrain the caprice of the men. The nuptial ceremonies practiſed by the Mahometans and Coptis.

To Mr. L. M.

Grand Cairo.

AMONGST Chriſtians, Sir, marriage, raiſed to the dignity of a ſacrament, becomes an indiſſoluble engagement. The laws in certain caſes ſuſpend its effect, but they never totally deſtroy it. (This holds good only amongſt Catholicks). It behoves the contracting parties, therefore, to be perfectly acquainted with each other, that their inclinations may be free, ſince their happineſs and that of their children depend on that knowledge and that freedom. The Oriental manners, ſo different from thoſe of Europe, have compelled their legiſlators not to make an inviolable contract of that act. Amongſt theſe people, the two ſexes live ſeparate, and do not

 converſe

converſe together. How can the young man and the virgin who have never beheld each other vow eternal love and inviolable fidelity? Such an oath, by expoſing them to perjury, would prove the ſource of the greateſt diſorder. Mahomet, who knew men well, and who was authorized by the example of Abraham, and the other patriarchs, has permitted repudiation. After endeavouring to prevent it by preſcribing to the married perſons thoſe attentions, that tenderneſs which ought to conſtitute the delight of their lives, he has ſaid, *Such as all ſhall have ſworn to have no further commerce with their wives, ſhall be allowed a delay of four months (q); if during that time they ſhould return to themſelves, the Lord is indulgent and merciful.*

If the divorce be firmly reſolved, God ſees, and knows every thing.

This precept, Sir, authorizes repudiation, but it leaves God to judge of the legitimacy of the action. In the remainder of that chapter, which is the ſummary of all the laws of the Mahometans, the Legiſlator ſtrives to fix ſome limits to the capriciouſneſs of man. A Mahometan cannot eſpouſe a woman without aſſigning her a dowry in proportion to his ability. If he wiſhes to ſeparate from her, he ſends for the Judge, and declares in his preſence that he repudiates her, and, at the expiration of his four months grace, he

(q) "When a Mahometan has made an oath to have no further commerce with his wife, he has four months delay, during which he may reconcile himſelf with her. If he lets that time elapſe, he is obliged to repudiate her, ſhe becomes free, and may contract new engagements." *Coran, chap.* 2

beſtows

bestows on her the portion stipulated in the contract of marriage, and whatever effects he has received from her. If they have any children, the husband retains the boys, the wife takes away the girls. From that moment they are free to contract fresh engagements. The women are not, as it is believed in Europe, subject to a perpetual slavery. When they have serious causes for separation they implore the protection of the laws, and break their chains. But in this case, they lose their dowry, and the wealth they may have brought into their husband's family; but they regain their liberty.

Sometimes a Mahometan vows, without just cause, that he will have no further commerce with his wife. Should he repent, he may be reconciled to her, without the intervention of the Cadi. The Legislator has fixed a period for this caprice, in the following verse: *He who shall repudiate his wife three times, shall not be allowed to take her back, until she shall have lain with another husband, who shall have repudiated her. They shall then be permitted to re-unite, if they believe themselves capable of observing the commandments of God (r).*

The guilty husband who finds himself thus circumstanced, and who dreads that separation, the sentence of which he has himself rashly pronounced, endeavours to evade the precept. He seeks for a friend on whose discretion he thinks he can depend, shuts him up with his wife, in the presence of witnesses, and waits at the door the event of this singular scene. The proof is delicate, and does not always succeed according to

(r) Coran, chap. 7.

his wiſhes. If the officious friend, on coming out, ſays, *Behold my wife, and I repudiate her*, the firſt huſband has the right to take her back; but if, forgetful of his friendſhip in the arms of love, he declares that he acknowledges her for his wife, he carries her off without any oppoſition. Such are the laws by which Mahomet has ſtrove to ſecure the peace and happineſs of marriages. He has made that ſtate a ſtate of ſociety, the mutual attentions of which, and the birth of children, muſt inceſſantly bind them more cloſely to each other. Parties once contracted, do not often avail themſelves of the liberty he gives them. Divorces are much leſs frequent amongſt them than is generally believed. Many of them are contented even with one wife, and do not profit by the privilege the law allows them of having four at a time. This moderation muſt be attributed to the ſeparation of the ſexes, to their mode of private life, to the charms of which they are highly ſenſible, and, above all, to that tenderneſs which attaches them both to their children, who, brought up in the paternal manſion, become at once the ſupport and conſolation of the authors of their being.

The female relations of a young man are the perſons who take upon them his eſtabliſhment. They have had the opportunity of ſeeing *naked* at the baths the principal part of the young women of the city. They paint to him the portrait of them *after life*. When his choice is fixed, they propoſe the alliance to the father of the young woman, the dowry is ſpecified, and if he he agrees to it, they make him presents. As soon as the parties are agreed, the female relations, the friends and acquaintances of the young virgin, conduct her to the bath. They strip her with great solemnity. She is bathed, shampoed, and perfumed. They tinge the nails of their toes and fingers of a gold colour, by means of the *henné*. They black her eye-lashes with *cohel*. They mix precious essences in her hair, and wash her whole body with rose-water. The women, naked, without any other ornament than the flowing locks of their beautiful long hair, lead the young novice round the apartment, and initiate her in the mysteries of Hymen. They appease the alarms of her timid heart, by telling her of the pleasures she is going to enjoy, and by celebrating the beauty and riches of her young spouse. The remainder of the day is spent in entertainments, in dances, and songs, suitable to the occasion. The next day, the same persons repair to the house of the betrothed girl, and tear her, as if by violence, from the arms of her disconsolate mother. They conduct her in triumph to the husband's house. The procession usually commences in the evening, which is preceded by hired dancers, with their feet fastened on long sticks, and balance-poles in their hands. A number of slaves display to the sight of the people the effects, the furniture, the trinkets, destined for the use of the bride. Troops of dancing girls advance, keeping time to the sound of instruments. Next to them, matrons, richly clad, march gravely in the procession. Then appears the

the young victim under a magnificent canopy, borne by four slaves. She is supported by her mother and her sisters. A veil of gold, enriched with pearls and diamonds, covers her entirely. A long train of flambeaux lights the whole, and from time to time chorusses of *Almé* sing couplets in praise of the new-married pair. I have seen the pomp I am now describing pass twenty times through the streets of Cairo. They always take the longest road, for they are very proud of shewing to the people all the magnificence they are capable of displaying on such occasions.

When they arrive at the husband's house, the women mount to the first story, from whence they perceive through the blinds of a gallery, every thing that passes below. The men, assembled in the saloon, do not mix with them. They pass a part of the night in banqueting, drinking coffee and sherbet, and in listening to music. The dancing girls descend amongst them, take off their veils, and display their wonderful activity and skill. They play *mute scenes* to the sound of the tabor, the cymbals, and the castanets, in which they represent the combats of Hymen, the resistance of the young bride, and the stratagems of love to gain the point. Nothing can equal the voluptuousness of their motions, and the licentiousness of their postures. There is no occasion for words to understand their pantomimes. Every thing is painted by them in so natural a manner, that it is impossible to mistake them. I have assisted several times at these representations, and never without being surprized how a people, who

who preſerve in public ſo much reſpect for the women, can be ſo paſſionately fond of theſe laſcivious dances. When they are finiſhed, a chorus of *Almé* ſing the epithalamium, ſo celebrated amongſt the Greeks, extolling the incitements of the young bride, more beautiful than the moon, freſher than the roſe, more odoriferous than the jeſſamine, and the felicity of the mortal who is about to enjoy ſo many charms. During the ceremony, ſhe paſſes frequently before her huſband, always in new dreſſes, to diſplay her gracefulneſs and riches. When the aſſembly are at length retired, the huſband enters into the nuptial chamber, the veil is taken off, and he ſees his wife for the firſt time. When ſhe is a girl, the tokens of her virginity muſt appear, otherwiſe he has a right to ſend her back the next day to her parents; and this is the greateſt diſhonour that can happen to a family. Accordingly there is no country upon earth where young girls are watched with more care, nor where one is more certain of marrying a virgin.

Such are the marriage laws and ceremonies amongſt the Egyptians. The poor, as well as the rich, obſerve them ſcrupulouſly. The daughter of the mechanic is conducted in the ſame manner to her huſband. All the difference conſiſts in the ſpectacle that ſurrounds her. Inſtead of flambeaux, the proceſſion takes place by the light of pinewood carried in iron chafing-diſhes, on the end of long poles. Inſtead of dancing girls, and muſicians ſhe is preceded by tabors and hired men-dancers. The daughter of the poor man, in ſhort, who can have neither canopy, nor retinue, borrows a veil, marches to the ſound of cymbals, or pieces of metal agitated in cadence by a ſet of low fellows.

The Coptis obſerve nearly the ſame ceremonies; but they have the cuſtom of betrothing young girls at ſix of ſeven years old. A ring which they put upon the finger is the ſymbol of this alliance. They frequently obtain from their relations the permiſſion to bring them up at their houſes, until they are marriageable. Repudiation, the baths, the pompous eſcort of the bride, are alſo in uſe amongſt theſe ſchiſmatic Chriſtians, only they are allowed but one wife at a time. You will find, Sir, in the *Arabian Tales*, deſcriptions which reſemble very much that I have been giving you, becauſe the author of that agreeable work, being perfectly well acquainted with the manners and uſages of his country, has deſcribed them like a ſkilful painter. Thoſe faithful pictures it is which render his book of infinite value. It is in this point alſo that thoſe romance writers err, who, never having travelled in the eaſt, give us, under the name of Oriental Tales, the fooliſh dreams of their own imagination. You there ſee the Turks, the Arabs, and the Perſians, metamorphoſed into French and Engliſhmen, and the moſt groteſque portraits inſtead of nature.

I have the honour to be, &c.

LET-

LETTER XLVII.

THE REVOLUTIONS IN THE COMMERCE OF EGYPT, FROM THE MOST REMOTE ANTIQUITY TO THE PRESENT TIME.

State of the Egyptian commerce under the Pharoahs, the Persians, and the Ptolemies, who created a powerful marine; and under the Romans, who guided by the Egyptians, penetrated as far as Bengal. Declension of this extensive commerce under the Princes of the lower empire. Almost annihilated during the government of the Arabs. Re-established by the Venetians, who opened to themselves the ports of Egypt. The Portuguese deprive them of this trade; in consequence of which the Venetians lose both their marine and their distant provinces. Actual state of the present commerce of this country.

To Mr. L. M.

Grand Cairo.

THE preceding Letters, Sir, present you with some particular details on the traffic of the principal towns in Egypt. These scattered notions would be insufficient in an age when every Court of Europe looks on commerce as an inexhaustible source of riches and of power. I shall attempt to trace out to you a rapid picture of the revolutions it has undergone, from the most remote antiquity to the present day. However difficult the undertaking, its *eventual utility* to my country encourages me to proceed.

The

The Egyptian Pharoahs were acquainted with the advantages of trade. The numerous canals they formed had a double object, that of diffusing fertility with the waters of the Nile, and of transporting with facility the produce of the country from one end of the empire to the other. The fairs they established in the Delta and the Thebais united the inhabitants of the most distant provinces. Each man brought with him the fruit of his industry, and the whole nation, by means of mutual exchange enjoyed the inventions of the arts, and productions of all the kingdom. The charms of these water-voyages, the cool air they breathed in them, the beauty of the banks of the river, the necessity of navigating during the innundation, rendered the Egyptians mariners; and one may be led to think, that the first vessels on which men dared to trust themselves to the inconstancy of the waves, were built in Egypt. Pleasure, interest, and religion, those powerful springs of human action, induced them to travel from one temple to another. Throughout the country there was nothing but festivals, illuminations, and assemblies, wherein the merchant as well as the rich man found his private advantage. The Egyptians must be regarded as one of the most ancient nations of navigators. They made voyages on the Red Sea long before the famous expedition of the Argoauts. Danaus *(s)* carried into Greece, then in a state of barbarism, the art of

(s) Herodotus.

navigation and of commerce. His brother, Sesostris, soon after set out with two armies, one by land, the other by sea, to conquer Asia. Whilst he reduced the interior kingdoms, a fleet of four hundred sail took possession of the ports of the Arabic Gulph, sailed through the straits of *Bab Elmandel (t)*, and penetrated into the Indian Ocean, which had never beheld vessels of such a size. It is from this æra that we must date the commerce of Egypt with Asia, which has never been interrupted since that remote period.

Sesostris founded several colonies in the course of his conquests; one of them fortified itself on the coast of Phœnicia. Tyre erected her ramparts, cut down the cedars of Libanon, to build vessels, and prepared to dispute the glory of navigation with the mother country. She sent her ships as far as the pillars of Hercules, and spread the arts every where with her commerce *(u)*. The Egyptians on their side, mounting the Bosphorus, entered the Black sea, exchanging with their brethren (*x*) settled in

(*t*) *Bab Elmandel* signifies *the Gates of the Handkerchiefs*, because it was by this streight that Egypt has at all times received the cottons, of which their *handkerchiefs* are formed, which are still called *Mandel*.

(*u*) Clement, of Alexandria, says, "Phœnicians received "letters from Egypt, and transmitted them to the Greeks." He adds in another place, "Cadmus, the Phœnician, carried "them into Greece, on which account Herodotus gives the "name of Phœnician to the Greek characters."

(*x*) Herodotus asserts that Sesostris also left a colony in Colchis, and that the Egyptians traded with them.

Colchis

Colchis, the productions of their country with those of the Northerns; whilst the fleets of the Red Sea went in search of the pearls, the diamonds, the perfumes, and the precious stuffs of the eastern world.

Commercial Egypt soon attained a high degree of power. She raised in every part those colossal statues, those temples, those obelisks, which cannot be contemplated without admiration. The colleges of priests continually applied to the study of the heavens, taught navigators that astronomy which served them as a guide through the immensity of the seas. Powerful without, rich in her own productions, Egypt with her trade propagated the light of the sciences. Having spread amongst the savage nations of Greece, the art of cultivating grain, she disposed them to civilization. It is thus that the hardy mariners of Europe, sent by Kings, friends to humanity, will reclaim from barbarism the islanders of the South Sea, by communicating our productions and our arts. The savage cannibal of New Zealand will cease, doubtless, to devour his fellow-creature, when our sheep, our cows, and our seeds, shall have procured him abundant and certain food. Agriculture will establish amongst them society and laws. They will one day enjoy the advantages of civilized nations. As their islands do not appear to contain any of the precious metals, they will not be reduced to that slavery which would nip their virtues in the bud. After the example of the Greeks, who deified their first benefactors, they will erect monu-

monuments to *George the Third* and *Louis the Sixteenth*. Theſe, indeed, are actions which immortalize Sovereigns, and the remembrance of which is for ever ſacred to poſterity.

Greece, enlightened by the great men who were taught in the ſchools of Memphis and Heliopolis, was divided into ſeveral republics. Each of theſe petty ſtates wiſhed to have commerce and a navy. Tyre continued to ſend forth her veſſels into the whole extent of the Mediterranean, and Kings were decorated with purple. Pſammeticus *(y)*, a friend to the Greeks, opened to them the ports of Egypt. Necos, his ſon, attempted to make a communication between the Nile and the Red Sea. The great obſtacles he met with, and the loſs of a multitude of workmen, made him abandon his project. He then formed another enterprize, which proves to what a degree the maritime art was then carried *(z)*. He fitted out ſome ſhips at Suez, the command of which he entruſted to Phœnician Captains, and ordered them to make the tour of Africa. Theſe ſkilful navigators ſailed out of the Arabic Gulph, *doubled the Cape of Goodhope*, aſcended to the northward, and after three years navigation, arrived at the Pillars of Hercules, from whence they returned to Egypt. This was the firſt time of circumnavigating this great continent. The difficulties of ſo long a voyage, at a time when veſſels were obliged never to loſe ſight of the coaſt,

(y) Herodotus.
(z) Herodotus, lib. 4.

made them abandon this route. They contented themselves with navigating in the Mediterranean and the Indian ocean. The marine of Egypt was then the most powerful, and that country the richest upon earth.

Apriès, the son of Necos, defeated in a naval combat the combined fleets of the Cypriots and the Tyrians, the two most renowned people in the art of navigation. Emboldened by these successes, Amasis sent a fleet to the conquest of Cyprus, and took it. He found there wood and every proper material for ship-building in abundance. This Pharaoh became the master of the Mediterranean. To give more activity to commerce, he called in the Greeks to his states, and permitted them to build Naucrates, almost at the entrance of the Canopic branch. In order to prevent those new allies from extending themselves too far into the country, he restricted their vessels from landing any merchandize but in the harbour of that town *(a)*. The fairs established there, and the continual arrival of ships, rendered it very commercial. The Ionians, the Dorians, the Eolians, built temples there at their joint expence. Whatever their magnificence might have been, they had not the solidity of the Egyptian edifices, and the traveller at this day seeks in vain for their ruins.

The prosperity of this kingdom was at its height. The arts were nearly brought to perfection. Astronomy predicted the eclipses with accuracy. The sculptor engraved fine stones,

(a) Herodotus, lib. 2.

and

and fashioned at his pleasure the hardest marbles. Mechanism elevated in the air masses of an astonishing size. Chymistry stained glass, gave more brilliancy to precious stones *(b)*, and printed indelible colours on stuffs by the means of corrosives. Agriculture had enriched this country with the productions of India, a present which it has subsequently made to Greece, to Italy, and all Europe. Yes, Sir, every time we see bread white as snow, rice, peas, beans, and several other vegetables, we ought to return thanks to the Egyptians; who first communicated these precious gifts to the Greeks, from whence they passed to the Romans, and were by them transmitted to the Gauls.

When famine was exercising its ravages amongst the neighbouring nations, like the children of Jacob they came to Memphis in search of their subsistence. These great advantages were partly owing to the commerce of the Pharaohs, who sent forth their fleets to trade from the Isle of Tatrobane, now called Ceylon, to the distant ports of Spain. The polished nations of Africa and Europe received from them the objects of utility, of luxury, and comfort. It is partly to the prodigious benefits of their trade that one must attribute their admirable works. Never did a nation collect so many treasures, nor cultivate the arts and sciences with more ardour. Never did a nation construct such noble monuments. The gold dust rolled down by the tor-

(*b*) Pliny.

rents of Ethiopia, the pearls of Ormuz, the perfumes of Arabia, the ſtuffs of Bengal arrived at Memphis, become the moſt commercial city upon earth.

Egypt enjoyed this flouriſhing condition, when Cambyſes attacked it with innumerable armies. Amaſis had the imprudence to give cauſe of diſcontent to the militia of the country, by giving the preference to the Grecian troops, and one hundred and fifty thouſand men abandoned their country. The deſertion threw this beautiful kingdom into the hands of the Perſian Monarch, who ravaged it with ſword and fire. Intoxicated with his victory, this ſavage conqueror deſtroyed the academies, and left on thoſe monuments he was unable to overthrow, the barbarous marks which are ſtill viſible. After ſacrificing thouſands of ſoldiers in the mad expedition he undertook againſt the temple of Jupiter Ammon, and the Ethiopians, he left a detachment of his army in Egypt, and returned into Perſia. Commerce ſuffered from his exceſſes, but its eſtabliſhment had taken deep root, and in ſpite of the ſhackles put upon it, it ſtill followed its courſe. Darius, the ſon of Hyſtaſpes, who knew its utility, reſtored it to its priſtine vigour, and favoured it in the whole extent of his empire. He was deſirous even of continuing the canal begun by Necos, and only relinquiſhed the enterprize on the falſe intelligence of his engineer, who informed him that the Red Sea was higher than the Mediterranean, and would conſequently overflow Egypt. Seylax having deſcended

ſcended the river Indus, by his order, diſcovered the coaſts of a part of Aſia, from eaſt to weſt, and after two years navigation, he returned to the Iſthmus of Suez. The diſcoveries he made for the King of the Perſians, determined him to carry his armies into India, where he made great conqueſts. The Egyptians availed themſelves of this opportunity to extend their trade, to repair their loſſes, and to reſtore their marine. They ſerved the ambition of this prince againſt the Greeks *(c)*, furniſhed his armies with proviſions and aſſiſted him in building that memorable bridge which joined the two banks of the Boſphorus, and in the ſea-fight near the Iſle of Eubea, they took five ſhips from the enemy. Their valour and maritime ſkill ſhone in the engagements of Salamin, and of Mycale; but the Republics of Sparta and of Athens were then enflamed by the love of liberty, the firſt and nobleſt of motives, and the great men they produced, withſtood the efforts of Aſia and Africa, conſpired together for their ruin.

In the following century, a prince born with an impetuous character, an elevated genius, and an undaunted courage, by fighting againſt Greece learnt the art of conquering all the nations of the world. Having attained the throne, he put himſelf at the head of forty thouſand men, overthrew the Satraps of Aſia Minor, deſtroyed haughty Tyre, which refuſed to acknowledge any maſter, and turned his arms againſt Egypt.

(*c*) Herodotus, lib. 4.

That nation ſupported with impatience the Perſian yoke. She ſubmitted willingly to Alexander, and the country was conquered without battle. Charmed with his reception amongſt the Egyptians, and intoxicated with the flattering promiſes of the Oracle of Ammon (*d*), he left them the ſame form of government and the ſame religion. This great prince, whoſe mind had been cultivated by a philoſopher, and whoſe ambitious views embraced the empire of the world, did not wiſh to conquer, in order to deſtroy. To ſecure Egypt, whoſe importance he felt, he founded there a large city, encompaſſed by three harbours, fit to receive the fleets of Greece, and the merchandize of all nations. He traced out himſelf the commercial plan which was to unite together the diſperſed members of his vaſt dominions; but he was carried off in the flower of his age, and paſſed like a torrent on the earth. His generals divided his ſpoils, and became powerful monarchs. Ptolemy, ſon of Lagus, having received Egypt for his ſhare, endeavoured to carry into execution the great projects of his maſter. He called the merchants of Syria and Greece into the city of Alexandria. The unremitting favour he ſhewed them, rendered his kingdom flouriſhing, and furniſhed him the means of engaging his enemies with advantage, and of conquering the Iſle of Cyprus. The Rhodians, his faithful allies, having refuſed to join their fleets with thoſe of Antigonus to

(*d*) Quintus Curtius.

make

make war againſt him, were beſieged by Demetrius Poliercetes. The powerful ſuccours of corn and naval ſtores ſent them by Ptolemy, aided them greatly in triumphing over that renowned warrior. Gratitude induced them to beſtow the name of *Soter* or Saviour on their defender.

Amidſt the tumult of arms, the firſt of the Ptolemies occupied himſelf with zeal in the proſperity of his new government. The approach to Egypt was extremely dangerous from the lowneſs of its coaſt. Veſſels were frequently daſhed on ſhore by tempeſts, before they were able to diſcover it. He built on the Iſle of Pharos, that ſuperb tower which overtopped the ſeas, and on which was written in large characters: *To the Saviour Gods, for the utility of navigation.* The white marble it was compoſed of, made it diſtinguiſhable from a great diſtance in the day time. At night, a lantern was lighted on it to direct the veſſels in their courſe. All antiquity has celebrated this magnificent work. It is thus too that the French will bleſs the memory of a protecting king, who is conſtructing a noble harbour in the middle of the waves. Poſterity will one day ſay, on beholding *whole ſquadrons* in ſafety, behind piers miraculouſly formed at Cherbourg, by a ſkilful engineer; *Here Louis* XVI. *enchained the waves of the ocean.*

Alexandria, by her ports ſituated to the weſt, the north, and ſouth, received the merchandize of the whole univerſe. She was, as Strabo calls her, the greateſt market in the world. Not content

content with these attentions, Ptolemy erected an academy, the learned men of which, by his orders, went to visit the different countries of the earth, to examine their riches and their productions. The monarchs of France have in our days imitated this brilliant example, by sending academicians from the Pole to the Equator, to measure degrees of the globe, and acquire useful knowledge for geography and navigation. Notwithstanding the wars in which the son of Lagus was engaged against Syria, he collected manuscripts from all parts to compose that famous library, the deplorable fate of which still excites our regret. The monuments of this prince have perished, but his glory is immortal, since at the same time that he was chasing the enemy from the frontiers of his dominions, he was indefatigable in securing the happiness of his people.

Ptolemy Philadelphus marched in the footsteps of his father, and rendered Egypt fruitful and happy. The pomp he displayed on his accession to the throne, proves the extent of the commerce of this kingdom. Athenæus describes it at length. I shall only select the leading traits. The productions of every climate were there seen collected together. The procession was opened by women slaves of Asia and Africa, dressed after the manner of their respective countries. They were followed by camels laden with frankincense, saffron, cinnamon, and precious aromatics. A band of Ethiopians carried four hundred

hundred elephants teeth and a great quantity of ebony. The Abyssinians were loaded with the gold dust which they gathered on the sides of their torrents. The Indians displayed to the eyes of the people the pearls, the diamonds, and the varied riches of their climate. A number of rare animals was led in procession by their keepers. The most beautiful birds of Africa, the sheep of Abyssinia, of the Yemen, and of Greece; the oxen of India, of the most brilliant whiteness; bears from the north; leopards, panthers, the lynx, the giraffe, the rhinoceros, decorated the cavalcade. These different objects can only be met with in a country which traffics with all the nations of the world.

Ptolemy Philadelphus, either better acquainted with the level of the sea, or more fortunate than Necos and Darius, continued the canal which was to join the Nile to the Red Sea, and had the glory of compleating it. He began at the Pelusiac branch, and extended it as far as Arsinoé, now called *Aggerout* (*e*). The waters were prevented from rushing into it too violently, by sluices placed at the entrance. It was made to pass by lakes which fed it, and served as resting places for the boats. History does not inform us whether this canal was of any great benefit to commerce; but as it was necessary to arrive there, to run along the whole length of the Arabic gulph, the extremity of which is very nar-

(*e*) Aggerout is at this day two leagues from the port of Suez. This is the space the Arabic Gulph has retired since the reign of Ptolemy Philadelphus.

row

row and extremely dangerous, Ptolemy opened another route for the merchants. He founded a city in the latitude of Sienna, and on the coast of the Red Sea, to which he gave the name of Berenice his mother. From that city to Cophtis, he constructed reservoirs, and places where the caravans found refreshment in the middle of the deserts. It was twelve days journey across burning sands, and Berenice presented nothing but an open shore exposed to every wind. These inconveniencies determined navigators in the end to repair to the port of Rat, now *Cosseir*, where they found good anchorage. From that period, the trade with India has been carried on by the way I have already described to you.

To protect the Egyptian merchants, the Ptolemies kept up a formidable navy in the Red Sea and the Mediterranean. Theocritus *(f)* assures us that they had ninety-seven ships of the first size, several of which were two hundred feet long, beside a multitude of small vessels, and four thousand barks, destined to convey their orders through the whole extent of their empire. It was by such means that Ptolemy Philadelphus extended his conquests very far into Ethiopia and the Yemen, and that he saw thirty-three thousand cities submitted to his sway. These facts would appear incredible, were they not attested by writers worthy of belief, and did we not know to what a degree of splendor commerce can raise a state, or were we unacquainted with

(*f*) Theocritus, Idyll. 17.

the infinite resources an enlightened Emperor might derive from the situation of Egypt, communicating with two seas, and possessed of the treasures of an inexhaustible soil.

Ptolemy Evergetes imitated the example of his predecessors, and founded his power on trade. He encouraged it with all his might, maintained fleets on the Red Sea, subjugated several of the Homerite Kings who reigned in Arabia Felix, enjoined them to look after the security of the highways, and powerfully protected the caravans against the Arabs. During his reign the wealth of the Egyptians was at its height. This abundance of gold, and goods of every kind, produced at Alexandria prodigious luxury, and corrupted the Court of the Kings. Men in general preserve their virtue best in mediocrity. Misfortune elevates their minds, and gives full scope for energy; but the excess of prosperity enervates, and by opening to them the door of the vices, closes on them that of happiness. The Ptolemies, at the pinnacle of power, resigned themselves to effeminacy and cowardice, and to a general relaxation, which influenced the manners of their subjects; for the corruption of states takes its rise invariably with the great; the fourth of these Princes, however, performed some meritorious actions. At the request of the Rhodians, he restored to liberty Andromachus, father of Achæus, Sovereign of part of Asia Minor, who had entered into a league with the Byzantines, to exact a duty on all vessels which should pass the Dardanelles. Achæus, from gratitude

tude for this bounty, detached himſelf from his allies, who renounced their pretenſions, and commerce, freed from this impediment, reſumed its uſual courſe. He maintained alſo the navy erected by his anceſtors, and augmented it. Under his empire were veſſels conſtructed of a prodigious ſize, and which have never ſince been equalled. Plutarch (*g*) deſcribes one of his gallies which had forty rows of oars, was three hundred and ſeventy feet long, and ſixty-four in elevation at the ſtern. This enormous veſſel, by the ſide of which our three-decked ſhips of war would appear only as ſmall frigates, contained four hundred ſailors to hand the ſails and rigging, four thouſand rowers, and about three thouſand ſoldiers deſtined for battle. The art of ſhip-building and navigation muſt have been brought to great perfection amongſt the Egyptians, to form and put in motion ſuch immenſe ſhips which muſt have reſembled floating cities.

The reigns of the remainder of the Ptolemies preſent nothing but a ſcene of unbridled luxury in the capital, and Princes abandoned to every exceſs; but even theſe facts demonſtrate the treaſures they muſt have drawn from commerce, ſince, in the midſt of their prodigious expences, the country was rich and flouriſhing. From the boſom of the pleaſures they were plunged in, they ſtill at intervals beſtowed ſome attention on its advantages. Ptolemy Phyſcon ſent Eudoxus,

(*g*) Plutarch's Life of Demetrius.

the

the Cyſicenian, on an embaſſy to ſeveral of the Potentates of India. The reports of this celebrated navigator added to the knowledge they already had of thoſe countries, and gave a new ſpur to the avidity of the merchants. They made freſh expeditions to the eaſt, and penetrated by the Ganges even into Bengal. After the King's death, his widow, Cleopatra, ordered Eudoxus to viſit the nations at the extremity of Africa. He embarked on the Red Sea, and viſited the inhabitants of the coaſt of Soffala. Having found on the beach the prow of a veſſel which was known to be of Cadiz, he formed the project of coaſting along the ſhores of this great continent. On his return to Egypt he found on the throne Ptolemy Lathyrus, by whom he was not liked, and he attempted therefore an enterprize which he had meditated. He ſailed out of the ſtraits of Babelmandel, doubled the point of Africa, and returned to the Pillars of Hercules. This was the ſecond time of performing this hardy voyage. In thoſe ages when there was no compaſs to direct the mariner's courſe, we may eaſily conceive how difficult ſuch an undertaking muſt have been, and what talents and intrepidity were neceſſary to ſurmount the obſtacles and perils to which he was expoſed. This voyage was then leſs eaſy of execution than the circumnavigation of the globe is at the preſent day.

Under Ptolemy IX. the merchants of Alexandria continued to navigate the Black Sea to Spain, in the Perſian Gulph, and even to the extremities

extremities of India. It was no longer to the wiſe adminiſtration of theſe Kings that Egypt owed her extenſive commerce; but it had been eſtabliſhed on ſuch ſolid foundations, that when they did not ſtraighten it exceſſively, it followed the regular routine.

During the war of Alexandria, carried on for ſome time by Ptolemy XII. againſt Julius Cæſar, that General burnt one hundred and ten large veſſels, yet the Egyptians ſtill had reſoures to equip a fleet capable of making head againſt the enemy; but who could reſiſt the ſublime talents of Cæſar? The Alexandrians made but a feeble ſtand againſt the conqueror of the Gauls. It was reſerved to a woman to triumph over this great great man. The famous Cleopatra overcame the victor, and entangled him in her net by irreſiſtible charms. This queen diſplayed during her whole life a magnificence and a prodigality, of which hiſtory does not afford us a ſecond example *(b)*. Summoned by Antony, then at Tarſus, in Cilicia, to render an account of her conduct, ſhe ſet out to wait on the Roman General. Having traverſed the Mediterranean, ſhe aſcended the river Cydnus in a veſſel, the brilliant deſcription of which reſembles what the poets tell us of the ſhell of Venus. The ſails were of purple, the head and the ſides ſparkled with gold. Plates of ſilver covered the oars, which were moved in cadence to the ſound of inſtruments. The Queen, careleſsly reclined under a canopy

(b) Plutarch's Life of Antony.

enriched with gold and jewels of an inestimable value, had adapted her dress to the richness of the vessel. Pearls, diamonds, and the richest habits, veiled her charms, without hiding them.—Like the Goddess of Cytherea, she was surrounded by a crowd of children, dressed in the manner of Cupids. With their fans they cooled the air, breathed by this new Divinity, whilst clouds of perfumes, which were perpetually burning, embalmed both the banks of the river. Antony, who wished to punish Cleopatra, soon experienced the power of her charms. He forgot that he was her Judge, to become her lover. Nor did the Queen of Egypt owe her victory only to her beauty; she had a great deal of understanding, and of the most ornamental kind. She knew all the languages of the eastern world. Speaking perfectly the Greek, Ethiopian, Hebrew, Parthian, Syriac, and Persian, she used to converse with the foreigners who were perpetually arriving at Alexandria, each of them in his native language. That city, since the fall of Carthage and of Corinth, was become the centre of the commerce of the world *(i)*. There were reckoned in it three hundred thousand free persons, and at least double the number of slaves.

Cleopatra had chained Cæsar and Antony to her car; but having made the same attempt in vain on Augustus, a cold and artful man, and dreading to adorn the triumphal pomp of this fastidious conqueror, she killed herself. Egypt

(*i*) Diodorus Siculus, lib. 1.

passed

passed under the dominion of the Romans. This conquest was for Rome, what Peru has been for Spain, and what Bengal is now for England. It diffused gold and silver there in such abundance, that lands, merchandize, and every article, doubled their prices. It hastened the downfal of that empire.

Deprived of their monarchs, and subjected to the Romans, the Egyptians became their factors. The people of Italy entered with ardour into the trade with India, which, according to Pliny, rendered *one hundred fold*. Their voyages were conducted by their guides. Some entering the Indus, penetrated into the interior of the country; others traded to the ports of the isle of Ceylon; and others again, doubling Cape Comorin, ascended the Ganges as far as Palibotra *(k)*, a powerful city with which the Egyptians had long carried on a great commerce, and where there was a general concourse of all the nations of the eastern world. They brought back with them cotton, and silk stuffs, of which Augustus wore the first dresses. After his example, the Romans became much addicted to the luxury of dress; and pearls, diamonds, and perfumes, became objects of necessity. Now that the mulberry-tree and the silk-worm are transplanted to Europe, precious stuffs unknown to the Roman Consuls, decorate men of every condition; we have not, however, yet attained the quality of those of Bengal, nor the unalterable permanency of their colours. Perhaps the little Indian colo-

(k) Strabo, lib. 15.

ny, which an Admiral *(Mr. de Suffrein)* whoſe virtues, whoſe talents, and whoſe victories, do honour to France, has tranſported into our country, may reveal to our artiſts the ſecrets of the Oriental countries.

In proportion as the Romans extended the limits of their empire, they adopted the uſages and the vices of the conquered people. Egypt, of all the kingdoms ſo circumſtanced, was that which influenced the moſt their manners, becauſe it procured them the greateſt riches. The beautiful linen and cotton manufactured at Alexandria, her magnificent tapeſtry, her chryſtals of various colours, were conveyed to Rome.—— The grain of the Thebais, and her abundant productions, fed the capital of Italy. From that period ſhe no longer ſtood in need of manufactures; from that period ſhe ceaſed to encourage the labours of the huſbandman. In a few years ſhe was environed with immenſe parks and ſuperb gardens. In thoſe places where the Dictators had not diſdained to conduct the plough; on thoſe ſpots where they had dwelt under ruſtic roofs, ſprang up places ornamented with flowery lawns, caſcades, and delightful groves. Aſiatic effeminacy enervated the vigour of theſe fierce Republicans. In vain did wiſe Emperors ſtrive to ſtem the torrent. The maſters of the world had taſted the charms of inactive life; the different nations paid them tributes; the corn of Egypt rendered it unneceſſary for them to cultivate their lands. They fondly imagined that they had nothing to do but to enjoy the homage of the world,

world, and the labours of the conquered nations. Liberty, the laſt ray of which was ſtifled by Auguſtus, gave place to ſlavery. All the vices that follow in her train boldly reared their heads, and the Romans became leſs jealous of commanding, than eager after feaſts and ſpectacles. The thirſt of gold completed their corruption. Every thing at Rome was venal; ſoldiers and armies muſt be bought, and even the empire was expoſed to ſale by the Pretorians.

Conſtantine tranſported the ſeat of it from Rome, and it was not long in being divided. The partition of this great dominion was followed by its deſtruction; that of the weſt fell firſt, becauſe it wanted the eſſentials which form the permanence of ſtates, agriculture, and manners. Italy was nothing but a garden. Its inhabitants, enfeebled by luxury, were unable to reſiſt the efforts of the Barbarians, who attacked it on all ſides. Egypt long ſupported the tottering throne of the Emperors of Byzantium. In ſpite of the ſeverities exerciſed by ſeveral of them upon her; in ſpite of the contractors who eſtabliſhed a deſtructive monopoly in that country, ſuch as is renewed in our days in great cities, where fortunes are infinitely diſproportioned, commerce ſtill continued to enrich her. She furniſhed her Sovereigns with great reſources againſt the different people who were contending for their deſtruction. Cous, in poſſeſſion of the trade of India, flouriſhed for ſeveral ages, and became the rival of Alexandria; her fleets had not loſt the route of Bengal; they ſtill went thither to load the merchandize

merchandize in request throughout the rest of the empire: but the time was at hand when the glory of this country must fall with commerce, agriculture, and the arts.

Mahomet, born with a genius calculated to change the face of the earth, created for the people of Arabia a religion which was to unite their tribes dispersed throughout the deserts, and arm them against the rest of the world. Emboldened by his successes, he sent Ambassadors to the Emperors of Persia, of Constantinople, of Abyssinia, and the Governor of Memphis, to invite them to embarce Islamism, or to pay him a tribute. There is not in the annals of history the example of so bold a mission. He must have been regarded as a madman, had he not possessed resources in his own mind capable of supporting this audacious enterprize. But his travels had taught him the weakness of the neighbouring nations, and he knew that the warriors educated in his school could undertake and execute every thing. The Greeks having slain one of his Envoys, he armed three thousand men. After this handful of men had traversed the solitudes of desert Arabia, Khaled seeing the three Generals, named by the Prophet, perish, put himself at the head of the Arabs, and by prodigies of valour overthrew one hundred thousand Greeks. Encouraged by this expedition, Mahomet set out with thirty thousand men, and reduced the whole country as far as the frontiers of Syria. Death terminated the course of his exploits; but his successors, animated by his example, and burning with the enthuſiaſtic fire he had communicated to them, overſet the neighbouring thrones, and conquered Egypt and a part of the Eaſt.

Egypt, become a province of the empire of the Caliphs, gradually loſt her commerce and the arts. The learned men eſcaped to Conſtantinople, and into the Grecian Iſlands. The fervour of the firſt Mahometans not permitting them to form any connections with the Chriſtian Princes, they neglected the commerce of the Mediterranean, and confined themſelves to that of the Red Sea, and the interior of the country. Agriculture, however, ſtill flouriſhed, and ſome of the Arab Princes encouraged the ſciences. At length the Venetians found means to open for themſelves the ports of this country, and to keep Conſuls there. They even obtained permiſſion to eſtabliſh in the internal cities, and carried on the trade with India under the protection of the Egyptians. They derived very great advantages from it, and became the firſt navigators of Europe, which they furniſhed with all the productions of Aſia and Africa. The Genoeſe partook with them for ſome time of theſe advantages; but the marine of the Venetians having rapidly encreaſed, reigned triumphant in the Mediterranean. Inſpired by their ſucceſs, they took advantage of the ruins of the Greeks to deſpoil the Ottoman Porte of ſome fragments of their empire. Having taken the Morea, Candia, and ſeveral iſlands of the Archipelago, they ſent their ſquadrons to the very ſtreight of the Dardanelles, and humbled the pride of the Creſcent.

At

At the battle of Lepantum, they fought, with their allies, the whole naval forces of the Turks. This Republic, enriched by the commerce of the Red Sea and India, ſaved Italy, and was for two centuries the bulwark of Chriſtendom.

Commercial Venice had nearly attained the ſummit of her proſperity, whilſt a courageous nation, excited by a Prince verſed in geography and aſtronomy, was endeavouring to open a new route to India. Henry, brother of the King of Portugal, knew, from hiſtory, that it was impoſſible to ſail round Africa. He fitted out ſeveral veſſels which, by the aid of the compaſs, diſcovered the weſtern Iſles and the Canaries. One of his Captains advanced as far as the Cape which terminates Africa; he was there aſſailed by furious winds, called it the *Cape of the Tempeſt*, and returned home. The Prince changed this name into that of *Good Hope*. Theſe attempts, ſo long fruitleſs, muſt give us a high idea of the art of navigation amongſt the Egyptians, ſince they had twice executed that enterprize without any other guide than the ſtars and their own genius. The glory of doubling this famous Cape was at length reſerved for Vaſco de Gama, a Portugueze Gentleman, who arrived on the coaſt of Malabar, and returned in triumph to Liſbon. The precious ſtones he brought back from his expedition, the pompous deſcription he gave of the treaſures of the Indian Kings, inflamed the Portugueze, and in a few years they conquered Cochin, Goa, and ſeveral other cities, from whence they drew immenſe riches.

The Ottomans had taken Egypt from the Arabs. Excited by the Venetians, who furniſhed them with wood for ſhip-building, and other materials, with which they equipped a fleet on the Red Sea, they tried to put a ſtop to the conqueſts of the Portugueze, and to drive them from their new ſettlements. Albuquerque, who then governed them, fought gloriouſly the Ottoman fleet, penetrated into the Arabian Gulph, and determined to deſtroy Egypt. Having concluded a treaty with the Emperor of Abyſſinia, he engaged him to turn the waters of the Nile into the Red Sea. To what horrors does ambition lead men! To ſecure to his nation the excluſive commerce of India, this Admiral did not heſitate to make four millions of inhabitants periſh, by converting their country into a frightful deſert. After what we have ſeen in theſe letters, on the poſſibility of diverting the courſe of the Nile, we have a right to preſume that the enterprize was practicable. Fortunately for Egypt, death carried off the impetuous Albuquerque, and the Emperor of Abyſſinia did not carry his infamous project into execution.

Whilſt the Portugueze were diſputing with the Venetians and the Egyptians the riches of the weſtern world, the Spaniards, led by the genius of Columbus, had diſcovered America. But their ambitious views were not to be limited by the poſſeſſion of the new world. The Liſbon mariners, following the path of Vaſco de Gama, touched on the coaſt of Malabar, and penetrated into the Indian Archipelago. The navigators from

from Cadiz made the Moluccas. These two rival nations setting out at nearly the same time from the same country, and each of them traversing half the circumference of the globe, arriving from opposite quarters, met together at the extremity of the world. They jointly partook of the treasures of these climates, not without bedewing them with their blood and that of the wretched inhabitants of the Celebes, whom, after reducing them to slavery, they rivalled each other in plundering. The aromatics, the spices, the gold and diamonds, with which they returned laden, awakened from their stupor the other Courts of Europe, which had rejected as a dream the glorious projects of the immortal Columbus. England and France formed a marine, and were desirous of participating in the new discoveries. This was the æra of the fall of Venice. The trade of Egypt and of India was the foundation of her power. The loss of this source of wealth plunged her into that insignificance from whence she had originally sprung. The ruin of her marine followed that of her commerce, and disabled her from defending her distant provinces. The Turks wrested from her the Morea, Candia, and the isles she held in the Archipelago. At present no more remains to her than one or two rocks, which the Porte leaves her, because they are of no utility.

At this day that the maritime powers of Europe found the prosperity of their states on the basis of commerce, each of them strives to incline the balance in her own favour. Russia, too high to the northward to send her fleets to India, by the Cape of Good Hope, and so enter into competition with the nations more favourably situated, is opening herself a route known to the Romans and the Genoese. She makes her ships descend by the Volga to the Caspian Sea, and her merchants endeavour to draw towards them the merchandize of Persia, and the northern provinces of the Mogul empire. The beautiful silks of the Guilan have already become objects of their speculations, and Catherine II. will, doubtless on the first revolution, become mistress of those rich countries. On the other side, England, France, and Holland, provide Europe with the productions of the east. The English, above all, having formed in Bengal a kingdom of a vast extent, are become, so to speak, the masters of this commerce, and dispute with all the other nations the glory of navigation.

In this state of things, Egypt, without arts, without a marine, and groaning under the tyranny of four and twenty Beys, is unable to derive any advantage from her situation, or to enter into competition with the Europeans. Her ignorant mariners no longer navigate to India; scarcely do they dare to make the circuits of the Red Sea. Their most distant expeditions are an annual voyage to Moka. Their Saiks ill equipped, and incapable of defence, load there the coffee of Yemen, the perfumes of Arabia, the pearls of the Baharem Isles, the muslins, and the linens of Bengal, which are brought them

by

by the Banians. Even this limited commerce procures them great advantages. The coffee which they buy at eight sols (or four-pence English) a pound at Moka, they sell at Cairo for thirty. This article alone is an annual object of eleven millions of livres. They export the principal part of it to Constantinople, into Greece, to Marseilles, and to the coast of Syria. The remainder is consumed in the country.

The English have already attempted to deprive them of this branch of commerce; but the Egyptians complained to the Government, and strenuously opposed them. When Ali Bey had established the safety of the caravans, and laid open Egypt to foreign merchants, some English ships touched at Suez, laden with Bengal stuffs, of which they made a very advantageous sale. *Political views* have again prohibited them from carrying on this traffic, and the Egyptians have retained possession of it. But without a marine, what can a people do against the European squadrons? They must inevitably, sooner or later, submit to receive from foreigners those precious effects, which they import at such heavy expence from Moka, and which can be furnished them much cheaper. Besides, means might be found to obtain from them the permission of undertaking this lucrative conveyance.

Egypt, however, notwithstanding her decline, may again appear with splendor amidst the powerful nations, because she contains within herself the source of genuine riches. Her abundance

dance of grain, with which ſhe feeds Arabia, Syria, and a part of the Archipelago; her rice, which ſhe ſends throughout the Mediterranean, and even to Marſeilles; the flower of the Chartame, with which the inhabitants of Provence yearly load ſeveral veſſels; her ſal-ammoniac which is conveyed throughout Europe; the kali produced there in abundance, her beautiful flax in ſuch requeſt in Italy; her linens, dyed blue, which ſerve a part of her neighbours for cloathing; all theſe objects, the produce of her own territory, ſtill procure her money from the principal part of the nations which trade with her. The Abyſſinians bring her gold-duſt, elephants teeth, and other precious ſubſtances, which they barter for her produce. The clothes, the lead, the arms, and ſome gold and ſilver lace of Lyons, exported thither by France are by no means ſufficient to pay the various articles ſhe receives in exchange. She pays the reſt with piaſtres of Conſtantinople. The copper veſſels, and the furs landed by the Turks in the port of Alexandria, do not balance the corn, the rice, the lentils, the coffee, the perfumes, they load there, which are chiefly paid for in ſpecie. In a word, excepting at Moka, and at Mecca, where the Egyptians leave every year a great quantity of ſequins, all thoſe who carry on a trade with them bring them gold and ſilver. Theſe precious materials are ſtill in ſuch abundance in the country, that Ali Bey, on flying into Spain, carried with him twenty-four millions of livres (a million

ſterling)

ſterling) and Iſmael Bey, who a few years after eſcaped in the ſame way, loaded 50 camels with ſequins, pataques (*k*), pearls, and precious ſtones.

If Egypt, deſtitute of a marine and manufactures, and nearly reduced to the mere advantages of her ſoil, ſtill poſſeſſes ſuch great riches, judge, Sir, what ſhe is capable of becoming in the hands of an enlightened people. What cloths might be manufactured with the beautiful wool of her ſheep! What linen with her delicate flax! What muſlins with the two different ſorts of cotton which grow there, one annual, the other perennial! What ſtuffs, with the ſilks which it would be ſo eaſy to introduce into a country, where the ſilk-worms could not but thrive, under a ſky free from rain and tempeſts! What an affluence of benefits might there not be procured by clearing the canals, repairing the dykes, and by reſtoring to agriculture the third part of her lands now buried under the ſands? With what ſucceſs might not her mines of emeralds be explored, ſo famous for their hardneſs, equalling almoſt that of the diamond? The granite, the porphiry, and the alabaſter, which are found in ſeveral of her mountains, would alſo form a valuable branch of commerce. With what utility the manufacturer might employ her indigo, her chartame, and other materials for dying, ſpread over her deſerts! Theſe advantages, Sir, are not chimerical. Egypt has poſſeſſed them for many ages. A wiſe Ad-

(*k*) A piece of money worth five ſhillings.

ministration would restore to her all the treasures that nature has lavished on her. Such, Sir, are the vicissitudes which the commerce of this country has experienced from the most remote antiquity down to the present day. Its former brilliant state cannot fail of leaving on your mind a forcible impression of what it still is capable of becoming.

I have the honour to be, &c.

LETTER XLVIII.

OF THE ANCIENT RELIGION OF THE EGYPTIANS, AND PARTICULARLY OF ATHOR, ONE OF THEIR DEITIES.

Athor, or the night, in the opinion of the Egyptian priests, represented the darkness which enveloped the chaos before the creation, which the creative spirit animated with its breath, and of which it formed the universe. The moon regarded as a symbol of this original darkness, and recommended to the veneration of the people. This idea extended to that period of time when the sun, during his progress through the signs of the southern hemisphere, renders the days shorter and the nights more long.

To Mr. L. M.

Grand Cairo.

RELIGION, Sir, is born with man. She is the daughter of necessity and gratitude.—— Placed on a globe where experience makes him feel his weakness every moment, he seeks for protectors who are able to defend his life from the dangers that surround him. When he has not been favoured with revelation, those objects which forcibly strike his attention, from which he receives great benefits, and which he dreads the most, alternately attract his veneration. He addresses his prayers to the sun, to the sea, to tem-

tempests, to rivers, and erects altars to them.—The less he is acquainted with the phenomena of nature, the more readily does he attribute them to superior beings. All the people of the earth have, under different names, adopted these invisible spirits, either to obtain their protection, or to divert their wrath; for it belongs only to man, enlightened by a sublime philosophy, to acknowledge one only first cause in the universe, and to regard the plurality of gods as absurd and contradictory. I am persuaded however, that prejudiced and superficial writers have frequently calumniated the worship of nations, by making them adore an insensible stone or vile animals.—The marble sculptured by their hands, the ox consecrated by religion, were emblems only of the divinity to whom they addressed their vows, similar to the statutes and images which fill our temples, which are no more than representations of the saints, or of the god for whom our incense burns. If the islanders of Otaheite, scarcely in any degree civilized, esteem their Bananas, and the animals deposited within their *Morais*, as offerings only to their *Eatoas (l)*, what should make us imagine that the Egyptians worshipped as gods the onion and the crocodile *(m)*? This

(l) Invisible gods of the inhabitants of the South Sea. See Cook.

(m) Herodotus, Strabo, Diodorus Siculus, Ælian, all speak of the sacred animals of Egypt. None of them bestow the name of gods on them. On the contrary, they expressly regard them as living images which remind the people of the deities to whom they are consecrated.

opinion,

opinion, destitute of foundation, can never be entertained for a moment by a sensible people. Is it possible that this people who were stiled wise, *per excellentiam*, who cultivated the sciences with such success, amongst whom Solon resided to collect the beautiful code of laws he gave to the Athenians, where Plato learnt to acknowledge the immortality of the soul, could ever adopt so barbarous a theology? No, Sir, the philosophers of Egypt have never deified animals; they have not even, like the Greeks, raised their heroes to the rank of Gods. Their religion was founded on astronomy, and the phænomena of nature.—But they placed above the stars an invisible being, to whom they attributed the wonderful harmony which pervades the universe. It is true that the vulgar, whose feeble sight cannot raise itself beyond sensible objects, frequently adored the symbol instead of the divinity. I shall attempt to unveil their religious opinions. The learned Jablonski has done this before me with great success. I shall tread in his foot-steps, and shall bring in testimony passages from the gravest historians of antiquity; for in a matter of such importance, as little scope shall be given as possible to imagination, to hazard, and conjecture.

One of the most ancient divinities of Egypt is *Athor*, which in the Coptic language signifies night (*n*). The priests did not originally indicate by this name the obscurity which reigns on the setting of the sun, but that darkness spread over

(*n*) Jablonski, Pantheon Ægyptiacum, tome premier.

chaos

choas previous to the creation, which the eternal Being animated with his breath, and from which he drew forth every being. This myſterious night was in their opinion the origin of things (*o*). Damaſcius, in ſpeaking of the theology of the ancient Egyptians, ſays: "They "eſtabliſhed as the firſt principle, that darkneſs "which the human underſtanding is unable to "comprehend, and which they celebrate three "times in their ſacred hymns." Sanchoniathon, impreſſed with this doctrine, ſays: "Mortals "were created from the wind *Kolpia* and his "ſpouſe *Baaou* (*p*)." Kolpia, a Hebrew word, ſignifies the breath of God, and Baaou, the void*. Thus it is the voice of the Creator which brings beings into exiſtence. This theology differs little from that of Geneſis, where the prophet thus expreſſes himſelf (*q*); "And the earth was with-"out form, and void; and darkneſs was upon "the face of the deep, and the ſpirit, (*or breath*) of God was upon the waters." Simplicius (*r*) accordingly pretends, that theſe words, *The Creator called the light, day, and the darkneſs, night,* were borrowed from the Egyptians; but ſhould Moſes even have adopted this doctrine from the prieſts of Memphis, as he has diſengaged it from all the abſurdities which enveloped it, it would be

(*o*) Damaſcius, quoted by Cudworth.

(*p*) Jablonſki, tome premier.

* Blackerel tranſlated from Sanchoniathon—*Colpias*, the voice of the mouth of God, and his ſpouſe *Baa* or *Bohou*, darkneſs or night. *Tranſlator.*

(*q*) Geneſis, chap. i.

(*r*) Ariſtotle's Phyſics, book 8.

the

the lefs divine*. This ancient people, defcended from Mifraim, the grandfon of Noah, might, as well as the Hebrews, have received the light of revelation from their common father. If they had obfcured its purity, the chief of the Ifraelites has reftored it to its proper luftre.

Orpheus, initiated in the myfteries of the Egyptians, firft conveyed into Greece their religious opinions, and fung them in harmonious verfes. "At the beginning of the word," faid he, "ap-" peared Æther, created by God; from her bo-" fom proceeded Chaos and the dark night. She " covered every thing that was below Æther." In the dialogue between Jupiter and the night, the poet availing himfelf of his privilege perfonifies her, and makes the Creator fay *(f)*: "Nurfe of " the gods, immortal night——How fhall I pro-" ceed with wifdom to the creation of the im-" mortal gods? How fhall I contrive to make the " univerfe one great whole, and each thing exift " feparately? *Night*. Surround the creation with " the immenfe æther, place the heavens in the " middle, and in the heavens the earth encom-" paffed by the fea, and ftars to compofe its " crown."

The Greeks eagerly received the religion fung by Orpheus. It flowed from the primitive ideas which the ancient Egyptians had of the origin of the world. The natural philofophers covered it

* A learned prelate well obferves: "That the fables which " were profane in other nations, were *fanctified* in *Syria*, and " confirmed by God himfelf!" *Tranflator.*

(*f*) See Efchenbach.

with

with a veil impenetrable to the people, and the poets having perſonified the elements, compoſed of them a fabulous Theogony, through which it was difficult to diſcover the truth, concealed under ſo many veils. The religious opinions of Egypt, however, long prevailed in the temples of Greece. Pauſanias, viſiting that country, ſaw at Megara *The Oracle of the Night*, where they taught probably every thing reſpecting *Athor*.

This ſymbolical deity, by which the Egyptians characterized the poſſible principle of things, became in the language of the Greek philoſophers, Venus, or the mother of the world. It was ſtill Orpheus who taught them this compariſon (*t*): "I ſhall ſing the Night, Mother of Gods and "Men, Night the origin of all created things, "and we ſhall call her Venus." The poets ſoon got poſſeſſion of this metaphyſical idea, and as they muſt have a deity fit to embelliſh their poems, they made her ſpring from the froth of the ſea, excelling in beauty, and created her goddeſs of Pleaſures. She animated the world; ſhe gave life to every thing that breathed, and Ovid celebrated her power in the following allegorical verſes:

The

(*t*) Jablonſki, tome premier.

(*u*) Venus rules the univerſe with her glorious ſceptre.
No divinity equals her power.
She gives laws to heaven, to the earth, and to the teeming waters.
She preſerves all beings by uniting the ſexes.
All the gods owe their exiſtence to her.
She makes the trees to grow, and matures the harveſts.

See

The Egyptian priests who had painted Night as a divinity, from whose bosom the Eternal had drawn forth all its creatures, aware that the minds of the vulgar required sensible objects, proposed to their veneration the moon in the midst of darkness. Doubtless they at first taught that this planet was only the emblem of the night, and a sign of the divine power; but as it often happens that the image effaces the divinity, the people addressed their prayers to the moon and erected altars to her.

The philosophers still farther extended this doctrine. They bestowed the name of Night, of Athor, of Venus, on the period when the Sun having passed the Equator, remains in the Southern Hemisphere, because then the days are the shortest, and the nights the longest. "The "natural philosophers *(x)*," says Macrobius, "have honoured with the name of Venus, the

See also *Lucretius.*

Alma VENUS cœli subter labentia signa
Quæ mare navigerum, quæ terras frugiferenteis
Concelebras; per TE quoniam genus omne animantum
Concipitur, visitque extortum lumina SOLIS:
Nam simul ac SPECIES patefacta est verna dieï,
Et reserata viget *genitalis*, aura favoni
Aëreæ primum volucres, te DIVA, tuumque
Significant *initium*, percussæ corda tuâ vi ——
Omnibus incutiens blandum per pectora amorem
Efficis ut cupide generatim sæcla propagent.

LUCRET.

Translator.

(*u*) Ovid, De fastibus, lib. 4.
(*x*) Lib. i. chap. 21.

" upper, and with the name of Proferpine, the " lower Hemifphere. The Phœnicians and the " Affyrians reprefent the former goddefs in tears, " when the fun, paffing through the twelve figns " of the Zodiac, enters the Southern Hemi- " fphere. All the time he remains there, and " renders the days fhorter, they pretend that " Venus weeps the abfence of the god carried off " by a temporary death, and detained by Profer- " pine. We fee her ftatue on Mount Lebanon; " (it is the celebrated Venus of Aphacitis) fhe has " her head veiled, and her countenance forrow- " ful. Befides that this ftatue reprefents the " afflicted goddefs, it is alfo the fymbol of winter.

The following paffage proves that this opinion came from Egypt *(y)*: " In the month of " Athyr (z), the Egyptians fay, that Ofiris (the " fun) is dead. Then the nights become longer, " the darknefs encreafes, and the force of the " light diminifhes. The priefts on this occafion " perform mournful ceremonies. They expofe " to the people a gilded ox covered with a black " veil, in token of the grief of the goddefs, (Ifis " or the Moon). For in Egypt the ox is the " fymbol of Ofiris, and of the earth."

You have feen the Egyptian *Athor*, Sir, at firft fignifying that myfterious night which covered Chaos before the creation, afterwards become the planet of the night, and at length marking the

(*y*) Plutarch, Treatife of Ifis and Ofiris.

(z) Athyr is the name of a month. The Egyptians call Venus, *Athor*, and from this name they have formed that of the third month of their year. *Orion the grammarian.*

period

period when the ſun is diſtant from us. You have obſerved, by what analogy the Orientals, the Greeks, and the Romans have called Venus the Queen of the World, and the Mother of Pleaſures. It is invariably the ſame doctrine; but changes forms, in paſſing amongſt different nations, and in the mouths of poets and philoſophers.

Athor had temples in Egypt. Herodotus, who gives us the Egyptian name of ſeveral remarkable places in the country, makes mention of *Athar, Beki*, the city of Athor, which Strabo (*a*), and Diodorus Siculus (*b*) render by the name of *Aphroditopolis*, the city of Venus. Ælian (*c*) in ſpeaking of a town ſituated in the Hermopolitan Nome, ſays: "In this town they worſhip Venus. "A peculiar worſhip is alſo paid here to the "cow." The ſame author informs us that Iſis, or the moon, was repreſented with the horns of a cow. Thus was this animal, or the ox, the emblem of the planet of the night; and the black veil with which they covered it, whilſt the ſummer was viſiting the ſigns of the winter, could only expreſs to the eyes of the people, the diminution of the days, and the grief of Iſis; but certainly it reminded the prieſts of the darkneſs ſpread over chaos before the creation. On caſting your eyes on the map of Egypt, you will perceive three towns called *Aphroditopolis* by the Grecian geographers, but which the natives call *Atharbeki*.

(*a*) Strabo, l. 17.
(*b*) Diodorus, l. 1.
(*c*) Ælian, Treatiſe on Animals, lib. 11.

Such, Sir, are the feeble lights we are obliged to extract from the fragments left us by the ancients, on the subject of the religious opinions of the Egyptians, respecting *Athor*. Had not their books perished in the conflagration of the Ptolemean library; did not their hieroglyphics hide from us the information they meant to transmit to posterity, we should have discovered amongst a people so learned, and situated near the common source of human nature, clearer and more satisfactory ideas. Let us enjoy however what still remains to us, and endeavour gradually to penetrate into the mysteries of their religion.

I have the honour to be, &c.

LETTER XLIX.

OF PHTHA, NEITH, AND CNEPH, NAMES UNDER WHICH THE SUPREME BEING WAS ADORED IN EGYPT.

The Supreme Being adored by the Egyptians, under the Names of Ptha, Neith, and Cneph. By these Appellations were denoted the power, the wisdom, and the goodness of that infinite spirit which created the world. The Temple of Ptha was at Memphis, that of Neith at Sais, and that of Cneph in the island of Elephantine. Purity of religion only among the Priests, and those who were initiated in the sacred mysteries. The people neglect the Creator, while they adored his works.

To Mr. L. M.

Grand Cairo.

I HAVE said, Sir, that the ancient Egyptians revered, under the name of *Athor*, or of Night, the darkness spread over the abyss before the creation. This Chaos, sung by the poets of Greece and Rome, could produce nothing of itself. The philosophers of Egypt acknowledged a mind which drew forth from it the universe, and established that admirable order which reigns in it without alteration. They gave it the name of of *Ptha*, Difpofer *(d)*. Jamblichus *(e)* gives us this information in the following words: "The "Egyptians call *Ptha* the creating fpirit, which "does every thing with truth and wifdom. "The Greeks have called it Vulcan, confider-"ing nothing but the art with which he produ-"ces." They placed their fpirit before every thing, taught that he firft gave to Chaos the *form of an egg* §, and that he afterwards created all beings. Thales, the Milefian, inftructed in the fchool of the Priefts of Memphis, faid *(f)*, "Water is the principle of things, and God is "that fpirit which has formed the universe out "of the humid principle." This paffage of Genefis has great fimilitude with the doctrine of the Egyptians on the creation *(g)*. *The fpirit (or breath) of God moved upon the face of the waters.* It is natural to imagine, that Mofes, brought up in the court of the Pharaohs, acquired there part of his knowledge, and that he afterwards extricated the true light from the myfteries and fables which enveloped it *. To paint the Creator in a

(*d*) La Croix, trefor epiftolaire, liv. 3. Jablonfki, liv. premier, fays, *Ptha*, in Coptic, fignifies, *Difpofer of things.*

(*e*) Myfteres Egyptiens, fection 8.

(§) The difcovery of the oviformity of the earth was brought from Egypt into Greece by Orpheus, from whence it was called the Orpic Egg.——Tranflator.

(*f*) Cicero, lib. 4. de natura deorum.

(*g*) Chap. 1.

* Blackerell, in his Letters concerning mythylogy, fays, "'Tis quite enough, if by comparing the Egyptian tradition "of the rife of things from *Sanconiathon*, or *Jaaut*, we find fome "traces of that affertion, That the Hebrew lawyers were in-"ftructed in all the wifdom of the Egyptians." Prax. Apoft. ——Tranflator.

manner

manner adapted to the ſenſes, the Egyptians attributed to him both ſexes, that is to ſay, they acknowledged in him the power of producing without the aid of any other being. Accordingly Syneſius, who was tainted with this ancient theology, has ſaid of the infinite mind, *Thou art the father, thou art the mother, thou art the male, thou art the female (h).*

On the obeliſk of granite, tranſported from Egypt to Rome, amongſt the hieroglyphics, of which Hermaphion has given the interpretation, is the following remarkable paſſage on the ſubject of Rameſtes, King of Heliopolis *(i): This is he whom Ptha, the father of the Gods, has elected.* Theſe words, father of the Gods, point out the ſtars which the Egyptian ſages regarded as the moſt ſtriking emblems of the divinity, and which the people really adored. From the time of Herodotus *(k)* fire, water, earth, the heavens, the moon, the ſun, the day, and night, received divine honours in this country: but theſe were the deities of the vulgar. Perſons initiated in the myſteries, had another belief. They acknowledged only the Author of Nature, who had drawn forth every being from non-entity.

The firſt dynaſty of Manethon comprehends the reign of the God in Egypt *(l)*. He places *Phtha* or Vulcan at their head, and after him, his ſon—the Sun. This paſſage, taken in an allego-

(*h*) Syneſius, hymn 3.
(*i*) Ammian Marcellin, lib. 17.
(*k*) Herodotus, lib. 2.
(*l*) Manethon, according to Syncellius.

rical

rical ſenſe, is by no means contrary to ſound theology. The ſun being the work of the Creator, may be conſidered as his ſon; and the Egyptians, to ennoble their origin, adored the Creator as the firſt of their Kings. Manethon aſſigns to each of theſe material Gods the year of their reign, which muſt be underſtood by the various Solar and Lunar Cycles, inverted by aſtronomers *(m)*. This dynaſty proves that *Phtha* precedes time and thoſe viſible deities, whoſe conſtant order ſuggeſted the regulation of their courſe when men ſtudied the heavens. The Egyptian Prieſt poſitively declares it *(n)*: "No "determined period can be aſſigned to *Phtha*, "becauſe he always ſhines in the midſt of dark-"neſs, as in the day." The ſtars of the firmament, in fact, appear and diſappear alternately. Their empire is not eternal, becauſe it had a beginning; but the inviſible mind exiſted before time. His power ſhines forth perpetually in his works, and his reign is immutable.

The Egyptian Prieſts confined within the ſanctuaries of their temples this ſublime doctrine, either tranſmitted to them by the firſt men, or to which they had, like Abraham *(o)*, elevated themſelves

(*m*) See Vignoles, tome 1.

(*n*) Manethon, according to Syncellius.

(*o*) St. Clemens, of Alexandria, aſſerts that Abraham raiſed himſelf to the knowledge of the only God by the ſtudy of aſtronomy. It appears that this alſo was the opinion of the Arabs. Mahomet, who had collected the traditions of his country, repreſents the patriarch of the believers, with his eyes turned towards heaven, and after obſerving, with aſtoniſhment, the

ſelves by the efforts of their reaſon, and by the ſtudy of aſtronomy. Having cloathed it in allegories, of which they only poſſeſſed the explanation, they left the people plunged in ignorance, and favoured their idolatry by pronouncing, at the death of each individual, this prayer *(p)*, " O Sun, ye and other Gods, who beſtow life on " man, receive me, reſtore me to the eternal " Gods, that I may dwell with them."

The Greeks pretended that, even in the opinion of the Egyptians, *Phtha* was nothing but fire, the pureſt, the moſt ſubtile of every thing, which they elevated above æther, from whence ſouls detached themſelves to animate bodies; for which reaſon they gave it the name of Vulcan, who preſides over that element. " The ſages of Egypt, ſays " Servius *(q)*, embalm the bodies, in order to " preſerve them; and that their ſouls remaining " long attached to them, may not quit them to " animate others. The Romans, on the contra- " ry, burn them immediately, that they may re- " turn to their firſt nature." This is the metempſychoſis which Herodotus *(r)* pretends has paſſed from Egypt into all the countries of the earth. If we may credit theſe authors, the Egyptians regarded *Phtha*, or the ſuperior part of æther,

the appearance and vaniſhing of the ſtars, the ſun, and the moon, which he had at firſt looked upon as divinities, he makes him exclaim, *No, I will not adore Gods who riſe, and who lie down.* See alſo Ab. Ecchellens. Arab. Hiſt. VI. [Tranſlator.]

(*p*) Porphyry, lib. 4.

(*q*) Servius on the Æneid, lib. 3.

(*r*) Herodotus. lib. 2.

as

as the divine eſſence, which ſucceſſively gave life to all the univerſe. The followers of Plato and the Pythagoreans profeſſed the ſame creed. They publiſhed that the ſoul, immortal in its nature, leaving the body, again returned to mix itſelf with the ſoul of the world, from whence it derived its origin (*s*).

However theſe opinions may be, they are Greeks who ſpeak, and it is not to be doubted, that they altered the religion of Egypt, by intermixing the reveries of their metaphyſicians. The facts I have cited in the firſt part of this letter, prove that *Phtha* was looked upon, in remote antiquity, as the ordaining ſpirit, and the great architect of the univerſe. The inhabitants of Memphis raiſed a temple to him, where he was principally worſhipped (*t*). But as I have related, the worſhip of the viſible Gods prevailed amongſt the people, over that of the Supreme Being, and the Prieſts alone burnt incenſe on his altars.

We ought not to ſeparate from *Phtha* the God whom the Egyptians adored under the name of *Neith*, ſince he is alſo the creative ſpirit. *Neith*, in fact, ſignifies *he who diſpoſes all things* (*u*). But by the firſt of theſe attributes, God was underſtood to be taken in a general ſenſe, and by the ſecond, his wiſdom was more particularly

(*s*) Plutarch, lib. 4, on the doctrine of the Philoſophers.

(*t*) Herodotus and Diodorus Siculus have deſcribed this temple. Suidas adds, the inhabitants of Memphis adore Vulcan, under the name of *Phtha*.

(*u*) Jablonſki, tome premier.

cha-

characterized. His worſhip flouriſhed at Saïs, a town of the Delta, where the Prieſts had a famous college. Plato *(x)*, who frequented it, expreſſes himſelf thus: "Saïs, the capital of "the Saïtic preſecture, is a conſiderable town, "of which Amaſis was King. *Neith*, to whom "the Greeks have given the name of Minerva, "is its tutelar Deity." The following inſcription engraved in hieroglyphic characters on the gate of the temple of *Neith*, marks the ſublime idea they had conceived of that divinity *(y)*: "I am what is, what ſhall be, what has been. "No mortal has lifted up my Tunica. The "fruit I have engendered is the Sun." This definition can be applied only to the Supreme Being, who exiſting by his eſſence, and having neither beginning nor end, contains in himſelf the paſt, the preſent, and the future *(z)*. This incomprehenſible ſpirit lies hid from the limited view of man, who cannot lift up the veil which covers him. Theſe words: *the firſt I have engendered is the ſun*, clearly demonſtrate, that *Neith* and *Phtha* are the ſame divinity; for Ma-

(*x*) Timæus of Plato.

(*y*) Proclus, the learned Commentator of Plato, gives us this inſcription in that work. Plutarch cites it in his Treatiſe of Iſis and Oſiris.

(*z*) Man may be conſidered as the image of God, for he contains within himſelf, in certain reſpects, the paſt, the preſent, and the future. The remembrance of what has been, the ſentiment of his actual exiſtence, the hope of what he ſhall be, make him enjoy at the ſame time theſe three modes of being; accordingly the Creator has ſaid in Geneſis, *Let us make man after our own image*.

nethon

nethon asserts also, in a figurative sense, that Phtha is the father of the sun. The Phœnicians, who received their religion and their knowledge from their brethren the Egyptians, likewise acknowledged (*a*) Minerva, or *Neith*, for the artist of nature.

The Egyptian Priests adoring more particularly, under the name of *Neith*, the divine wisdom, which directs the course of the world, and enlightens human beings, had placed the arts under his protection The warrior wore on his finger a ring, on which was engraved a scarab or beetle. Horapollo gives us the reason of it (*b*). "The Egyptians, says he, pretend that the world "is composed of males and females. They "paint a scarab to represent Minerva (*c*)." This ring which distinguished the soldiers, was a sign by which they did homage to the Divinity, whose emblem they bore, and who held in his hand the fate of battles. One of the Pharaohs, *Psammenites (d)*, instructed by *Neith*, announces that the Kings put themselves under the protection of the Supreme God, believing that they held their knowledge from him.

Cadmus, the Phœnician, was the first who carried this worship into Greece. He gave the name of *Neith (e)* to one of the seven gates of

(*a*) Julian, Or. 4.

(*b*) Horapollo, Hieroglyphics, lib. 1.

(*c*) I have already said that the Egyptians, to mark in a sensible manner the productive power of the Creator, described him with two sexes; now as they attributed the two sexes to the scarab, or beetle, they made that insect the symbol of *Neith*.

(*d*) Jablonski, tome premeir.

Thebes,

Thebes, in Bœotia. The Egyptian theology was taught there. The poets ſoon mixed with it their brilliant allegories. They called *Neith* Minerva, made her proceed, completely armed, from the brain of Jupiter, celebrated her as the Goddeſs of Combats, and the Mother of the Arts. Philoſophers ſtill ſaw the truth through the veil with which it was obſcured; but the people were unable to diſcover it, and beſtowed incenſe on a fabulous Deity.

"The firſt woman, ſays Euſtathius *(f)*, who "formed a web, was an Egyptian. She was "ſeated; it is for this reaſon that the Egyp-"tians repreſented Minerva ſeated." They intended, doubtleſs, by giving her this attitude, to remind men that ſhe had taught them the arts, and that all their knowledge came from her. The ancient Greeks, imitating their Preceptors in every thing, repreſent Minerva ſeated, in their ſculptures and engravings *(g)*.

The Egyptians, after adoring the power of the Creator, under the name of *Phtha*, his wiſdom under that of *Neith*, honoured his beneficence by calling him *Cneph*, or *Good*, *per excellentiam (h)*. "The Prieſts of Egypt, ſays Eu-"ſebius *(i)*, call Cneph the Architect of the Univerſe." Strabo ſpeaks of his temple built in the iſle of Elephantis. This beautiful monument

(*e*) Jablonſki, tome premier.

(*f*) Euſtathius's Obſervations on Iliad, lib. 1.

(*g*) Strabo, lib. 13.

(*h*) Jablonſki, tome premier.

(*i*) Euſebius, Evangel. Prepar. lib. 3.

is ſtill remaining, ſuch as I have deſcribed in my thirteenth Letter. The ſymbol of this God was a ſerpent, as Euſebius teſtifies. " The ſerpent " in the middle of a circle, which it touches in " the two oppoſite points of its circumference, " indicates the Good Genius." For this object, they choſe a particular ſort of ſerpent, of which Herodotus (k) gives us the following deſcription: " There are found, in the environs of Thebes, " ſacred ſerpents which are not venomous (l). " They have two horns on the top of their head. " When they die, they are buried in the temple " of Jupiter." The name of *Cneph* (m), or Good Genius, was beſtowed on them, as well as on the divinity they repreſented, and the veneration of the people extended no farther than to the image. " One day, ſays Plutarch (n), I ſaw two men " diſputing; one of them perceiving a ſerpent, " called it *Agatha Daimon*, Good Genius, and " tried to take it."

We muſt not here confound the Good Genii of the Greeks and Romans with thoſe of the Egyptians. The former, by this denomination, underſtood intermediate beings between the divine and human nature; the latter employed it

(k) Herodotus, lib. 2.

(l) This ſpecies of ſerpents, honoured by the name of *Haridi*, ſtill play a brilliant part, as we have ſeen in our days in the hands of the Prieſts of Achmin.

(m) Euſebius Prepar. Evangel. lib. 3, ſays, The Phœnicians call this ſerpent the Good Genius; for this ſame reaſon the Egyptians call him *Cneph*.

(n) Plutarch's Treatiſe of Iſis and Oſiris.

to point out the benevolence of him who presides over heaven and earth, and whose all-powerful will gives motion to the stars through the immensity of space.

Such, Sir, are the religious opinions of the Egyptians on the subject of *Phtha*, of *Neith*, and of *Cneph*, three attributes under which they adored the same God, but by which they respectively characterised his power, his wisdom, and his goodness. This worship was gradually effaced. It remained buried in the Temples, and the people, either deceived by the Priests, who presented nothing to their senses but symbolical figures, or incapable of elevating their minds to a knowledge of the infinite Spirit, who is every where present, and every where escapes our senses, honoured his works, and addressed their prayers and their offerings to them.

I have the honour to be, &c.

LETTER L.

OF THE VISIBLE GODS OF THE EGYPTIANS, AND CHIEFLY OF OSIRIS, A SYMBOLICAL DIVINITY, WHICH REPRESENTED THE SUN.

At first the Egyptians worshipped the Sun, under the designation of Phré, and afterwards under that of Osiris. This Deity very famous. His temples and Priests in every corner of the kingdom. His origin derived from astronomy, which having observed his course more regular than that of the moon, made use of it for the measuring of time. The name of Osiris, derived from Osch Iri, *the Author of Time, shews the design of the Priests in introducing this allegorical divinity.*

To Mr. L. M.

Grand Cairo.

"THE ancient Egyptians," says Diodorus Siculus (*o*), "contemplating the arch of the "heavens, raised above their heads, and ad-"miring the marvellous order which reigns in "the universe, regarded the sun and moon as "eternal Gods, and honoured them with a parti-"cular worship. They called one Osiris, and "the other Isis." The assertion of this historian is too general. To have written in a manner more conformable to truth, he should have ex-

(*o*) Diodorus Siculus, lib. 1.

cepted

cepted the Pharaohs, the perſons initiated in the myſteries, and eſpecially the Prieſts, who did not believe in that idolatry to which they had ſubjected the people. Beſides, it is reaſonable to believe, they at firſt taught them, that theſe brilliant bodies were the works of the Moſt High. However that may be, the Egyptians worſhipped the ſun and the moon, under the pompous titles of the King *(p)* and Queen of heaven. The ſtar of the day was firſt called *Phré (q)*. The father-in-law of the patriarch, Joſeph, was called, according to the verſion of the Septuagint, *Petephre*, Prieſt of the Sun. The aſtronomers obſerving his courſe, and his principal effects, gave him the ſymbolical name of Oſiris, which was conſecrated by religion (*r*). " It is acknow- " ledged," ſays Macrobius, " that Oſiris is no " other than the ſun. When the Egyptians wiſh " to deſcribe him in their hieroglyphic charac- " ters, they paint him with a ſceptre and one " eye."

They could not figure in a manner more ſenſible the ſtar which enlightens the world, and to whom they attributed the empire of the ſky. Accordingly Martian Capella (*s*), in the beautiful hymn which he compoſed in honour of the father of the day, ſays,

(*p*) Jeremiah, chap. 7, and 44.
(*q*) Jablonſki, tome premier.
(*r*) Macrobius, Saturnal, lib. 1.
(*s*) Martian Capella, lib. 2.

Eye of the world, brilliant torch of Olympus;
Latium calls thee the Sun, for, after thy author,
Thou art the ſplendid cauſe of light. The Nile calls thee
Seraphis;
And Memphis adores thee under the name of Oſiris.

Some authors have alſo called the Nile Oſiris. Plutarch explains this opinion (*t*). "The "Egyptians look upon the Nile as the preſerver "of their country, and as deriving its ſource from "Oſiris." In fact, the vapours exhaled by the ſun, and then condenſed in the atmoſphere, fall down in rain, and form the great river which conſtitutes the riches of Egypt. It is accordingly in this ſenſe that Homer always calls it *the emanation of Jupiter* (*u*). The Egyptians, ſays Herodotus, (*x*) pretend that Oſiris is the ſame as Bacchus. This ſentiment has many partizans amongſt the Greeks, and is not without probability. The Prieſts of Egypt made Oſiris travel from one end of the world to the other. They painted him as a powerful King, who had conquered the earth, and loaded men with bounties. The Greeks, who attributed the ſame gifts, the ſame conqueſts, to Bacchus, have ſaid that he was the ſame with Oſiris. But in the ſacred language of Egypt, theſe journies only repreſented the courſe of the ſun, and the advantages he procures to mortals. Theſe allegories have been at

(*t*) Plutarch's Treatiſe of Iſis and Oſiris.
(*u*) Jupiter was the ſame with the Sun, or Oſiris.
(*x*) Herodotus, lib. 2.

at all times in uſe amongſt the Orientals, and the Pſalmiſt makes uſe of one when he thus expreſſes himſelf (z): The ſun "is as a bridegroom coming out of his chamber, and rejoiceth as a ſtrong man to run a race. His going forth is from the end of the heaven, and his circuit unto the ends of it; and there is nothing hid from the heat thereof." Tibullus, following literally the opinions of the Greeks, has rendered them in verſes full of grace and harmony (*a*).

Primus aratra manu Solerti fecit Oſiris,
  Et teneram ferro ſollicitavit humum.
Primus inexpertæ commiſit ſemina terræ,
  Pomaque non notis legit ab arboribus.
Hic docuit teneram palis adjungere vitem:
  Hic viridem durâ cædere falce comam.

A fact admitted by the graveſt writers of antiquity, evinces to a demonſtration how far the Greeks were deceived in attempting to eſtabliſh a perfect reſemblance between Bacchus and Oſiris. The firſt was honoured as the author of the vine, and the Egyptians, ſo far from attributing its culture to Oſiris, abhorred wine as poiſon. "The Egyptians," ſays Plutarch (*b*), "had never drank wine before the time of Pſammeticus (*c*). Regarding this liquor as the "blood of the giants, who, after making war "againſt the Gods, had periſhed in the com-

(z) Pſalm 19.
(*a*) Tibullus, lib. 1. elegy 8.
(*b*) Plutarch's Treatiſe of Iſis and Oſiris.
(*c*) This Prince was one of the laſt Egyptian Pharaohs.

" bat, they did not offer them any in libations, " imagining it was odious to them. They aſ- " ſerted even, that the vine had ſprung from " this blood, mixed with the earth."

This ſacred fable had paſſed from Egypt into Perſia, and as far as the extremities of India (*d*). St. Clemens, of Alexandria, reports that the Magi abſtained from wine with the utmoſt attention. The Arabs had a law which prohibited them the uſe of it (*e*). Ovington (*f*), in ſhort, who has travelled in India, aſſures us, that in our days the Brachmins deteſt that liquor, and hold it in no leſs horror than Manes, who regarded it as the blood of demons. It is difficult to ſay whence aroſe this averſion of the Orientals for wine; but it really exiſts, and this is probably one of the reaſons which induced Mahomet to prohibit it (*g*). Perhaps we ought to ſearch for the cauſe of this prohibition in the curſe pronounced by Noah againſt his ſon Cham, who, having ſurprized him in his drunkenneſs, inſulted his ſituation. However this may be, the Egyptians, who hold it in horror, never could attribute the culture of the vine to Oſiris.

But what does this ſignify? On what occaſion was it given to the ſun? This queſtion has excited the reſearches of the ancients and the moderns,

(*d*) Stroma 3.

(*e*) Diodorus Siculus, lib. 1.

(*f*) Ovington's Voyage, Vol. I.

(*g*) Wine is an abomination invented by Satan.——*Coran.*

moderns, and they have laboured to resolve it. Diodorus Siculus (*h*), and Horopollo (*i*), say, that Osiris signifies *Poliophthalmus*, he who has many eyes. This interpretation applies to the sun, but does not explain the word Osiris. For if *Os*, or *Osch*, may be translated in Egyptian by *many*, *Iris* has no connection with *eye*. "The "name of Osiris," says Plutarch (*k*), "indi-"cates a great number of things, and may be "interpreted in various ways. It expresses ef-"ficacious strength and bounty." This still does not render the literal sense. The learned Jablonski (*l*) interprets this word in a more natural manner. "Osiris," says he, "comes from "*Osch*-Iri, he who makes time." The Egyptians understood by this expression what God declares in speaking of the sun and of the moon (*m*): "And God said, let there be lights in the "firmament of the heaven, to divide the day "from the night, and let them be for signs and "for seasons, and for days and for years." The following passage of Clemens, of Alexandria, favours this sentiment (*n*): "The Egyptians "paint the sun, borne in a vessel, or on a croco-"dile. This emblem gives us to understand

(*h*) Diodorus Siculus, lib. 1.
(*i*) Horopollo, Hieroglyphics, lib. 1.
(*k*) Treatise of Isis and Osiris.
(*l*) Jablonski, tome premier.
(*m*) Genesis, Chap. i. verse 14.
(*n*) St. Clemens, quoted by Eusebius, Prep. Evangel. lib. 1.

"that

" that the ſtar of the day, journeying through " the mild and moiſt air, engenders time."

The Egyptian aſtronomers, after repeated obſervations, regulated the year by the courſe of the ſun. The great circle of gold, of 635 cubits, which they placed on the ſummit of the tomb of Oſimandué, and where was ſeen the riſing and ſetting of the ſtars for every day of the year, is a ſplendid proof of their labours, and of their diſcoveries. " The Prieſts of Thebes," ſays Strabo (*o*), " applied themſelves princi-" pally to the ſtudy of aſtronomy and philoſo-" phy. They made uſe of the ſun, and not " the moon, to meaſure time." Julius Cæſar, who paſſed a year amongſt them, made himſelf acquainted with their learning, and reformed the Roman Calendar, which was extremely defective. " This Prince," ſays Macrobius (*p*), " imitating the Egyptians, who alone were per-" fectly acquainted with divine things, formed " the year from the motion of the ſun, who fi-" niſhes his revolution in 365 days and a quar-" ter." The ſame author, entering into the ſpirit of the aſtronomers, looks upon that meaſure of the year as the chief virtue of the ſun.

The ſolar year was found by the academy of of Heliopolis, under the reign of Aſeth (*q*), 1325 years before J. C. and 320 after the departure of the Iſraelites. The Prieſts who till

(*o*) Strabo, lib. 17.

(*p*) Macrob. Saturnal. lib. 1.

(*q*) Vignoles, Chronologie, tome premier

then

then had honoured the ſun under his proper name of *Phré*, beſtowed on him, in memory of ſo important an event, that of *Oſiris*, or the *Author of Time*.

I have the honour to be, &c.

LETTER

LETTER LI.

OF AMMON AND HERCULES, EMBLEMS OF THE SUN.

Amoun, *called by the Greeks* Ammon, *and by the Latin*, Jupiter Ammon, *was particularly worſhipped at Thebes, which the ſcriptures ſtyles* the city of Ammon, *and the Greeks* Dioſpolis *the city of Jupiter. His ſtatue decked with the ſkin and head of a ram. This ſymbolical divinity, which repreſented the vernal ſun, delivered oracles in a temple, ſituated in the midſt of the deſerts of Lybia. The ſtatue of Hercules, which partook of the worſhip of its deity, at the Vernal Equinox, denoted the force of the ſun when he had reached the Equator.*

To Mr. L. M.

Grand Cairo.

THE Egyptians, Sir, verſed in the ſtudy of Aſtronomy, perceived that the ſun appeared under different aſpects according to his ſituation in the Zodiac. They obſerved that he ſlackened his motion towards the ſolſtices, that he haſtened them at the equinoxes, and that his influence was greater or leſs under theſe various circumſtances. They expreſſed theſe different phænomena by characteriſtic denominations. Having adopted in their theology the uſe of the hieroglyphic language, which ſpeaks only by ſymbols,

bols, they alternately painted the ſun under the form of a child, of a man grown up, and an old man, now joyous, now ſad, or ſplendid, in the midſt of light. The prieſts by theſe emblems alluded to aſtronomical or phyſical effects. The vulgar, accuſtomed to ſee theſe figures in the temples, forgot the object they repreſented, and adored them as divinities. Macrobius, who had penetrated into the myſteries of this ancient religion, unveils them to us in the following terms (*r*): "The Egyptians, at the winter Sol-"ſtice, wiſhing to mark the ſhorteſt day of the "year, drew from the ſanctuary, the ſun, repre-"ſented under the form of an infant. His "growth is rapid, which they indicate by re-"preſenting him at the ſpring Equinox in the "figure of a young man. At the ſummer Sol-"ſtice, when he has reached his maturity, his "age is diſtinguiſhed by a full face, ornamented "with a long beard. At length they diſplay "him with the features of an old man, to point "out the diminution of the days."

Theſe repreſentations, adopted doubtleſs before the uſe of writing, and preſerved by the prieſts, expreſſed emblematically the four ſeaſons of the year. Firſt let us examine what the Egyptians underſtood by the name of Ammon, ſo celebrated in antiquity. *Amoun*, ſays Plutarch (*s*), of which we have made Ammon, is

(*r*) Macrob. Saturnal. lib. 1.

(*s*) Treatiſe of Iſis and Oſiris. Herodotus and Diodorus Siculus, give Jupiter alſo the name of Ammon.

the

the Egyptian name of Jupiter. This god was particularly worſhipped at Thebes, called by the ſacred books *Hamon-no*, the poſſeſſion of Hammon, and by the Septuagint (*t*) the city of Ammon. Herodotus tells us under what form he was honoured (*u*). "The inhabitants of "Thebes regarded the ram as ſacred, and do not "feed on its fleſh. Every year however, on the "feſtival of Jupiter, they cut off the head of a "ram, and take off its ſkin, with which they "cover the ſtatue of the god." Proclus teaches us the object of this ceremony (*x*): "The Egyp-"tians," ſays he, "had a ſingular veneration "for the ram, becauſe the image of Ammon "bore his head, and that this ſign, the firſt of "the Zodiac, was the preſage of the fruits of "the earth." Euſebius (*y*) adds that this ſymbol marked the conjunction of the ſun and moon in the ſign of the ram.

You recollect, Sir, the ceremony obſerved by the prieſts of the temple of Ammon, when men went to conſult that oracle. Faithful obſervers of the opinions adopted by their anceſtors, who made the ſun travel in a veſſel, they carried in a boat the ſtatue of that god, formed of precious ſtones, and bearing the head of a ram. So many anthorities and facts, evidently demonſtrate, that amongſt the aſtronomers of Egypt, Ammon re-

(*t*) Ezechiel, chap. 30. The Greeks and the Romans called it *Dioſpolis*, the city of Jupiter.

(*u*) Herodotus, lib. 2.

(*x*) Timæus of Plato.

(*y*) Euſebius, prep. Evangelic. lib. 3.

preſented

presented the sun. It is in this sense that Diodorus Siculus has said (z): *Osiris is the same with Ammon.* Notwithstanding, these two names did not represent the same phænomena. The former, as you will have observed, announced this luminary the author of time; the latter, the spring, and the commencement of the astronomical year which happen in the sign of the ram, and was pointed out by the symbolical figure of that divinity. The word *Amoun*, composed of *Amouein* (*a*) *shining* denoted, the desired effects produced by the sun on attaining the Equator, such as the encrease of the days, a more splendid light, and above all, the fortunate presage of the inundation and abundance.

The priests, on the festivals of Ammon, were accustomed to associate Hercules in his worship. After covering the statue of Jupiter with the skin of the ram, they brought near to this emblematical god, the representation of Hercules (*b*), whom they called in their language *Dsom* or *Dsiom* (*c*), *strength*. This expression characterized the virtue of the star of the day, when arrived at the Equinoctial line. Accordingly, Plutarch (*d*) says, they asserted that Hercules, placed in the sun, turned with him. This observation has not escaped Macrobius (*e*): "The name alone of

(*z*) Diódorus Siculus, lib. 1.
(*a*) Jablonski, tome premier.
(*b*) Herodotus, lib. 2.
(*c*) Jablonski, tome primier.
(*d*) Plut. Treatise of Isis Osiris.
(*e*) Macrob. Saturnal, lib. 1.

"Hercules

" Hercules (Heracleos) proves that he indi-
" cated the ſun. In fact, *Heras* ſignifies *of the air*,
" *cleos*, *glory*; and to whom attribute this epi-
" thet, if not to the body which fills the univerſe
" with his fire, and which on retiring, leaves it
" plunged in darkneſs?" Hence have ariſen the
brilliant allegories of the Greeks, who themſelves
acknowledge, that the twelve labours of this hero, allude only to the ſun paſſing through the
twelve ſigns of the Zodiac, in his annual revolution.

I have the honour to be, &c.

LETTER LII.

OF HORUS, A SYMBOLICAL DEITY WHICH REPRESENTED THE SUN.

Horus, as well as Osiris, had a hawk for his symbol. The same attributes frequently ascribed to both. His throne supported by lions, because he represented the sun at the summer Solstice. His education at Butis, on the border of the great lake, denoted his great power in raising vapours into the atmosphere, whence they fell down in dew upon the earth. The victory of Horus over Typhon, depicted the happy effects produced by the sun in his progress, through the summer signs, such as the inundation, the extinction of the north winds, and the excitement of those named the Etesian.

To Mr. L. M.

Grand Cairo.

HORUS, a renowned deity of ancient Egypt, was also, Sir, an emblem of the sun. Plutarch positively affirms it (*f*): that virtue which presides over the sun, whilst he is moving through space, the Egyptians called *Horus*, and the Greeks Apollo.*.

The

(*f*) Plut. Treatise of Isis and Osiris.

* Job also calls *Ur* or *Orus* the sun—" If I gazed upon the " sun (*Ur*, *Orus*) when he was shining, or on (*Järècha*) the " moon walking in brightness, and my heart hath been severely " enticed

The veneration of the people for this god (*g*) appears from the circumſtance of three cities being called by this name (*h*) in the Thebais. The ſparrow-hawk repreſented equally Oſiris and Horus. It was their common emblem, and they had ſometimes the ſame attribute. The interpretation left by Hermapion of the hieroglyphics engraved on the obeliſk of Heliopolis, offers theſe remarkable words (*i*): *Horus is the ſupreme lord and the author of time.* You know, Sir, that theſe qualities were chiefly attributed to Oſiris; that they may apply to Horus, he muſt neceſſarily denote the ſtar of the day, in certain circumſtances; this is what is explained to us by the oracle of Apollo of Claros:

Learn that the firſt of the gods is *Jao*.
He is called *inviſible* in winter, Jupiter in the ſpring (*k*),
The *ſun* in ſummer, and towards the end of autumn, the tender *Jao*.

The ſtar of the day, on attaining the ſummer Solſtice, and called per excellentiam *the ſun*, is the ſame as Horus. In fact the Egyptians repreſented him borne on lions (*l*); which ſignified

"enticed (i. e. to worſhip) or my mouth hath kiſſed my hand; "this alſo were an iniquity to be puniſhed by the judge, for I "ſhould have denied the God who is above." Job, chap. xxxi. ver. 26, 27, 28. *Tranſlator.*

(*g*) Horapollo, Hieroglyphics, lib. 1.

(*h*) Their Egyptian name was *Cities of Horus*. The Greeks called them Cities of Apollo.

(*i*) Ammian Marcellinus.

(*k*) That is to to ſay *Amoun*. Thoſe various denominations will be explained in the courſe of theſe letters.

(*l*) Horapollo, Hieroglyphics, lib. 1.

his

his entrance into the ſign of the lion. They who preſided over the divine inſtitutions, then placed ſphynxes at the head of the canals and ſacred fountains to warn the people of the approaching inundation. Macrobius, who informs us why the Greeks gave Horus the name of Apollo, confirms this ſentiment (*m*): " In the myſteries," ſays he, " they diſcover as a ſecret, which ought " to be inviolable, that the ſun arrived in the " upper hemiſphere, is called Apollo." Theſe teſtimonies concur in proving, that this emblematical deity was no other than the ſtar of day, paſſing through the ſigns of ſummer.

Theſe lights may lead us to the explication of the ſacred fable, which the prieſts publiſhed on the ſubject of Horus; for they enveloped in myſtery every point of their religion. Plutarch (*n*) gives it at length. I ſhall only quote the principal traits. They ſaid that he was the ſon of Oſiris and of Iſis; that Typhon, after killing his brother Oſiris, took poſſeſſion of the kingdom; that Horus leaguing himſelf with Iſis, avenged the death of his father, expelled the tyrant from his throne, without depriving him of life, and reigned glorioully in Egypt. A perſon who has travelled ever ſo little in Egypt, eaſily diſcovers natural phenomena, hid under the veil of fable. In the ſpring, the wind *Khamſin* frequently makes great ravages there. It raiſes whirlwinds of burning ſands, which ſuffocate travellers, darken the air, and cover the face of the ſun in ſuch a man-

(*m*) Mabrob. Saturnal, lib. 1.
(*n*) Plut. Treatiſe of Iſis and Oſiris.

ner

ner as to leave the earth in perfect obſcurity. Here is the death of Oſiris, and the reign of Typhon. Theſe hurricanes break looſe uſually in the months of February, March, and April.—When the ſun approaches the ſign of the lion, he changes the ſtate of the atmoſphere, diſperſes theſe tempeſts, and reſtores the northerly winds, which drive before them the malignant vapours, and preſerve in Egypt coolneſs and ſalubrity under a burning ſky. This is the triumph of Horus over Typhon, and his glorious reign. As the natural philoſophers acknowledge the influence of the moon over the ſtate of the atmoſphere, they united here with this god, to drive the uſurper from the throne. The prieſts conſidering Oſiris as the father of Time, might beſtow the name of his ſon on Horus, who reigned three months in the year. This is, I believe, the natural explication of this allegory. Beſides, all enlightened men muſt have underſtood this language, which was familiar to them. The people only, whoſe feeble ſight extends no farther than the exterior, without diving into the true meaning of things, might regard theſe allegorical perſonages, as real gods, and decree prayers and offerings to them.

(*o*) Jablonſki, who has interpreted the epithet of *Arueri*, which the Egyptians gave to Horus, pretends that it ſignifies *efficacious virtue*. Theſe expreſſions perfectly characterize the phænomena which happened during the reign of this god. It is in ſummer, in fact, that the ſun manifeſts

(*o*) Jablonſki, tome premier.

all

all its power in Egypt. It is then that he swells the waters of the river with rains, exhaled by him in the air, and driven against the summit of the Abyssinian mountains; it is then that the husbandman reckons on the treasures of agriculture. It was natural for them to honour him with the name of *Arueri*, or *efficacious virtue*, to mark these auspicious effects.

I have the honour to be, &c.

LETTER LIII.

OF THE CELESTIAL SERAPIS, A SYMBOL OF THE SUN.

The worſhip of Serapis flouriſhing under the Ptolemies, who built a ſuperb temple in honour of him. Adored in Egypt before their reign. His origin on the banks of the Nile. This emblematical divinity denoted the Sun in his progreſs through the autumnal ſigns. Said to be inviſible, becauſe ſeen only for a ſhort time by the inhabitants of the north. The ſame with the Pluto of the Greeks, but diveſted of the fables with which their poets involved him.

To Mr. L. M.

Grand Cairo.

THE Ptolemies having brought from Synope, a city of Pontus, to Alexandria, the ſtatue of a god, who on his arrival received the name of Serapis, propagated his worſhip throughout Egypt. The magnificent temple they built in his honour, and which for grandeur, the beauty of its ornaments, and the majeſty of its architecture, was compared to the capitol, the feſtivals they eſtabliſhed, the brilliant ceremonies they inſtituted, attracted the veneration of the people to this deity. Serapis, become the god of the court, made the Egyptians almoſt forget their ancient gods. The provinces emulated each other in building

building temples to him, and burning incenſe on his altars. It is to this celebrity that we muſt attribute the opinion of thoſe writers, who have pretended that his worſhip was firſt introduced into this country by the Ptolemies, and that he was a ſtranger there before their reign. Various paſſages, extracted from better informed hiſtorians, prove the contrary. Plutarch *(p)* in his Life of Alexander the Great, introduces a man, who ſays to him: Serapis has appeared to me, and after breaking my chains, has ſent me to thee. The Athenians having decreed to this conqueror the honours of Bacchus, Diogenes the Cynic *(q)* exclaimed: *Let them make me Serapis then.* Theſe circumſtances prove that Serapis was known before the Ptolemies. Other paſſages inform us that he had his birth on the banks of the Nile. One ſees in Egypt, ſays Pauſanias, ſeveral temples of Serapis *(r)*. Alexandria poſſeſſes the moſt magnificent; the *moſt ancient* is at Memphis. Laſtly, Tacitus, whoſe evidence cannot be called in queſtion, expreſſes himſelf thus, in ſpeaking of the god of Synope tranſported to Alexandria *(s)*: "A temple wor-"thy the grandeur of this city, was built on a "ſpot of ground called *Rachotis (t)*. There "was

(p) Plutarch, Life of Alexander.

(q) Diogenes Laertiu Life of Diogenes the Cynic.

(r) Pauſanias, Attic.

(s) Ann. Tacit. lib. 4.

(t) In the time of Alexander, Rachotis was only a hamlet inhabited by fiſhermen It ultimately became a conſiderable ſuburb

"was at this place an ancient chapel consecrated "to Serapis and Isis." These authorities leave no doubt of the antiquity of the Egyptian Serapis. History informs us also that he was in certain respects the Pluto of the Greeks, and one of the symbols of the sun.

"When the god of Synope," says Plutarch (*u*), "was transported to Alexandria, the "interpreter Timotheus, and Manethon of Se-"bennytus, conjectured on the sight of the cer-"berus and the dragon which adorned his statue, "that it represented Pluto, and persuaded Pto-"lemy that this god was *the same with Serapis*; "for he did not go under that name in the coun-"try from whence he was brought. He re-"ceived therefore on his arrival that of Serapis, "which the Egyptians give to Pluto." It must not be imagined however that the Egyptian Pluto was the sovereign of hell, king of ghosts, and judge of the dead, like that of the Greeks. This theology of Grecian origin was unknown at Memphis (*x*). Porphyry tells us so in express terms: "The priests of Egypt understood by "Pluto, the inferior sun, which remaining un-"der the earth the winter solstice, passes over "and enlightens the unknown regions." It is for this reason that Callisthenes calls Serapis *the invisible god of Synope*. For the same reason, Ju-

suburb of Alexandria. At this day we see there a hill of rubbish of near one hundred feet in elevation, and under which are burried the remains of *Serapeum*.

(*u*) Plutarch, Treatise of Isis and Osiris.

(*x*) Prophesy quoted by Eusebius, Prepar. Evangel. lib. 3.

lian,

lian, in ſpeaking of Pluto, ſays *(y)*: "Plato "aſſerts that the ſublime ſouls of virtuous men "are carried before that god, whom we call alſo "Serapis, becauſe he is inviſible."

The epithet of inviſible was given him, becauſe the ſun, in approaching the winter ſolſtice, remains longer concealed under the earth, and ſeems to haſten to conceal himſelf from the ſight of the northern nations. To mark his abode of ſix months in the northern, and the other ſix in the ſigns of the ſouthern hemiſphere (z), they painted him in two different colours, ſometimes luminous, at other times of a dark blue. The former was called ſparkling or ſuperior *Amoun*; the latter, *Serapis* or inferior. This is what the ancients, but particularly Jablonſki amongſt the moderns, have left us as the moſt probable account of this emblematical deity. Nor is it unlikely, that in the opinion of the ancient philoſophers of Greece, Pluto was no other than the inferior ſun, but that under the brilliant pencil of the poets, he became the monarch of the infernal regions.

I have the honour to be, &c.

(*y*) Julian, Or. 4.
(*z*) Macrob. Saturnal. lib. 1.

LETTER LIV.

OF HARPOCRATES, AN EMBLEM OF THE SUN.

Harpocrates repreſented, in Egypt, the Sun at the winter Solſtice, and, in Greece, the God of Silence. Delineated by the Egyptian Prieſts with his feet joined together, in ſuch a manner that he could ſcarcely walk. This emblem of the ſlow, and almoſt inſenſible motion of the ſun, when verging to the Tropic of Capricorn. Repreſented ſitting on the Lotus flower, becauſe it never opens till towards the end of autumn.

To Mr. L. M.

Grand Cairo.

MACROBIUS informs us, Sir, that the Egyptians drew from their ſanctuary the ſun, repreſented under the form of an infant, to announce to the people the ſhorteſt day of the year. This emblematical deity was called *Harpocrates (a)*. The Greeks made of him the God of ſilence, becauſe he was born holding one of his fingers on his mouth. Iſis, ſays Plutarch (*b*), brought forth at the winter Solſtice the tender Harpocrates. This Egyptian name ſignifies *lame (c)*. He was repreſented with this infirmity to

(*a*) Saturnal. lib. 1.
(*b*) Treatiſe of Iſis and Oſiris.
(*c*) Jablonſki, Pantheon Egyptiacum, tome premier.

mark

mark the ſlow, and almoſt imperceptible motion of the ſun, when at the Tropic. Horapollo, in the explanation he has left us of the hieroglyphics, aſſures us of this in the following terms *(d)*: "The two feet of Harpocrates were "joined together, ſo as to form only one. The "Egyptians figuratively expreſſed by this em-"blem the courſe of the ſun at the winter Sol-"ſtice." Plutarch adds *(e)* that he was painted, ſeated on the flower of the Lotus. A more expreſſive ſymbol could not be given this God, for the calix of this ſuperb lily of the Nile, does not blow before the end of autumn.

The Prieſts, who enveloped with the veil of fable the moſt ſtriking phænomena of nature, and who had compoſed an ænigmatical theology, ſaid that Jupiter (Ammon) having originally had his feet joined together, could not walk freely; that the ſhame he felt at this deformity induced him to live in ſolitude; that Iſis, touched at his ſituation, reſtored him the uſe of his legs by ſeparating them. Through this allegory we diſcover Harpocrates, or the ſun, ſtationary at the winter Solſtice; and by the operation of Iſis, Ammon, or the ſtar of the day, advancing with a more rapid motion, when he reaches the Equator.

But the Egyptians were not the only people who expreſſed themſelves in a ſymbolical manner. All the ancient nations, eſpecially in the

(*d*) Horapollo, Hieroglyphics, lib. 2.

(*e*) Plut. Treatiſe of Iſis and Oſiris.

infancy of language, were compelled to adopt the uſe of parables and allegories. Before the invention of letters, ſenſible ſigns were neceſſary to ſpeak to the underſtanding; and the metaphors employed ſo frequently by the Hebrew and the Arab, ſtamp the ſeal on their antiquity. "The Paphlagonians, according to Plutarch *(f)*, "ſaid that the ſun ſlept in winter, and was "awake in ſummer; and the Phrygians, that he "was chained during the winter, and that in the "ſpring he walked free from his irons."

I have the honour to be, &c.

(f) Treatiſe of Iſis and Oſiris.

LET-

LETTER LV.

OF MENDES, THE SYMBOL OF THE SUN.

Mendès the first emblem of the sun. Denoted the fecundating influence of this planet. The he goat sacred to him, because the most prolific of animals. The Priests initiated in the mysteries of Mendès. The Phallus, *an emblem of generation, adorned their habits, and decorated the statues of other deities. Named by the Greeks, Pan, but improperly, for he bore little resemblance to that demi-god.*

To Mr. L. M.

Grand Cairo.

THE deity I am about to treat of, Sir, was probably the first symbol of the sun. The Egyptians having discovered that they owed the riches of their country to that star, that he was the principal cause of the inundation, that his beneficent rays conveyed heat and life throughout nature, that made the plants spring up, and ripened the harvests, looked on him as the first source of fertility. They worshipped him under the name of *Mendès*, which signifies *very fruitful* (*g*). To point out in a sensible manner the

(*g*) Jablonski, Pantheon Egyptiacum, tome premier.

pro-

productive power with which they believed him to be endowed, they consecrated the goat to him as the most prolific of animals. This animal was fed in the Temple of Mendès, as the living image of the God he represented. The inhabitants of the Mendesian province celebrated festivals in his honour, wore mourning at his death, and held him in such extraordinary veneration, that * *decency* forbids me to relate what Herodotus, Pindar, Plutarch, and several other historians, have written concerning them, to such a pitch can superstition mislead feeble mortals !—The father of history (*h*), deceived by this worship; thought that *Mendès* really signified *a he-goat*. Several Grecian writers have adopted this mistake. Others have discovered it, and have observed that *Mendès* was the symbolical deity for fecundity, the goat his living image, and the sun the principle. Suidas positively asserts it (*i*). " The Egyptians, says he, honour the goat, be-" cause he is consecrated to the generative vir-" tue." § Diodorus Siculus (*k*) and Horapollo (*l*) are of the same sentiment.

The Greeks, who represented Pan with the horns, the feet, and the tail of a goat, discovered

* *Preterea Mendes ubi Pan colitur, et Hircus animal—Hoc in loco Hirci cum mulieribus coeunt.* Strabo, lib. 17. [Translator.]

(*h*) Herodotus, lib. 2.

(*i*) Suidas, at the word Mendès.

§ *Hircum autem deificarunt, ut apud Græcos, Priapum, propter genitalem partem..* Diodorus Siculus, lib. 1. [Translator.]

(*k*) Diodorus Siculus, lib. 1.

(*l*) Horapollo, Hieroglyphics, lib. 1.

a strika ſtriking analogy between him and the Egyptian God. They gave to Mendès the name of Pan, and called the city of *Chemmis*, now *Achmim*, *Panopolis*, in which Pan had a temple. But this reſemblance was only in appearance. Their Pan, the guardian of the woods, the caverns, and mountains, had only the title of demi-god, and that of Egypt was in the number of the eight divinities. " Hercules, Bacchus, and Pan," ſays Herodotus (*m*) " have been newly received " into the temples of Greece. Pan (that is to " ſay, Mendès) is the moſt ancient of the eight " great Gods of Egypt." Diodorus Siculus adds (*n*), " The Egyptians honour Pan with a " particular worſhip. Almoſt all the temples " have his ſtatue, and the Prieſts who inherit the " prieſthood, firſt initiate themſelves in his my- " ſteries."

Theſe paſſages authorize us to regard *Mendès* as the firſt emblem of the ſun. Indeed, reaſon itſelf leads us to this concluſion. Before men were aſtronomers, before they had conceived the idea of the Tropics and the Equator, and obſerved the various phænomena produced by the revolution of the ſun, the Egyptians muſt have remarked his productive virtue. To paint this ſenſibly, they created an emblematical divinity which they called *Mendès*, *very prolific*, and of which the goat, from his procreative quality, was the image. It is for this reaſon that Dio-

(*m*) Herodotus.
(*n*) Diodorus Siculus, lib. 1.

dorus

dorous Siculus (*o*) declares that *Mendès* is the ſame with Oſiris. In truth, both one and the other repreſent the ſtar of the day, but each of them has different attributes. What adds a freſh degree of evidence to this truth is, that the *Phallus*, the ſymbol of generation, and particularly of *Mendès*, decorated all the Gods I have been ſpeaking of, and ſerved as an ornament to the ſacerdotal dreſs of the Egyptians.

I have laid before you, Sir, the different denominations under which the ſun was adored in ancient Egypt. You have ſeen, that under the celebrated name of Oſiris, he was regarded as the author of time; that Ammon marked his paſſage to the Equator, announced the ſpring, and the renewal of light; that Hercules indicated his beneficent power; that the glorious reign of Horus, repreſenting him in the ſigns of the ſummer, announced to the people the extinction of the ſoutherly winds, and the progreſs of the inundation; that Serapis was the emblem of this luminary, returning from the Equinoxial Line towards the Tropic of Capricorn; that Harpocrates marked the ſlowneſs of his courſe when he had reached the winter Solſtice, and that Mendès was the ſymbol of his generative virtue. Theſe various attributes, perſonified by the Prieſts, compoſed a fabulous theology which the people looked upon as ſacred, and which made them offer incenſe to chimerical deities. In the following letters I ſhall give you ſome

(*o*) Diodorus Siculus, lib. 1.

account

account of Iſis, and the deities connected with her. Through the whole, you will diſcover the ſame ſpirit of myſtery; through the whole, you will ſee the Prieſts ſtudying nature, obſerving aſtronomical and phyſical effects, and concealing their diſcoveries from the eyes of the vulgar, with an impenetrable veil.

I have the honour to be, &c.

LETTER LVI.

OF ISIS, OR THE MOON, AN EGYPTIAN DEITY.

The moon anciently worſhipped by the Egyptians under its proper name Joh; *the adoration of which, when introduced into Greece, gave birth to the fable of Job's being changed into a cow. Its influence on the atmoſphere being obſerved, they afterwards named it* Iris, *which ſignifies* the cauſe of abundance. *The inundation of the Nile aſcribed to the tears of this deity; that is, to the dew, of which ſhe excites a fermentation in the waters. To this day the Coptis pretend that the dew which falls at the Solſtice, makes the waters ferment, and by that means produces the inundation.*

To Mr. L. M.

Grand Cairo.

THE Egyptians, Sir, had a boundleſs veneration for the moon. From the moſt remote antiquity, ſhe was honoured by them as the Queen of Heaven *(p)*. At firſt they worſhipped her under her proper name of *Job (q)*. Inachus, the firſt king of Argos, carried this worſhip into Greece, one hundred and twenty years before the birth of Moſes *(r)*: "It is there," ſays

(*p*) Jeremiah.

(*q*) *Ioh*, in the Egyptian language, ſignifies the moon. Pantheon Ægyptiarum de Jablonſki, tome ſecond.

(*r*) Jablonſki, tome ſecond.

ſays Euſtathius *(s)*, "that a cow is the ſymbol "of Jo or the moon; for in the Argian language "the moon is called *Jo*." John Malala *(t)* confirms this ſentiment. "In our days the Greeks "call the moon Jo, in a myſtic and hidden "ſenſe." After the Greek language prevailed over the Egyptian, this foreign name appeared myſterious, and was only made uſe of within the walls of the temples, where the origin of the ancient modes of worſhip was preſerved; it is for this reaſon that Malala calls it myſtic.

In the end, the Egyptian prieſts, employed in obſerving the phænomena of nature, having remarked that the moon has a direct influence on the atmoſphere, the winds, and the rains, regarded it, like the ſun, as one of the ſources of the inundation. They ſought therefore for an expreſſion which might characterize this effect, and called it *Iſis*, which, in the Egyptian language, ſignifies *(u)*, *the cauſe of abundance*. This happened 320 years after the departure of the Iſraelites. At this period they beſtowed ſurnames on the ſun and moon, proper to fix their diſcoveries, and preſented the people with a new theology. It is to this change that we muſt attribute the origin of the Grecian fable, which makes *Jo* croſs the ſea, metamorphoſed into a cow, and conducts her into Egypt, where ſhe receives the name of *Iſis (x)*. Lucian, who was

(*s*) Commentary on Dion. Perigetes.

(*t*) Chronologie de Jean Malala.

(*u*) Jablonſki, Pantheon Ægyptiacum, tome ſecond.

(*x*) Lucian, Dialogue of the gods, book i.

perfectly

perfectly versed in ancient mythology, puts these words into the mouth of Jupiter: "Conduct *Io* to the banks of the Nile across the "waves of the sea. Let her become *Isis*; let "her be the goddess of the Egyptians; let her "augment the waters of the river and let loose "the winds."

The swelling of the Nile being the event, the most important for this country, since the lives of the whole nation depend upon it, the causes of it were sought after with the greatest attention. The priests, initiated in the mysteries, that is to say, acquainted with the natural sense of the allegories with which they amused the credulity of the vulgar, knew every thing which was connected with the inundation, and by what signs it might be conjectured how far it would be moderate or favourable. Their intimate connections with the Ethiopians, had procured them most valuable information on this head, which they reserved to themselves: "The abundant rains," says Eustathius *(y)* "which fall during the summer in Ethiopia make the Nile swell, as Aristotle and Eudoxus assure us, who say they derive this knowledge from the Egyptian priests." They knew also that these rains owed their origin to the northerly winds. "The rains of "Abyssinia," says Pliny *(z)*, "are attributed to "the northerly winds, which convey thither "during the summer the clouds of the northern "countries." These effects being merely phy-

(*y*) The learned commentator of Homer, Odys. lib. 4.

(z) Plin. lib. 5. and Pomponius Mela, lib. 1.

sical,

ſical, were not unknown to the ſacerdotal tribe; but to rule over the minds of the people, and hold them in ſubjection to the yoke of religion, the prieſts enveloped their own knowledge in myſteries, and were the ſole depoſitaries of ſcience.

The Nile beginning to encreaſe at the new moon which follows the ſolſtice, the prieſts, who regarded this planet as the mother of the winds, (the vulture, the ſymbol of Iſis, announced her power of engendering and letting looſe the winds) *(a)* decreed to her the honour of this phænomenon. "Iſis," ſays Servius *(b)*, "is the Genius of "the Nile. The ſiſtrum ſhe bears in her right "hand, indicates the encreaſe and the flowing "of the waters. The vaſe ſhe holds in her left, "marks their abundance in all the canals." Temples were erected to her in the different provinces, and ſhe had altars and ſacrifices throughout the country. "Coptos," ſays Euſtathius *(c)*, "is a city of the Thebais, where *Jo* is ador-"ed under the name of Iſis. It is on her feſ-"tivals that they celebrate with the ſiſtrum the "increaſe of the Nile." The people, from the allegorical language of the prieſts, imagined that they owed this bounty to the tears of that divinity. The Egyptians, according to Pauſanias, were perſuaded that the tears of Iſis had the virtue to augment the Nile, and to make it riſe up into the country. The Coptis are not

(*a*) Euſeb. prep. Evangel. lib. 3.
(*b*) Servius, Obſervations on the Æneid, lib. 8.
(*c*) Euſtathius the grammarian.

 yet

yet cured of this ſuperſtition. In our days, they ſay that at the ſolſtice there falls a dew which makes the waters of the rivers ferment, and produces their overflow. Are not theſe the tears of the goddeſs ſo celebrated amongſt the ancient Egyptians, their anceſtors(e)? They afterwards attempted to eſtabliſh a pointed analogy between the phænomena of the courſe of the moon, and thoſe of the inundation. They ſaid, as Plutarch *(d)* aſſures us, "That the degrees of the elevation of the waters "correſponded with the phaſes of that planet; "that at Elephantinos they roſe to the height of "twenty-eight cubits, a number equal to the "days of her revolution; that at Mendès, where "the encreaſe was the leaſt conſiderable, they "approached to ſeven cubits, correſponding to "the number of days in which ſhe decreaſes; "that the mean term of the inundation at Memphis, was fourteen cubits, and was relative to "the period of the full moon." This paſſage proves with what attention they endeavoured to become acquainted with every thing, concerning an event ſo particularly intereſting to the public felicity.

The Egyptians having called the moon *Iſis*, or *the cauſe of abundance*, beſtowed this epithet on the earth, as on the mother of fruits. We know, ſays Macrobius *(f)*, that Oſiris is the ſun,

(*d*) Treatiſe of Iſis and Oſiris.

(*c*) Servius on the Æneid, lib. 8.

(*f*) Macrob. Saturnal. lib. 1.

and

and Isis the earth *. Isis, in the Egyptian language, adds Servius, means the earth. Considered in this point of view, she has a striking affinity to the Ceres of the Greeks. This observation has not escaped Herodotus *(g)*, who declares that it is the same divinity. But not to wander from the Egyptian theology, we must not extend this denomination to the globe in general *(h)*. Plutarch, who was well acquainted with this matter, informs us that the priests honoured only with the name of Isis, that part of Egypt watered by the Nile, and in allusion only to her fecundity; he adds that, in the sacred language, they termed the inundation, the marriage of Osiris with Isis.

I have the honour to be, &c.

* The gods, says Blackwell, in whose worship all the Egyptians agreed, were no more than *Isis* and *Osiris*, the sun, moon and earth: for Isis is sometimes *Diana*, though for the most part *Ceres*.——See also Herodotus, *Euterpe*.

Translator.

(*g*) Herodotus, lib. 2.

(*h*) Plutarch has composed a compleat treatise on Isis and Osiris, where much curious matter is to be met with.

LETTER LVII.

OF SOTHIS, A STAR SACRED TO IRIS.

Some writers call Sothis *by the name of Iris; but ſtar, denominated Sirius by the Greeks, and Canicula by the Latins, was only ſacred to that goddeſs. The Egyptians marked the riſing of Sothis by two ſtated periods. The veneration of the people for this ſtar aroſe from a particular circumſtance; namely, that at its heliacal riſing, they could judge of the degree of inundation. On this account, it was named* the ſtar which makes the waters increaſe.

To Mr. L. M.

Grand Cairo.

ASTRONOMY having obſerved the courſe of Sothis, and its connections with Iſis and the inundation, offered this ſtar to the veneration of the people. It became conſecrated by religion, and poſſeſſed ſuch celebrity that ſeveral authors have called it by the name of Iſis. Horapollo (*i*) thus expreſſes himſelf: "Iſis is alſo the name "of a ſtar, called in Egyptian, Sothis, and in "Greek, Aſtrocyon." The Egyptians, adds Damaſcius (*k*), aſſert that Sothis is the ſame with Iſis.

(*i*) Horapollo, Hieroglyphics, lib. 1.
(*k*) Damaſcius, Life of Iſidone.

However

However theſe opinions may be, it is certain that Sothis did not indicate Iſis, but only the conſtellation of the dog-ſtar, and particularly the ſtar which ſhines at the head of it. The Egyptians dated the commencement of their civil year from his riſing. "In Egypt," ſays Plutarch (*l*), "that ſtar was called Sothis, to which the Greeks "give the name of the dog-ſtar, and Sirius. "The conſtellations of Orion and of the Dog, "are conſecrated to Horus and to Iſis." The aſtronomer Theon (*m*), comes in ſupport of this ſentiment. "The Dog riſes towards eleven "o'clock at night. It is at this epocha that the "Egyptian year begins. This ſtar and his riſing "are conſecrated to Iſis." Porphyry (*n*) goes farther. "Aquarius," ſays he, "is not at Memphis, as at Rome, the commencement of the "year, but Cancer. Near to this ſign is Sothis, "called by the Greeks, the dog. The Egyptians regard the riſing of this ſtar as the firſt "day of the month, and as the inſtant of the "birth of the world." We may join to theſe authorities, that of Macrobius (*o*): "Antiquity "aſſigns to the ſun and to the moon, the lion "and the crab, becauſe they were in thoſe ſigns "at the creation of the world." We may believe that theſe laſt words mark the period when men, after numerous obſervations on the movement of the heavenly bodies, formed from their diſcoveries a ſyſtem of doctrine, to which

(*l*) Treatiſe of Iſis and Oſiris.

(*m*) Phænomena of Theon.

(*n*) Porphyry, of the cave of the Nymphs.

(*o*) Macrob. Dream of Scipio, lib. 1.

they

they gave the name of aſtronomy. They dated from this epocha, *the birth of the world.* If this conjecture be juſt, it proves that the Egyptians are the moſt ancient aſtronomers on earth, for it is to them that writers attribute this allegorical language.

The quotations I have laid before you, Sir, demonſtrate that Sothis did not repreſent Iſis, but was only conſecrated to her. The aſtronomers formed two periods which they called Sothic, becauſe they commenced with the riſing of that ſtar. In the former, which comprehended 1461 years, they conſidered principally the courſe of the ſun, who after his long revolution returned to the ſame point of the heavens from whence he ſet out. In the latter, the duration of which was twenty-five years, they paid attention to the courſe of the ſun, and of the moon. They remarked that after this ſpace of time the new moons returned to the ſame days of the year, without being however in the ſame point of the zodiac. They made uſe of this cycle, which comprehended exactly 309 lunar revolutions, to regulate the feſtivals; for they paid great attention to the new moons.

The following was the principal reaſon which led them to conſecrate the dog-ſtar to Iſis: they regarded this divinity as the cauſe of the inundation, and as they were able on the riſing of Sothis to judge of the degree to which the waters would riſe, they dedicated it to this ſtar. Horapollo gives us to underſtand this indiſputably (*p*):

(*p*) Horapollo, Hier. lib. 1.

"The

" The riſing of the dog-ſtar announces by certain ſigns, the events of the year." This paſſage muſt be underſtood as relative to the increaſe of the Nile, the moſt important phænomenon for Egypt. Accordingly Diodorus Siculus (*q*) tells us, that the Egyptians called Sothis, *the ſtar which makes the waters increaſe.*

Bochart and Kircher, who knew that amongſt the Greeks, Sothis was called *Cynos*, Dog, and amongſt the Romans, Canicula, have pretended that this word had the ſame meaning in Egyptian. But this is an error that Jablonſki (*r*) has refuted in a convincing manner. He proves that this name is derived from *Soth-ois*, *the beginning of time.* It is impoſſible to give a more proper deſignation of a ſtar, from whoſe riſing was dated the renewal of the civil year, and in an allegorical manner the creation of the world.

I have the honour to be, &c.

(*q*) Diodorus Siculus, lib. 1.
(*r*) Pantheon Ægyptiacum, tome ſecond.

LETTER LVIII.

OF BUBASTIS, A SYMBOLICAL DEITY OF THE EGYPTIANS.

Great honours paid to Bubastis in Egypt. A city distinguished by her name. She was reputed the patroness of pregnant women, and known to the Greeks and Romans by the name of Diana *and* Ilithyia. *This symbolical deity represented the new moon. Her festival celebrated the third day of the month, because then her increase is visible over all the world.*

To. Mr. L. M.

Grand Cairo.

YOU know, Sir, that the Egyptians bestowed different names on the sun, either to characterize his effects or his relations with respect to the earth ; they followed the same method respecting the moon. Chæremon, a sacred writer of Egypt, leaves no doubt on this subject.—— "*(s)* Every thing which is published of Osiris "and Isis, all the sacerdotal fables, allude only "to the phases of the moon, and the course of "the sun."

Bubastis was one of the principal attributes of Isis. Theology having personified her, formed of

(*s*) See Porphyry, Epist. to Anebon.

of her a divinity, in whose honour a city of that name was built, as described by Herodotus *(t)*, and where the people collected from all parts of Egypt, at a certain period of the year. A cat was the symbol of this deity. The priests fed it with sacred food, and when it died, they embalmed its body, and carried it in pomp to the tomb prepared for it. The ancients have explained this worship variously, all of them in a manner by no means natural, and which I shall not relate. The Greeks pretend that when Typhon declared war against the gods, Apollo transformed himself into a Vulture, Mercury into an Ibis, and Bubastis into a Cat, and that the veneration of the people for the latter animal took rise from that fable; but they ascribe their own ideas to the Egyptians who thought very differently. However that may be, the cat was greatly honoured in Egypt, and a Roman soldier having imprudently killed one, was immediately put to death by the populace.

Bubastis, in the language of the priests, was deemed the daughter of Isis, and even represented her in certain circumstances. It is for this reason that the Greeks, who honoured the moon by the name of Diana, bestowed it also on this Egyptian divinity. Bubastis, says Herodotus *(u)*, is called Diana by the Greeks. The Egyptians attributed to her the virtue of assisting pregnant women, as antiquity testifies *(x)*. Nicharchus

(*t*) Herodotus, lib. 2.
(*u*) Herodotus, lib. 2.
(*x*) Antolog. lib. 1.

says

ſays alſo, in ſpeaking of a lady who had been happily delivered, without invoking her, "Thus "has the office of Bubaſtis been rendered uſe-"leſs. If all women were to produce children "like *Philænium*, what would become of the "worſhip of the Goddeſs?"

The Greeks and Latins, diſciples of the Egyptians, aſcribed the ſame power to Diana; and Horace does not think it unworthy of his pen to addreſs the following Strophe to her (*y*):

Montium Cuſtos nemorumque, Virgo,
Quæ laborantes utero puellas
Ter vocata audis, adimiſque letho,
Diva triformis:

The philoſopher will ſeek for the origin of this ancient worſhip in the laws impoſed by nature on women, and which in ſome meaſure follow the lunar revolutions. The natural philoſophers, and the poets, buried it under allegories, unintelligible to the people.

A perfect reſemblance does not exiſt between the two deities I have been ſpeaking of. The Greeks conſtituted Diana Goddeſs of the Chace, and of the Foreſts, an attribute the Egyptians did not acknowledge in Bubaſtis. The former added, that ſhe was the daughter of Jupiter and Latona, and Bubaſtis was produced by Oſiris and Iſis.

A barbarous cuſtom was introduced at the feſtivals celebrated in honour of Bubaſtis, called by

(*y*) Horace, lib. 3, Ode 16.

the

the Greeks alſo, *Ilithyia*, or *Lucina*, to mark her preſiding over childbed. The Egyptians adored her under this name in the city of *Ilithyia*, ſituated near Latopolis (z). "In this city, ſays "Plutarch (*a*), they burnt men alive, calling "them Typhons, as Manethon aſſures us.— "Their aſhes were thrown to the wind."—— "Amaſis, continues Porphyry (*b*), who cites "the ſame fact, aboliſhed theſe ſanguinary ſacrifices, and eſtabliſhed figures of wax of the "natural ſize, for the human victims." Herodotus (*c*), on the other hand, warmly maintains that the Egyptians were never guilty of this crime. "How could a people, exclaims he, "who can ſcarcely prevail on themſelves to ſacrifice a few animals, ſhed human blood upon "the altars of their Gods?"

The teſtimonies being very poſitive on one ſide and the other, the moſt rational conjecture is, that the paſtoral Arabs who ſubjugated Egypt, long before the arrival of the Iſraélites, brought with them that barbarous cuſtom eſtabliſhed amongſt them from the moſt remote antiquity (*d*). What gives

(z) Strabo, lib. 17, makes mention of this city, the ruins of which are not now to be ſeen.

(*a*) Treatiſe of Iſis and Oſiris.

(*b*) Porphyry, of Abſtinence.

(*c*) Herodotus, lib. 2. According to this hiſtorian, the Egyptians ſacrificed only ſwine, calves, oxen, and geeſe.

(*d*) The Dumatenian Arabs annually ſlew an infant, and buried it under the altar. They made uſe of its carcaſe as of a divine image. *Porphyry, of Abſtinence, book ſecond.* I could cite many other examples to prove that the Arabs ſacrificed human

gives an air of probability to this opinion is, that the Egyptians ceaſed ſhedding human blood as ſoon as the Pharaoh Amaſis had taken Heliopolis from theſe ferocious conquerors, and had driven them to the frontiers of Arabia.

It remains for me, Sir, to reſolve a queſtion which naturally ariſes here. How could Bubaſtis be called the daughter of Iſis, ſince ſhe alſo was a ſymbol of the moon? The Egyptian theology eaſily explains theſe apparent contradictions. Iſis was the general appellation of the moon, Bubaſtis a particular attribute. The ſun, in conjunction with the ſtar of the night, formed the celeſtial marriage of Oſiris and Iſis; the creſcent which appears three days after, was allegorically called their daughter. It is in this ſenſe that the Hebrews called this ſame phænomenon, *the birth of the moon*, and that Horace ſays,

> *Cælo Supinas ſi tuleris manus,*
> *Naſcente lunâ, Ruſtica Phidyle,* &c. &c.

Theſe obſervations inform us, why in the city of Ilithyia, where Bubaſtis was adored, the third day of the lunar month was conſecrated by a particular worſhip *(f)*. In fact, it is three days after

human victims. Mahomet, who forcibly reproaches them with this abominable cuſtom, has abſolutely put an end to it amongſt them. On ſurveying the earth from one extremity to the other, and on recurring to the origin of nations, one ſees with aſtoniſhment that there is not one in which ſuperſtition has not offered up human ſacrifices to the gods.

(e) Horace, Ode 17.

(f) Euſebius, prep. Evangel. lib. 3. relates this fact.

after the conjunction that the moon, disengaged from the rays of the sun, appears as a crescent, and is visible to us. The Egyptians celebrated therefore a solemnity in honour of Bubastis, which in their tongue signified *New Moon (g)*. The crescent with which her head was crowned, expresses palpably the intention of the priests in creating this symbolical divinity.

I have the honour to be, &c.

(g) Jablonski, Pantheon Ægyptiacum, tome second.

LETTER LIX.

OF BUTIS, A SYMBOLICAL DEITY WHICH REPRESENTS THE SUN.

This Goddess, named by the Greeks Latona, had a famous temple in the city of Butis, where the sanctuary consisted of an enormous block of granite. Here she delivered her oracles. The Egyptians placed her in a moving island; and in this they were imitated by the Greeks. This deity was the symbol of the full moon; and as the dew is at that time most copious, they ascribed it to her influence. It was believed she had educated Horus, and saved him from the ambushes of Typhon, which ought to be understood in an allegorical sense.

To. Mr. L. M.

Grand Cairo.

THE Egyptians, Sir, revered also, under the name of *Butis*, or *Buto*, an emblematical divinity, who, in some respects, was the same with Isis. They built in her honour the city of Butis on the branch of the Nile, which running near to Sebennytus, now called *Samanout*, discharges itself into the lake of Bourlos. This goddess was adored there in the magnificent temple I have described to you from Herodotus *(b)*, and the sanctuary of which, composed of a single block of granite of sixty feet every way, is the

(*b*) Letters on Egypt, Vol. I.

largest

largeſt and the heavieſt ſtone mentioned in the hiſtory of nations *(i)*. The oracle of Butis became very famous, and they flocked from all parts of Egypt to conſult it. The Greeks, who derived their mythology from the ſacerdotal fables, gave to this divinity the name of Latona *(l)*. The Egyptians pretended that ſhe had nouriſhed Horus and Bubaſtis, and that the iſland on which her temple was built, floated on the water. The Greeks, imitating their Preceptors, ſaid that Latona, the mother of Apollo and Diana *(k)*, took refuge at Delos, which floated with the waves. The reflection of the Father of Hiſtory *(l)*, how an iſland can be moveable, and ſwim, was no obſtacle to them. They adopted the Egyptian allegory, and accommodated it to their theology. The poets cloathed it in brilliant colours, and the people who could not penetrate the real meaning, offered up their incenſe to chimeras.

(i) The block which compoſed this ſanctuary had only five ſides, for the roof was formed of another ſtone. Theſe ſides were 60 feet ſquare, and ſix in thickneſs, which gives 84,808 cubic feet. Now, this number multiplied by 184 pounds, which is the weight of a cubic foot of granite, gives 15,604,672 pounds; and, deducting from this calculation 604,672 pounds for the opening of the door, the dimenſions of which are not given us by the hiſtorian, there will remain for the weight of that enormous ſtone 15,000,000 of pounds. This maſs greatly ſurpaſſes any which have been moved on earth by human power.

(l) Herodotus, lib. 2.

(k) You have ſeen that Apollo and Diana, worſhipped in Greece, were the ſame with Horus and Bubaſtis.

(l) Herodotus, lib. 2.

Let

Let us examine, Sir, what was the object of the priests in publishing it, for that ought to be the object of our enquiries. You know that they studied with attention all the phænomena of nature. Under a climate, whose temperature is much more constant than that of Europe, they pursued its variations with more facility. The observations of many ages *(m)*, preserved in the sacred archives, and deposited in the sanctuaries, had taught them to foresee what was to happen at each season of the year. They had remarked, that during the new moon the dews were less frequent, and that they became extremely abundant when it was at the full. They attributed to this planet a great influence over the atmosphere, the virtue of attracting the vapours from the lakes and rivers, and of afterwards diffusing them over the earth in imperceptible drops. They made of the full moon, therefore, a divinity, which they called Butis. Conformably to their principles, they placed her abode on the bank of a great lake, as if she might more easily drench herself with its waters. This doctrine, whether it has passed from Egypt into other parts of the world, or whether natural philosophers have deemed it to be founded on real phænomena, has been adopted by several of the ancients and moderns.

" *(n)* The Stoics pretended that the sun en-
" flamed his rays with the waters of the sea, and

(*m*) A people who had a period of 1461 years, must have observed the heavens and all the phænomena of nature for a great number of ages.

(*n*) Plutarch.

" that

"that the moon attracted to herſelf the mild humidity of the lakes and fountains. It is imagined, ſays Pliny (*o*), that the freſh waters are the aliment of the moon, and that the ſun is fed by thoſe of the ſea." "When the moon is full, ſays Macrobius (*p*.) the air either diſſolves itſelf into rain, or if the ſky be ſerene, it diſtils an abundant dew. This is what has made the Lyric Poet, Alcman, ſay, that the dew was the daughter of the air." Amongſt modern naturaliſts, Mr. Mile (*q*) has adopted this ſentiment: "On a fine day, and eſpecially in the ſpring, a ſubtile and cold vapour is attracted by the moon into the middle region of the air. Condenſed ſhortly into imperceptible drops, it moiſtens the earth with abundant dew, and furniſhes plants with proper nouriſhment."

I do not quote theſe authorities, Sir, as unqueſtionable facts: It cannot be denied that the moon has great influence on the atmoſphere ſurrounding our globe; but I think it would be difficult to prove that ſhe is endowed with the power of attracting towards herſelf the exhalations from the water. This is the virtue of the ſun, who dilating the particles of the humid element, and rendering them lighter than the ambient air, forces them to riſe into the atmoſphere, until they are in equilibrio. But were the ancients ignorant of this attraction? Do not the

(*o*) Plini. lib. 2.
(*p*) Macrob. Saturnal. lib. 2.
(*q*) Hiſtoire Naturelle, tome ſecond.

 paſſages

passages I have quoted tend to prove that they were acquainted with this phænomenon, and that they knew that it was more sensible when the two great bodies which enlighten us are in opposition? However that may be, the Egyptians, placed under a burning sky, were hardly ever refreshed by the salutary rains which fall in other climates, and whose country would be uninhabitable, did not the nocturnal dews (r) restore life to vegetables, attentively observed the causes which might produce them. Perceiving that they were more abundant during the full moon, they created of it a divinity, who presided over the dews.

It is at the full moon especially, says Plutarch (s), that the dew falls in the greatest quantity (t). In Egypt, at Butis, and at Babylon, adds Theophrastus, where the rains seldom moisten the earth, the dews furnish the aliment of the plants. This is the reason why the holy scripture (u) frequently promises the Israelites, who inhabited a climate pretty similar to that of Egypt, the dew of heaven, as a signal favour, and announces the refusal of it as a chastisement. To have a more lively idea of the effect of these promises and threats, let us for a moment suppose the devouring sun of these countries tran-

(r) These dews are so copious, especially in summer, that the earth is deeply soaked with them, so that in the morning one would imagine that rain had fallen during the night.

(s) Plutarch, lib. 3.

(t) Theophrastus's History of Plants, lib. 8.

(u) Genesis, chap. xxviii.

sported

ſported to France, and let us examine what would happen in that rich kingdom, if for one year only the ſky, become like iron, poured down neither rain nor dew. We ſhould ſoon ſee the country burnt up, every ſource of fecundity exhauſted, and all animals periſh.

The Egyptians, in ſhort, who were attentive obſervers, had divided (*x*) the time from the creſcent to the full moon, into three equal parts. They called the firſt period *an imperfect gift*, and the third, which comprehends from the eleventh to the fifteenth day, was named per excellentiam, *the perfect gift*, becauſe the dews then fall in abundance. The name of Butis, under which they honoured their ſymbolical deity, preciſely marked the phænomenon of which they believed it to be the cauſe, for it ſignifies, *the ſtar which attracts humidity*, or *the mother of the dew* (*y*).

You will conceive, Sir, from the genius of the Prieſts, that they concealed theſe natural effects under allegories. This is the fable they intended, and which Herodotus has preſerved (z). " The Egyptians ſay that Latona (Butis) whom " they place in the number of their eight great " divinities, dwelling in the city of Butis, where " we ſee her oracle, received Horus as a depoſit " from the hands of Iſis, and concealed him in a " floating iſland. She preſerved him from the " outrages of Typhon, who, ſearching after the " ſon of Oſiris, repaired to this place; for they

(*x*) Proclus, Tim. of Plato.

(*y*) Jablonſki, Pantheon Ægyptiacum, tome ſecond.

(*z*) Herodotus, lib. 2.

" pretend that Horus, or Apollo, and Bubastis, " whom we call Diana, were the children of " Osiris and Isis."

You know, Sir, the destructive effects of the south wind which raises whirlwinds of burning dust, and suffocates men and animals in the midst of the sands. One of its most pernicious effects, too, is totally to prevent the dews from falling, and depriving Egypt of that aliment so necessary to vegetable life. This scourge is the tyrant Typhon, who seeks for the son of Osiris, to put him to death. But Isis has entrusted him to the care of Butis, whose habitation is placed in the midst of waters; that is to say, that the sun, by attracting their exhalations, and the full moon, by exercising her influence on the atmosphere, put an end to those evils produced by the *Khamsin*, and restore to the earth those salutary dews which give new life to nature. This I imagine is the natural interpretation of this sacerdotal fable.

I have the honour to be, &c.

LETTER LX.

THE NILE ADORED AS A GOD BY THE ANCIENT EGYPTIANS.

The Nile raised to the rank of gods. A city built in honour of him. His priests, festivals, and sacrifices. At first he bore the general name of Jaro, *which signifies a river. When the phænomena of his inundation were observed, he received the epithet of* Neilon, *that is,* one who grows in a stated time. *At the winter solstice, they invited him to a feast, which was publicly prepared for the purpose; and the people believed, that without this ceremony he would never overflow their fields.*

To Mr. L. M.

Grand Cairo.

I Have represented the Nile to you, Sir, as a river to which Egypt owes her fertility and her riches; I am now going to paint her to you as a divinity to whom superstition erected altars.—You may conceive of what importance he is to this country, since without the aid of his fertile waters, it would soon be converted into a desert. The veneration of the people was proportioned to the wonderful advantages he procured them. They carried it even to the most fantastic excess *(a)*. Religion, says Plutarch, afford to none of

(*a*) Treatise of Isis and Osiris.

of the gods a more solemn worship than to the Nile. Nor have the Egyptians been the only people who have deified rivers *(b)*. The ancient Greeks and the Indians also granted them divine honours. But the priests of Egypt surpassed them all by the pomp of their ceremonies. They seemed to worship Osiris and Isis only from their connection with this river, and from their decided influence on its waters.

They at first called it *Jaro (c)*, which signifies river. It long retained that general denomination, and we may conclude that when Homer wrote, it had no other, as this poet and geographer calls it simply the river of Egypt. After they had observed, perhaps for ages, the phænomena of its increase, they bestowed on it the epithet of *Neilon, which increases at a certain period (d)*. This characteristic expression, adopted by all the nations of the earth, obliterated the ancient name. Hesiod is the first author who has employed it, from whence we may conjecture that this poet was posterior to Homer. Thetis, says he, has produced from the ocean, the great rivers the Nile, the Alpheus, and the Eridanus, famous for its deep whirlpools (*e*).

(*b*) Maxime de Tyr.

(*c*) Genesis, chap. 41. This name in Coptic signifies also, River. Jablonski, Panthæon Ægyptiacum, tome second.

(*d*) This word comes from the Egyptian *Nei Alei, which encreases at a certain period.* The Greeks have made *Neileon* of it, and the Latins, Nilus. Jablonski, Pantheon Ægyptiacum, tome second.

(*e*) Theogony of Hesiod.

The

The Ethiopians and the Egyptians deſcribed it under different names. Dionyſius Periegetes (*f*) tells us this in theſe words:—"The river "which waters in its long windings the country "of Ethiopia, is called *Siris*, but the inſtant he "bathes with his azure waters the walls of Sye-"na, receives the name of Nile." The rivulets, adds Priſcian (*g*), which form this great river, ruſh from the mountains ſituated to the eaſt of Lybia. The Ethiopians call it *Siris*, and the huſbandmen of Syena, the *Nile*.

The people of Egypt thought they could not make too ſtriking a diſplay of their gratitude towards a river to whom they owed in great meaſure their exiſtence. Accordingly the pompous denominations of (*h*) father, of preſerver of the country, and of the terreſtrial Oſiris, were laviſhed on him. They declared that the gods were born upon his banks (*i*); which muſt be taken allegorically. Nilopolis (*k*) was founded in honour of him, and a ſuperb temple was there built to him. Herodotus (*l*) informs us that in all the conſiderable cities, there were prieſts conſecrated to the Nile, whoſe principal occupation it was to embalm the bodies of ſuch as were killed by crocodiles, or who were drowned in his waters. "In a town

(*f*) Dion. Perieget. Deſcription of the univerſe.

(*g*) Priſcian, Pliny, lib. 5. and Solinus confirm theſe authorities.

(*h*) Treatiſe of Iſis and Oſiris.

(*i*) Diodorus Siculus, lib. 1.

(*k*) The City of the Nile. See Stephen of Byzantium.

(*l*) Herodotus, lib. 2.

"of

"of Egypt," ſays Palladius (*m*), "was to be "ſeen a temple remarkable for its grandeur, "wherein was a wooden ſtatue famous for the "adoration of the Nile." "The fecundity of "this country," adds Libanus (*n*), "is a gift of "the Nile. This god is invited by ſacred cere-"monies to aſſiſt at the ſplendid feſtival which "is annually prepared for him, that he may "overflow the lands. If they who preſide over "divine things, fail to obſerve this ſolemnity at "the appointed time, he would ceaſe to carry his "fertility over the plains of Egypt."

It is evident, Sir, that the prieſts abuſing the credulity of the vulgar, inſtituted this ſuperſti-tious worſhip, the abſurdity of which they knew, in order to eſtabliſh themſelves as the mediators between heaven and earth, and to be regarded as the diſpenſers of abundance. The enigmatical theology which they compoſed, and which they hid from the people under the veil of hierogly-phics, was wonderfully ſubſervient to their views, and they employed all the light of their underſtanding to render it reſpectable. *Theſe obſervations may be applied to many other nations.*

The grand feſtival of the Nile happened at the ſummer ſolſtice, the time when the inundation commenced. "This ſolemnity," ſays Heliodo-rus (*o*), "is the moſt celebrated of the country. "The Egyptians grant divine honours to their "river, and revere him as the firſt of their divi-

(*m*) Pallad. chap. 57.
(*n*) Libanius, Ov. pro Templis.
(*o*) Heliodorus, lib. 9.

"nities.

"nities. They declare him to be the rival of "heaven, ſince he waters the country without "the aid of clouds and rain."

A Nilometer was the ſymbol of his encreaſe. At the moment it commenced, the prieſts brought it forth from the temple of Serapis, and carried it in pomp through the towns and cities. This is the ſtatue of wood againſt which Palladius declaims. When the waters ſubſide, they depoſit it in the ſanctuary. Beſides theſe emblems, they had alſo ſculptured on ſtone, an image of the inundation, conſecrated to the god of the Nile (*p*). Pliny ſpeaks of it as follows in treating of the Baſaltes. "The largeſt we know of, is "that which is placed in the temple of Peace by "the Emperor Veſpaſian. It repreſents the "Nile with ſixteen children playing around him. "They repreſent the number of cubits to which "his waters mount."

Such, Sir, were the religious opinions of the ancient Egyptians reſpecting the Nile, and the feſtivals eſtabliſhed by ſuperſtition in his honour. They are not entirely extinct in our days. The pomp with which the canal that conveys the waters to Grand Cairo is annually opened, ſtill preſerves their memory.

I have the honour to be, &c.

(*p*) Pliny, lib. 36.

LETTER LXI.

OF APIS, THE SACRED OX OF THE EGYPTIANS, ADORED BY THE PEOPLE.

Apis renowned over the world. Kings and princes ſolemnly offered ſacrifices to his godhead. Deſcription of his diſtinguiſhing marks, his inauguration, the place where he was kept, and the temple to which they removed him at his death. Feſtivals celebrated at the birth of a new Apis. This allegorical deity was created by the prieſts to be the guardian of the ſolar year of 365 days, the type of the cycle of 25 years, and the ſymbol of the inundation.

To Mr. L. M.

Grand Cairo.

APIS became famous in Egypt, and renown conveyed his name to the neighbouring nations. Pomponius Mela (*q*), and Ælian (*r*), and Lucian (*s*), who report the teſtimonies of the prieſts, tell us that he was generally worſhipped throughout the country, and that his divinity was proved by evident characters (*t*). Alexander, after conquering this kingdom, did not diſdain to of-

(*q*) Pomponius Mela, lib. 1.
(*r*) Ælian, lib. 11.
(*s*) Lucian.
(*t*) Arrian's Expedition of Alexander.

fer

fer facrifices to him. Titus (*u*), Adrian (*x*), and Germanicus (*y*), went to vifit him, and rendered homage to him. Thefe great Princes were undoubtedly fully fenfible of the folly of this worfhip; but curiofity led them to become acquainted with the myfteries with which the priefts encompaffed their God, and the defire of acquiring the love of the Egyptians, induced them to offer incenfe to their idol.

The wifeft and beft informed writers on the Egyptian religion, inform us, that Apis was only a fymbolical deity. " Amongft the animals " confecrated to ancient rites, fays Ammianus " Marcellinus (z), Mnevis and Apis are the moft " celebrated: the firft is an emblem of the fun, " the fecond of the moon." Porphyry (*a*) tells us that Apis bore the characteriftic figns of the two ftars; and Macrobius (*b*), who confirms this opinion, adds, that he was equally confecrated to them both.

You may fuppofe, Sir, that this Bull, become the object of public adoration, could not be born like other animals; accordingly the priefts publifhed that his origin was celeftial. " An Apis " is feldom born, fays Pomponius Mela (*c*). " He is not produced by the ordinary laws of

(*u*) Suetonius's Life of Titus.
(*x*) Spartian's Life of Adrian.
(*y*) Annal. lib. 2.
(*z*) Ammianus Marcellinus, lib. 22.
(*a*) Porphyry, quoted by Eufebius, Prep. Evangel. lib. 3.
(*b*) Macrobius, Saturnal.
(*c*) Pomponius Mela, lib. 1.

" gene-

"generation. The Egyptians ſay he owes his "birth to celeſtial fire." Plutarch (*d*) explains this paſſage: "The prieſts pretend that the "moon diffuſes a generative influence, and as "ſoon as a cow who takes the bull is ſtruck by "it, ſhe conceives an Apis. Accordingly we "diſcover in him the ſigns of that ſtar."

Such were the fables induſtriouſly ſpread by thoſe who preſided over the divine inſtitutions. The vulgar, to whom this emblematical deity preſaged abundance, received them eagerly, and implicitly believed them. Pliny (*e*) has deſcribed the characters which diſtinguiſhed this ſacred Bull: "A white ſpot reſembling a creſcent, on "the right ſide, and a lump under the tongue, "were the diſtinguiſhing marks of Apis." When a cow, therefore, which was thought to be ſtruck with the rays of the moon, produced a calf, the ſacred guides went to examine it, and if they found it conformable to this deſcription, they announced to the people the birth of Apis, and fecundity.

"Immediately, ſays Ælian (*f*), they built a "temple to the new god, facing the riſing ſun, "according to the precepts of Mercury, where "they nouriſhed him with milk for four months. "This term expired, the prieſts repaired in "pomp to his habitation, and ſaluted him by the

(*d*) Treatiſe of Iſis and Oſiris. Herodotus, lib. 2, ſays the ſame thing.

(*e*) Pliny, lib. 8. Ælian, lib. 11, confirm this deſcription.

(*f*) Ælian's Treatiſe on Animals, lib. 11.

"name

"name of Apis." They then placed him in a veſſel magnificently decorated, covered with rich tapeſtry, and reſplendent with gold, and conducted him to Nilopolis, ſinging hymns, and burning perfumes. There they kept him for forty days (*g*). During this ſpace of time, women alone had permiſſion to ſee him, and ſaluted him in a manner which I ſhall not relate, but which is deſcribed by reſpectable authorities. They were never after admitted into his preſence for the remainder of his life. After the inauguration of the god in this city, he was conveyed to Memphis with the ſame retinue, followed by an innumerable quantity of boats, ſumptuouſly decked out (*h*). There they completed the ceremonies of his inauguration, and he became ſacred to all the world (*i*). Apis was ſuperbly lodged, and the place where he lay was myſtically called *the bed*. Strabo (*k*) having viſited his palace, thus deſcribes it: "The edifice where "Apis is kept, is ſituated near the temple of "Vulcan. He is fed in a ſacred apartment, be-"fore which is a large court. The houſe in "which they keep the cow that produced him, "occupies one of its ſides. Sometimes, to ſa-"tisfy the curioſity of ſtrangers, they make him "go out into this court. One may ſee him at "all times through a window; but the prieſts

(*g*) Diodorus Siculus, lib. 1. Euſebius, prepar. Evangelic. lib. 3, relates the ſame fact.

(*h*) Ammian. Marcellinus.

(*i*) Pliny, lib. 8.

(*k*) Strabo, lib. 17.

"produce

" produce him alſo to public view." Once a year, ſays Solinus, they preſent *a heifer* to him, and the ſame day they kill her.

A bull, born in ſo marvellous a manner, muſt be poſſeſſed of ſupernatural knowledge. Accordingly the prieſts publiſhed, that he predicted future events by geſtures, by motions, and other ways, which they conſtrued according to their fancy. " Apis, ſays Pliny (*l*), has two temples " called Beds, which ſerve as an augury for the " people. When they come to conſult him, if " he enters into a particular one, it is a favour- " able preſage, and fatal if he paſſes into the " other. He gives anſwers to individuals by " taking food from their hands. He refuſed that " offered him by Germanicus, who died ſoon " after." It would be unjuſt to conclude, that this reſpectable writer gave credit to ſuch auguries. He relates the opinions of the Egyptians, and contents himſelf with citing facts without offering his judgment.

(*m*) Diogenes Laertius informs us, that during the ſtay of the aſtronomer Euxodus, in Egypt, Apis appeared to lick the edge of his garment, and that the prieſts predicted his celebrity; but that his career would be of ſhort continuance. Several hiſtorians relate, that ſome children who were playing round the ſacred Bull, feeling themſelves ſuddenly inſpired, ſaw into futurity, and revealed events that were to happen. What

(*l*) Pliny, lib. 8.

(*m*) Diogenes Laertius, lib. 7.

empire

empire has superstition over the minds of men! yet they boasted of their knowledge!

You have seen, Sir, the installation of Apis. His anniversary was always celebrated for seven days (*n*). The people assembled to offer sacrifices to him, and, what is extraordinary, oxen were immolated on the occasion (*o*). This solemnity did not pass without prodigies. Ammianus Marcellinus, who has collected the testimonies of the ancients, relates them in these words (*p*): "During the seven days in which the priests of "Memphis celebrate the birth of Apis, the cro-"codiles forget their natural ferocity, become "gentle, and do no harm to any body."

This Bull, however, so honoured, must not exceed a mysterious term fixed for his life. "Apis, says Pliny (*q*), cannot live beyond a cer-"tain number of years. When he has attained "that period, they drown him in the fountain "of the priests; for it is not permitted, adds "Ammianus Marcellinus, to let him prolong his "life beyond the period prescribed for him by "the sacred books." When this event happened, he was embalmed, and privately let down into the subterraneous places destined for that purpose. In this circumstance, the priests announced that Apis had disappeared; but when he died a natural death, before this period arrived,

(*n*) Nicetas.

(*o*) Herodotus, lib. 2, relates this fact.

(*p*) Ammianus Marcellin. lib. 22, to which may be added the testimony of Solinus, who cites this fact.

(*q*) Pliny, lib. 8.

rived, they proclaimed his death, and solemnly conveyed his body to the temple of Serapis.

(r) "At Memphis was an ancient temple "of Serapis, which strangers were forbidden "to approach, and where the priests themselves "only entered when Apis was interred. It was "then, says Plutarch (s), that they opened the "gates called *Lethes* and *Cocythe* (of oblivion and "lamentation) which made a harsh and piercing "sound."

Ammianus Marcellinus, and Solinus, paint with great energy the general despair of the Egyptians, who with cries and lamentations, demanded another Apis from heaven; and Lucian (t) represents this very pleasantly. "When "Apis dies, is there any one so enamoured of "his long hair as not immediately to cut it off, "or to display on his bald head the symptoms of "his sorrow?"

It is of some consequence, Sir, to know the term prescribed for the life of Apis, since that will point out to us the object of the priests in creating this symbolical divinity. Plutarch throws some light on this subject (u). "The "number of five, multiplied by itself, gives the "number of the letters of the Egyptian alpha- "bet, and the age of Apis." His life therefore was twenty-five years. Now you know that this number marked a period of the sun and

(r) Pausanias.

(s) Treatise of Isis and Osiris. These were the gates of Serapis.

(t) Lucian, of sacrifices.

(u) Treatise of Isis and Osiris.

of

of the moon, and that this Bull was consecrated to these two bodies. The following observation of Syncellius (*x*) may still farther aid us: When he comes down to the thirty-second Pharaoh, called Aseth, he says, "Before Aseth, the solar "year consisted but of 360 days. This Prince "added five to complete its course. In his reign "a calf was placed amongst the gods, and named Apis." The following passage will furnish us with an additional explanation (*y*): "It was "customary to inaugurate the Kings of Egypt "at Memphis, in the temple of Apis. They "were here first initiated in the mysteries, and "were religiously invested; after which, they "were permitted to bear the yoke of the god, "through a town, to a place called the sanctuary, the entrance of which was prohibited "the profane. There they were obliged to "swear that they would neither insert months "nor days in the year, and that it should remain composed of 365 days, as had been established by the ancients."

These facts authorize us to believe, that Apis was the tutelary divinity of the new form given to the solar year, and of the cycle of twenty-five years, discovered at the same time. Nor can it be doubted that he had a marked relation to the swelling of the Nile, for it is testified by a great number of historians. You know that the new moon which followed the summer solstice, was the æra of this phænomenon, on which

(*x*) Chronography of Syncellius.
(*y*) Fabricius, Bibliothec. Latin.

the eyes of every body were fixed. Pliny ſpeaks as follows on this ſubject (*a*): "Apis had on his "right ſide a white mark, repreſenting the cre-"ſcent: this mark, continues Ælian (*b*), indi-"cated the commencement of the inundation." Ammianus (*c*) confirms theſe authorities. If Apis poſſeſſed the characteriſtic ſigns which proved his divine origin, he promiſed fertility and abundance of the fruits of the earth. It ſeems demonſtrated therefore that this ſacred Bull, the guardian of the ſolar year of 365 days, was alſo regarded as the genius who preſided over the overflowing of the river. The prieſts, by fixing the courſe of his life to 25 years, and by making the inſtallation of a new Apis concur with the renewal of the period, of which I have been ſpeaking, had probably perceived, as the reſult of long meteorological obſervations, that this revolution always brought about abundant ſeaſons. Nothing was better calculated to procure a favourable reception of this emblematical deity from the people, ſince his birth was a preſage to them of a happy inundation, and of all the treaſures of teeming nature.

The ſolemnity of this inauguration was called *Apparition*. That which was renewed every year towards the twelfth or thirteenth of the month *Payn*, which correſponds with the ſeventeenth or eighteenth of June, was called *the birth of Apis*. It was a time of rejoicing, which Ælian

(*a*) Pliny, lib. 8.
(*b*) Ælian's Treatiſe on Animals, lib. 11.
(*c*) Ammian. Marcellin.

describes in the following manner *(d)*: "What "festivals! what sacrifices take place in Egypt "at the commencement of the inundation! It "is then that all the people celebrate the birth "of Apis. It would be tedious to describe the "dances, the rejoicings, the shews, the ban-"quets, to which the Egyptians abandon them-"selves on this occasion, and impossible to ex-"press the intoxication of joy which breaks "forth in all the towns of the kingdom."

The name of this respectable Bull may still throw a fresh light on the observations you have been reading. *Api*, in fact, in the Egyptian tongue, signifies *number (e), measure*. This epithet perfectly characterizes an animal established as the guardian of the solar year, the type of the cycle of twenty-five years, and the presage of a favourable inundation *(f)*.

I have the honour to be, &c.

(d) Ælian's Treatise on Animals.

(e) Jablonski, Pantheon Égyptiacum, tome second.

(f) Monsieur Huet, Bishop of Avranche, has endeavoured to prove that Apis was a symbolical image of the Patriarch Joseph, and has supported his opinion with all his erudition.—— Some authors, misled by the authority of this learned man, have adopted this system, which I have not thought proper seriously to combat, because it falls of itself. It proves only to what point a prejudiced man may abuse his knowledge, when his pen is not guided by sound reason and the spirit of impartial criticism.

LETTER LXII.

OF MNEVIS AND ONUPHIS, SACRED BULLS OF ANTIENT EGYPT.

Mnevis and Onuphis consecrated to the sun. The worship of the former began in remote antiquity, but the epoch of its commencement is unknown. The latter, brought up in the temple of Apollo, at Hermunthis, had no degree of celebrity, if we may judge by the silence of historians. Apis, deified with the view of preserving the remembrance of ancient observations, became famous, and eclipsed the other two.

To Mr. L. M.

Grand Cairo.

MNEVIS and ONUPHIS were two bulls, consecrated to the sun. The former was the tutelary divinity of Helipolis; the latter, fed in the temple of Apollo, of *Hermunthis*, now called *Armant*, had relation to the increase of the Nile.

"The city of Heliopolis, says Strabo *(g)*, "built on an artificial eminence, possesses a temple of the sun. The bull Mnevis, is fed there "in a sacred precinct. The Heliopolitans regard "him as a god." The ancients unite in affirming

(g) Strabo, lib. 17.

ing that this bull was consecrated to the sun (*h*). The epocha of his consecration is lost in the obscurity of time. It is much more ancient than that of Apis. Mr. de Vignoles (*i*) makes it mount as high as to Menes, the first of the Pharaohs; but this opinion, being unsupported by the authority of history, must be regarded as a conjecture. It was very probably, however, prior to the departure of the Israelites, who, accustomed to the Egyptian idolatry, moulded a golden calf in the desert, to serve them as a guide. The worship of Mnevis gradually disappeared, when Apis, who was consecrated to more important events, became the general deity of the country. Accordingly Macrobius (*k*) informs us that Mnevis held only the second rank amongst the sacred Bulls. Ammianus Marcellinus (*l*) adds, that they related nothing memorable of him.

Strabo (*m*) relates that Cambyses, the scourge of Egypt, overthrew the magnificent temple of Heliopolis. It is doubtless from this æra that we must date the downfal of the worship of Mnevis (*n*). Jablonski, who has interpreted his name, says that it signified, *dedicated to the sun*. The city of Hermunthis, which possessed a nilome-

(*h*) Diodorus Siculus, lib. 1. Ælian's Treatise on Animals, lib. 11, and Porphyry cited by Eusebius, Prep. Evang. lib. 3.

(*i*) Chronologie de Vignoles, tome second.

(*k*) Macrob. Saturnal. lib. 1.

(*l*) Ammian. Marcellin. lib. 22.

(*m*) Strabo, lib. 17.

(*n*) Jablonski, tome second. He derives it from *Mneein*, dedicated to the sun.

ter,

ter, admitted alſo the worſhip of a bull, called *Onuphis* (o), the Good Genius, becauſe he was honoured as the ſymbol of abundance. The prieſts fed him in the magnificent temple of Apollo, which I have deſcribed to you in my twelfth Letter. At the bottom of one of its apartments are ſtill to be ſeen two marble bulls, ſurrounded by women who ſuckle their children. Doubtleſs they celebrated in his honour the feſtivals practiſed on the birth of Apis. But as this city was leſs conſiderable than Memphis, become the capital of the kingdom, after the Kings of Thebes had transferred thither the ſeat of empire, Onuphis did not enjoy ſo much celebrity as Apis. This is the reaſon why none of the ancients, except Strabo, Macrobius, and Ælian, make any mention of him. Such, Sir, were the bulls conſecrated by the prieſts, to preſerve the memory of their diſcoveries, and which the vulgar worſhipped as divinities.

You muſt have remarked, Sir, that, from the moſt remote antiquity, the Egyptians conſecrated the ox or the bull, as the ſymbol of fecundity. The ancient Greeks followed this example. In the end they contented themſelves with painting the horn of that animal, filled with ears of corn, and fruits, to expreſs this emblem, and the poets ſang the Cornucopia in their verſes. Thus have the greateſt part of the ancient cuſtoms been derived from Egypt.

I have the honour to be, &c.

(o) Ælian's Treatiſe of Animals, lib. 12.

LET-

LETTER LXIII.

OF THE TERRESTRIAL SERAPIS, A SYMBOLICAL DEITY WHICH BORE A RELATION TO THE NILE.

The terreſtrial Serapis regarded by the Egyptians as a deity that preſides over the encreaſe of the waters. His emblem a Nilometer of wood, divided into cubits. A feſtival celebrated in honour of him at the commencement of the inundation. The Nilometer named by the prieſts Sari Api, the pillar of menſuration. *Brought forth from his ſanctuary at the beginning of the inundation, and led back when it was on the decline. Such was the origin of this emblematical deity, to which the Greeks gave the name of Serapis.*

To Mr. L. M.

Grand Cairo.

THE Egyptians, Sir, acknowledge two deities of the name of Serapis, one celeſtial, of whom I have ſpoken, the other terreſtrial, which ſhall be the ſubject of this letter. The former repreſented the ſun of autumn, the latter was connected with the inundation *(q)*. "The people of "Egypt," ſays Gregory of Nazianzen, "mea-"ſure the encreaſe of the Nile by cubits." "Some authors," ſays Suidas *(r)*, "aſſert

(*q*) Gregory of Nazianzen, Or. 29.
(*r*) Suidas, on the word Serapis.

"that

"that Serapis is the ſame as Jupiter, others "that he repreſents the Nile, becauſe he bears on "his head a buſhel, and a cubit, ſymbols of "the inundation."

The writers from whom he has gathered theſe opinions were all equally in the right. The celeſtial Serapis might be called Jupiter, as an emblem of the ſun, and that of whom I ſpeak, was thought to preſide over the over-flowing of the river; accordingly Ariſtides, the rhetorician (s), calls him the god who makes the waters ſwell in ſummer, and calms the hurricanes. The ancient Chriſtian authors agree in this point with the Gentiles. They attribute, ſays Ruffin (t), to Serapis, that virtue of the Nile which procures riches and fertility to Egypt. Socrates (u) confirms this ſentiment: "The Egyptians award to "Serapis the glory of watering their fields."

It may be proper to enquire into the origin of this deity. By following the rays of light ſcattered through the annals of hiſtory, we ſhall be able to tread upon his footſteps, and arrive at his cradle. You know that the Egyptians, attentive to every thing which could give them an inſight into the progreſs of the inundation, had conſtructed ſeveral Nilometers in different parts of the kingdom. There was one in the Iſle of Elephantinos, at Hermunthis (x), now called Ar-

(s) The rhetorician Ariſtides, Or. pro Serapis.

(t) Hiſtoire de l'Egliſe, lib. 2.

(u) Socrates, Hiſtory of the Church, lib. 1.

(x) Heliodorus, lib. 19. deſcribes the Nilometer of Hermunthis.

mant,

mant, at Memphis, and even in the Lower Egypt; at firſt they contented themſelves with building a hall on a level with the bed of the river, and the height of the water was marked by lines traced out on the walls at ſtated diſtances. They afterwards erected in the middle of this baſon, which the ancients called a well, a column divided into cubits and digits, and which ſerved by way of Nilometer. It was called *Sari Api (y)*, *column of meaſurement*. This place became ſacred, and the prieſts, the depoſitaries of all knowledge, had the excluſive right of entering it. Their obſervations, and their diſcoveries, written in ſacerdotal characters, ſerved by way of guide to their ſucceſſors. Enlightened by theſe meteorological tables, continued for ages, and more and more improved, they predicted from this ſanctuary the phænomena of the inundation long before it reached its term. Maſters of this important ſcience, they announced to the people, either abundance or ſterility, and were looked upon as oracles. In order to give more authenticity to their predictions, they declared that they received them from Serapis, the divinity under whoſe protection they placed the column of meaſurement. Aware that the vulgar muſt be gratified with ſenſible objects, they compoſed a Nilometer of wood, which was the emblem of Serapis, and to which they attributed a divine virtue.— The prieſts carried it about with ſolemnity on the feſtivals of Apis.

(*y*) Jablonſki, tome ſecond, gives this explication of theſe Egyptian words of which the Greeks have made Serapis.

"It

" It was the cuſtom," ſays Ruffin (*x*), " to " carry the meaſure of the Nile into the temple " of Serapis, as to the author of the inundation. " The Nilometer was afterwards depoſited *in the* " *church* to render homage to the ſovereign of the " waters." Zozomene (*a*) adds that this change took place under the Emperor Conſtantine — From that moment the cubit with which they meaſured the increaſe of the river, ceaſed to be carried into the temples of the Gentiles, and it was placed in the churches. Julian (*b*), called the apoſtate, reſtored things to their former ſituation; but the Emperor Theodoſius, having overthrown the magnificent temples of Serapis at Alexandria, aboliſhed this ſuperſtitious ceremony. Theſe and ſeveral other authorities I could cite, if it were neceſſary, to prove that the Egyptians at firſt called the Nilometer, *Serapis*, the column for meaſurement; that they beſtowed the ſame name on the god under whoſe protection they placed it, and to whom they attributed the power of encreaſing the waters; and laſtly, that they carried the ſymbolical image of it in their ſolemnities. Thus did they abuſe their knowledge to keep the people in idolatry, and to render themſelves reſpectable in their eyes.

(*c*) There is ſtill remaining an Alexandrian crown piece, on one face of which, the Nile, under the form of an old man, is repreſented in a

(z) Ruffin, Hiſtoire de l'Egliſe, livre ſecond.
(*a*) Zozomene, Hiſtoire de l'Egliſe, livre premier.
(*b*) Zozomene, Hiſtoire de l'Egliſe, livre 4.
(*c*) Pignorius, expoſition de la table Iſiaque.

recum-

recumbent attitude. He bears a bushel on his head, holds in one hand the cornucopia, and in the other a piece of papyrus with this inscription: *To the Holy God Nile.* On the reverse of the medal, is a head of Serapis, covered with a bushel, with this legend: *To the Holy God Serapis.*

I shall not lay any stress, Sir, like Jablonski, on the situation of the ancient temple of Serapis, as that question appears to me a matter of indifference. I shall only observe that this learned man, to whose knowledge I do homage, and whose valuable researches have been so serviceable to me, is deceived in placing that edifice in the Isle of *Raouda*, where we at present see a Mekias, the sole remains of the Nilometers of Egypt. I could present you with a long dissertation on this subject, and combine with the testimonies of the ancients my own local knowledge; but I should be apprehensive of abusing your patience. My object was to trace the origin of the terrestrial Serapis, which I hope I have fulfilled.

I have the honour to be, &c.

LET-

LETTER LXIV.

OF ANUBIS, A SYMBOLICAL DEITY OF THE EGYPTIANS.

Anubis had in Egypt temples and priests, and a city was built in honour of him. His statue bore the head of a dog; and this animal, from being his living image, was consecrated to him. This allegorical divinity, invented by the astronomers, represented the horizon. Hence he was regarded as the inseparable companion of Osiris and Iris. Called in the sacred language their illegitimate son, because he is not luminous of himself, and shines only by borrowed lustre.

To Mr. L. M.

Grand Cairo.

ANUBIS, who was regarded as the faithful companion of Osiris and of Isis, received divine honours in Egypt. Temples and priests were consecrated to him, and his image was borne in all religious ceremonies. Lucian puts these words into the mouth of Socrates (d): Do you not see with what respect the Egyptians adore the god Anubis? They give to his statue an emblematical form, which is the head of a dog upon

(d) Lucian, tome premier.

a hua human body *(e)*. Accordingly Virgil *(f)* and Ovid call him the *Barker Anubis.*

The ingenious Lucian, who diffuſes ſuch a delightful vein of pleaſantry over every object that falls under his pen, and who in his exquiſite ſarcaſms, ſpares neither heroes nor gods, introduces Momus on the ſtage, and makes him ſpeak as follows: "O thou whom Egypt repreſenteth "with the head of a dog! Who art thou? Speak. "Since thou barkeſt, how haſt thou preſumed "to ſuffer thyſelf to be placed in the rank of "the immortal gods *(g)*?"

(h) Cynopolis, the preſent *Minieh*, ſituated in the lower Thebais, was built in honour of Anubis. The temple wherein he was worſhipped no longer ſubſiſts. The prieſts celebrated his feſtivals there with great pomp, and conſecrated the dog to him, as his living repreſentation *(i)*. "Anubis," ſays Strabo, "is the city of dogs, "the capital of the Cynopolitan prefecture.— "Theſe animals are fed there on ſacred ali-"ments, and religion has decreed them a wor-"ſhip." An event however, related by Plutarch, brought them into conſiderable diſcredit with the people. Cambyſes having ſlain the god Apis, and thrown his body into a field, all animals re-

(*e*) Diodorus Siculus, lib. 1. ſays, The god called Anubis is repreſented with the head of a dog.

(*f*) Virgil, Æneid, lib. 8. Ovid, Metamorphoſis, lib. 9.

(*g*) Lucian, tome ſecond.

(*h*) Cynopolis, the city of the Dog.

(*i*) Strabo, lib. 17. Stephen of Byzantium, adds, Cynopolis is the city in Egypt where Anubis is adored.

ſpected it except the dogs, which alone eat of his fleſh. This impiety diminiſhed the popular veneration for them.

Cynopolis was not the only city which burned incenſe on the altars of Anubis. He had chapels in almoſt all the temples, which made Juvenal ſay (*k*), So many cities venerate the dog!—On ſolemnities, his image always accompanied thoſe of Iſis and Oſiris. Rome having adopted the ceremonies of Egypt, the Emperor Commodus (*l*), to celebrate the Iſiac feaſts, ſhaved his head, and himſelf carried the god Anubis. His ſtatue was either of maſſive gold or gilt, as well as the attributes that accompanied him. The ancients are agreed in this point, and Lucian, who relates an outrage committed by a Syrian ſlave, confirms this ſentiment. This ſlave, ſays he, formed a connection with ſome ſacrilegious perſons. They entered the ſanctuary of Anubis, robbed the gods of two vaſes, and a caduceus of gold, with two cynocephati of ſilver. Even the name of Anubis ſignifies *gilded* (*m*). It was myſterious, and the Egyptian prieſts, as we ſhall ſee, had not given it without reaſon.

But what was the ſignification of this emblematical deity? what is the natural meaning concealed under it? Plutarch explains this (*n*).

(*k*) Juvenal, Sat. 13.

(*l*) Lampridius, chap 9. Spartian quotes the ſame fact.

(*m*) Jablonſki, Pantheon Ægyptiacum, tome 3. Anubis, ſays he, comes from *Nub*, *Gold*, and *Annub*, *gilt*. The Greeks have made Anubis of it.

(*n*) Treatiſe of Iſis and Oſiris.

"The

"The circle which touches and ſeparates the "two hemiſpheres, and which is the cauſe of "this diviſion, receiving the name of *Horizon*, is "called Anubis. He is repreſented under the "form of a dog, becauſe that animal watches day "and night." St. Clemens of Alexandria, who was well informed in the myſtic theology of the Egyptians, favours this explication. The two dogs, ſays he *(o)*, (the two Anubis) are the ſymbols of two hemiſpheres, which environ the terreſtrial globe. He adds in another place: Others pretend that theſe animals, the faithful guardians of men, indicate the tropics, which guard the ſun on the ſouth and on the north, like porters.

If you adopt, Sir, the former of theſe interpretations you will ſee that the prieſts, regarding Anubis as the horizon, gilded his ſtatue, to mark that this circle receiving the firſt rays of the ſun, appears ſparkling with brightneſs on his riſing, and that at his ſetting, he reflects his laſt rays upon the earth. They ſaid in their ſacred fables, that Anubis was the ſon of Oſiris, but illegitimate. In fact, he only gives to the earth a borrowed light, and he never can be eſteemed, like Horus, as the father of the day, or as the legitimate offspring of Oſiris. We may add, that the viſible horizon turning with the ſun is his inſeparable companion.

In the latter of theſe explications, where Anubis repreſents the tropics, he is alſo the faithful

(*o*) Clemens of Alexandria, ſtroma 5.

guar-

guardian of Isis and Osiris. In fact, the course of the sun and of the moon is contained between the circles wherein the solstices are performed. They neither deviate to the right nor left.—These limits assigned by the author of nature, might therefore, in hieroglyphic language, be represented by a divinity with the head of a dog, who seemed to oppose their passage on the side of the two poles. The other opinion, notwithstanding, seems to me more natural, and to be more analogous to the ideas of the priests.

You see, Sir, that those authors who have amused themselves at the expence of the Egyptians, have either been insincere, or did not comprehend their allegories. It is reasonable to imagine that Anubis, at first, was only a symbolical image, invented by astronomers, to give a sensible expression of their discoveries; that afterwards, the people, accustomed to see it in their temples, which were the depositaries of science, adored it as a deity; and that the priests favoured their ignorance by connecting it with their religion. The worship of Anubis introduced that of the dog, become his emblem.—Almost all the gods of the Gentiles have originated in this manner. Before the invention of writing, men made use of imitative figures to convey their ideas. This representative language was at first intelligible to every body.—When characters were discovered, adapted to transmit the thought by sounds, the people employed them, because they were more easy.—The hieroglyphics remained in the sanctuaries,

and

and the priefts alone preferved the knowledge of them. In the end, thefe allegorical figns no longer reprefented the real meaning of things to vulgar underftandings, but the exterior forms and figures only, which became the objects of fuperftition.

I have the honour to be, &c.

LETTER LXV.

OF TYPHON, A SYMBOLICAL DEITY OF THE EGYPTIANS.

Typhon regarded as an evil genius. The Crocodile and Hippopotamus consecrated to him. His statue insulted, when the calamities, of which they believed him to be the cause, did not cease. This allegorical deity is represented, in the imagination of the priests, winter, and the fatal effects produced in Egypt by the blowing of the south and south-east winds. The sacred fable on the subject of Typhon is propagated into Phœnicia, Greece, and Italy. It is decorated with new allegories by the natural philosophers and poets of those countries, and accommodated to their religion. Notwithstanding the veils with which they have covered it, its origin is still perceptible.

To Mr. L. M.

Grand Cairo.

I HAVE already spoken to you, Sir, of Typhon, because his history is connected with that of all the gods of Egypt. I am going to lay before you the principal traits of them. Their combination will throw a new light on the enigmatical theology of this country. Hitherto you have seen it offer incense only to beneficial deities, adoring the sun, moon, the Nile, and consecrating

ſecrating animals to them. Theſe acts of homage were dictated by gratitude. The worſhip of Typhon was the reſult of anxiety and fear. The beneficial gods received thankſgivings and offerings. They ſtrove to appeaſe this malignant genius by artifices; and when the calamities which were imputed to him did not ceaſe, they inſulted his image.

The Egyptians regarding Typhon as the evil principle, conſecrated to him the crocodile (*p*), the hippopotamus, and the aſs, on account of his duſky colour. Theſe animals, which they imagined were agreeable to him, were worſhipped in ſeveral cities. They were fed in ſacred precincts, and they imagined that theſe religious marks of attention would calm the fury of Typhon, whoſe ſoul was thought to animate them (*q*). The Egyptians, ſays Plutarch, ſtrove to appeaſe this evil genius by ſacrifices.—— When this failed, they treated him as follows (*r*): "On certain feſtivals they loaded him with opprobrious terms, abuſed him with invectives, "and ſtruck his ſtatue. If any extraordinary "heats happened which occaſioned peſtilential "diſorders, or other calamities, the prieſts, "holding Typhon in horror, conducted into "ſome gloomy place one of the animals dedi-"cated to him. Firſt, they tried to terrify

(*p*) Treatiſe of Iſis and Oſiris. Herodotus, lib. 2.

(*q*) Treatiſe of Iſis and Oſiris. Herodotus confirms this opinion: The crocodile, ſays he, dedicated to Typhon, received worſhip in certain cities, becauſe the Egyptians were perſuaded that his ſoul animated them, lib. 2.

(*r*) Plutarch in the ſame treatiſe.

"him by menaces, and, if the contagion did "not cease, they sacrificed him to the public "vengeance."

It is clear that the object of these ceremonies was to appease the alarms of the people, and to raise their hopes. During the time of practising them, the mischiefs resulting from the southerly wind might cease, and the nation, who concluded that Typhon was neither appeased by sacrifices nor intimidated by menaces and insults, ascribed the glory of it to the priests.

Let us examine the natural meaning of the word *Typhon*. Jablonski *(s)* tells us, it is composed of *Theu*, *wind*, and *Phou*, *pernicious* (*t*). The testimonies of the most ancient authors confirm this interpretation. Hesychius says, "They "give to a violent wind, the air of which is "scorching, the name of Typhon." Eustathius renders the same expression by that of *(u) burning winds*, and Euripides employs it to express a whirl of burning wind (*x*).

The ancient Egyptians, to characterise its violence, gave it the epithet of *Apoh*, *(y)* Giant.

I have mentioned to you more than once, in the course of these Letters, its destructive ef-

(*s*) Jablonski, Pantheon Ægyptiacum, tome 3.

(*t*) Hesychius.

(*u*) Eustathius's Iliad of Homer.

(*x*) Euripides, Phenisses. The same wind is called by Job, chap. 27 (Latin version) *burning wind*; by the Greeks, *breath of fire*; by the Latins, *Eurus*; by the Arabs, *Sem*, poison; lastly, by the modern Egyptians, *Merisi*, south wind, and more generally *Khamsin*.

(*y*) Jablonski, Panth. Ægypt. tome 3.

fects;

fects; but however forcible the expressions I have made use of may seem, they fall greatly short of the reality. Whole caravans suffocated in the deserts, whole tribes of Arabs extinguished in one day, the sky obscured by a dust which burns the eyes, destroys the functions of the breast, and hides the face of the sun; showers of sand with which the surface of all Egypt has sometimes been covered, the sandy hills, in short, which rolled along from the depth of the deserts, threaten to swallow up every living being; such is the calamity they called *the giant Typhon*. I have read in the history of the Arabs (z), of a hurricane from the south which lasted three days and three nights, and Egypt was on the brink of ruin. Had it continued with the same violence, this beautiful kingdom would have been converted into a frightful solitude. The Priests, to express the fury of Typhon, published in their allegorical language, that he was not born in the same manner as Osiris and Horus; but that, having burst open the side of his mother, he escaped by that opening (*a*).

Herodotus (*b*) gives the following description of two statues, which in his time were placed in the temple of Vulcan, at Memphis "One "which faces the north, and which is called "Summer, is adored by the Egyptians, and is "encompassed with marks of their respect and

(z) Elmacin, History of the Arabs.

(*a*) Treatise of Isis and Osiris.

(*b*) Herodotus, lib. 2.

"gra-

" gratitude; the other turned towards the ſouth, " and called Winter, meets with a very diffe- " rent fate." The latter is that which they ſcourged on certain occaſions, becauſe it repreſented Typhon. It is in the month of February, in fact, that the ſoutherly wind begins to be felt, and to cauſe the misfortunes I have mentioned. During the ſummer, the northerly winds prevail in their turn, purify the air, and procure the happieſt effects for this country. The knowledge of theſe circumſtances will furniſh us with the means of giving a ſatisfactory explanation of the ſacred fable, circulated by the prieſts, on the ſubject of Typhon, and of which I have already, in part at leaſt, delivered to you my ſentiments. Plutarch relates it at length. It will be ſufficient to cite ſome of the moſt remarkable particulars of it.

(*c*) Oſiris, having mounted the throne of Egypt, reigned there with glory, and became celebrated for his beneficence and juſtice. He travelled over the univerſe to load men with his bounties. Typhon, his brother, did not dare for ſome time to undertake any thing againſt his intereſt, becauſe Iſis watched over the ſafety of the kingdom; but when Oſiris returned from Ethiopia, Typhon lay in wait for him with 72 conſpirators, attacked and ſlew him, encloſed his body in a wooden coffin, and threw it into the Nile. It deſcended into the Mediterranean by the Tanitic branch. Iſis found it on the coaſt

(*c*) Treatiſe of Iſis and Oſiris.

of

of Phœnicia, and brought it back to Egypt. But the uſurper perceiving it at night, whilſt he was chaſing the wild boar, broke it, divided the body into 14 parts, and diſperſed the ſcattered members over the country. Iſis collected them all (*d*), and carefully preſerved them. Delivered from all his enemies, Typhon exerciſed his deſpotic ſway over Egypt. To make ſure of the crown, he tried to kill Horus, ſon of Oſiris, and induſtriouſly ſought after him But Latona, who had concealed him, and who brought him up at Butis, evaded his reſearches. This god became ſtrong, declared war againſt the murderer of his father, vanquiſhed him, and delivered him over, loaded with irons, to the care of his mother. Iſis ſet him at liberty. Horus, full of indignation, wreſted from her her crown, fought freſh battles with the tyrant, and, after overthrowing him a ſecond time, enjoyed a glorious and peaceable reign.

A few ſhort obſervations will ſuffice to explain this fable, which muſt be already partly underſtood. Oſiris is the general name of the ſun, who diffuſes his favours from one end of the world to the other, and who peculiarly manifeſts his power in Egypt. His return from Ethiopia marks the period when returning from the Tropic of Capricorn, he proceeds towards the Equa-

(*d*) "Except the private parts, which being thrown into "the river, were devoured by the Lepidote, the Phagre, and "the Oxyrinchus." Perhaps this circumſtance was added to denote the prodigious fecundity of thoſe fiſhes which became ſacred.

tor,

tor, and paſſes through the winter ſigns. This is the ſeaſon when the ſoutherly wind prevails. The ſeventy-two conſpirators (e) indicate the number of days during which it uſually blows. This is the epoch of the death of Oſiris and the triumph of Typhon. Horus, brought up near the lake of Butis, denotes, in the opinion of the Egyptians, the ſun, who attracts towards him the benignant vapours, to ſhed them in dews upon the earth. The ſtrength he has acquired, and his victory over the tyrant, point out his entrance into the ſummer ſigns, and the northerly winds which begin to repulſe the tempeſts from the ſouth. In ſhort, Typhon, ſet at liberty by Iſis, teaches us that this ſcourge ſometimes recurs even to the end of the month of June, eſpecially at the full moon (f); but the ſun having reached

(e) At this day, the time during which the ſoutherly wind prevails is called *Khamſin*, or *fifty*; but this number, as well as that of *ſeventy-two*, does not mark its duration with preciſion. It is ſometimes of longer, ſometimes of ſhorter continuance. This epoch, therefore, could only be marked by a number approaching the truth, and that of 72 appears to me the moſt accurate. I have already apprized you that this phænomenon was not continued, for it would render Egypt uninhabitable, and that it ſeldom laſts three days ſucceſſively.

(f) I have ſeen in Egypt inſtances when this phænomenon has become tremendous; for then the ſoutherly wind drives back towards the north the clouds which are to cauſe the overflowing of the river, and the country is threatened with ſterility. As this event frequently happens during the full moon, the prieſts ſaid that Horus, enraged at Iſis for releaſing Typhon, had wreſted her crown from her, and was obliged to fight new battles with the tyrant, in which he was victorious; that is to ſay,

reached the Tropic of Cancer, the north wind refumes its empire, cools the air, puts an end to contagious maladies, drives the clouds towards the lofty fummits of the Abyffinian mountains, and fwells the Nile with the rains which fall there in torrents. This is the glorious reign of Horus.

The Greeks, the difciples of the Egyptians, greedily received thefe allegories, and, by adapting them to their theogony, cloathed them in foreign colours, and in frefh fables. Some of them changed the names of Typhon into Typheus; others left him his ancient denomination.

Hefiod (*g*) painted him with a hundred dragons heads coming out of his fhoulders. Pindar fays (*h*), that he was buried under Mount Ætna, whence he launches forth his fires. Apollodorus (*i*), who lived 140 years before Chrift, gives us the following defcription of him. "The "enormous giant Typhon, foaming with rage, "and making horrid bellowings, launched burn-"ing rocks towards heaven. He vomited from "his mouth a torrent of flames. The gods fee-"ing him ready to fcale Olympus, were terri-"fied, took to flight, and efcaped into Egypt. "Their enemy purfuing them, they concealed

fay, that the moon being in conjunction, and travelling in the day with the fun, had loft her light, and that in this interval, the north wind refumed its fuperiority.

(*g*) Hefiod, Theogonia.

(*h*) Pindar, Ode firft.

(*i*) Apollodorus, Bibliotheca, lib. 1.

"them-

" themselves under the form of animals; but " Jupiter, perceiving Typhon at a distance from " him, struck him with lightning, and buried " him under Mount Ætna (*k*). Hyginus adds, " that since that time the mountain vomits " forth flames."

Next come the Romans. They still improved upon their models, and Ovid thus sung the war of the giants (*l*):

> Emissumque ima de sede Typhoea terræ
> Cælitibus fecisse metum cunctosque dedisse
> Terga fugæ, donec fessos Ægyptia tellus
> Ceperit, & septem discretus in ostia Nilus.
> Huc quoque terrigenam venisse Typhoea narrat,
> Et se mentitis superos celasse figuris:
> Duxque gregis, dixit, fit Jupiter, unde recurvis
> Nunc quoque formatus Libys est cum cornibus Ammon (*m*).
> Delius in corvo, proles Semeleïa capro,
> Fele soror Phœbi, nivea Saturnia vacca,
> Pisce Venus latuit, Cyllenius ibidis alis.

You see, Sir, how the truth, in proportion to its distance from its first source, and in passing from one people to another, becomes obscure, and covers itself with so thick a veil, that it is hardly possible to discern it, and how the poets who employ the same allegories to adorn their

(*k*) Fables of Hyginus.

(*l*) Ovid Metam. lib. 5.

(*m*) It is unnecessary to tell you, Sir, how far the Latin poet here wanders from the truth. The statue of Ammon was represented with horns, because that symbolical god denoted the sun when in the sign of the ram.

verses,

verſes, fill them with words, with the true ſenſe of which they are totally unacquainted. It is evident, however, that the Greeks and Latins, deſirous of explaining the worſhip the Egyptians paid to different animals, pretended that the gods aſſumed their forms to eſcape from the purſuit of Typhon. This error has been lately renewed by the learned *Warburton*, but it has obtained no more credit on that account. Neither Herodotus nor the ancient authors have written any thing reſembling it. Hyginus (*n*) aſſerts the contrary. "The Egyptians, ſays he, allow no violence to "be committed on animals, becauſe they regard "them as *images* of the gods." In fact, they conſecrated ſome animals to them, either in acknowledgment of their bounty, or in commemoration of important diſcoveries, and they honoured them as living emblems of their divinities.

The prieſts related in a very different manner the tragical end of Typhon, whom they drowned in the waters of a peſtiferous lake. "The lake "Sirbon, ſays Euſtathius (*o*), is ſituated at a "ſmall diſtance from Peluſium. They ſay, that "Typhon was buried there." Accordingly the Egyptians, as Plutarch tells us (*p*), called it *the breath of Typhon*. This lake, whoſe malignant vapours was very injurious to the health of the inhabitants of Peluſium, is no longer to be found

(*n*) Fables of Hyginus.

(*o*) Euſtathius's Commentary on Dionyſius Periegetes.

(*p*) Treatiſe of Iſis and Oſiris.

in

in Egypt. It muſt, as well as many others, have been choaked up by the ſand.

The fable of Adonis appears to have been copied from that of Oſiris. Let us hear Macrobius (*q*), who has unveiled with wonderful ſagacity the myſteries of the worſhip of ancient nations. "When we attentively conſider the "religion of the Aſſyrians, it is no longer doubt-"ful that Adonis was the ſun. Philoſophers "have given the name of Venus to the upper "hemiſphere, a part of which we inhabit. Re-"garding the wild boar as the ſymbol of win-"ter, becauſe he loves wet, muddy, and frozen "places, they feigned that this animal had ſlain "Adonis. The winter, which diminiſhes the "light and heat of the ſtar of the day, is the "wound therefore of Adonis." It is unneceſſary for me to point out to you, Sir, in what particular this fable reſembles that of the Egyptians. In one and in the other it is winter which deſolates theſe countries, and cauſes the death of the ſun. This myſterious language is embelliſhed by the painting of the Greeks, who have ſung in verſes breathing grace, ſentiment, and nature, the tears of Venus for her lover *. You have

(*q*) Macrob. Saturnal. lib. 1.

* See an account of the mourning of Venus for her lover, in Bion's Ode, the Euterpe of Herodotus, and in Plutarch de Iſide & Oſiride, when he was ſuppoſed to be ſlain in hunting amongſt the monſters of the Zodiac, on approaching too near Arctos, the North—*the Frozen Bear.* But Adonis was unqueſtionably an emblem of the ſun amongſt the Aſſyrians, the Phœnicians,

have remarked how an allegory, under the veil of which the phænomena of nature were alluded to, was metamorphosed, so to speak, in passing from Egypt into Phœnicia and Greece, and even to Rome; but by collecting with discernment the testimonies of the ancients, we recover it pretty nearly as it was at first invented.

I have the honour to be, &c.

nicians, and Egyptians, in the language of the two first of which countries, *Adon* signified Dominus, and *Adoni*, Dominus meus. Blackwell's Letters on Mythology.

[*Translator.*]

LET-

LETTER LXVI.

OF NEPHTHYS, A SYMBOLICAL DEITY OF THE EGYPTIANS.

Nephthys was, in the sacred language, the barren spouse of Typhon. Not prolific till Osiris had commerce with her. This word, in its natural signification, denoted the sandy plains which stand between the Nile and the Red Sea, and are greatly exposed to the south-east wind. When in years of an extraordinary inundation the river stretched to those parts, the phænomenon was imputed to the adultery of Osiris with Nephthys. *By* Thueri or Aso, *Queen of Ethiopia, reputed the concubine of Typhon, was denoted the south wind, which, uniting with that of the east, formed the* south-east, *a wind extremely formidable to the Egyptians, on account of its scorching breath, and the torrents of sand which it rolls upon the country.*

To Mr. L. M.

Grand Cairo.

THE Egyptian priests, Sir, continuing their allegory, gave Typhon a spouse called *Nephthys (r)*, the sister and rival of Isis. She was struck with a perpetual sterility, and only became fruitful, when Osiris, deceived by appearances, had commerce with her. The crown of

(r) Treatise of Isis and Osiris.

Lotus,

Lotus, which decorated the head of the god, and which he forgot in the apartments of Nephthys, expofed his crime. Such was the fable on the fubject of the fpoufe of Typhon, and which I fhall endeavour to explain.

You recollect, Sir, that the Nile fometimes received the name of Ofiris, and that Ifis, in certain circumftances, denoted the plains he overflowed. Accordingly this goddefs was regarded as his legitimate fpoufe, and the inundation, in the facerdotal language, was called their marriage. When the river, in years of extraordinary increafe, rofe higher than the hills which bound its courfe on the eaft, and flowed into the deferts, it carried fecundity with it even thither, and the fands were covered with verdure and with plants, the moft remarkable of which was the Lotus. Here is the crown which difcovered the adultery of Ofiris. "The Egyptians," fays Plutarch *(s)*, "beftow on the confines of "their kingdom, which ftretch towards the fea, "the name of Nephthys; he adds: When the "Nile fpreads itfelf over this part of the coun-"try, they call this overflowing, the commerce "of Ofiris with Nephthys, a commerce an-"nounced by the Lotus which grows amongft "the fands."

The characteriftic expreffion of *Nephthys*, which fignifies *(t) country expofed to winds*, explains the

(*s*) Plutarch, in the fame treatife.

(*t*) It is compofed of the Egyptian words, *Neph Theu*, *country expofed to the winds.* Jablonfki, Pantheon Ægyptiacum, tome 3.

natu-

natural ſenſe concealed by the prieſts under the emblem of the fable. All that part of Egypt, in fact, which extends from the Red Sea to the Nile, from Sienna to the Mediterranean, being unprotected by lofty mountains, is greatly expoſed to the winds from the ſouth-eaſt. It was allegorically, ſtiled therefore, the barren ſpouſe of Typhon, becauſe he there roves at liberty, and rolls over the fields of Egypt, the ſands of theſe vaſt ſolitudes.

This malignant genius had alſo a concubine, not leſs dangerous, called *Thueri* or *Aſo*, Queen of Ethiopia *(u)*. When Oſiris returned from his travels, Typhon, as I have already related, prepared an ambuſh for him, aided by ſeventy-two conſpirators, and by Queen Aſo *(x)*. Plutarch, profoundly verſed in the Egyptian theology, gives this explanation of that paſſage: "Queen Aſo, who aſſiſted Typhon, denotes the "ſouth wind which comes from Ethiopia. If "he repulſes the northerly winds which convey "the clouds towards that burning country; if "he prevents the rains from falling, which pro-"duce the ſwelling of the Nile, then Typhon, "victorious, deſtroys the plains with his fiery "breath."

Such was the allegory circulated by the prieſts, on the ſubject of the ſpouſe and concubine of Typhon. The former repreſented the ſandy

(*u*) *Thueri* comes from *Thuris*, ſouth wind. *Aſo*, in the ancient dialect of the Thebais, ſignifies Ethiopia. Thus the Queen *Aſo* denoted the wind which uſually prevails in Ethiopia, that is to ſay, the ſouth wind. Jablonſki, tome 3.

(*x*) Plutarch, Treatiſe of Iſis and Oſiris.

deſerts,

deſerts, which ſeem abandoned to the winds from the ſouth-eaſt; the latter, the ſoutherly ſtorms. When theſe two winds combined (*y*), it was Typhon who came accompanied by Nephthys and Aſo, to dethrone Oſiris, and ſpread deſolation over the rich valley watered by the Nile. We perceive that theſe allegorical perſonages have been invented by the firſt men, who ſtood in need of ſenſible images, to make themſelves underſtood. Homer, the poet who approaches the neareſt to that antiquity, frequently expreſſes himſelf like the prieſts of Thebes and Memphis. At this day Typhon, Nephthys, and Aſo, are unknown in Egypt, but the ſame winds, known there under the general denomination of *Khamſin*, continue to cauſe the ſame ravages, and to deſolate this delicious country.

I have the honour to be, &c.

(*y*) When the ſouth wind, and that of the eaſt blow at the ſame time, they form the ſouth-eaſt wind; this is preciſely what the Egyptians moſt dread, becauſe it is the moſt fiery, and rolls along with it a greater quantity of ſand. As ſoon as it begins to blow, the thermometer mounts to above thirty-three degrees, and if it continues ſome days, it exceeds thirty-ſix.

LETTER LXVIII.

OF CANOBUS, A PRETENDED DEITY OF THE EGYPTIANS.

Canobus, named by the writers of the Lower Empire Canopus, was the pilot of Menelaus. He died on the coaſt of Egypt, and they erected to him a tomb. This place, called in the Egyptian language Cahi noub, *the* golden land. *A city and temples were built here. The Greeks, miſled by this appellation, ſpread a report that they had been erected in honour of the ſtranger; but this was a miſtake. Ruffin relates a long fable, by which he affects to prove, that the deity which they worſhipped in the temple of Canobus was a pitcher: but this was only an offering made to the god of the Nile, the water of which it ſerved to purify.*

To Mr. L. M.

Grand Cairo.

CANOPUS, Sir, became famous under the empire of the Ptolemies. It is of importance therefore to inquire into his origin, the motives that induced ſome hiſtorians to deify him, and what he really ſignified in the opinion of the Egyptians. Several of the writers of Greece and Italy, building on the teſtimony of Homer and Heca-

Hecateus, make Menelaus land in Egypt, and ſay that Canopus, his pilot, dying of the bite of a viper, that hero erected a tomb to his memory on the ſide of the beach. This brilliant fact, ſupported by grave authorities, cannot be called in queſtion. They add, that a city was afterwards built on this ſpot, called Canobus (z), in honour of the ſtranger. Dionyſius Periegetes (a) improving on their reports, expreſſes himſelf in theſe terms: "In the moſt northerly gulph "of Egypt, we ſee the famous temple of the "Spartan Canobus."

It would be very remarkable for the Egyptians, who from the formal teſtimony of Geneſis (b), had an utter averſion for ſtrangers, to have elevated to the rank of god-head a Grecian pilot, whilſt we know that they never awarded divine honours to any mortal. Herodotus, who lived for ſome years with the prieſts of Heliopolis and Memphis, learnt from their mouth, that Menelaus, after receiving Helen from the hands of King Proteus, repaid this ſervice by outrages, and pillaged the coaſt before he ſet ſail (c).

(z) I have hitherto called it Canopus in conformity with the modern uſage, but the real name is Canobus.

(a) Dion. Periegetes.

(b) Geneſis, chap. 43.

(c) The teſtimony of Herodotus cannot be invalidated, who, a Greek by birth, never would have invented a falſehood to throw diſcredit on his nation, in whoſe preſence he read his hiſtory. This muſt have been a well known fact in his time, and the love of truth alone could have made him ſpeak of it.

Besides this, he makes no mention of Canobus. Is it credible that such ingratitude should have been rewarded by the apotheosis of his pilot, even supposing that the religion and the manners of the Egyptians were not directly repugnant to it? Let us give no credit therefore to the improbable assertion of Dionysius Periegetes, the only writer among the Gentiles who has decreed the honours of a temple to the Lacedæmonian pilot.

(d) Ammianus Marcellinus tells us, that the city of Canobus possessed several temples. The most celebrated was that of Serapis; the most ancient built in one of the suburbs, was in honour of Hercules (e). These are the only ones mentioned by antiquity. Strabo (f) describes the temple of Serapis, which the Ptolemies decorated with a truly royal magnificence. They made an addition to it of several buildings, in which they formed an academy where the Belles Lettres were taught, and above all, the mysteries of the religion, and ancient language of Egypt. A great number of learned men flourished there, and Ptolemy, the astronomer, rendered it very famous. "He passed," says Olympiodorus (g),

(d) Ammianus Marcellinus, lib. 22.

(e) Herodotus, lib. 2. This town built before Canobus, was called Heraclea, the city of Hercules.

(f) Strabo, lib. 17. See letter 3 of the first volume of Letters on Egypt, where I have described from Strabo, the ceremonies practised in this temple, and the prodigious increase of people who repaired thither from Alexandria and all parts of Egypt.

(g) Commentaries of Olympiodorus.

"forty

"forty years in the wings of the temple of Canobus, during which he dedicated himſelf to the ſtudy of aſtronomy. His ſyſtem and diſcoveries were engraven there on the columns." Serapis was its tutelar deity, and his worſhip, encouraged by the Ptolemies, propagated itſelf into Greece (*h*). Pauſanias, in travelling through that charming country, ſaw in the citadel of Corinth, a temple dedicated to Serapis the Canobite. The ſciences as well as the Pythagorean and Platonic philoſophy, were for ages cultivated at Canobus. But the Emperor Theodoſius, having deſtroyed her colleges and her temples, a part of human knowledge was buried under their ruins, and the learned were diſperſed.

Ariſtides, the rhetorician, wiſhing to know the origin of the name of Canobus, queſtioned an Egyptian prieſt (*i*). He gives the following account of it. "I learnt from a prieſt of diſtinction in his order, that this place was called Canobus, long before Menelaus landed there. He proved by invincible arguments that this word could not be perfectly written in gold characters, and that it ſignified *land of gold*. It is to be preſumed," adds Ariſtides, "that the Egyptians are better acquainted with their own hiſtory than Homer and Hecateus." Mr. de la Croix (*k*) thus corroborates his teſtimony: the monuments we have now remaining of the Coptic language, leave no room to doubt the

(*h*) Pauſanias, Corinthian.
(*i*) Ariſtides the rhetorician.
(*k*) Diſſertation Philologique.

fidelity

fidelity of this relation. *Kahi*, in fact, a word which on account of its aspiration cannot be written in Greek, signifies *land*, and *noub*, *gold*.

The Greeks, knowing that the chief part of the Egyptian cities bore the name of the divinities they adorèd, and that Canobus had his tomb in a place called *Cahinoub*, deceived doubtless by the resemblance of these expressions, affirmed that this city was built in honour of him; and Dionysius Periegetes has made them dedicate to him a temple. We see how greatly he has strayed from the truth. The Christians of the first ages of the church, who were inclined to throw a ridicule on the idolatry of the Gentiles, endeavoured to establish this error. " Canobus," says Epiphanius (*l*), " and his spouse *Eumenouth*, " were buried on the sea shore, twelve miles " from Alexandria (*m*), and honoured with divine " worship." He is the first author who hazarded this assertion. Ruffin expatiates largely on the subject, and his zeal leads him still farther astray.

(*n*) " How paint the crimes committed by " superstition at Canobus? There, under pre- " text of studying sacerdotal literature, (the " name given to the ancient language of Egypt) " magic was almost publicly professed. This " place, which may be termed the source of " dæmons, became more celebrated amongst the

(*l*) Epiphan. tome second.

(*m*) This is the exact distance from Alexandria to *Abouker*, formerly Canobus.

(*n*) Ruffin, Histoire de l'Eglise, livre second.

" Pagans,

"Pagans, than Alexandria itſelf. It will not be "improper to unfold the origin of theſe mon- "ſtrous errors. It is ſaid, that the Chaldeans, "tranſporting the fire, which was their god, into "all the provinces, offered to let him combat "thoſe of other nations, on condition that if he "remained conqueror, they ſhould adore him. "The prieſts of Canobus accepted the challenge, "and deviſed this ſtratagem. They fabricate in "Egypt pitchers of an extremely porous earth, "through which the water filtrates and is puri- "fied. He took one of them, ſlopped up the "pores with wax, and painting it of various co- "lours, filled it with water, and made it his god. "He covered it with the head of an ancient "ſtatue, ſaid to be that of the pilot of Menelaus. "The Chaldeans preſented themſelves; the "conteſt began; they lighted fire around the "vaſe; the wax melts; the water runs through "the pores and extinguiſhes the fire. The fraud "of the prieſt gave the victory to Canobus over "the Chaldean deity. From that moment his "image has been repreſented with very ſhort "feet, a narrow neck, and the belly and back "rounded like a pitcher. It is under this form "he is worſhipped as the vanquiſher of all the "gods."

I do not know where Ruffin has met with this fable, for he does not cite his authorities; but it is ſo puerile, that it is unneceſſary to refute it. Beſides that, it formally contradicts the worſhip of the Egyptians, who have never adored water. If this pretended conteſt had any real foundation,

foundation, certainly St. Clemens of Alexandria, who knew the religion of Egypt much better than the prieſt of Aquileia, would not have forgot it.—This tale, however, will aid us at leaſt in diſcovering ſome truths. The Egyptians have fabricated from the remoteſt antiquity, veſſels of porous earth, which ſerve to filtrate water and to clariſy it. The Greeks call them *Beaucalion*, the Arabs call them *Bardak*. This invention was very intereſting in a country where for five months of the year the Nile brings down a great quantity of ſand, mud, and inſects. Before they drink its water, they let it ſubſide in great jars, into which they throw powder of almonds bruiſed, which precipitates in a few hours the heterogeneous particles. But to make it more agreeable, they expoſe it on their windows to the north wind, in *Bardaks*. It penetrates the pores, and as it is conſtantly ſtruck by the refreſhing breath of the north wind, it contracts a coolneſs which is delicious in this burning climate. The poor as well as the rich, drink with a ſort of voluptuouſneſs, of the water which has remained for ſome days in theſe vaſes. This art therefore was a valuable diſcovery for Egypt. The ancient inhabitants who made it, were ſenſible of its importance. To mark their gratitude for it to the god of the Nile, they conſecrated one of theſe pitchers in the temple of Serapis at Canobus. This is the offering which Ruffin, aided by a fable, ſtrives to paſs for a divinity. Several monuments concur in proving what I have advanced. We ſee on a crown piece ſtruck in the time of of the Emperor Adrian, by the inhabitants of Canobus, one of these vases (*o*) with a serpent twisted round the mouth of it. Now we know that this figure was the emblem of *Cneph*, the good genius, and in a more extensive sense, the author of nature. Even the Canal which came from the Nile, and discharged itself into the sea near Canobus, was called (*p*) *Agatho Daimon*, the good genius, doubtless, because it touched upon a city where the people adored Serapis, and the priests the supreme Being. It is natural to suppose, therefore, that the earthen vessel deposited in his temple, was nothing else than a testimony of homage done to his beneficence (*q*). We find similar consecrations in the greatest part of the Egyptian monuments. The sacrifice engraved on the rock near Babain, and offered to Jupiter Ammon, or the sun of the spring season, presents us with seven pitchers of this kind, bearing the three piles, on which repose the lambs that were offered in sacrifice.— The obelisks were symbols of the rays of the sun, and their shade served to mark his course, whilst he was above the horizon. All these facts testify that the Egyptians were very attentive in consecrating to God the fruit of their inventions. The

(*o*) Cotelerii Monumenta, vol. 1.

(*p*) Ptolemy's Geography.

(*q*) Amongst the rarities which Mr. Dombei, who has travelled with glory for nine years in South America, has just brought back to France with him, I have remarked some vases, taken from the tombs of the people of Peru, which greatly resemble those we find in the vaults of Saccora; and some idols of gold, similar to those the Arabs tear from the mummies, which their avarice leads them to pull to pieces.

name

name of *Cabi Noub*, land of gold, beſtowed on the country which produced the clay, the beſt adapted to the compoſition of theſe pitchers, for filtrating the water, ſhews us that it was with reaſon the prieſts offered one of them to the gods in the very place where they were fabricated, and perhaps even invented.

I have the honour to be, &c.

LET-

LETTER LXIX.

OF THOTH, A SYMBOLICAL DEITY OF THE EGYPTIANS, AND REGARDED AS A CELEBRATED MAN BY THE GREATER PART OF WRITERS.

Thoth was held to be an extraordinary man by a great number of writers. To him they aſcribed the invention of all arts, ſciences, and human inſtitutions; and dignified him with the name of Triſmegiſtus, *or thrice great. This alone might be ſufficient to prove that the perſonage was allegorical.* Thoth, *in the Egyptian language, ſignifies a pillar; and as it was uſual to engrave approved works upon pillars, they all received the general appellation of* Thoth. *The three* Thoths *or Mercuries might denote the infancy, the progreſs, and the perfection of human knowledge.*

To Mr. L. M.

Grand Cairo.

AFTER offering you, Sir, ſome notions reſpecting the principal divinities of Egypt, it remains that I ſhould treat of *Thoth*, that ſymbolical divinity, or famous perſonage who received the homage of antiquity, and who was regarded as the inventor of almoſt the whole of human know-

knowledge. The ages in which his exiſtence is placed, are ſo very remote, that it is almoſt impoſſible to throw upon them any light, capable of clearing up the objects which lie hid in the obſcurity of time. Plato, who wrote upwards of two thouſand years before us, and who was educated in the ſchool of the prieſts of Heliopolis, did not himſelf know what judgment to form of Thoth, already of too ancient a date for him to diſcover his origin *(r)*. " *Theuth*, ſays he, in-" vented letters, diſtinguiſhed the vowels from " the conſonants, the mutes from liquids; a " diſcovery which alone ſhould make him be re-" garded as a god, or as a divine mortal. Fame " ſays that he lived in Egypt." In this ſtate of uncertainty the moſt prudent meaſure is faithfully to report the paſſages of the ancients, and to examine them with the ſpirit of impartial criticiſm.

Thoth was differently named by different nations. " The Greeks, ſays Philo, of Biblos *(s)*, " gave the name of Hermes, or Mercury, to " *Taaout*, whom the Egyptians call *Thoith*, and " the Alexandrians *Thoth*." Hiſtorians agree in attributing to him the invention of almoſt all the arts. " *Thoth*, ſays Lactantius *(t)*, remounts to " the moſt remote antiquity, and though a man, " he poſſeſſed all the ſciences, which juſtly ob-

(*r*) Plato calls him *Theuth*.

(*s*) A Phœnician Hiſtory aſcribed to Sanchoniathon, tranſlated by Philo, of Biblos, and quoted by Euſebius in his Preparation for the Goſpel, lib. 3.

(*t*) Lactantius, lib. 1.

" tained

"tained him the surname of *Trismegistus*, three "times great." He created the different parts of discourse *(u)*, and first gave names to many things. He discovered numbers *(x)* and measures, and reduced arithmetic to a system *(y)*. The Egyptians said that he taught them geometry, which was absolutely necessary for them; likewise astronomy and astrology: they added, that being the first who observed the nature and harmony of sounds, he composed the lyre.—— Clemens of Alexandria *(z)* speaks of the code of laws entrusted to the care of the priests, and Ælian points it out under the denomination of *the body of law of Mercury* (Thoth). The creation of theology, the establishment of divine worship, and the orders of sacrifices, were also attributed to him *(a)*; this doctrine was contained in the books of Mercury, deposited in the temples, and the priests there found every thing concerning religion. In short, Diodorus Siculus tells us, the Egyptians asserted that all the sciences, institutions, and arts, were invented by *Thoth*, or Mercury.

When we reflect on the nature of the human mind, which advances only step by step from one

(*u*) Diodorus Siculus, Plato, and Eusebius, affirm that he was the inventor of letters, and the first who wrote books.

(*x*) Plato in Phædro.

(*y*) Diodorus Siculus, lib. 1.

(*z*) Clemens of Alexandria, lib. 6. Stroma. Cicero de Natura deorum, and Lactantius, lib. 1, say that he gave laws to the Egyptians.

(*a*) Diodorus Siculus, lib. 1.

truth

truth to another, when viewing the annals of hiſtory, we perceive but a ſmall number of creative geniuſes, widely diſperſed, and at great intervals from each other on the earth, making a few important diſcoveries; when Plato, an enlightened judge, conſidering *Thoth* ſimply as the author of letters, and of writing, calls him god, or a divine mortal, one is compelled to believe that this perſonage, whom they endow with univerſal ſcience, never has exiſted; but that the learned men of a nation, verging on the origin of the human race, publiſhed under his name the various knowledge they had acquired for many thouſand years. This ſentiment, dictated by reaſon, is confirmed by the authority of ſeveral great men. Jamblichus (*b*) makes *Abamon* (or Anebo) a prieſt of Egypt, ſpeak thus: "Mercury, the god of eloquence, is with reaſon regarded as the common divinity of prieſts; for it is the ſame ſpirit which preſides over the genuine ſcience of religion. This is the reaſon why our anceſtors, on dedicating to him their works, the produce of their wiſdom, graced them with the name of Mercury."

Here then we have the books of the Egyptians, publiſhed under the name of Thoth *. Galen, trained up to the ſciences in the academy of Alexandria, informs us of the manner in which

(*b*) Jamblichus, Myſt. Egypt.

* Sonchoniathon ſays, *Taaut*, the inventor of *letters*, and firſt *recorder* amongſt men, wrote that part of it relating to the riſe of things, in ſigns or *ſacred ſculpture*. φοινικων θεολογια παρα ευονϭ. [Tranſlator.]

this

this was practiſed : "All the diſcoveries made "in Egypt, ſays he, muſt be ſtamped with the "approbation of the learned. Then they were "engraved on the columns (*c*) without the names "of the author, and depoſited in the ſanctuary. "Hence the prodigious number of books *aſcrib-* "*ed to Mercury*. The diſciples of Pythagoras "imitated this example by putting the name of "Pythagoras at the head of their works."

Theſe paſſages evidently prove that *Thoth* was not a man, but that they engraved the works, approved by the colleges of prieſts, on columns (*d*) called *Thoth*, as we ſhall hereafter ſee, and that they went under this general denomination. The ſpirit by which the learned ſaid they were inſpired, and to which they aſcribed their knowledge, was *Phtha*, the artiſt of nature, the ſource of all information. "The Egyptians, "ſays Diogenes Laertius (*e*), affirmed that Vul-"can (*f*) had taught them the principles of "philoſophy, and that the Pontiffs and the Pro-"phets aſſumed to themſelves the honour of "being his prieſts." Accordingly, in the Chronicle of Scaliger, Vulcan is called *the Legiſlator of* Egypt.

It is of importance to examine theſe columns on which are engraven diſcoveries worthy of

(*c*) Galen, lib. 1. contra Julian.

(*d*) They are uſually called pillars of *Thoth*; but as Galen knew that this Egyptian word ſignified *column*, he did not chuſe to be guilty of a pleonaſm.

(*e*) Diogenes Laertius, Hiſtory of Philoſophers.

(*f*) The ſame as *Phtha*.

being

being tranſmitted to poſterity. Mercury (Thoth) ſays Manethon (*g*), invented the myſterious columns, and ordained that the laws by which the ſtars are governed in their motions ſhould be written on them §. Achilles Tatius (*h*) corroborates this: "The Egyptians are the firſt who "have meaſured the heaven and the earth, and "tranſmitted this knowledge to their deſcen- "dants by engraving them on columns." * Proclus adds that remarkable actions (*i*), as well as intereſting inventions, were alſo written on them.

(*g*) Manethon, lib. 5.

§ Sanchoniathon ſays, "Before this the god *Taaut* had, in "imitation of heaven, expreſſed the appearances (aſpects) of "the gods *Time* and *Dagon*, and the other deities in the *ſacred* "*engravures of letters.* To him (TAAUT, or LETTERS) Time "going afterwards to the land of the ſouth, gave all the king- "dom of *Egypt* to be his royal ſeat." (The land of learning and parent of writing). Blackſtone remarks on the fragment of Sanchoniathon he has given us, what a valuable writing that work would have been entire, and free from the interpolations of Philo and other commentators; and how the ſpecimen we have of him, ſuch as it is, ſhews us the irreparable loſs we have ſuſtained in the extinction of the records kept by the prieſts in the chief cities in Egypt, and all over the eaſt; but eſpecially in the grand temples of *Memphis*, *Thebes*, *Babylon*, and *Tyre.* Sanconiathon ſays, too, of *Myſou*, liberty came, *Taaut letters.*—[Tranſlator.]

(*h*) Achilles Tatius, Commentator of Aratus.

* Sanchoniathon tells us, "Then the God HEAVEN made BAITYLLIAS, having produced *animated ſtones.*" Compare this with the Bible—"and he gave unto Moſes, when he made "an end of communing with him upon Mount Sinai, two tables "of teſtimony, tables of ſtone, written with *the finger of* "*God.*" Exodus, chap. xxxi. v. 18. [Tranſlator.]

(*i*) Proclus, Timæus of Plato, lib. 1.

These

These stones, which were remarkably hard, composed an immortal book, a sort of Encyclopedia, containing all the sciences, all the arts invented or improved for ages: it is for this reason the priests undertook nothing without previously consulting them (*k*). Pythagoras and Plato who read them, drew thence the foundation of their philosophy, which made Theophilus, of Antioch, say (*l*), " What use has it been to Pythagoras " to have penetrated the sanctuaries of Egypt, " and to have consulted the columns of Mer- " cury (*m*)?" Sanchoniathon, the most ancient historian after Moses, boasts of having derived his knowledge from the monuments of the temples of *Taaout*, and from the mysterious books of the Ammonians.

The practice of imprinting on marble, in indelible characters, the discoveries of science is almost as ancient as the world. We may conclude that stone was the first book of man *. The historian Josephus speaks thus of it (*n*):

(*k*) Jamblicus, Egyptian Mysteries.

(*l*) Theophilus, lib. 3.

(*m*) Sanchoniathon cited by Eusebius, prep. Evangel. lib. 3.

* Blackwell says, the word מצבה, which the Jews are prohibited to erect, does not strictly mean a *statue* or *image*, but what the Greeks called ςιλη (Cippus, Titulus,) a *pillar or column*; may not this be the custom in question, though differently applied by Blackwell? Persons, initiated in the Eleusynian mysteries were instructed out of the πετρωμα (two stone tablets.——See also, Deuteronomy, chap. xxvii. verse 8. &c. &c.

Translator.

(*n*) Jewish Antiquities, book 1.

"The Patriarch Seth knowing that Adam had "foretold that every thing on earth would pe- "rish either by fire, or by a general deluge, and "fearing left philofophy and aftronomy fhould "be effaced from the memory of men, and "be buried in oblivion, engraved his knowledge "on two columns, the one of brick, the other "of ftone, that if the waters fhould deftroy the "former, the latter might fubfift, and inftruct "human race in aftronomical difcoveries.— "This column is ftill to be feen in the *Siridiac* "land."

Let us now attend to Manethon, a celebrated hiftorian, and facred writer of Egypt, who flourifhed more than three centuries before the Jewifh author (*r*). He teftifies, "that he derived his "knowledge from the *ſteles* placed in the *Siri-* "*diac* land, where *Thoth*, the firft Mercury, had "engraved them in facred language, and in "hieroglyphic characters, and that after the de- "luge, the good Genius, fon to the fecond Mer- "cury, tranflated them into the dialect made ufe "of by the priefts, and wrote them in facerdotal "letters." Here, Sir, are two men or two nations, who imprint their difcoveries on marble. I fhall not examine whether *Seth*, as Jablonfki (*p*) pretends, is the fame with *Thoth*, and whether Jofephus, who was pofterior to Manethon, was defirous of giving a Patriarch the honour of

(*c*) Manethon in the book of Sothis, dedicated to Ptolemy Philadelphus. See the chronography of Syncellius.

(*p*) Jablonfki, Pantheon Ægyptiacum, lib. 3. chap. 20.

an

an invention, the glory of which the Egyptians had long arrogated to themſelves. This would be a reſearch of pure curioſity. The important matter would be to aſcertain from authentic monuments the place where theſe columns were ſituated, and their exiſtence. Both the hiſtorians call it the *Siridiac* land, but that was unknown to the ancients as well as to the moderns, which has led ſome of the learned to imagine that inſtead of *Siridiac*, we ſhould read *Siringic*, an expreſſion which denotes ſubterraneous paſſages. This idea muſt have ariſen from the following paſſage of Ammianus Marcellinus (*q*): "It is "affirmed that the Egyptian prieſts, verſed in all "the branches of religious knowledge, and ap-"prized of the approach of the deluge, were "fearful leſt the divine worſhip ſhould be effaced "from the memory of man. To preſerve the "remembrance of it, they dug in various parts of "the kingdom, ſubterraneous and winding paſ-"ſages, on the walls of which they engraved "their knowledge under different forms of ani-"mals and birds, which they called hierogly-"phics, and which are unintelligible to the La-"tins."

It ſeems as if this writer had decided the queſtion, and that by the *Siridiac* land, we are to underſtand theſe ſubterraneous paſſages in the rocks, in the environs of Thebes and Memphis. In fact, we find in theſe immenſe labyrinths,

(*q*) Ammian. Marcellinus, lib. 22.

formed under the plain of Saccora, a great number of figures of men, of birds, and various animals ſculptured on the walls. Near Thebes we meet with ſimilar hieroglyphics in the numerous caverns of the mountains. Amongſt theſe ſacred characters, ſome are painted, ſome engraved, ſome cut in relief, divided into compartments, or arranged in columns. Are not theſe the ſanctuaries into which the prieſts alone had the right of entering, and where they committed to ſtone, the different epochas of hiſtory, the inventions of the ſciences, and the prodigies of art? I know the Scholiaſt of Sophocles (*r*) pretends, that the *ſteles* on which theſe remarkable events were conſigned, were ſquare ſtones. Perhaps they had that form in Greece; but the obeliſks, the columns, the walls of the temples, and of the ſubterraneous paſſages covered with innumerable hieroglyphics, divided into compartments, were the *ſteles* of the Egyptians, according to the teſtimony of Sanchoniathon, Manethon, and the moſt ancient hiſtorians. The monuments deſcribed by Ammianus Marcellinus are ſtill ſubſiſting. The traveller contemplates them with a ſterile admiration, as the firſt efforts of human genius to immortalize the fruit of its labours.

The teſtimonies of the authors I have cited, are not deciſive enough to perſuade us that theſe hieroglyphics are antecedent to the deluge. The reading of the events they contain could alone

(*r*) Scholiaſt of Sophocles on Electra.

aſcertain

ascertain the truth or the falshood of that assertion. That would undoubtedly inform us, both of the era in which they were engraved, and the unknown history of the first ages of the world. But we may at least form a reasonable conjecture that these characters preceded writing, and that they are the most ancient monuments that have reached us.

It is proved then, that *Thoth*, that so much boasted personage, never had any real existence, but that the Egyptian priests published their works under this general title, after they had been honoured by the unanimous approbation of the colleges. The interpretation of this word, leaves no doubt upon the subject. Jablonski (*s*) has proved that *Thoth* signifies column. The Greeks by translating it by the word στηλη (*t*), have retained this meaning. As the learned of

(*s*) Jablonski, tome 3, says, *Thoth*, *Theuth*, or *Thoith*, comes from the Egyptian *Thouthi*, column.——Blackwell says in his Letters on Mythology—" I am inclined to think that *Taaut* is " pure *Egyptian* for LETTERS, from דוה *Taau, signum nota*, such " as the *Egyptian* letters especially were: thence גהדה *Ottoth* " SIGNA LITERÆ, and with the ה transposed from the middle, " or the *Coptic* article T' put before it Taaöt." N. B. This is translated from the Phœnician by Blackwell, and has neither been paraphrased by Philo, nor truly deduced by subsequent commentators.——See Blackwell's Letters, page 348, in the notes.

Translator.

(*t*) *Stele* signifies also *column*.—στηλη (Cippus, Titulus) a *pillar* or *column*. Blackwell.

Translator.

Egypt

Egypt were accuſtomed to write their books without putting their names to them, it was natural that they ſhould bear that of the monuments by which they were to be tranſmitted to poſterity. It appears even that this honour was granted only to ſuch as made important diſcoveries, ſince the approbation of all the academicians of the country was neceſſary to enjoy it. When the Latins therefore, and perſons who had but a ſuperficial acquaintance with the Egyptian hiſtory, ſpeak of the columns of *Thoth*, they are guilty of the ſame pleonaſm as thoſe geographers who call Ætna Mount Gibel (*u*). Obſerve, I requeſt you, that Sanchoniathon, Manethon, Galen, and the other writers who penetrated into the myſteries of Egypt, and drew their information from the genuine ſources, do not commit this fault, but only relate that they carved on columns or *ſteles*, the remarkable events, and prodigies of art.——Thus when, according to Ælian (*x*), *the prieſts aſſerted that Seſoſtris was taught the ſciences by Thoth* or *Mercury*, it ſignified, that on initiating him into the myſteries, they had taught him to read the hiſtory of human knowledge impreſſed in hieroglyphic characters on the columns. They bore at firſt that ſimple denomination; the cuſtom of conſulting them, the ſacred places where they were kept, the depoſits they preſerved, all rendered them reſpectable. They became conſecrated by religion,

(*u*) Gibel is an Arabic word for mountain.
(*x*) Ælian, lib. 12.

and

and were placed under the immediate protection of *Phtha*, or the creative spirit.

These principles established, we are enabled to give a probable explanation of the three *Thoth* or Mercuries reckoned by the Egyptians. They placed the most ancient before the deluge, and the others subsequent to that event. The first marked the infancy of human knowledge, whether it be, that some monuments have escaped the destruction of the human race, or whether those they raised shortly after, ascended beyond that terrible epocha. The second *Thoth* denotes the efforts of the Egyptians to discover physical and astronomical truths, the translation of the hieroglyphics into sacerdotal characters, and the fixed establishment of divine worship, and the laws. The third again, pointed out the flourishing state of the sciences, the progress of the arts, and the perfection to which they were carried, as testified by the pyramids, the temples, and obelisks, the immensity and magnificence of which have never been equalled by any people. The Egyptian priests expressed these eras in a sensible manner by the epithet of *Trismegistus*, *three times great*, which they bestow on their allegorical *Thoth*.

You must have observed, Sir, that the books of *Thoth* or Hermes, were the collection of the productions of all the learned men of Egypt, and formed their Encyclopedia. They have unfortunately perished in the conflagration of the Ptolemean library, and the originals which remain engraved on the marbles of Egypt, in a thousand

thousand places, are unintelligible. Of so many treasures we have only a few fragments preserved by the ancients.——As to the Hermetical books, boasted of by those who sacrifice their time, and their money in seeking after the philosopher's stone, they are merely supposititious works, and falsely attributed to Hermes, or the Egyptian *Thoth*.

I have the honour to be, &c.

LETTER LXX.

OF THE VOCAL STATUE OF MEMNON.

The ſtatue of Memnon greatly celebrated in ancient times for the ſound which it emitted at ſun-riſe. Called by the prieſts the Son of the Day. The ſon of Aurora, the conqueror of Antilochus, celebrated by Homer. His interpreters, and the poets ſince his time, have applied thoſe expreſſions to the Egyptian Memnon. This is a miſtake; the Thebaic ſtatue bore the name of Amenophis. The Memnon who came to the ſiege of Troy a little after, was ſent from Suſa by Teutam, king of Aſſyria. The vocal ſtatue of Egypt was broken by Cambyſes. The mutilated figure ceaſed to emit any ſound for a long time, but reſumed its vocal power under the Ptolemies. After its diſgrace, it pronounced ſeven notes. The prieſts, who gave the harmonic courſe of the ſeven planets the name of celeſtial muſic, *and who conſecrated to them the notes, called this ſtatue the image of the ſun, and the couſin of Oſiris, becauſe it pronounced the ſeven notes which compoſed the terreſtrial muſic. It received the name of* ame nouphi, to tell good news, *becauſe it pronounced the notes at the vernal equinox, a ſeaſon dear to the Egyptians.*

To Mr. L. M.

Grand Cairo.

I HAVE briefly mentioned to you, Sir, the ſtatue of Memnon, in deſcribing the ruins of Thebes;

Thebes; but the wonders which are related of it are atteſted by ſo many great names engraven on its pedeſtal, that I cannot conclude theſe letters without attempting to extricate from obſcurity ſome circumſtances of its hiſtory. A hundred Greek and Latin, and a few Egyptian authors have celebrated it in their writings. Their opinions frequently differ, and are ſometimes impreſſed with the character of a blind credulity. Others, more wiſe, unable either to reject the teſtimony of their ſenſes, or to believe in miracles, remain in a ſtate of ſuſpenſe. I ſhall give you a faithful account of their various narrations, which will enable you to form a judgment reſpecting this ſtatue, ſo celebrated in antiquity.

You have remarked, Sir, amongſt the ruins of Thebes, ſeveral coloſſal figures, almoſt all mutilated, or lying on the earth. The largeſt was placed at the entrance of the veſtibules of the tomb I have deſcribed to you *(y)*. Diodorus Siculus calls it *Oſimandué*; Strabo *(z)* ſay it was called by the Egyptians *Iſmandes*; but writers in general give it the name of Memnon (*a*). This ſtatue, ſtill leſs remarkable for its gigantic ſtature, and the hardneſs of the granite of which it is compoſed, than for its property of producing a ſound at the riſing of the ſun, was broken by

(*y*) Diodorus Siculus, lib. 1.

(*z*) Strabo, lib. 17.

(*a*) Oſimandué and Iſmandes were probably the vulgar names of this coloſſus, among the Egyptians. Theſe words are derived from *Ou Smandi*, *to give a ſound.* Memnon may alſo come from *Emnoni*, *of ſtone.* The Greeks have made of it, *Memnon Iſmandes*, *the vocal ſtone.* See Jablonſki de Memnone.

Cambyſes.

Cambyſes. Half of it is overthrown, the other half remains upon its baſe. Philoſtrates thus deſcribes it (*b*): "The coloſſus of Memnon re-"preſented a young man in the flower of his "age, whoſe face was turned towards the riſing "ſun. When his rays fell upon it, it was ſaid "to ſpeak." Dionyſius Periegetes ſays (*c*), "The "people who inhabit Thebes, famous for her "hundred gates, and for the vocal ſtatue of "Memnon which ſalutes his mother Aurora on "her riſing." The prieſts of Egypt called it the Son of Day (*d*), and, according to Diodorus, *the Couſin of Oſiris*.

Homer is the firſt who ſpeaks of the ſon of Aurora (*e*). "Neſtor preſerved in his heart "the memory of his generous Antilochus, ſlain "by the illuſtrious ſon of Aurora." His commentators have all been of opinion that the latter expreſſions related to the Egyptian Memnon; but the prince of poets might have made uſe of them to point out one of the chiefs who came to the releaſe of Troy from the eaſtern countries. This metaphorical language was familiar in his time. The ſcripture employs it in the ſame manner by calling the people of thoſe climes *the children of the eaſt*. The poets who flouriſhed after him, gave a different explanation of his

(*b*) Philoſtrates, Life of Apollonius of Thiones, lib. 6.

(*c*) Dionyſius Periegetes, Deſcription of the Univerſe.

(*d*) In the old Egyptian tongue, the day was called *Eho*; the Greeks made of this, *Eos*, the morning, and called Memnon the ſon of the morning. Jablonſki de Memnone.

(*e*) Homer's Odyſſey.

expreſ-

expreſſion: "Aurora, ſays Heſiod *(f)*, brought "forth by Tithon, the valiant Memnon, who "wore a brazen helmet, and was King of Ethi-"opia." Pindar aſcribes to him the victory over Antilochus *(g)*: "The brave Antilochus, "endowed with a magnanimous ſoul, deſirous "of ſaving his father's life, fell in the combat "he ſuſtained with Memnon, the leader of an ar-"my of Ethiopians *(h)*. One of Neſtor's "horſes, pierced by a ſpear thrown by the hand "of Paris, ſtopped his car."

Building on theſe authorities, the poets of Greece and Italy confounded the Trojan with the Egyptian Memnon. Virgil *(i)* ſpeaks of the troops of Aurora, and of the arms of the black Memnon. This colour, employed to mark the country of the hero, muſt not be regarded as a ſign of deformity; for the poet of Achilles, in celebrating Euripilus, ſays *(k)*, He was the handſomeſt of mortals, after the divine Memnon.

(*f*) Heſiod. Theogonia.

(*g*) Pindar, Ode 2.

(*h*) Theſe paſſages relate to the Egyptian Memnon. In fact, the ancient Greeks long called the Delta by the name of Egypt, and all the country farther to the ſouthward, Ethiopia. Homer puts theſe words in the mouth of Menelaus, ſpeaking to Telemachus: *I penetrated Egypt as far as Ethiopia.* Now, as he only conducts his hero to Thebes, it is evident that he underſtood the Thebais by this expreſſion. Damis, the companion of Apollonius of Thianes, declares that he ſaw the temple and the ſtatue of Memnon, in Ethiopia, that is to ſay, in Upper Egypt.

(*i*) Virgil's Æneid, book 1.

(*k*) Odyſſey, lib. 5.

Ovid

Ovid *(l)* expreſſes himſelf thus in his Metamorphoſes: "Aurora, who favoured the Trojan "party, is no longer touched with the misfor-"tunes of Ilion, nor of Hecuba; a nearer con-"cern occupies her ſoul; ſhe mourns her own "loſſes, and bewails in tears the death of Mem-"non." On the baſe of the ſtatue is the following beautiful epigram, written by the poet Aſclepiodorus: "Live, Thetis, goddeſs of the ſea! "Learn that Memnon, who died fighting under "the walls of Troy, daily utters a pleaſing ſound "near the tombs dug out of the Lybian moun-"tains, at the ſpot where the impetuous Nile "interſects Thebes, celebrated for her gates; "whilſt Achilles, thirſting inſatiably for battles, "no longer ſpeaks, either near the walls of Ili-"on, or in the Theſſalian plains."

Here, Sir, is the Egyptian or Ethiopian Memnon (for the ancients gave the name of Ethiopia to the Thebais) generally acknowledged to be him who glorioufly fell in repulſing the Greeks. But theſe are teſtimonies of the poets, who are more anxious to preſent us with moving pictures, and brilliant fables, than accurate hiſtorical truths. Let us purſue the fable of his birth *(m)*. Aurora, amorous of Tithon, carried him into Ethiopia, where ſhe bore to him Emathion and Memnon *(n)*. Iſacius Tzetza adopts the ſame allegory. Tithon, ſon of Laomedon, was beloved by the Goddeſs of the Day. From this com-

(l) Ovid. Metam. lib. 5.
(m) Apollodorus, Biblioth. lib. 3.
(n) Iſacius Tzetza.

merce

merce ſprung Memnon and Emathion (*o*). Diodorus Siculus explains theſe paſſages: "Tithon, "ſon of Laomedon, was brother to Priam, car"ried his arms into the eaſtern parts of Aſia, and "into Ethiopia, from whence the fable of Mem"non produced by Aurora, took its riſe."

But who is this hero who aſſiſted the Trojans; for the allegories of the poets are always founded on ſome truth? Diodorus (*p*) will tell us, "Mem"non came to the ſuccour of Troy, at the head "of the troops of Teutam, Emperor of Aſſyria. "Priam, ſovereign of Troas, a dependency of "that empire, oppreſſed by the weight of the "war, had implored his aſſiſtance. Teutam ſent "him twenty thouſand Ethiopians and Suzians, "and two hundred chariots, commanded by "Memnon. This warrior, a favourite of his "King, then governed Perſia. He was in the "flower of his age, and already celebrated for "his bodily ſtrength and greatneſs of mind. He "had built a palace in the citadel of Suza, which "bore his name until the empire of the Perſi"ans, and formed a public highway, ſtill call"ed in our days *the Memnonian way.*" Suza, adds Strabo (*q*), was founded by Tithon, father of Memnon. This city was ſix leagues in circumference. Its form was oblong, and its citadel called *the Memnonium* (*r*). Herodotus (*s*)

(*o*) Diodorus Siculus, lib. 4.
(*p*) Diodorus Siculus, lib. 2.
(*q*) Strabo, lib. 15.
(*r*) That is, *the citadel of Memnon.*
(*s*) Herodotus, lib. 5.

alſo

also calls Suza *the city of Memnon*. Pausanias *(t)* assures us that this General came to the siege of Troy from Suza, and not from Ethiopia, and that he subdued all the nations of Media to the river *Choaspes*.

These authorities, the number of which I could augment, if necessary, evidently prove, that, during the memorable siege, the heroes of which are immortalized by the vast genius of one man, the Emperors of Assyria sent to the aid of Priam, a brave Captain, called Memnon, who had nothing in common with the Egyptian Memnon *(u)*. It is probable, as I have already said, that Homer, in calling him the son of Aurora, meant only to indicate the east from whence he came. The poets after him invented the fable you have just read, solely to adorn their verses.

Let us now examine what was the real name of the statue which is the object of your enquiries, the opinion entertained of it by the ancients, and the end which the Priests had in view in erecting it. Herodotus *(x)* is the first who calls it Memnon, and he scarcely speaks of it, because it was mutilated when he visited Egypt. Since the days of that historian a crowd of travellers have cited it with enthusiasm, and they

(*t*) Pausanias in Phocicis, ch. 31.

(*u*) Philostrates positively says, Memnon was an Ethiopian (Theban) and reigned in that country before the Trojan war. He who came to that siege is greatly posterior to, and different from the former. *Life of Apollonius of Thianes.*

(*x*) Herodotus.

have

have almoſt all concurred in beſtowing on it the name of Memnon, which only proves that this was the denomination generally adopted by foreigners; but to come at the real name, we muſt attend to the Egyptians, who muſt certainly be better acquainted with their own monuments. We read the following words in the chronicle of Alexandria (*y*): "Cambyſes ordered *Amenophis*, the vocal ſtatue, vulgarly called Memnon, to be cut in two." Pauſanias, an accurate obſerver, comes in ſupport of this authority (z). The Thebans aſſure us that the ſtatue we call Memnon, is that of the Egyptian *Phamenophis*. The *Ph* (*a*), in the language of the country, is the article maſculine; its true name therefore was *Amenophis*.

After Cambyſes had knocked down the half of this coloſſus, it ceaſed probably for a long time to utter any ſound; for Herodotus, who travelled through this country ſhortly after the Perſian conqueſt, would not have omitted ſo extraordinary a fact. The Ptolemies having founded a kingdom in Egypt, favoured the arts and ſciences. From that period, the remains of the ſtatue, ſtill upon its baſe, continued to make its voice be heard, as Manethon informs us (*b*), but not ſo diſtinctly as before its misfor-

(*y*) Chronicle of Alexandria.

(*z*) Pauſanias in Atticis.

(*a*) Jablonſki de Memnone.

(*b*) Chronographia Syncelli. Manethon, a ſacred writer of Egypt, flouriſhed under the firſt of the Ptolemies. He had retained the knowledge of the hieroglyphic language.

tune.

tune. Three centuries after, the Romans conquered Egypt, and they flew with admiration to visit antiquities. Germanicus was of this number. "He could not resist," says Tacitus (*c*), "the desire of contemplating the wonders of "Egypt, the most astonishing of which are the "statue, in stone, of Memnon, which at the in-"stant of being struck by the rays of the sun, "pronounces vowels; and the pyramids which "rear their heads like mountains in the midst "of almost inaccessible sands." The report of this historian is confirmed by numerous inscriptions. We read the following on the right leg of the colossus: *I, Cai Lælia, spouse to the African Prefect, heard the voice of Memnon at half past six in the morning, the first year of the Emperor Domitian, &c.* The following is inscribed on the left leg: *I, Publius Balbinus, heard the divine voice of the vocal statue of Memnon, otherways Phamenoph. I was in company with the amiable Queen Sabina (the wife of Adrian).* We read afterwards: *Julius Camillus commanded me to engrave these words, at the instant when Adrian Augustus heard the voice of Memnon.* And on the same side: *I, Mithridates, tribune of the twelfth legion, heard the voice of Memnon at six in the morning.*

A thousand other inscriptions testify the same fact; it is needless therefore to recite them.— When to these authorities we add those of Strabo, and of Tacitus, incredulity itself cannot resist such testimonies. The marble which has preserved them for upwards of sixteen hundred

(*c*) Annals of Tacitus, lib. 2.

years, is a durable book which depoſes in favour of the voice of *Amenophis*. But what are we thence to conclude? Is this phænomenon owing to the nature of the ſtone? Pauſanias leans to this opinion *(d)*. " The ſtone they ſhew at " Megara, when ſtruck with a flint, produces a " ſound which reſembles the vibration of the " ſtring of an inſtrument. The coloſſus I have " ſeen at Thebes, on the other ſide of the Nile, " ſurprized me much more. It produces every " day at the riſing of the ſun, a ſound *as ſmart* " *as that of the cords of a guittar, or of a lyre,* " *which ſnap on being ſtretched*." * Philoſtrates, miſled

(*d*) Pauſanias in Atticis.

* Without preſuming to offer an opinion concerning this enquiry, the *Tranſlator* could not reſiſt the inſertion of the following extract from one of the notes to Blackwell's Letters on Mythology.—The real wandering *Jew, Benjamin*, one of the greateſt travellers of the eaſt, has given this curious deſcription of the ſolar worſhip in his Itinerary. " There is a people," ſays he, " of the poſterity of *Chus*, addicted to the contempla-" tion of the ſtars; (perhaps the people of whom Zephaniah " ſays, chap. i. verſe 5. *And them that worſhip the hoſt of hea-* " *ven on the houſe-tops*). *Tranſlator.* They worſhip the ſun " as a god, and the whole country for half a mile round their " town, is filled with great altars dedicated to him. By the " dawn of morn they get up, and run out of town to wait the " riſing ſun, to whom, on every altar there is a conſecrated " image, not in the likeneſs of a man, but of the ſolar orb, " framed by magic art. Theſe orbs, as ſoon as the ſun riſes, " take fire and *reſound with a great noiſe*, while every body " there, men and women, hold cenſers in their hands, and all " burn incenſe to the ſun." One would ſuſpect theſe orbs to have been filled with ſome nitrous compoſition, and kindled by a col-

misled by his love of the marvellous, sets no bounds to his credulity (*e*). "The colossus of "Memnon, though of stone, was gifted with "speech. At the rising of the sun, joyous to "behold again his mother, he saluted her in a "pleasing voice. Towards the setting sun, he "expressed his sorrow in a sad and mournful "tone. This marble had also the property of "shedding tears at pleasure. It is pretended, that "echo answered to its voice, and imitated per- "fectly the events of its joy and grief." Lastly, an ancient grammarian (*f*) says that this statue was so marvellously composed, that it saluted the king and the sun.

a collection of the rays. It nicely explains, not the shrine of *Moloch*, which is easily understood to be a portable tabernacle, such as was used by the Egyptians; but *the image of* KIUN, *the* STAR *of your gods, which you have made to yourselves.* Amos, chap. v. verse 26. Blackwell adds, this piece of idolatry committed by the *Jews* in the wilderness, soon after they had come out of Egypt, and on the borders of the sun's votaries, the posterity of *Chus*, is not as I remember recorded in the Pentateuch.—The *Translator* will only take the liberty of suggesting, as matter of reflection, that VULCAN, who among the Phœnicians and Assyrians, was the same with *Saturn* or the *Sun*, and, as Herodotus observes, was among the most ancient and most honoured of the Egyptian deities, is derived from BAL-KIUN or BUL-KAN, the LORD FIRE. May not some combination be thence formed, respecting the origin of this famous statue, as well as the causes of its voice, which is represented as similar to the snapping of the cords of a musical instrument? In a country also, abounding in nitre, like Egypt, an early discovery must have been made of its explosive quality.

Translator.

(*e*) Philostrates, Life of Apollonius of Thianes.

(*f*) Quoted by Jablonski de Memnone.

These passages, however, will never induce us to believe that marble is capable of producing such a sound as is attributed to Memnon. I know that the empty sarcophagus of the great chamber of the pyramid, resounds in a very sonorous manner, when struck with a stone or piece of metal; but in whatever manner it might be disposed, the rays of the sun shining upon it, never could produce any such effect. Let us suppose, therefore, that the priests of Thebes had carried the mechanic art to the degree of perfection it has attained in our time, and that with as much ingenuity as Vaucanson, and other celebrated artists, they had fabricated a speaking head, the springs of which were so arranged, that it should pronounce vowels at the rising of the sun.—Cambyses destroyed this wonderful mechanism, by overturning the upper part of the statue; and all the testimonies I have quoted, speak only of the trunk, which we see at this day upon the pedestal. It is natural therefore to attribute the sound of the mutilated colossus to the artifices of the priests, who opposed this pretended miracle to the rising progress of Christianity. At all events, it is very certain that since the commencement of the fourth century of the church, when the inhabitants of Egypt became Christians, no more has been said of the voice of *Amenophis*. [Does not the supposition of a nitrous preparation furnish an easier solution, and render the deceit as practicable on the trunk of the statue, as from the head? Translator.]

Let

Let us try to discover the object of the priests in framing this vocal statue. We know that they consecrated their secondary deities to preserve the memory of their most important discoveries. *Amenophis* was undoubtedly created with the same intention. The comparison of some passages extracted from the ancients, may give weight to this conjecture. You recollect, Sir, that in the temple of Abydus, which Strabo (*g*) calls also *the temple of Memnon*, the priests repeated the seven vowels in the form of hymns, and that musicians were forbid to enter it. Demetrius of Phalerus confirms (*h*) this important fact: "In Egypt the priests make use of "the seven vowels instead of hymns, to celebrate the gods. They repeat them successively "with such an accent as they think proper.— "This continuity of sounds, thus modulated, "serves them instead of the flute and the guittar, and produces an agreeable melody."— The ancients, and Jablonski (*i*), who has collected their testimonies with extreme attention, assure us that these vowels were consecrated to the seven planets, and that the statue of *Amenophis* repeated them at a certain epocha. Lucian (*k*) introduces Eucrates on the stage, and makes him say: "In Egypt I have heard Memnon, utter, not according to custom, *an insignificant* sound, but pronounce from his mouth

(*g*) Strabo, lib. 17.
(*h*) Demetrius Phaler.
(*i*) Jablonski de Memnon.
(*k*) Lucian, vol. 2.

"an oracle in ſeven ſounds." This paſſage, probably, is no more than a pleaſantry of Lucian, but it is founded on the general perſuaſion, that before Cambyſes broke this Coloſſus, it pronounced the ſeven vowels. The following dialogue written in Greek on the left leg, is a freſh proof of this:

A. *Cambyſes has mutilated me, me, this marble, formed after the image of the ſun. I formerly poſſeſſed the melodious voice of Memnon. Cambyſes deprived me of the accents by which I expreſſed my joy and grief.*

B. *What thou relateſt is deplorable. Thy voice at preſent is obſcure and incomprehenſible. Wretched as thou art, I lament the misfortune that has reduced thee to this condition.*

The Egyptians regarded the ſpring equinox as the moment of the creation of the univerſe (*l*). "They ſaid, that at the birth of the world, when "the ſtars began to move through ſpace, the "ram occupied the middle of the heavens, the "moon was in the ſign of the crab, the ſun roſe "with the lion, Mercury with the virgin, Ve-"nus with the ſcales, Mars was in the ſcorpion, "Jupiter in the archer, and Saturn in capri-"corn." Syncellius (*m*) has diſcovered in an ancient Egyptian chronicle, that after a revolution of thirty-ſix thouſand five hundred and twenty-five years, the zodiac would be reſtored to its firſt poſition, that is to ſay, that the firſt minute of the degree of the equinoctial line would commence with the ſign of the ram.

(*l*) Macrobius, Somnium Scipionis.
(*m*) Chronographia Syncellii.

I leave

I leave the truth of these facts to the discussion of astronomers; but they announce at least, that in Egypt the attention of the learned and the people was chiefly directed to the spring equinox. *Amoun*, a symbolical divinity, was consecrated to it, and all the festivals they celebrated in his honour, related only to this interesting period. It was thence the astronomical year took date. It was thence, that, according to the priests, the seven planets recommenced their course, which they allegorically stiled *the cœlestial music*. It was at this moment also, that *Amenophis* pronounced the seven vowels which were the symbols of the planets, and which composed *the terrestrial music*. This famous statue may be called in sacred language *the cousin of Osiris (n)*, and *the image of the sun (o)*, since it imitated on earth the office he performed in the heavens *. The priests, by making him repeat the seven sounds, of which all languages are formed, and which marvellously paint our thoughts, were desirous of immortalizing the most beautiful of their discoveries, a discovery, which, according to Plato, could only be invented by a god, or by a divine mortal. Perhaps also, the shadow of this lofty colossus served to mark the instant of the equinox. Its name at

(*n*) Diodorus Siculus.

(*o*) See the inscription I have mentioned.

* This accords perfectly with the suggestion hazarded by the translator in his note respecting BAAL-KIUN, the LORD FIRE or the SUN, &c. *Translator.*

least composed of *Ame Nouphi (p), to tell good tidings (q)*, leads me to think so. The Greeks adopted these ancient ideas, in attributing to Apollo, who was no other than the sun, the invention of the lyre and of music. The fictions of the poets observed this allegory, which painted the admirable harmony which reigns amongst the stars, and it was no longer heard of.

I have the honour to be, &c.

(*p*) Jablonski de Memnone.

(*q*) The sun attaining the Equator, promised the Egyptians a cessation of the southerly winds, and the approach of the inundation, which made them so anxiously attend to it.

LET-

LETTER LXXI.

REFLECTIONS ON THE RELIGIOUS WORSHIP OF THE EGYPTIANS.

The Egyptians had only two dogmas in their religion, namely that of a God the Creator, and that of the immortality of the ſoul; all the reſt was allegorical. This religion was preſerved pure and untainted within the temples; but the neceſſity they were under of uſing repreſentative figures before the invention of letters, induced the people by degrees to adore them; which happened when the art of writing having become eaſy, they forgot the ſenſe of the hieroglyphics. The gods of Laban were nothing but hieroglyphics, of which he had loſt the meaning. They were to him the objects of worſhip, becauſe they had been tranſmitted by his fathers, and he did not comprehend them. The ſame thing happened in Egypt.

To Mr. L. M.

Grand Cairo.

YOU will now permit me, Sir, to make a few ſhort reflections on the religion, the myſteries of which I have been endeavouring to lay before you. It contains only two dogmas, that of the infinite Spirit, author of the creation, and that of the immortality of the ſoul. The temples of *Phtha*, of *Neith*, and of *Cneph*, conſecrated to the power,

power, the wisdom, the goodness of the Supreme Being, are a demonstration of the first. The care with which they embalmed the bodies, the prayer repeated on the death of an Egyptian, furnish a proof of the second. The temple of *Cneph*, situated in the isle of Elephantinos, may be regarded as the most ancient of the country. In fact, before the Egyptians descended into the valley where the stagnant waters of the Nile formed impenetrable morasses, until they had drained them by the most prodigious labours, and rendered them fit for agriculture, they dwelt, according to Herodotus, on the mountains bordering on the cataracts. This monument therefore, testifies, that amongst them the worship of the Creator preceded every other. We are justified even in asserting, that the priests retained it in its purity; for men who had once risen by the sublime efforts of reason to the knowledge of one only God, or who had received it by tradition, could never, whilst they continued to compose an enlightened body, fall back into idolatry, which invariably implies a profound ignorance.

The rest of the Egyptian theology was purely allegorical. It embraced the course of the sun, the moon, the stars, and the most striking phænomena of nature. All these objects were personified in the sacred language of the priests; but far from making them the objects of adoration, they considered them only as admirable signs by which the Most High manifested his omnipotence to their senses. It is very probable that they at first taught this religion in its

its purity, but that it became insensibly corrupted, because the vulgar, accustomed to behold in the sanctuaries, the symbolical figures I have spoken of, and to offer sacrifices and thanksgiving to the Creator, at the periods when they were produced, forgot the invisible object of their veneration to worship his works, hidden under these emblems §.

But why did not the priests extinguish this blind worship? Why did they hold the nation in subjection to the yoke of so deplorable a superstition? Doubtless this was not originally their design. The necessity of expressing their ideas, previous to the invention of letters, by allegorical figures, the practice of confining them to the

§ A Christian writer of abilities, makes the following *arch*, but pertinent answer to the despisers and too-zealous calumniators of the ancient mythology. "Suppose that amidst the "calamities that frequently besel the *Jewish* nation, the book "of their law, whose preservation is almost a miracle, had perished, and with it, as of other incidents, the memory of "the Brazen Serpent, erected by their law-giver, had been "irretrievably lost, what idea could we have now entertain-"ed of the serpents erected at this day as Talismans all over "the east, *in imitation* of that divine pattern? We might have "groped in the dark, attributed them perhaps to the power "of *Mercury's Caduceus*, the magic rod with twining snakes, "or to Æsculapius's badge of life and health, a single serpent "wreathed round his staff; or to the mystical veneration of "the Egyptians, who have most of these Talismans, for that "reptile, which they still venerate, amidst all the strictness of "the *Mahometan* doctrine concerning the unity of God and the "preciseness of the *Christian Coptis*." See Dr. Pocock, and our author, for an instance of this veneration for the serpent *Haridi*—[Translator.]

temples,

temples, accuſtomed the people to look on them as ſacred. When the leſs difficult art of writing had made them entirely loſe the meaning of theſe figures, they ſet no bounds to their veneration, and paid real homage to theſe ſymbols, which were only reſpected by their fathers. Then Oſiris and Iſis became tutelary divinities of Egypt; Serapis preſided over the inundation; Apis foretold abundance; and the evil genius, Typhon, threatened the country with the moſt deſtructive calamities. Theſe ideas, once deeply impreſſed on the minds of the people, it would have been difficult to eradicate them, without involving the total overthrow of the eſtabliſhed worſhip: perhaps, alſo, (for men have been the ſame in all ages) the prieſts adroitly availed themſelves of this ignorance to become the mediators between heaven and earth, and the ſole diſpenſers of the divine oracles. But what ſhould render men circumſpect when they take upon them to condemn a learned body, who publiſhed thoſe wiſe laws which formed the glory of the Athenian code, and who erected a great number of durable and uſeful monuments, is that the Hebrews, though reſtricted to the ancient creed of Abraham by their elders and their prophets, no ſooner found themſelves in the deſert, than taking advantage of the abſence of Moſes, who was waiting on the mountain the oracles of heaven, they compelled Aaron to caſt a golden calf to ſerve them as a god; ſo true it is, that the view of ſenſible objects has more empire over the multitude than all the precepts of the pro-

foundeſt

foundest wisdom. In short, if we reason impartially, we shall perceive that it is sometimes no less difficult than dangerous to shew mankind the truth. The principal philosophers of Greece and Rome, as well as the Egyptian Priests, acknowledged only one God. Mythology, in their eyes, was no other than a tissue of allegories, implying effects and natural causes They bowed their head, however, before the statues of Jupiter, of Pallas, and of Venus. Socrates alone had the courage to lift up his voice against these fabulous divinities, and Socrates was compelled to swallow poison. Do you wish for another and more recent example of the danger of enlightening our fellow-creatures? Galileo proclaims a most important discovery to the world; and Galileo, after being obliged to ask pardon on his knees for having dared to tell the truth, was persecuted for the remainder of his life, and died in exile. It is doubtless very noble to be a martyr at this price, but few minds are equal to so sublime an effort.

These facts, with many others I could cite, prove that if the Egyptian priests were culpable for having concealed the light from a people whom it was their duty to instruct, we should not condemn them with too much rigour. For in these distant ages, when men spoke only by symbols, idolatry made a rapid progress, and it was almost impossible to destroy it, without oversetting all religion. Recollect the gods of Laban stolen by Rebecca. These idols were hieroglyphics. Laban, who had probably lost the key of their real signification, adored them, because he had received them

them from his anceſtors. The ſame circumſtance occurred in Egypt, where the hieroglyphics became the deities of the people, as ſoon as they had loſt the comprehenſion of their real meaning. The ſole means of extinguiſhing the ſuperſtition would have been by deſtroying them; but the prieſts, in making ſuch a ſacrifice, muſt have annihilated all their knowledge, and above all, their abſolute controul over the minds of men. Now, if there are examples of a few individuals who have been generous enough to renounce the charms of dominion, from the pure dictates of humanity, we never yet have ſeen a body of men capable of ſo noble an act of virtue.

I have the honour to be, &c.

LET-

LETTER LXXII.

OBSERVATIONS ON THE HIEROGLYPHICS.

Hieroglyphics, the first-written language of man. Their antiquity more remote than the deluge. The meaning of them entirely lost under the princes of the lower empire. The recovery of it would render us acquainted with the language of the Coptis, or ancient vulgar Egyptian, by which we might attain to a knowledge of the sacerdotal dialect, used for explaining the hieroglyphics, and which is found on the Egyptian monuments. A Journey might likewise be attempted to the temple of Jupiter Ammon, inhabited by an Egyptian colony, which may have preserved their ancient language, their books, and the knowledge of hieroglyphics.

To Mr. L. M.

Grand Cairo.

HIEROGLYPHICS, Sir, are the first written language of mankind. They are imitative and allegorical characters. They differ from letters in this, that the latter paint the thoughts by strokes and sounds, while the former represent them by figures. Their antiquity approaches the era of the deluge, if it be not prior to it; for the human race possessed the arts and sciences before that disaster, and since they were carv-

ed

ed on ſtone, ſome of theſe monuments may have eſcaped the general ruin. Clemens of Alexandria reckons a great number of books aſcribed to *Thoth*, that is to ſay, approved by the academies, and publiſhed under that title. He even gives an account of ſome of them. The firſt, ſays he, contained the ſacred hymns; the ſecond, rules for the lives of Kings: the four following treated of aſtronomy, and the obſervations of the Egyptians; ten others contained the ſcience of hieroglyphics, geography, and coſmography. A like number compoſed the code of laws, the religion, and the diſcipline of the prieſts. Laſtly, the remaining ſix formed a complete treatiſe on medicine.

Theſe works have undergone the fate of many others, which a barbarian, whoſe name muſt be ever odious to poſterity, made uſe of for ſix months to heat the baths of Alexandria; but the chief part of the Egyptian books were only copies. The originals remain engraven in a thouſand places on the marbles of the temples, the obeliſks, and the walls of the ſubterraneous paſſages. Theſe are the monuments which the learned of all nations ſhould endeavour to read. Manethon, a high-prieſt and ſacred Egyptian writer, drew thence the hiſtory he wrote, under the reign of the Ptolemies. About three centuries after, Hermapion decyphered the obeliſk of Heliopolis, tranſported by Auguſtus to the capital of the Roman empire. Since that author, no other has poſſeſſed the knowledge of hieroglyphics, or, if any one has been ſo gifted, his works have not reached us. Ammianus Marcellinus,

linus, who flouriſhed under the Emperor Julian declares, that in his time theſe characters were unintelligible to the Romans. Are there then no means of tearing off the veil that covers them, and of explaining the facts which they contain? The man who ſhould make this diſcovery would acquire immortal honour, by reſtoring to the arts, to ſcience, and to hiſtory, ſo many diſcoveries now loſt to the world. I do not pretend to this ſublime effort, but ſhall content myſelf with expoſing ſuch ideas as the ſtudy of the ancients, and the frequently-repeated view of the monuments of Egypt, have given birth to, in my mind.

We know that the prieſts invented the letters which they called ſacerdotal, and by means of which they tranſlated the hieroglyphics: they were in univerſal uſe in the temples, and it was in thoſe letters they wrote every thing reſpecting religion and the ſciences. This partial dialect was intermediate between the hieroglyphics and the common language of the country, which fortunately is not loſt; for the fact is, that it ſtill exiſts in the books of the Coptis, with Greek and Arabic tranſlations. It is to be found in a great number of manuſcripts ſcattered through Egypt, and in the European libraries. In order to arrive, by means of it, at the knowledge of the ſacerdotel dialect, we muſt diſcover either alphabets or paſſages common to the two languages. Now, we diſcover on the walls of the temples, and the ſouterrains, certain letters interſperſed amongſt the hieroglyphics, different from all thoſe we are acquainted with, and which form probably part

 of

of the sacerdotal dialect. These are the characters we should endeavour to comprehend; for they would give us the key of the hieroglyphics, of which they are either the continuation or the interpretation. Perhaps some learned man, perfectly well versed in the Coptic, the Arabic, and the Hebrew, who would dedicate some years to the study of the monuments of ancient Egypt on the spot, might accomplish this noble enterprize §.

The

§ The scriptures furnish many proofs that the Jews brought the hieroglyphics with them out of Egypt, as well as the worship of the sun.——Ezekiel, in his vision, chap. viii. verses 9, 10, and 16, says, "And he said unto me, Go in, and behold "the wicked abominations that they do here. So I went in "and beheld every form of creeping thing, and abominable "beasts, and all the idols of the house of Israel, pourtrayed on "the wall round about."—And he brought me into the inner court of the Lord's house, and behold, at the door of the temple of the Lord, between the porch and the altar, were about five and twenty men, with their backs towards the temple of the Lord, and their faces towards the east; and they worshipped the sun towards the east.

The Bishop of Clogher, in 1753, published a Journal from Grand Cairo to *Mount Sinai*, and back again, translated from a manuscript written by the Prefetto of Egypt, in company with the Missionaries *de propaganda fide* at Grand Cairo; spoken of by Dr. Pocock, and wherein mention is made of *great numbers* of ancient unknown characters in the wilderness of Sinai, at a place well known by the name of *Gebel-el-Makatab*, or *the Written Mountains*. Likewise of the second stone struck by Moses, as related in the twentieth chapter of Numbers, is still lying there. The celebrated Mr. Edward Wortley Montague made this journey a few years since, expressly to view these objects, but declared himself *greatly disappointed* at finding them every where *interspersed* with figures of men and beasts, which convinced him that they were *not* written by the Israelites.—

With

The following is another reflection with which I have been greatly struck, since I have travelled in this country.——The Ammonians were an Egyptian colony. The priests who gave Jupiter Ammon his celebrity, had the same religion, and possessed the same knowledge with those of Egypt. Their God has ceased to utter his oracles, but his temple may still subsist; the country around it being extremely fertile, must be inhabited. This tribe not having experienced the revolutions which have overturned every thing in Egypt for upwards of two thousand years, may have retained its customs, its worship, and its native language. It is probable that the arts and sciences, no longer fostered by celebrity, have fallen into decay; but tradition may have preserved their memory. Sanchoniathon affirms that he derived his knowledge from the monuments of Egypt, and the books of the Ammonians. These books might still be found in the heart of the country which gave them

With great deference to so ingenious an observer, is it not almost evident that these are neither more nor less than the Egyptian hieroglyphics; and that, from the passage above cited from Ezekiel, as well as the Egyptian education of Moses, they *may have been* written by the Israelites, and that the characters *interspersed* with the figures of men and beasts, are the sacerdotal characters or dialect mentioned by our author? Mr. Montague had certainly no reasonable cause of *disappointment* at finding these stones covered with unknown characters; for what else was to be expected? But these very curious and highly interesting monuments are not for that reason the less deserving the attention of the learned, whether they be of Israelite or Egyptian origin.——[Translator.]

birth, and possibly in the sanctuary of that ancient temple, protected by immense deserts. It should be towards this memorable spot, therefore, that a learned man should bend his course with any hope of success. The way that leads to it is beset with dangers. Alexander, followed by a numerous retinue, and by camels laden with water and provisions, was on the point of perishing with thirst. One of the armies of Cambyses remained buried under the sands, and not a single soldier who composed it ever again beheld his country. But what is not an intrepid individual capable of performing, enlightened and enflamed by the love of science? Until some well-informed European, in short, shall have visited the temple of Ammon ; until he has communicated to enlightened nations the treasures or the ruins it contains, it is natural to imagine that it is surrounded by an ancient Egyptian colony, who speak the mother tongue, and who have preserved the science of hieroglyphics. But what leads us to believe that this tribe is not extinct is, that *the Oasis* which I have traced on the chart, are still inhabited in our days, and that the Bey of Girgé sends to the Oasis, which corresponds with that town, a Cachef to govern it. A traveller who should venture to traverse the deserts which separate the *Oasis* from the banks of the Nile, must infallibly find there monuments hitherto unknown, and infinitely curious.

I have the honour to be, &c.

LETTER LXXIII.

To Mr. LEMONNIER, *Physician to the* KING *of* FRANCE, *First Physician to* MONSIEUR, *and* MEMBER *of the* ACADEMY *of* SCIENCES.

PLAN OF AN INTERESTING VOYAGE, AND WHICH HAS NEVER BEEN PERFORMED.

To take a survey of the great lake of Menzale *in a boat. To examine the ruins in its isles. To visit Pelusium, Farama, the Oasis; to Siéne for the wells of the solstice, and to ascertain the ancient observation of the Egyptians. To pass through the interior parts of the Imen, with the view of procuring information and manuscripts. To go to Mecca; to stay there during the pilgrimage, and to bring thence and from Medina the works and information that are unknown in Europe. To travel over both Arabias, Petræa and Deserta; and after remaining some time at Damas to return to Europe.*

To Mr. L. M.

Grand Cairo.

MANY things still remain, Sir, to be verified in Egypt. The following is the project I propose to the man who is desirous of being eminently useful to the arts and sciences, and to pro-

procure most valuable information for his country.

To survey in a boat the great Lake of Menzalé; to sound its outlets into the Mediterranean; to touch at the Isle of Tanis, where, according to the testimony of Arabian writers, and the natives of the country, there are vast ruins and antique marbles; to navigate to the extremity of the lake; to visit the remains of Pelusium, and of Farama, where the Arabian geographers describe a tomb, which must be that of the great Pompey.

To descend the canal of Sebennytus, now called *Samanout*, as far as the borders of Lake Baurlos; to search for the ruins of the ancient Butis, where Herodotus places the sanctuary of Latona composed of the astonishing block of granite, the description of which I have given from that historian.

To discover the ruins of Naucrates, and of Sais, situated in the environs of Faoué, and those of Phacusa and Bubastis, where the famous canal of the Ptolemies passed.

To make a treaty with a tribe of wandering Arabs in order to penetrate to the Oasis of Ammon, at no great distance from Lake Mæris, and thence to the temple of Jupiter Ammon, so celebrated in antiquity; where there are hopes of recovering the ancient language of Egypt, and possibly the books which served to decypher the hieroglyphics.

To visit the three Oasis, and describe the people and the monuments they contain, and which are lost to the world.

To

To ſtop eight or ten days at Sienna to diſcover the well of the ſolſtice, and to verify the admirable obſervation of the ancient Egyptian prieſts, who, when the ſun deſcribed the Tropic, ſaw his entire image at noon reflected on the water, which covered the bottom of this aſtronomical well. For eighteen hundred years paſt no European has verified any of theſe circumſtances, or viſited the places I have mentioned. Theſe reſearches, however, ſuppoſe a man verſed in antiquity, and thoroughly acquainted with the manners, the religion, and the language of the Arabs; ſuch a man would not content himſelf with theſe limits to his travels. He might embark on the Red Sea in the capacity of a Mahometan merchant, ſurvey all its ports, remain ſome months at Moka, where he would meet with precious manuſcripts, then repair to Sannaa, the ancient capital of the Homerite Kings, who governed Yemen in the time of the Ptolemies; viſit the interior parts of that rich country; join one of the caravans, and arrive at Mecca. He might remain there under the pretext of religion and of commerce; examine the library begun long before Mahomet; he might purchaſe, or procure copies of the moſt intereſting manuſcripts; and, after obſerving the worſhip, the trade and the monuments of that city, the antiquity of which is coeval with Iſmael, he might ſet off with the caravan for Damaſcus, and repoſe himſelf after his fatigues in that beautiful capital of Syria, where he would procure likewiſe a great number of ſcarce books, &c. &c.

The

The learned man who ſhould ſucceed in this journey, the difficulties and the perils of which are innumerable, would furniſh Europe with an abſolutely new hiſtory of the nations of Arabia; for the interior of that country is as little known as the foreſts of New Zealand. He would procure a great quantity of intereſting diſcoveries for natural hiſtory and geography, and might poſſibly have the good fortune to reſtore to Tacitus, to Livy, and to Diodorus, the complement of their immortal works, for they have all been tranſlated by the Arabs.

After I had given to the publick a *tranſlation of the Koran*, and *the life of Mahomet*, full of enthuſiaſm for the ſciences, I did propoſe to undertake this journey. My project met with obſtacles which prevented me from carrying it into execution, and which gave me much uneaſineſs. But we muſt ſubmit to the law of neceſſity. From that time I have totally abandoned the thoughts of it, and I confeſs that at preſent I ſhould not have the courage to undertake it, becauſe I know from experience the perils of ſuch an enterprize, and that after a few years reſidence in my native country, to the climate of which I am again habituated, my health probably would not be proof a ſecond time to the deſtructive heats of Africa and Arabia. But I hope that ſome European, inflamed with the love of glory, and wealthier, or more favoured than me, will immortalize himſelf by collecting the information and the manuſcripts I have mentioned; and above all, by procuring for enlightened nations the unknown

hiſtory

hiſtory of the people of Yemen, of Mecca, of Medina, and of the interior parts of Arabia.

Such is the knowledge I have been able to obtain by five years travels in the eaſtern world, and by the ſtudy of the ancients. May you, Sir, who, in the charming retirement, which your labours and your talents have enriched with all the rare plants of the world, and a collection of valuable books, who afforded me the leiſure neceſſary to arrange theſe Letters, publiſhed under the auſpices of an auguſt Prince, who honours you with his eſteem; may you, Sir, derive ſome pleaſure from their peruſal, and regard them as a teſtimonial of my gratitude.

I have the honour to be,

With reſpect, Sir,

Your moſt obedient, humble ſervant,

SAVARY.

END OF THE LETTERS ON EGYPT.

www.ingramcontent.com/pod-product-compliance
Lightning Source LLC
Chambersburg PA
CBHW030942110726
47900CB00004B/1088

* 9 7 8 3 3 3 7 2 3 8 5 6 8 *